RAD SICK
RECORD

HYSTERICAL BOOKS

RAD SICK RECORD

Michael Trammell

HYSTERICAL BOOKS

TALLAHASSEE, FLORIDA 2020

Design, production: Jay Snodgrass

Library of Congress Cataloging-in-Publication Data
Rad Sick Records — First Edition
ISBN — 978-0-940821-11-8
Library of Congress Cataloging Card Number — 2019936771

HYSTERICAL BOOKS
1506 Wekewa Nene
Tallahassee, Florida 32301
Website: www.hystericalbooks.com
mail: hystericalbooks@gmail.com
Published in the United States by

Hysterical Books
First Edition, 2020

Acknowledgements

Thanks to my mom for always encouraging my love for all things literary.

Thanks to my dad for instilling me with discipline and perseverance.
I miss you.

Thanks to my brother, Barry, for his generous, imaginative spirit.

And thanks to all writers and teachers in the communities I've been fortunate enough to be a part of, especially the members of the 4th Quarter / Wings group over the past 25+ years, including R. Franklin, J. Reynolds, C. Miranda, L. Kitchen, C. Hayes, P. Laffan, R. Wiginton, M. Gearhart, G. Clark, T. McWhirter, M. McClelland, D. Newman, J. Clark, N. Stuckey-French, V. Suarez, P. Busby, T. Schneider, M. Rychlik, P. MacEnulty, M. Hobson, R. Smith and J. Needle.

Dedication
For Ariel, Dylan, and Mary Jane

RAD SICK
RECORD

This record chronicles how I joined Wings, tackled the impenetrable clouds of TallaTec, and battled the mysterious machinations manipulating my kind who'd mutated from wombs across South Florida.

I begin with this entry, in what I call my "Rad Sick Record," late summer, August 27, 2000.

--JULY 15, 2001

Sunday, August 27, 2000

Always this thought lingers, annoys and haunts: yeah, the Great Next War never happened—and sure, thank God.

But for me, down south where I grew up—I can never forget "The Accident," even if they labeled it "Incident '80," guaranteeing that few recall that night.

But let me stop remembering. Makes the hate demons in my head pitchfork my stomach. A good way to cure the ache is a stroll in the grass.

All day I'd been feeling trapped inside my room in this Aluminum Village apartment, so I clambered outdoors to the green space between the brick buildings, the original bones of a military barracks. All old colleges in Florida hide artifacts from the never-ending Cold War. Including here in Tallahassee, T-town, where Anti-H-bomb detonators, according to urban legend, were hidden beneath meter boxes, ready to deliver a strong, counter blast.

The detonators. The history. The people have forgotten that college towns were targets for H-bombs. *Incinerate the scientists!* the generals advised. That was before the Davos 1995 agreement.

But pre-'95, Army personnel, incognito, were at the ready to fire shoulder-launched missiles set to counterpunch a hydrogen bomb.

In theory, the Anti-H's would prevent the worst of the Big-H's, but those small payloads were packed with lots of iffiness.

I stepped outside into searing heat and brooding thunderclouds. There was a 30-something guy sitting beneath a tree, maybe fifty feet away. Couldn't tell if he was a resident or just visiting. The grounds here are so park-like. Scenic. Oaks, with long curtains of moss, tower over Bahia grass lawns.

I thought he was smoking, but it was a pencil. He stared up into the branches and jotted something in a spiral notebook. I thought he might be like me—a frustrated prose writer turned briefly to poetry. But I didn't ask. He looked too deep into it. After a few minutes, he closed the notebook and flung it into the branches above. The pages sprang white— flapped like gull wings. The paper ripped against the bark and tumbled back to grass. He ignored it, as if it were a pine cone that had fallen.

His eyes closed. I got tired of looking at him and went back inside.

Five minutes later I opened the door and peeked out. He was gone. But the notebook remained. I walked across the lawn and snatched it.

Wednesday, August 30, 2000

I track the Cold War because I feel fused to the events.

Here's the latest, buried on the newspaper's page four.

Reuters reports a U.S. submarine collided with a Russian military cruiser in the north Atlantic off the coast of Greenland. The U.S.S. Stonewall Jackson was forced to surface after the incident. The Soviet's took the captain and chief navigator into custody. The Pentagon sees the incident as an accident. Moscow views it as hostile. Apparently, neither vessel was damaged. A Pentagon spokesperson warned the Soviets to avoid escalation.

On this news, markets fell 2%.

I'd hate to be in that numbskull navigator's shoes.

*   *   *

I've just jolted awake, a nightmare from an undersea pinging fallen silent. I realize my hometown friend Taylor Velázquez (and fellow *sufferer*—we're called Rad Sicks) navigates the *Stonewall Jackson*. She's First Lieutenant, Chief Navigator and Operations Specialist, always on duty. Oh my God, she might become a major player in Cold War history. Probably not. Still, I can't get it out of my head, the possibility.

But most likely, the collision will be another disremembered incident, like so many before in an endless chain of small skirmishes and accidents, ranging from tank battalion standoffs along the Suez Canal to military reactor "mini-meltdowns." These occasions made and make us briefly tense but steadfastly blasé.

Hell, in the U.S. alone, as far as incidents and accidents go, there's a no-longer-famous series. In my mind, obviously, is what I call The Accident, the one that affected me, what the powers-that-be branded *Incident '80*, placing it in a forgettable continuum.

The Accident is one of five mishaps, each labeled by year, *Incident '75, '79, '80, '83* and *'85*. They include everything from contained terrorist attacks to radiation leaks.

What they share: casualties: death and illness, from dozens to hundreds.

What they also share: no one remembers them.

But what if something happens with the *Stonewall Jackson*? Certainly it will be forgotten too.

But Taylor Velázquez I'll never forget. As children, she and I were friends. We'd sneak off to play spies behind rows of Spanish bayonet plants that choked a vacant lot. Our chats meandered, but I liked how she listened to me intently, and as she talked, I loved how she held my forearm with her strange, long-fingered hands, making me feel connected. I was too often a loner, and our friendship was good for me. Even as we grew older and spoke less, we always talked as if we'd returned to our world within the bayonet plants made uglier from radiation, though they truly weren't.

Dear Taylor, stay free from harm.

I'm not a big prayer person, but I'm praying now.

Thursday, August 31, 2000

Can't stop thinking about Taylor.

Will try.

Forgot to mention classes started, and though this is my new plan, going to school not to critique literature but to create it, I can't say I have felt any different.

That guy beneath the tree, I met him. He, like me, has switched from "crit" to "create."

I still need to return his notebook—haven't mentioned I found it, if he even wants it. I've skimmed pages, but not carefully. Feels weird.

In his notebook, I read a passage that implied his misgivings about *novel workshops*. In class he keeps his arms folded across his chest. We're both wrestling with the same doubts. Or maybe I'm projecting.

After class today we ran into each other at the tavern across the street from campus, Ravensview. Hot as hell here in late summer, so thirst hovers like a vulture. By coincidence we both had the same aim for a draft. His name is Randal Salt. He's got good sarcasm. He'll occasionally pull his fingers through his hair (an almost-mullet), a girlish gesture.

"Just call me Rand," he said. "That'll work." His voice was a dead mumble, not girlish. Good thing I've an ear for invisible voices, another result of Rad Sickness. These voices, spoken or written, that should be heard but aren't. I can sometimes hear the future in them.

We talked a bit. He said he had a girlfriend who not only had a child from a previous relationship but was pregnant.

"Yours?" I asked.

He looked at me funny, glanced at the tavern's bare stage, then ordered another beer. I stared hard at an ashtray.

"Yes," he said.

I have to admit, I was caught off guard. I figure all youngish guys have to be single with maybe a serious girlfriend, and that's about it, at least very youngish guys, like me, in grad school. Of course, what is my real age? That's somewhat of a mystery. Incident '80 fucked with my growth, my entire aging process. I've only been on Earth for a score, but the docs who've examined my skin, drawn blood, scanned my brain, drilled into the bone marrow, all say my cells are *ahead of their time*. Like the phrase *Incident '80*, this line from the M.D.s obscures the truth. I'm older than I look. I may die earlier than I should. The hematologist said I have the blood of a 40 year old. The brain doc says I'm early thirties. Some days a brief but harsh exhaustion hits, and I feel 90. No matter. I'm actually healthy. No major complaints. But I'm at least 35, not 20.

Rand looked maybe 30. Too young for babies. Nevertheless, he seemed calm, but I sensed he was overwhelmed. Now didn't seem a good time to mention his notebook. Anyway, I'm sure he'd deliberately ditched it.

He said he'd see me later and took off without finishing his second beer.

I finished it for him.

Friday, September 1, 2000

As an exercise, I'm trying to learn to write about place, comparing home with here. Here's my starter cluster:

South Florida.

1. Flat. Bridges are the only hills.

2. Heat. Even in the winters, you sweat.

3. Subtropical flora. Nothing but jungle plants. The Amazon as V.D. on North America's penis. Crazy large ass flowering trees: Floss Silks, Hong Kong Orchids, Royal Poinciana, Pink Trumpet Trees. And Banyans with roots like giant worms slowly cracking asphalt roads to black debris until the colossi are chain-sawed.

4. Burrowing Owls. Birds living underground. And weirdly, mainly on South Florida Campuses.

5. Mullet are for bait.

6. Suburbs extend for hundreds of square miles, all crisscrossed by perfectly symmetrical intersecting grids of roads, streets, highways.

7. Oaks = small, gnarled things, resembling bushes crippled from radioactive drinking binges.

T-town.   *(from what I've seen and been told)*

1. Endless hills. I keep looking for mountains. From the fifth floor of the library I swear I see the first muscular ridge of the Appalachians.

2. Cold. True cold. Nights that turn dew to frost and make pipes burst.

3. Deciduous forest plants. Some trees that actually color and drop their leaves in autumn and winter. Unbelievable to a South Floridian.

4. Barred Owls. Bad ass birds which hoot back and forth from pine tops in a cacophony of monkey phrases and almost-human cackles.

5. Mullet are fried or smoked and eaten with raw oysters and pitchers of beer.

6. Suburbs thin quickly beyond city limits (except in the north where they extend a lake or two further). Roads make no sense. Finally figured all roads simply spokes on a wheel with university as hub, T-town's G-spot.

7. Oaks = giant, majestic, moss-filled beauties with cavernous overhangs of branches.

I sense this landscape will try to own me, if I don't resist it.

Saturday, September 2, 2000

My Ex called. Dumb-selfish-girl-I-still-care-about. The whole time she talked about her new place in Kansas City, I kept thinking about the last time we'd had sex. Right here in this apartment. I kept weirdly trembling because I was so messed-up since I knew this was it, and I really did love her, though I was glad we were over. She ignored my shakes. I think she felt the same about us. Who knows.

I'm supposed to submit a chapter of something soon for the novel workshop, and since I definitely don't want to write about Ex, all I've got is crap about South Florida temp jobs. I met the weirdest people at those temp jobs, from a black guy who thought it was hilarious that I'd eat pussy to a warehouse foreman who instructed me that *If I say, "Shit," you better ask, "What color?"* That's what I've been working on. Though lately I've been tooling with poetry, taking a break from prose.

So why am I in a novel class?

I went out to the tree where I first saw Rand and stood there, looking into the leaves. This was right after my Ex called. No news fell, not even a pine cone; instead, it started to rain.

Sunday, September 3, 2000

I will write a poem about stalemates: (1) with my Ex, (2) at the Arctic.

Associated Press: The standoff continues between the U.S. and the Soviets, as the Russians have yet to release the two U.S. naval personnel. State Department officials have implied a U.S. response may follow. The aircraft carrier U.S.S. Dwight D. Eisenhower, already in the region, has reportedly altered its course, though its actual destination remains unclear.

In business news, the manufacturing sector of the U.S. economy sagged in the last quarter; economists worry about investors' reaction on Monday.

My poem, a haiku:

Ex is like a bomb: / A flash above a Soviet ship, / my Arctic up in smoke

      *   *   *

Can't leave it there. I'm still wondering about Taylor Velázquez aboard that Russian cruiser. Are the pair held as prisoners or guests? Are they being fed Siberian gruel or sturgeon eggs with a splash of Stolichnaya? Taylor would tongue each caviar bubble and maybe tell how each proto-sturgeon might have swum the River Kızılirmak or the River Dniester and eventually settled quietly in the Black Sea or the Sea of Azov.

Oh, Taylor Velázquez, a poem for you:

I fret / on every note of news / for a dirge that contains your name.

Thursday, September 7, 2000

Ventured to Ravensview tonight, and discovered they had readings. I recognized many people from hallways on campus. About a half dozen read. But the audience was huge. Dozens and dozens and dozens.

Incredible!

First writer was a professor. Wild-eyed and nutty. I didn't recognize him. He read postmodern sonnets. Big irony. They were smart, but they were shit. Criticism in stanza form. No matter. I laughed anyway.

A skinny red-haired girl appeared next. Her poems weren't half bad, but she was a terrible reader. Anxiety shook her. Her voice and legs trembled; she ran off the stage after two short poems. Nevertheless, the audience gave good applause. An intermission fell. The PA speakers, looking like floating fishbowls, drifted into the ceiling's cigarette smoke.

I was adrenalized. I didn't know about these happenings. I've been keeping too much of my own company. The reading fired me up because I'd never attended a literary event with so much vibe. Real energy lit the room. The people crowded into the space as if it were a rock concert. I was lucky to snag a spot at the bar. No tables had empty seats. And it wasn't just relatives and a few close friends as audience. An entire in-the-groove critical mass filled the joint!

And they did this *at least twice a week* the bartender said when I asked her.

I recognized a few people. My prof from the novel class, a few folks I'd seen outside the department, cigarette smokers. This tavern is like a smoker's black lung. I've been trying to quit. My Ex said she still hasn't—why did we make that promise to each other to quit when we broke up? That was weird.

And I spotted Rand at a table. With a pregnant but beautiful woman. A couple of long-haired guys joined them. The dudes looked familiar.

I tried to catch Rand's eye but gave up.

I'm too tired to write about the rest of the readers. They did OK. I'm just stoked about Ravensview!

Saturday, September 9, 2000

Taking a break from scene-writing this morning. I've fallen back into the novel, and I'm glad.

A moment ago as I paced outside my front door, I leafed through Rand's spiral notebook. I was curing my curiosity. I'd only glanced at the writings once, figuring they were private. I planned to hand it back to him soon. But of course that hasn't happened. I have found passages I like. Will jot them down here:

-- *I told my boy to watch for stingrays, the winged bird-fish of the shallows that whip their barbed tails.*

--*My son dreams without covers, the blankets wrestled off as R.E.M. blends to deeper plunges, his long white nightshirt grants him a manta ray's wings.*

--*My boy saw the tilled sand of ocean bottom slightly lined and ridged. My son wants to work as a marine biologist.*

--*I imagine my baby daughter's grin arching like the upside-down top of a heart.*

Yes, I need to give this back to Rand. Should carry it with me to campus, but I keep forgetting. I'd like to talk to him about these lines. There's potential.

O.K. Back to my scenes.

Sunday, September 10, 2000

Was going crazy as soon as I got up this morning. I couldn't face more pages of warehouse temp jobs as novel source. Yes, I've wholeheartedly decided to return to it. The poetry jag has lost its groove. But this A.M., I couldn't do prose.

Also, I'm bugged by Taylor's confinement on the Soviet vessel. Since the standoff is in stasis, the news has reported nothing. I'm sure both governments are glad. Make it all ho-hum. *See*, they might say, *it's not even newsworthy. Stop worrying!* I'm probably the only person on the planet, with the exception of her mother, concerned about Taylor Morgan Velázquez. She's bilingual, looks like a Cuban princess, and yet she's got the two most Anglo-American names in the world. Her parents were super-big on assimilation, but they hadn't anticipated The Accident, hadn't anticipated a Rad Sick baby, a kid who'd have a tough time assimilating on so many levels. But she took her first and middle name in stride, acted as though it gave her gravitas, a unique connection to the Anglo world.

I probably should have written another poem for Taylor. But I couldn't do that either. Instead, I went for a drive. When I thought about buying cigarettes, I staunched the craving by driving to the coast.

Quiet. White sand, soft-brown water. Gulls.

The weather, surprisingly, was cool this morning. What? Maybe 59 degrees? That would be mid- winter sweater-weather in Miami.

I met a woman. She seemed drunk, or just spacey, but I felt attracted to her anyway (she gave me her phone number). Said she lived near Fishton, a coastal town. She looked 30, a little sun-washed. Her eyes were sad blue and wonderful. Long black hair. Cute bangs. I liked the way her body curved. I would call it dolphin-like, but I think the Gulf Coast has completely screwed-up my sensibilities. I thought about kissing her, and for a few moments I thought she might like me to, but I froze. Plus, she seemed so dazed. Her open, friendly body language might have been her status quo.

Ryanna Font. Local name. Saw a Font on a store sign near the turnoff for the beach.

She pronounced it, *Rye . . . anna.*

We talked a lot about the coast. I compared my east coast haunts with her gulf coast juts of land. We laughed a lot. I can't remember about what. I was shy with her, and she was shy too.

I plan to call her, but I don't know when. Maybe in an hour. No, maybe tomorrow.

September 11, 2000

Not tomorrow.

September 12, 2000

Not this tomorrow either.

Wednesday, September 13, 2000

Sometimes, just for fun and self-torture, I write out a synopsis of "The History of the World as Relevant to *Me*." I do it over and over. Must be both therapy and rewriting practice. It's different every time.

Rewriting myself into context makes me feel less sorry for myself, other times it makes things worse. I keep doing it anyway. Here we go: "The History of the World. . . ."

I was born 1980. In that year, humanity was big-time sweating the Cold War and the Bomb, the Berlin Wall and ICBM-loaded submarines.

The Cold War had been simmering hot since '73. Vietnam's proxy battles were fading, politicians on both sides kept retreating from handshakes.

First they tried the Nuclear Arms Restriction Talks (NART, they called it). But those failed. Next, a joint space venture was proposed, the Apollo-Soyuz Test Project, but it never got off the ground (ha, ha).

Things grew hottest in late 1979. By then both sides had created the harshest H-Bombs imaginable, and had additionally developed Anti-H mini-missiles that could short circuit the worst of an atomic rocket's explosion with a counterpunching radioactive plume of its own. Both sides were more tempted than ever to fire a first nuclear strike since each believed an Anti-H would water down counterattacks.

Maybe this cockiness grew more in Moscow than D.C.

Russia took a radical risk in '79. After feigning disinterest in Afghanistan's year-old civil war, the Soviets launched Operation Storm on Christmas Day. Special forces stormed the Tajbeg Palace in Afghanistan and captured the sitting president. Next, a surprise attack with a small H-bomb stunned provinces in northern Pakistan, allowing Soviet infantry in radiation-proof suits to take territory coveted by Mother Russia.

Weirdly, northern Pakistan is a new country: Moskowistan.

Operation Storm stayed on the radar past New Year's. Commentators ranted on U.S. media; many news outlets demanded retaliation. The U.S. government and its citizens were freaked. Nerves popped and frayed.

Anything could happen.

Mistakes. Accidents.

Especially accidents.

Lucky for the planet and the human race, no gigantic accident splattered the Earth. Things cooled; tempers and tensions went from flames, and then changed, of course, to ice. More Cold War. The one we're still in today.

But the U.S. had time a few months after Operation Storm for one small accident.

The blame rested solely on the shoulders of one poor guy. Who could fault him, right? Think about all the unfortunate, anxious souls at the control panels of those missiles hidden in underground silos, bombs waiting in the bellies of swooping jets, Anti-H-bombs lying in wait in civilian locations.

Can you blame one jumpy soul for making a mistake?

In September 1980, someone jumped. The Accident exploded.

The Accident, immediately labeled "Incident '80" by the government and the media, happened in my hometown, Miami.

Right as I was being born.

And yes. I blame him.

Thursday, September 14, 2000

I went to Ravensview last night, hoping for a reading, but the place was dead. The bartender offered me a drink and said a guitarist would play later. Her boyfriend. I didn't want to seem like a jerk, so I grabbed a beer and let a shot of Jack boil beside me. She didn't charge for the beer.

A girl showed up, tall with straight, long brown hair, and sat at a table near the front, reading the latest issue of *Rolling Stone*. She wore glasses. The bartender brought a vodka tonic.

I focused on my shot glass, trying hard to ignore two ashtrays to my left. I must have been deep inside my head, because when looked around, I saw two guys sitting at a nearby table, as if they'd drifted from the ceiling's graveyard of ashes. Rand and a guy from the other night shared a pitcher.

Rand recognized me and waved me over. Why was I the happiest dumb-shit in the world when Rand with his almost-mullet beckoned?

The other guy was tall and blue-eyed. A beard. A German-Jesus look. He was serious but not unfriendly.

"This is Van Gear," said Rand. "He's just finished his collection. We're celebrating."

"Collection of what?" I asked.

"Stories," said Van Gear. "Are you not going to drink that shot? If not, I will."

I let him. Then they shot me a few questions. I summed me up—with absolutely no mention of my overlapping history with *Incident '80*. I even lied about my birthplace.

Born in Bama, I said (I don't know why; mainly, I liked the alliteration), *moved as teen to Lauderdale* (slight lie of dislocation), *dad still working for UPS* (truth), *mom, an exec assistant at a local college* (more truth). *Undergrad in zoology for no reason with a minor in English for some reason but not logical* (mostly true), and *older sis just finished accounting degrees* (true too). I left out how high school dual enrollment allowed me to start at Burrowing Owl U as a junior and graduate at twenty. Though I'm a Rad-Sick space cadet, I've always been decent at school. I watered the summation down to keep it from morphing to a main topic of talk. I asked about them, but at the moment it all blurs, because a few minutes later a man walked in with a guitar.

As the guitarist skidded past the table, Van Gear said, "Don't tell me this asshole is playing tonight."

The guy stopped. Froze. Dropped his guitar case on the bar. Ordered a vodka straight. Then glared.

I'd basically just met Jesus and the Mullet (a fucking *great* band name!), and I wasn't sure I knew them well enough to justify joining in a scrap—Van Gear's stare was intense.

"Van Gear," said the guitarist. "The poet. Was looking forward to you taking my workshop again. But you didn't have the guts, did you?"

I suddenly recognized the man. A faculty member. I'd thought he was a janitor, till I'd heard someone in the hall whisper about his new book due in February and his class filled to the gills. Dirk Falter, listed as co-teacher for my Literary Theory class, but yet to appear. In the meantime the course was taught by a prof named Jones in black jeans and red beard, directing discussion and referencing Dirk's eventual appearance.

Didn't know Dirk did tunes too. Couldn't believe it. Couldn't quite believe he had a new book either. Or would show up to teach Theory. He smelled like a mix of high-end restaurant garbage and weak bleach.

Van Gear stood up.

"Sit down," Rand said, but Van Gear ignored him.

How scrap-ready was I? My fingers balled to fists.

"Sing us a song, piano man," said Van Gear.

Van Gear walked to the bar and said, "I'll have what he's drinking." He pointed his chin at Falter. The bartender glared at him. I'd forgotten the music guy was her boyfriend.

Falter paid no attention and popped open his guitar case. He appeared completely uninterested in fisticuffs. Thank God.

Van Gear downed the vodka and asked for another.

Falter walked to the stage, pried open a folding chair, and lowered. He tuned his guitar.

"Bring the drink back here," said Rand to Van Gear. "And get us a pitcher."

Van Gear nodded but did nothing.

Suddenly Falter was playing. The tall, brown-haired woman at the front table put down her magazine. I noticed Melissa Etheridge on the cover. She adjusted her glasses with both hands.

He was playing something he wrote, because I sure as hell didn't recognize it. He could sing a little and strum the bar chords OK, but his lyrics were all James Taylor re-dux without a strut from the banal.

"Can you believe this guy is recording a record?" whispered Rand.

Van Gear started to cry. First a soft whimper and then actual sobbing. I was alarmed. But then Rand laughed, spraying beer all over the table. Van Gear cranked his voice's volume, revving up his weird, ironic mockery of Dirk's song. The bartender threw an ice cube at V.G. that he ignored, and Falter played louder for ten seconds and then stopped.

The woman in the front returned to her magazine. She flipped through pages, deciding Falter's tune was a sound check.

My fists squeezed back to stones. Why was I so ready to help these guys in a fight? If it came to that?

"Let's hear you try, asshole," said Falter. "Could it be any worse than your poetry?"

Van Gear marched to the stage and gleefully took the guitar from Falter. The prof stood there. Glaring.

The bartender made to throw another ice wad, but Falter waved

15

her off.

"Let's hear it, Ginsberg," said Falter.

I could see that the *Ginsberg* barb stung, but Van Gear closed his eyes and broke into "Norwegian Wood" as if he'd been born playing the tune. His voice encircled the room with a rich tenor; he hit every strum with crisp precision.

He finished and handed the guitar back to Falter.

The woman up front said, "You can sing, man."

Two people standing in the back applauded; they'd entered half-way through the song.

The bartender was silent, but she was clearly surprised. Falter sat down on the stage and retuned his guitar.

Rand started laughing, and I couldn't figure out why. Van Gear smirked as he walked to the table.

"Let's go," he said. Rand flew to his feet and pulled my arm, and we slipped onto the sidewalk along Highway 90.

We walked for miles along the strip of four lanes and then walked back again. We'd tagged a two-thirty 9-pack from a gas station; Rand crammed it in his backpack, and we each snagged a can as we got thirsty—hiding the cans in jacket pockets when the occasional cop rolled past. We talked of Beats and the shapes of our own novels and poetry of the Bishop, the prose of Virgin-Woolf. And as we stood beside Ravensview's door again, Rand suddenly said to Van Gear, "We should get this guy in *Wings*," and German-Jesus concurred. And before I knew it, I was invited to be a Wing.

Friday, September 15, 2000

I remember better now. They'd invited me into a Wings group.

I have to admit, I am gleeful. These guys seem particularly honest, genuine, real, and that's what I need, straight-shooters to set me straight. When I went on a ramble about Murakami's *Wind-Up Bird Chronicle* and Naslund's *Ahab's Wife*, predicting long term greatness for both, especially Murakami's *Sputnik Sweetheart* which was yet to debut in English, Rand's and Van Gear's eyes got bigger. Something about my monologue impressed.

Wings. What is a Wings group? Maybe they actually *are* a band? Jesus and the Mullet as a Wings tribute—without McCartney?

Now I'm afraid to ask.

No, not true. I feel as though I've found something.

I'm suddenly on the inside. And this is good.

I've been too long an outsider.

Let me count the ways.

1. An outsider long annoyed by Nuclear Fear Era (NUFE) reminders such as two-thirty 9-packs, the beer pack of choice (nine 23-ouncers), invented in the early 80s to celebrate ICBMs. At that time, everyone knew that the plutonium isotope Pu-239 was the core ingredient to make a bomb. Booze-buying customers felt patriotic. Nowadays, people have forgotten the allusion; but the pack-size remains popular.

2. An outsider long annoyed by any references to radiation sickness (*Rad Sick, for short*) by jokers who'd invent phrases that simply sounded cool (*a rad sick trick, dude*) but had completely forgotten what the term meant.

3. An outsider long annoyed by others' assumptions based on half-remembered history. At first, Miami wanted to help our plight, wanted local TV stations to sponsor Rad Sick telethons, drafted public radio to sponsor fundraisers, demanded newspapers print childhoods-in-progress articles. Billboards were plastered around town, photos were front-paged in the *Herald*, commercials featured us crawling across blankets. However, there was one problem: the Rad Sick orange glow in our eyes. Even though the glow wavers, most cameras capture it. The images spooked people, no matter how cute we looked. The 1980s had no *Photoshop*, so the ghostly spark couldn't be perfectly edited. Thus, the telethons, fundraisers, features all died, disappearing so quickly that the initiatives had dropped off the radar by '85. Miami's public preferred to let it fade—after all, we

Rad Sicks became somewhat normal. Everyone wanted to forget Incident '80. It was easier. But, of course, a lot of people half-remember, get the facts wrong, ask us stupid questions.

I want to stop being annoyed.

I want to finally be an insider.

Sunday, September 17, 2000

I returned to Ravensview tonight hoping to find Rand and Van Gear and learn about Wings, but the place was dead. Different bartender. Less friendly. Tattoo of a mitochondria swam on the back of her neck. I remember that from a cell structure class—the powerhouse of the cell.

I was feeling a powerhouse of guilt: I'd missed a lot of class last week for no good reason. I'd felt glued to the linoleum floor, a strange inertia, as if I were as imprisoned as Taylor in the Arctic.

A menu leaned against a napkin dispenser near where I sat at the bar, and I studied it.

"Where's the kitchen?" I asked.

The bartender pointed down. A prickly flagellum blued her index finger.

I'd just realized Ravensview had a downstairs.

"Will they bring it up?"

"If you order and pay first."

She was the customer service A-team. I gave her good thumb.

I picked a steamed vegetable plate and broiled clam sandwich. She knocked a draft in front of me. When she turned, I noticed the vacuoles of her mitochondria roiling with sweat.

Two servers brought up each platter. A tall, brunette-touch-of-henna-haired girl with a glorious smile held the clam and bread and hummed a soft melody as she neared the table. Her hair was pinned at the top of her head in a bun; glasses graced her face. She looked familiar. A short dude with a black mustache trailed a yard behind her; he balanced the cauliflower and beets plate on his fingers.

"Hi!" said the girl.

"Where you want these?" said the guy, friendly enough.

"Good anywhere," I said.

They bent at the knees to place the food, crowning the table.

"You were here a few nights ago, didn't I see you?" asked the girl. "I'm Elly."

"Yeah, I remember you," said the dude. Neither moved.

I knew I'd seen her somewhere; the guy I was less sure of. Must have been from the other night.

Why would they recognize me? Were they from Miami?

Did they recall my face from the early, post-Accident telethon days?

When I was a toddler, my parents brought me to the local TV studio that hosted the telethon. I'd sit in a high chair and wave at the camera. People have told me I've kept my baby face. Makes me easy to recognize.

But this was exactly the motherfucking notoriety I was trying to escape.

I prayed this was some fluke, that they had me confused with someone else.

The girl dropped an ashtray on my table.

"No thanks," I said. "Trying to quit."

"You were the guy who didn't smoke," said the dude. He scratched at his mustache.

"Trying to quit," I repeated.

The girl sat on the table beside mine, and the guy leaned on the back of a nearby chair.

"We were trying to guess where you're from. You're new, right?" said Elly.

I stared. If they said *Miami*, I knew they were on to me.

"I'm sorry," she said. "It's a slow night, and we're just curious. This is Kelt." Elly pointed at the dude.

"Hey," I said to him.

They were silent.

"Are you hungry?" I asked.

Kelt snapped a cauliflower, and Elly shook her head.

"You're not from New York," asked the woman, "are you?"

"No."

"I didn't think so," she said.

"He's from Florida, clearly," said Kelt.

"What makes you say that?" I asked. I was already sick of the conversation, and I didn't want to have to bring up Rad Sickness.

"You have a beach-vibe," said Elly.

I wasn't sure what she meant. I stared at my meal. The clam sandwich looked damn good. I wanted these two to disappear, so I could taste the Gulf's tannins and not feel interrogated.

"Well," I said. "I'm going to eat. Good talking to you."

"But we haven't figured out where you're from," said Elly with honest disappointment. "Something about you is so familiar."

"Did you have a brother who worked at the Seaquarium?" asked Kelt.

"No, I have a sister. She's afraid of the ocean," I said.

"I bet you're from Kendall," said Elly.

"No, you're wrong." I sighed. "I'd like to eat my sandwich now, OK?"

Kelt yawned.

"Is your last name Needle?" Elly asked.

My gut filled with acid. She did recognize me. Even my name. Fuck.

"I'm from Miami, OK? The Kendall guess was close enough." I granted them a partial victory, hoping they'd finally leave me alone.

Elly pursed her lips and peered into my eyes.

"This one's a needlefish," she said to Kelt. "Prickly."

I was being fucked with. There's nothing I hate more. That's why

I'd left Dade. And all these other bad associations made it worse: my Ex was good at fucking with me, in a different sort of way. And my sister before that. Big Sis would peg me with thin innuendo until I cried. I was born with arms the width of popsicle sticks, though they're normal now. Another result of Incident '80.

"All right," I said. "I've had enough games. Go fishing somewhere else."

Elly looked hurt; her eyes widened in an odd way, and she frowned. She wiped the bridge of her glasses with a thumb.

Kelt shrugged and strolled away as if he'd never said a word. Perhaps he'd been stoned off his ass. Elly followed but suddenly reappeared at the top of the stairs.

"Sorry, Needlefish," she said. Her eyes held tears.

She took a few steps toward me. Stopped.

"I . . . I," she stuttered. "Maybe I'm not so unfishy either." She dashed downstairs.

What the fuck did that mean?

I suddenly recognized her. She'd been at the front table when Falter and Van Gear had their guitar duel.

My anxiety, though, wouldn't settle. I wolfed down my sandwich and left.

Monday, September 18, 2000

I wound my way to Ravensview tonight, half wanting to say something to Elly, half wanting to find Christ and the Mullet, half hoping for a reading, but I got distracted 1.5 yards from the doorway.

I was worried about someone stealing my bicycle. A couple of smokers leaned against a faded H-Bomb shelter sign. They eyed my U-bar as I snapped my bike to the roadside railing.

Rand appeared from nowhere, clutched my arm, and scared the shit out of me. The kid standing beside him laughed. A real kid. Eight or nine. Rand put a hand on the boy's shoulder.

"Sorry, man. You going inside?" Rand asked.

"No, I changed my mind," I said.

"O.K. Suit yourself," he said. He and the boy rambled to the entrance.

Rand turned.

"Hey, and I was just going to tell you about Wings." Rand widened his eyes. "And the *Thing*."

I shrugged. Rand winked and waved goodbye.

I unplugged my U-bar and pedaled back to Aluminum Village.

And here I am, an antisocialist prince, king of unfriendliness.

All because of my birthday.

It's today.

I tell no one. I hate the reminders, but I've been told to process it. It was at the heart of last night's impatience with Elly and Kelt—today's anniversary of Incident '80.

But, as psychologists have asserted, I must write my way through.

At this moment it hurts and annoys that I'm crying. Me, one of the lucky unluckies born in Miami that year. *Far enough from fire but close enough to kink*, some said. *Kink* as in what a beer can does in flames—shrivels, turns ugly.

Some called it *La Fiebre*.

I was a hot baby. Beneath the blue of our newborn *ojos* was a pinprick of orange ember. I was struck with *heat*. Docs said it messed with the molecules in my body, our bodies, my brain, our brains. Things go in and out. Memory, mood, perception. The older kids called us *Rad Sicks* as we meandered our way through school and childhood, and the phrase stuck.

Yes, I am a *Rad Sick*. I've proclaimed it here, written it a million times, become so weary of it I could scream. And this is precisely why I'm here, so I can escape my label. I no longer want the notoriety or the pity.

Yes, I was born when the bomb popped.

Yes, some jumpy spook misheard a phone call and launched

an Anti-H. And because he'd set the range too close to ground as he'd launched it from the dorms of Burrowing Owl U, the fucking thing blew just above the downtown skyscrapers, at the same height as sinking fog.

Yes, there was no Big-H. Only one Anti-H. But that was enough to fuck us up.

I've been told the sky that night lit up like noon.

So many of us were born in Miami's hospitals when the explosion's fission material snaked through walls, slipped between molecules in cinder blocks, and fizzled into our newborn genes, messed with our genetic codes before the first bit of nurture could get influence on the nature.

We were born bathed in radiation. We all turned red or gold and our eyes yellowed, and in some cases, we glowed like protozoa; phosphorescent like the tiny fireworks of splash lines above the shore break on the Gulf at night.

Then *ojos* got orange.

We were all diagnosed with Radiation Sickness. Of course, so were many others, the many who'd been strolling the streets that night, under no shelter. They were hospitalized. Expected to die. Most did.

Us too. Expected to die. We were watched, given weeks, maybe months, to live the life we might never remember.

But we survived, as if the radiation had given us new life, had added an indestructibility to our cells.

Our parents, our mothers especially, had their emotions pushed and pulled and stretched.

But parents whooped with joy when they saw we Rad Sick hundreds refused to die!

I can't believe I wrote this much about my birth, our birth. I am *trying* to forget it!

My stomach hurts now. I have to stop. Maybe this "writing-cure" will make me better later.

Tuesday, September 19, 2000

I have been thinking about Big Sis today. She can't find a job. She's got a Bachelor's and Master's in Accounting from Burrowing Owl U, the most in-demand degree in the universe, but still . . . nothing. It's the Recession. It's very weird in Miami. At first, the Dow Jones wouldn't save the Nasdaq and then *really* had to, but then it was too late.

Tech stocks fell, the jobless numbers soared. Economically, the western world is in the I.C.U. Just like we Rad Sick babies in 1980.

Last year I had an internship at a stock trading firm in Boca Raton, some fly-by-night operation. The internship director at Burrowing Owl U mixed me up with a finance major who had the same initials, so he got the desk job, and I got the bonds job. We were both so stupid—and the employers too—that things weren't righted for weeks. Even though I didn't know finance, I detected deceit in the Boca boiler room. They were selling what they titled *investment vehicles*, and they wanted me to cold call kooks with bucks, warm them up for an *investment facilitator*. Of course, I was terrible at it: all the potential clients—*whales* they called them—hung up on me, so I had plenty of time to listen to the traders' jive. They laughed about *the total shit* they were selling, bonds based on mortgages paid by people with bum credit who'd eventually default and thus make the bonds worthless. The boiler guys thought it was hilarious. They didn't care. They simply wanted their commissions. Swine.

Since Big Sis often treats me like swine, I'm not sure why I'm so worried about her. She wasn't always mean, but particular moments specifically stung. Not especially important instances, but little moments when all seemed well between us, and then I'd catch her glaring at me with disgust.

Once in out teens, mom had demanded I tag along with her and her boyfriend on a mall trek. Her boyfriend always talked Dolphins football with me, never mentioned the Rad Sick stuff. Sis would get tired of us yacking about QB ratings and always wanted me to scram. On that day in the mall, we wandered into an ice cream joint called the Orange Bowl.

Sis's guy and I immediately started Dolphins talk. As I stepped away from the counter with my cone, Big Sis bent down, picked up a mutant scuzzy bug and planted it at the tip. The insect seemed poised to stab a flag on "Mount Zebra." She and her boyfriend laughed. I ditched my ice cream into an ashtray, roach-first. Her face had been so full of hate—that look haunts me even now.

Ridiculous or not, I feel guilty that Big Sis can't find a job. After all, over the years she fought off a number of bullies.

Having a Rad Sick sibling had weighed on her a lot, I suppose, as if Rad Sickness had rubbed off on her like tar.

We're albatrosses, harbingers of never-ending bad luck.

Wednesday, September 20, 2000

With weird serendipity, Big Sis called this evening as if last night's journal entry had channeled her from her glum recession depression.

"What 'cha doing?" she asked.

"Studying poetry for class tomorrow. Audre Lord, Gloria Fuentes, and Pablo Neruda."

"Sounds like a Miami Channel 4 news team."

"Yeah. Except it's poetry."

"Right. Well, I called 'cause I'm kinda bored."

"Oh. Sorry. No luck on the job front, huh?"

"No. I had an interview yesterday, but I could tell they weren't interested. This guy kept staring at my chest, and every time he asked a question and I answered it, he'd just rephrase the question as if I hadn't said anything. Extremely annoying."

"Sorry. That sounds terrible."

"Yeah. Listen, you wanna play a phone-version of Trivial Trials?"

Big Sis loved clobbering me at all sorts of games. It was her number one pastime. She especially liked crushing me at checkers. Always Big Sis clicked her red disks at the end of the board and for some reason always shouted, *King me! King, double king!*

But she truly sounded depressed now, so I played along.

"O.K., sure," I said and sighed.

"Don't be a baby. I will make it easy for you. I will choose your favorite category: Literature."

"How are we going to play and keep score? You're the one with all the questions."

"If my question stumps you, I get a point. If you guess the question right, you get the point. The first to three wins."

"Whatever."

"Ready?"

"Hmmmmm, uh huh."

"From Geoffrey of Monmouth's *History of the Kings of Britain*, name the chapter from which this passage derives: "*. . . it is easier for a kite to be made to act like a sparrow-hawk than for a wise man to be fashioned at short notice from a peasant.*"

I don't know jack-shit about Medieval English literature.

"I'm stumped," I said.

"Come on. Part of the answer's in the question, and the other is a perfect adjective for you."

"Don't know."

"The Stupid Britons."

"Ha, ha, ha."

"Question Two. In Chaucer's "General Prologue" in *The Canterbury Tales*, the Reve is introduced as someone who made his workers "*adrad of hym as of the deeth.*" What is Chaucer referring to?"

"Teeth?"

"No, stupid Briton, the Black Death. The Plague. Sorta what you got. Back in 1980." I was used to this kind of meanness from her, so it didn't bother me.

"Ha, ha. Got in a nice double-dig there. Why don't you stop asking questions about books from a million years ago?"

"O.K. Here you go. Easy one. Question Three. The first chapter, titled "A Noiseless Flash," from this book starts *"At exactly fifteen minutes past eight in the morning, on August 6, 1945 . . ."* Name the book.

"Flash Gordon Meets G.I. Joe?"

"That's not even a book, retard."

"It's on the tip of my retarded tongue."

"Hiroshima, atom-boy."

"I knew that."

"Too bad. I won! Three in a row! King me! Double king me! Triple king me!"

"Good for you."

"Thanks! I feel a lot better now. Well, good-bye, little brother."

Click.

I feel terrible.

Sunday, September 24, 2000

At this instance I feel terrible again because up until this morning I'd forgotten about Taylor Velázquez. I've heard few details in three weeks; today new news arrived, buried on page 5.

Reuters: Because the Soviets continue to hold the two U.S. sailors in custody, the aircraft carrier U.S.S. Dwight D. Eisenhower is now within three miles of the Soviet/U.S. standoff in the Arctic. Sources report the Russians' missile-carrying nuclear submarine KERSKI has reportedly surfaced ten miles due south.

The U.S. government has remained mum. No newspapers have reported the administration's official reaction. As a country, we're so numb to these clashes.

But this one has gone on longer than usual. Even if everyone ignores it, it's bugging me.

I need some kind of radical escape.

Monday, September 25, 2000

Well-timed, radical escape found: the *Thing*.

Van Gear tapped my shoulder as I waited outside the department's building tonight, and I jumped like a nervous cat.

I'd been working up the nerve to return to class. It's been awhile. Modern poetry / peels / petals / from the black boughs / of my / brain / and leaves me / terrified / of the female professor.

She reminded me a lot of Big Sis.

"You going to class?" he asked. I'd just realized that Van Gear was one of the 30 bodies that packed the sepulcher-sized room.

"I'm thinking on it," I said.

Van Gear nodded. Then he shrugged.

"Spending too much time on Pound and the Imagists," said Van Gear.

A few smokers nestled beyond the stairwell tossed their stubs and crept by us to return to class.

"Fuck it," said Van Gear. "You up for a ride?"

"Yeah," I said.

Van Gear has a huge motorcycle, a Kawasaki souped-up with special Hiroshima-made parts. A huge, iron horse.

I had no helmet, and Van Gear gave me his and rode bareheaded.

We rambled deep into neighborhoods I did not know. Since I've only been in town a few months, I disassociate easily from landscape. Trees and streets were vague and alive. Alive with words. More alive at least than the words in the sepulcher.

We pulled up at a house squeezed into a shelf of magnolias. We found a crevice in the siding and slid in. Here was the *Thing's* home.

There were a dozen people circled around outdated computers. I thought of moths fluttering near glowing screens, but these machines lacked monitors. A pair or trio kneeled beside each black box. They were the black boxes of Titan Instrumental computers from the early 80s. Someone would plug a cartridge into each machine and then others would pull at IV hoses fountaining from the top. Mouths sucked away. I didn't see any smoke. I didn't know what the fuck they were doing.

"You want to try it?" Van Gear asked.

"What is it?"

"TallaTec."

"Right."

"You can only get it here, you know."

"This place?"

"This town, brother."

So I tried it, and I can't tell what the fuck happened to me. I remember nothing sparking when I kissed the tube. I felt ridiculous, sucking air. The tube tasted of plastic and copper, as if I were licking pennies. Then the world loomed large, or so I thought.

Van Gear raved about the ice in his freezer.

A woman behind me spoke in Swahili, and then translated herself back into English.

I was finished.

Tuesday, September 26, 2000

I can remember last night with Van Gear, but the memory is somehow sliced like fruit, thin fruit for the world's most frugal salad. I recall how the TallaTec funneled into me a vision in wedge-shaped glimpses. Things were the same but harshly brighter through all senses, from tactile to auditory, from sight to smell. Van Gear had said it made him want to be a writer. I'd understood, then didn't.

"But I thought you already were one," I'd said.

"S'like that Brandelsonna film, the one with the tiger and the Samurai. The tiger's left with nothing to eat but corn, and chooses the Samurai's brother instead."

I couldn't could follow that.

Last night we spent hours on the iron horse, peeling down Old

29

Bainbridge, a stolen TallaTec machine pinched against my back. The hoses were pink and prickly.

Van Gear said something, and I leaned forward to get words, but the black box squirted to pavement, and the tubes sprang to life as legs, and the square chased us for half a mile. Then gave up.

Good riddance.

Or no, we desperately wanted it back!

Or not.

Van Gear flew me down Devil's Dip at 90 +, shook us past Big Dismal in a spray of sugar sand and moon leaves, and screamed past the palm frond siding of San Luis Mission. Hours and hours were all spotted detail and the itch of wind. I breathed spikey humidity.

I know this sounds like an acid trip, but somehow it's much more complex than that; I will have to write a better description soon.

I'm writing this now to remind myself that I do remember everything, but instead of it being inside the lens of over-focus, hours bring the scope back into frame, vivid images bubble from memory, and I can see the minutes within the piston rod of night. That's bad poetry, but it's actually the way I remember it. So be it.

Thursday, September 28, 2000

I keep rehashing my deeper past. I think the TallaTec lingers as a parasitic hangover and makes my brain whir with old memories. Old playground rhymes.

You're insane, you're insane, Rad Sick is now your middle name.

In T-town, I'm keeping mum about my Rad Sickness. In Dade, I got sick of people's condescension, questions, pity, prejudice. Here I can make a new start.

The contact lenses help. They cloak the glow in Rad Sick eyes. Our eyes are not continually lit; after 10-20 seconds a glow will flash before disappearing. Imagine a flickering lighthouse, one flashing sporadically because drunk and tired men turn a crank. These contacts hide that flame.

The procedure was slow and painful, done with a tear-drying lubricant that burned for days. God, what terrible throbbing. The ache tore through as if tiny H-bombs in my tear ducts. Maybe that's why I'd never heard of others trying.

You're insane, you're insane, Rad Sick is now your middle name.

Insane stupid stubbornness explodes within me. (*Stupidorness*, Big Sis called it.)

When I applied to Ph.D. schools in Seattle, Toronto, Boston, Bloomington, Los Angeles, and Tallahassee, I stuck to a specific pattern for packaging my applications. It was a strange ritual that did not allow for double checking because that might create some curse.

Perhaps that's why only my *back-up* plan worked: T-town accepted me. No one else.

My *stupidorness* packaged the wrong writing sample, a first draft written in blank verse with a joke or two in Pig Latin.

I have no idea why T-town's school accepted me based on that sample. But here I am and here I remain. Ex reminded me I could go anywhere. I didn't need a grad school scholarship; I could just hunt for editor jobs.

But no. Once I lock in, I'm doomed to the decision.

You're insane, you're insane, Rad Sick is now your middle name.

I over-brood on The Accident, what Incident '80 did to us. The bad and the odd.

Odd? Some Rad Sicks believe we have expanded senses.

For me, I hear unheard voices, important ones. Hear how? By an inner ear as I read another's words and sing them to myself. Through sound, I know what's truly brilliant and what's not.

As a kid, I wondered if all Rad Sicks heard truth in voices. We never talked too much about our oddnesses, especially as youngsters. We were too busy trying to act normal. But as adolescents, we stuttered revelations, and realized each of us has a different skill. My friend Pedro, terrible in kitchens, always tasted the winner of any chili cook-off before the judges did their rounds. What about Gabriella? Though she knew zero about fabrics and style, she could always tell by touching the new clothes in the racks in late winter which skirts and blouses everyone would wear in spring. And Amelia? She could smell gangbangers' guns and sweat coming from blocks away, and she'd shout to clear the streets, allowing dozens to avoid bullets. One of our group, a black, Dominican kid, Blanco, with a missing bicuspid and a poetic soul, believed our talent for hearing, smelling, tasting, or touching *the invisible* tapped into what he called *the epicenter of the sixth sense* that tunneled directly to the *heart of the fourth dimension.*

What? We could predict the future? Blanco had some imagination.

Our brave navigator Lt. Taylor Velasquez had always grown quiet during these talks. She hinted that these abilities, whatever they were, if they even existed, couldn't be trusted.

Did her special sense fail her in the Arctic? Is that why the sub scraped the ship? Back then, she'd always told Blanco to shut up. Blanco wouldn't. He'd rant passionately about our sensed songs that *weaved the unheard future before the first note flashed from God's baton.*

Blanco's rants, though poetic, always struck me as complete bullshit, but as the years passed, I wondered if they might be true. Possibly, each of us could predict, in some distorted way, the sounds or smells or tastes or feel of the future.

Right.

I'm insane, I'm insane. Rad Sick has been my middle name.

Crap, crap, crap. I hope the dregs of TallaTec disappear soon.

Monday, October 2, 2000

I made it to my first Wings meeting.

Meeting of the Wings. We ate wing meat.

I'd bumped into Rand outside the campus library two days before, and he asked me and why I hadn't been showing up at Wings. I said I didn't know the where & when, and he looked puzzled, then said to go tonight at 7 p.m., and I did. To Wings.

It's a joint. Opposite the causeway from Raven's, more or less within walking distance. I must have passed it the night Rand, Van Gear, and I rambled after Dirk Falter's serenade. A 12 x 12 palimpsest of black and yellow fallout shelter signs plastered the wall by the entrance.

Through the doorway, I saw cooks on a smoke break teasing rats with rancid French fries. My kind of place, grease & beer.

Rand and Van Gear were there. The other long-hair I'd seen before, Willington, an ex-journalist, sat beside me. He moaned about needing a job, an academic post, *soon* because of loans and his wife's complaints. Also in attendance, a red-haired fellow, Jack, with a mutating overseas accent, and planted beside him, a philosopher golden boy, Ash, who'd once played college football.

There was good flow at our corner booth's round table, and electric words ran full circle.

The conversation belted back and forth, and people shouted over one another.

I loved it.

*   *   *   *

I've stepped outside my Aluminum Village door and opened a beer, downed it, and tossed it in the green recycle bin, and now I've decided to pen some of tonight's talk. The electric words.

Rand was jazzed, juiced because Professor Brockberry, the true heart of the lit scene, would be back in town. Rand couldn't get the others as enthused, but they listened. He quoted from a Brockberry piece called "In the Jaguar" (*dived into that brother // to enter an unlidded eye / never to lessen the lake / though they grappled it*) and how it was hot when it hit the *The Big Yorker's* pages in the '70s—what Rand considered North America's golden age of arts and letters—how Brockberry still had the inside connections with all journals' editors. Thus, Brockberry was the man.

Van Gear was oddly silent during Rand's rant. As if a secret had picked a quiet place inside his throat to sleep.

"Brockberry's not going to leave Italy," said Jack, the red-headed guy. "Even if his fellowship runs out. He'd be a fool to come back here. I'd give my eyeteeth to live in Florence." Jack's accent floated toward Aussie. Or was it Bosnian?

"You already gave those up," said Willington. "That's why you can't speak a word of intelligible English."

"Florence would be cool," said Ash.

"But he knows things are languishing here. Need revitalizing," said Rand. His voice verged on the desperate. "We need him! The guy invented this place!"

"Come on. We've got plenty of good fac here," said Jack, now sounding French. "Man's not God."

"Jack has a point," added Willington, the ex-journalist. "We've got big G Gods, Professor K-Facto and Bella. They rocked Ravensview last week."

I realized I'd missed it—K-Facto and Bella; I'd napped on the wrong night of the wrong week. I wanted to crown myself *moron, double moron*. Rand mumbled that Willington had introduced the pair well; Willington had been the night's host. He smoothed his long, tangled, greying hair behind his ears and looked pleased.

Talk.

Laughter.

I'd lost the thread, my Rad Sick brain falling overboard with lack of focus, so I snuck my head to the surface with an interrogative.

"What makes Brockberry king?" I asked.

Everyone got quiet. Van Gear glanced at me and smiled. Waved to the server to bring us another pitcher.

"He's not," said Van Gear.

Silence.

"I am."

We broke into furious laughter. The woman slapped the pitcher on the table. Jack clutched the handle to pour a round.

But Van Gear's face remained dead serious. We settled down.

"OK, Van Gear, your lordship, please explain," said Willington.

The German-Jesus reached into his leather jacket and removed an envelope. He methodically slid a sheet of paper from the top and gently unfolded the page. Ash looked on intently. Willington stared at the ceiling, and Jack watched bubbles dance in the half-empty pitcher. Rand looked worried, but also, oddly, hopeful.

"This, gents," said Van Gear, "is a letter I received yesterday from Kurt Mitchell."

"Of *the pacific*?" asked Rand. He looked dumbfounded.

I'd once had a year's subscription to *the pacific*. My mom got it for me when I was an undergrad, knowing my interest in fiction. I'd read it in bed instead of studying my parasitology and zoology texts. My roommate said, "Second best stories in North America, next to *The Big Yorker's*." He was an English major, so I guess he knew. I have to admit, I did like the fiction.

"Kurt Mitchell," said Willington. "Of *the pacific*. No shit. What does he say?"

"Did he accept a story from your collection?" Rand asked.

Jack's forehead crinkled. Ash continuously nodded.

Van Gear rolled his eyes.

"No, but listen to this."

And then Van Gear plowed into a long paraphrasing of the letter. Kurt Mitchell had read Van Gear's story and loved it. He'd passed it to the fiction board, and there'd been one hold out. But the story was fine, deserved a place in a fine magazine. Next, a long riff on their shared love for basketball came to light. As Van Gear had sent stories to Mitchell for over a year, he'd added long hand written letters, often noodling about the

Bulls, the Celtics, or Van Gear's years as C-town's big prep star. Finally, Van Gear had made an offer to Mitchell, one V.G. had promised in a previous letter, one contingent on Doc Primus, the writing department's chair, offering a nice sum for Mitchell to fly down and do a talk to the grad student flock. But the real offer: Van Gear would have an all-star B-ball outfit ready for a pick-up game every day of Mitchell's visit.

Van Gear stopped talking, looked up.

We were the basketball team.

"You're kidding," said Willington.

"Have you asked Primus about this yet?" asked Rand. His voice was as querulous as a giant injured rat. He ran his fingers once through his almost-mullet.

"Of course not," said Van Gear. He waved his hand dismissively. "But he'll agree."

Everyone stared at the ceiling or his beer glass.

Van Gear's face mutated to deadly serious.

"He fucking better. For God's sake, it's *the pacific's* Kurt Mitchell!"

Tuesday, October 3, 2000

Turned up at Ravensview tonight and stumbled onto another beautiful reading.

A woman swayed onto stage in jeans, bangs, long black hair, and sudden bright smiles.

She read poems that made my skin sizzle. She read poems that burst the top of my skull. She read poems that lifted the ceiling into the night sky and made the sky paint the stars with the gentle grace of long-leaf pines.

The black lung of the ceiling cleared.

And then the shock shook. I hadn't caught her name as she'd been introduced.

I'd been too busy scanning the joint: spotting Rand with his beautiful and pregnant girl (met her too, she's J.A.M., short for Jessie-Ann

Merry, and I suddenly realized that when people murmured *Jess is the best!* (as in writing) they'd meant JAM); seeing Ash, the philosopher, girl-friend-seeker, with a tall feminist scholar at his sleeve; nodding at Van Gear, Willington, and Jack as they nursed pitchers at a back table by the stairwell.

I stared at this woman, not recognizing her, and then, line by line, poem by poem, it finally clicked! This poet, this person, was Ryanna Font who I'd met at the coast in September.

How could we have talked for hours on the sand and never mentioned poems?

Her every word fired from the gun of her gut, true and resounding. The echo was pure music, all meaning. I was in the presence of genius.

I swam through bodies to talk to her after she'd read her coda piece.

"Hey," I shouted over the noise, "Remember me?"

"Sure. The boy at the beach. How are you?"

"You soared!"

Ryanna smiled and her eyes became Jupiter-big. "Well, thanks." She looked away and back at me. The bar hummed with delicious din. "What have you been doing?"

"Trying to write a novel."

"Oh, you're a writer too."

She'd just beaten me to my line.

"Poetry," I said, "That too, but you're stuff's on fire!"

"That's kind to say."

"I mean it."

She smiled again and shrugged her shoulders.

"Hey, I promised some people I'd talk to them, but call me, O.K.? You still have my number?"

I nodded, feeling mute. My throat was dry, but I felt giddy.

She slipped into the crowd. Hugged JAM. Hugged others.

I want to be hugged by her long black forest of hair.

Thursday, October 4, 2000

The standoff got press today. On page three. The photography had snow in the foreground and the dark outline of three vessels in the background.

United Press International: *Yesterday reports surfaced concerning a Russian Losos-class Piranha submarine appearing beside the Soviet and American vessels. The U.S.S. Stonewall Jackson remains roped to the Communist ship. An officer in formal uniform, said to be KGB operative Egor Volkov, was seen exiting the Piranha.*

Sources claim that captive U.S. personnel, Russian sailors, and the Piranha's party were observed at dusk on the cruiser's deck. A driving snowstorm made visibility difficult.

The Artic cold must be brutal, so bitter they can't think for the pain, are sick from it, noses raw like beef jerky. Freezing dew must stick to their hair. If sleet drummed atop the ships, the cold would become an encircling, unsolvable misery.

As I imagine the drumming sleet, I hear within my mind the clang of a fork against a plate. I'm not sure how, but a vision surfaces of a large man wearing a formal uniform and a red hat serving kulebyaka, a sturgeon spine-stuffed pastry, and bread wine, tasting of rye and malt, to the American captives. The man makes a toast.

I stopped writing to rub my eyes.

Remains of the damn *Thing* must still haunt me.

Thursday, October 5, 2000

My Ex called early. Before dawn. She sounded depressed, contradicting the letter she'd sent two weeks earlier. Kansas City's luster had faded.

I felt bad for her. The editing job at the college press sounded unpleasant. Too much gossip, a pit of snippy and sarcastic quippers. Nevertheless, she was pleased being employed. After all, joblessness had ticked up to 12.9% last month.

I wonder if she remembers Taylor Velázquez; they'd been in the same Brownie troop as kids. Taylor the scout. Taylor the navigator. It figures Taylor is sub's navigator. As a kid she could navigate abandoned buildings still partially irradiated from The Accident (we Rad Sick stupidly thought we couldn't get any more mutated). As if a cat, she found entrances and exits that were "safe" in the debris. Maybe her hyper sensitive tongue could taste "hot and cold" air columns. Of course, Ex wasn't adventurous in that way, even as a child. She'd rather stay inside and watch *Cabaret* on VHS.

I told Ex I was fine. I talked about Ravensview and Wings, but not TallaTec.

I wanted to ask her if she'd started smoking again, but I didn't.

The memory of Ryanna's big smile burst into my head at one point, and I wondered if Ex would get jealous if I mentioned Ms. Font, the fab poet, my new friend. But did I want to make Ex jealous? Not really.

Ex rambled, halfheartedly suggested that I visit KC. I had neither interest nor money. But I didn't say that. I moaned about upcoming essay deadlines, and she sighed.

I imagined a trip to KC as Ex taking me to a kitsch Dante's *Inferno*. She'd introduce me to her colleagues at an editorial party, and then spend the entire night flirting with greeting card composers who'd crash the gig wearing top hats with pitchforks. I hated top hats, but that's the kind of thing she loved.

"Too bad you're so busy," she said.

See you soon, she whispered before she hung up. That was weird. She never said shit like that. She preferred *Ciao*. *See you soon* sounded too earnest for a Miami girl.

Friday, October 6, 2000

I was the only one who showed up for Van Gear's B-ball practice.

I biked to the court early, saw him shooting jump shots from the top of the key. They rained, nonstop. He wore a blue headband that kept his hair from his eyes. He moved like a 1st round draft choice. He wowed me.

"Let's see your shot," said Van Gear. He threw a hard pass that stung my palms. I hesitated, examined the ball. I didn't want to reveal my lack of talent. I'd never played much B-ball. Some soccer, a lot of sandlot gridiron, a smattering of tennis.

I stepped back and catapulted a one-armed rainbow in the direction of the goal. Completely missed the rim, but it did boom the backboard.

"You seem nervous," said Van Gear.

"Not a hoops junkie."

"A shame. You got the height."

"Does Kurt Mitchell really play?"

"We're going to find out, aren't we?"

Or we weren't, because the *we* would only mean me and Van G. We waited an hour. No one else appeared.

Van Gear was pissed.

We played some one-on-one, and he drove past me like a Sunfish sailing past driftwood. To ease his frustrations, he constantly stole the ball from me. We were gassed. After a lightning move past me and a textbook reverse-layup, Van Gear stopped and leaned forward to catch his breath, hands on knees. He became cloud-white for five seconds, and I almost said something, but then he picked up the ball and chucked it at my head. I caught it two millimeters from my nose.

"Let's do more shooting," he said.

We practiced foul shots. I could hear Van Gear cursing under his breath.

"I don't get these pussies," said Van Gear. "Here's a perfectly reasonable opportunity to get to know Kurt Mitchell, an editorial *powerhouse*, and they fuckin' chicken-out. Who the fuck wouldn't want to play basketball with Kurt Mitchell? Who?" He shook his head in disgust. "I'm even giving them a chance to practice, so they won't embarrass themselves."

I stayed quiet. Actually sunk one with my weak hand.

"And Rand is all excited because Brockberry might return. That guy's not coming back. Who'd want to come back to this shit?"

That stung. *This* was *shit*? I was falling in love with T-town, the people, the places, the hum. Dade had been dross. T-town was time as rocket ship.

The sun was setting. A mild chill iced the wind.

Van Gear returned to mumbling. He missed shots now.

"I like it here," I said, sinking my third free throw in a row.

Van Gear missed a bomb from way out. The ball clattered off the rim, shook the entire backboard as if a nuke gale had swirled across the asphalt.

"That's enough," he said. "Let's go."

Monday, October 9, 2000

Wings met. Full contingent. Full quorum.

After pitcher-plentiful and food-full, we stood around in the empty parking lot—we'd closed the joint—and kept talking. We word-danced, double time.

Van Gear didn't mention the wallying on the B-ball session, and no one skated near *rim*, *pacific*, or *Mitchell*.

Ash suddenly had an unlit cigarette in his hand. I didn't think he smoked. Willington did, always solo, standing along Highway 90 during the lulls between beers.

"Did you guys know they've just started *bottling* this?" Ash said.

A white pick-up swished by going 60. Moths orbiting the lot's one light broke their Milky Way nimbus for a moment.

"What's that?" asked Rand. He kept checking his watch.

"I'd heard a rumor," said Van Gear. He stared intensely at the insect cloud.

"He's holding a bottle?" asked Jack. His accent was slipping Glasgow tonight. "That looks like a bloody cigarette to me."

"Yes, it's a joint, Jack. It's their *expression*." said Ash, "They're *bottling* TallaTec. You know, *the Thing*."

Everyone was silent for a beat.

"I think I'd like to try that," said Willington.

"Huh. Bottled it in a cigarette," said Rand.

"That's what they're calling it," said Ash. "Look, no label, no brand, no filter lines." Rand leaned towards Ash to study it. He frowned.

Ash lit the stick. Hit it.

Rand glanced at his watch a fifth time. "Guys, I've got to go. JAM's stomach again. The baby." Everyone nodded. He jumped in his car and rolled off.

Ash toked again. Then Van Gear. Next Willington. Finally Jack.

"You up, man?" asked Ash. He hungered for it.

"Sure," I said. But I wasn't. I suddenly wondered why I hadn't called Ryanna yet. I hated telephones, but at the moment, I'd been happier awkwardly talking with Ryanna than standing in a lot with Wings smoking TallaTec. The shit unnerved me.

Like a Rad Sick dumbass, I inhaled anyway.

Unlike the TallaTec from the I.V. hoses, this was actual smoke. I coughed ferociously.

"Take it easy," said Willington. "It'll punch your lungs out."
He slapped me good-naturedly on the back.

"Speaking of taking a punch, or throwing one, for that matter . . . Mr. Van Gear, will you be ready next week?"

I remembered Willington was hosting at Ravensview again, and apparently Van Gear would be the main attraction.

I suddenly wanted to read at Ravensview. Intensely. Like I'd wanted my Ex that last night before she left. I had to fully bond with the

T-town scene, and doing a reading would cement things.

"Who's after that?" I asked.

"Dirk Falter, I think," said Willington. "Then our man Jack the next week." He took a TallaTec hit. The joint glowed like an eye. I looked at the ground. "Rand and I read together after that."

"Oh," I said. "Cool."

"You looking to read?" Willington asked.

My face flashed up too expectantly, because Willington immediately backpedaled.

"Well, the list is set for this year. But whoever rides herd in January, get on 'em. We need to get you in."

Ash nodded his head and handed me the TallaTec.

"It's like that Brandelsonna film," said Van Gear. "The one with the samurai and the two horses. Before the battle scene, he must choose between the mare and the mustang. But a stray arrow kills him as he begins to point."

Willington gave a thumbs-up, clearly as stoned as Van Gear.

Ash left next. He had to work on his dissertation on Derrida and Nietzsche. A philosophy degree sounded like uphill plowing through a whole lot of words, but all the wrong ones. He drifted on foot beyond the glow of the overhead multi-winged nimbus.

After that point, my memory resembles a collage.

Van Gear and Willington had both arrived on Kawasakis, and I ended up on the back of W's, and Jack rode sidesaddle on Van G's, and we streaked into the T-town night.

I'm not sure which point in the night we arrived at the den with the black boxes, but I know we did. I thought I saw my ex sucking on three tubes, a red cartridge snuggled in the machine, but she became plaster-white and disappeared or turned into a camera-bulb flash the size of a cantaloupe.

Or both. I'm not sure which.

Perhaps later, we were on a pier somewhere, Jack standing on the edge of the boardwalk, staring out into a swamp called Lake Jackson. We were polishing two-thirty 9 packs. The TallaTec had washed from our systems; however, I thought I saw giant model Pu-239 isotopes playing bumper boats in the muck. Nine beers with 23 ounces each. So clever. Jack cleverly strapped our empties together with vines to make three-can boats. *Beer-subs,* he called them. Next, he had the brilliant idea of pissing behind the 3-can vessels to give them a push, soap-like suds bubbling beside each homemade craft. We had a few races but tired of it quickly, having emptied ourselves. At Wings the urinals stank of lavender toilet pucks, but here the lake smelled of old bait.

"You ever fish here?" asked Van Gear. He had his chin angled at Willington.

"Can't remember," said Willington. "Maybe in a boat once. Not on this dock."

"We should go fishing now," said Jack. He glanced back at the Kawasaki bikes as he teetered at the end of the dock. He'd been saying he was scanning the surface for schools of mullet. That's what he'd been saying all night, though the K-riding kings and I insisted mullet didn't live in freshwater.

Jack was suddenly wading in the water around the dock, and we laughed as he snatched at invisible minnows in the moonlight. I tossed a crumpled can in the water, and yelled *snook!* Which seemed out of proportion hilarious, and everyone was laughing, even Jack.

But then things weren't funny.

Jack was in chest deep water. Moaning, crying.

"Oh God! Where's my son, my son?!?!"

Van Gear and Willington were mumbling panicked whispers to one another, and they crashed into the black soup to fetch Jack and send us home.

Tuesday, October 10, 2000

Didn't know what to make of Jack the other night, but I guess it will surface before too long. Maybe it was the TallaTec. He'd taken stiff hits. Mine were shallow, because I didn't trust the stuff. My sanity had tiptoed around the warping *mind*-fields, but it'd still made me feel like hell. The drug must have affected Jack the same. The chemical could potentially unearth nightmares, deeply buried fears and bogeymen. What did TallaTec dig up from Jack?

He's been hiding something. Perhaps he too wants to keep the past concealed, has some shadow he wishes no one to know because he too is making a fresh start. I don't want TallaTec to raise the curtain on my Rad Sick history. I'm having a hard enough time adjusting to T-town, grad school, Alum Village, and even though I've recently been enjoying this New World's offerings, each step, with my tired Rad Sick feet, has been a trial. I don't need to make it harder.

Today's trial: getting over my phone-phobia—in the context of calling Ryanna. I held my breath, closed my eyes, and dialed from memory.

And it worked! I'd made the call.

And we'd made a date.

Ryanna suggested we meet at the Confluence in the late afternoon, the neck of water where the Wakulla and St. Marks rivers meet.

The day was surprisingly bitter. An early fall cold front pushed through last night, strutting down from Canada like the kick of a TallaTec high riding Arctic high pressure (no new news on Taylor moored in the Arctic). I was shivering, so I pulled on a long sleeve shirt with a hole in the right elbow that I hoped Ryanna wouldn't notice.

She'd arrived early, had already toured the remains of the tiny Spanish fort that boxed-in the grounds to the west. The distant smells of sea water and campfires mixed in the air.

"Let me show you something," she said.

We slogged through a nest of trees and ambled to a point, the crux where the two rivers met. The point arrowed to the Gulf of Mexico.

Her blue eyes sang beneath her black bangs, and her smile was continuous, friendly. She seemed as open as the clear sky.

I wanted to talk to her about her poems, about her reading at Ravensview, but every time I mentioned the subjects, she changed the topic. She was too engaged in the present, in this quiet, beautiful landscape, and any other matter, she implied, was unwanted distraction.

"Watch this," she said.

She grabbed a tree branch from the sand and heaved it into the St. Marks, making a huge splash. The stick drifted to the middle of the stream and then followed the current and floated to the heart of the Confluence. Once the branch lined up with the point, the stick swirled as if caught in a low-suction whirlpool. The wood turned slowly, like the needle of a compass trying to find north.

We watched the branch turn.

"Will it leave that spot?" I asked.

"Oh, eventually. But only when you're not looking." Ryanna grinned.

I could have kissed her at that moment. Should have. But some Rad Sick kink in my stomach triggered an eye-twitch, so I rubbed my face with both hands, hoping to regain my nerve. I self-consciously fingered the hole in my shirt's elbow, killing time.

Then my luck dipped south, because in the distance echoed the noise of drunken voices. They grew steadily louder.

Out of nowhere came a marauding gaggle of—I couldn't fucking believe it!—graduate students from the program, all walking bicycles through the maze of trees and brush. A few clutched liquor bottles. A dozen tromped in our direction, half of them singing Christmas carols for some asinine reason. They'd pedaled the sixteen miles on the old train tracks the government had buried and paved, a route that led from T-town to the tiny Spanish fort.

"Deck the balls with dread and fairies, La-la-la-la-la-*Laaaaaaa*,

Da bim, boom, bum!" sang a guy with an orange ski cap I recognized from the novel workshop. He'd spent each session slashing and burning everyone's prose; then when others targeted his uneven work, he got as defensive as a cornered snake.

A few of the group I knew from the poetry lit class, and maybe another from the Theory course I'd only attended thrice.

They mostly nodded at us and milled bashfully along the shore just north of where we lingered. Ryanna stepped away from me. I suddenly hated every grad student.

"Those your friends, huh?" Ryanna whispered. "They act much younger than you."

"Some of them are just kids," I said, which is ridiculous, because at all of 20 years, I'm just a child, but as the docs explained, my Rad Sick condition means I look, act, feel 35. Or older. That's one of the things I really like about Wings, all the guys are over 30.

"But they're your people," she said.

"No way."

O.K. I didn't really hate this group. But at this moment, they were a true kettle of kiss-killers. The drunk bastards! One pale-cheeked girl wearing ear muffs—oh yeah, she's in the novel class too—waved to me and smiled, and I nodded back. I couldn't remember her name, so I didn't want to introduce her to Ryanna (I did remember Ms. Ear Muffs was always kind), so I stared at the Confluence to catch a glimpse of the tree branch, trying to avoid her eyes.

But the branch was gone.

"Damn," I whispered.

"What?" Ryanna asked.

I pointed.

"I told you," she said. "But that's O.K." She paused a beat. "You've heard how nature wants to pull against itself, go from disorder to order?"

"Huh?"

"It's like that."

"What?"

"Well . . . I can show you another way."

"How's that?"

"I can take you to where the aquifer is tapped."

"You're changing the subject," I said. "What's that got to do with the stick vanishing?"

"Come on," she said. "I can show you."

"Where?"

"Come on."

As we rustled past the trees, all the grad students hurled their souls into a rousing chorus of "I Saw Three Ships Come Sailing." Some of the women were nicely nailing high harmonies. Their voices faded to a hum as we shuffled to Ryanna's car.

The temperature had dropped quite a bit, and my hands felt numb.

"So we're driving somewhere?"

"Yes. Let's go. I'll take you."

I hesitated. Something about abandoning my car gave me pause. My auto is my security blanket. In the past if punks' Rad Sick innuendo got too much, I could always speed off and surround myself with Zeppelin's "Your Time is Gonna Come."

At this moment, I stood silent, thinking.

A couple of local fisherman strolled by, warm in their flannel shirts, ball caps tight on their skulls, fishing poles and bait buckets firmly gripped. One had a faded atom-symbol on the front of his hat. They gave us a quick, curious glance as they walked through the parking lot and headed to the Confluence. They winked at us.

I took it as a sign. I acquiesced. I liked being with Ryanna, even if she did seem a touch spacey. Her blue eyes had innocent, child-like magnetism.

"Where we going? Near here?"

"To my work. It's not far."

"What you do?"

"I do boat tours at Skull Springs."

"Really. That's cool. You're a naturalist? A naturalist and poet?"

She didn't answer, only smiled to herself as she opened the door for me and soon steered her Ford onto the main highway.

We arrived at Skull Springs in the late afternoon. The gates were padlocked. A large wooden sign showed a bass leaping over a limbo bar and grinning its gills off. The letters of Skull Springs were painted a bright blue and stood out against the brown background.

This place was super dense with forest, armies of magnolias, pines, oaks, and sweet gums, and saw palmettos cluttered the ground. We were entering a north Florida jungle. I recalled old roadside attractions around Miami. They were as much about nature as amusement, which I thought was a good thing. And they always called themselves *jungles*: Monkey Jungle, Parrot Jungle, Miami's Jungle Serpentarium, Jaguar Jungle Safari—all now disappeared into the cement and silicon jungle of glass and cinderblocks. I miss those places.

We stared at the padlock on Skull Springs' gate.

"They close up early?" I asked.

"Yeah, Tuesdays are slow. The two guys on shift must have left at 4. Missed them by 30 minutes."

"Out of luck."

"Don't worry," said Ryanna. "I can get us in."

She pulled a large skeleton key from a pocket and unlocked the gate.

"Where'd you get that key?" I asked.

"Yeah, it's something special. Can open about anything." She grinned.

Glancing at her watch, she pushed the gate wide. After we rolled through, she shut it behind us and snapped the lock tight.

We meandered a mile along a gravel road and rolled to a dock where a gaggle of boats sat moored.

Empty, the 30-seat crafts looked haunted. Each needed a paint job along the hull's waterline, in contrast to the bright blue words *Skull Springs* and the shiny image of a bass bursting from the bows.

"I want to show you the view," said Ryanna. Her smile was broad.

"Of what? The aquifer?"

"You'll see."

She walked across the dead-silent cement dock where the five full-roofed boats sat moored. Two at the far end were boxy, with white panels making a fence-like wall around the sides; foot-wide slits marked an opening between each yard-long panel. They appeared under-used; a thick algae-like growth marked each hull's perimeter at the waterline.

Inside benches faced inwards along the perimeter of a 30 foot glass-topped coffin that covered the midline.

Ryanna walked the docks as if she owned the place. Yes, she worked there, but since it was after hours, I wondered if our visit was slightly iffy. Or maybe I was being Rad Sick paranoid.

She hopped onto the boat at the dock's far end.

"All aboard," she said. She pulled out a key, adjusted an engine priming lever, and checked a few gauges on the foot-long dashboard. She fidgeted with the steering wheel, clicked a few toggle switches.

"You sure this is OK?" I asked.

"Yes. Don't worry." She gave me a dismissive wave.

The engine cranked with the sad-sounding half-cough of an older era motor. The air stank of burnt oil. The boat quaked at first, a tremor I felt in my achy bones. A rattle echoed from the stern. But once Ryanna gave it a little more gas, everything quieted.

Ryanna steered us in the direction of the large pool—a lake, really—that marked the source of the river. An oddly curving cypress hung over one side of the springhead like a vulture. The majority of the banks were walled with cypress, except for a swimming area that had sugar-white sand. I stood next to Ryanna as she steered to a spot 50 feet from the curving tree.

As she drove, her blouse rolled up her torso, revealing her trim stomach, and the beautiful couple of ribs at the lower half of her rib cage. I kept going back and forth between her skin and the spring's surface.

She turned around and pointed to the boat's glass-topped coffin. I realized it had a glass bottom too, the perfect sarcophagus for viewing a 30-foot human corpse. But no—the glass was for viewing Skull Spring's secrets. I leaned over to see what lay beneath. Ryanna said the glass top protected the new surface a pair of university scientists had added to the bottom pane to increase magnification and clarity.

"Spectacular view there," she said.

"It's getting too dark."

"Got a floodlight attached to the stern." She popped a switch.

I stooped over again.

"Take a look," she said.

As I twisted my body onto the bench along the perimeter of the glass coffin, my shirt rose up, and I self-consciously pulled it down as my gut slid atop the transparent surface (What a hypocrite, yes? I got the *show*, but I was too shy to give her one?). The chilly air made my hands shiver.

The floodlight brightened the depths; things came into view.

"This is what they call a glass-bottom boat?" I asked.

"Yes, of course," she said and smiled.

Ryanna adjusted the throttle to near idle; the fifty foot craft drifted in one place.

I leaned over the box and stared into the depths of Skull Springs.

For a moment, the clarity of the water seemed dodgy, but as the floodlight warmed up, its beam struck the columns of molecules at just the right angle as if I was looking through air. We traveled above a bright-white sandy bottom, watching small bream glide along.

Ryanna inched us forward. Quickly, the landscape underneath changed from sand to the rim of a huge hole dropping yards and yards into the spring's darkness. The water worked to magnify things—or was it the coating on the coffin's glass bottom?

Then I saw the skull!

A colossal skull stared up at me with empty eyes, a mastodon or mammoth. Tiny silver fish darted through a hole near the skeleton's thinking-cap. A few ribs and a tusk bent around the space beneath the magnificent head. The bones were streaked with fuzzy growth.

The tusk reminded me of a scimitar or a warped spear or a sequence from a short strand of humungous DNA. Ryanna said the State had decided decades ago to not disturb the skull, leaving the spectacular view as a wonder all could enjoy.

Mysteries hid in the water, as if the sheer clarity of the fluid marked some barrier between the real and unreal. The water was so clear it made the conscious mind wonder if only *imaginary* water could be so transparent.

Ryanna adjusted a lever on the far side of her dashboard, and a whirring shuddered from the hull. The floodlight was moving, tracing changing landscapes along the sandy bottom near the lip of the hole where the skull rested.

The spotlight tilted and pierced the center of the spring's opening and paused. The beam stretched and diffused light into fragmented streaks.

In the barely lit gloom near the bottom, the opening to a cave appeared, a dark but toothless mouth that spewed water instead of words.

"Can you see the source?" she asked.

"The cave? Yes. What's it the source of?"

"Everything," said Ryanna.

I wondered about her mysterioso-schtick, but I let it ride, filed it away. Inside my head, the word *everything* hung in the gloaming and dampness, engulfed the lake's silence.

"You see the swirl of the tape grass, the *Vallisneria floridana,* at the edges of the spring's mouth?" She cut the motor again.

I tightened my focus, squinted. My Rad Sick contacts were bugging me. I concentrated, aware of movement that caught the shards of light from the spot's beam. Something danced, like streamers attached to a fan—fluttered in the darkness of the spring source, in the darkness of *the everything*.

Glancing over my shoulder, I caught Ryanna leaning over the side of the boat, her eyes wide with wonder, as if she'd never seen this all before. Was every time like the first time for her? Was it always new? She had a never-ceasing sense of wonder. I was jealous. If the world were always new, the ceaseless wonder could cushion all hurts.

I stared down through the boat's windowed bottom, gazed into the cold currents, down where all became blurry. An angular shadow crept into view, as if the cone-shaped nose of an underwater dog or the tip of a V2 rocket. The tip looked too pointy to be an alligator. In another moment, I thought I spied the spindly arm of an octopus or maybe the tail of an American crocodile. The shadow halted, revealing little. Maybe it was simply one corner of the boat's stern caught and distorted by the spotlight.

"Even with the light beam, I think it's hard to see what's what," I said.

Ryanna nodded. But she kept staring over the side as if trying to spot some shy, rare fish.

Bubbles fizzed from the cave mouth, a big burst, as if underwater smoke. Each mushroom of air dispersed from the center and steamed upward. Each bubble was shaped like a jellyfish. The water changed from blue to white.

Ryanna frowned.

Silence. Then the song of frogs and cicadas seared the air. Alligators lurking near clumps of cypress coughed to mark territory.

The wind had shifted, blowing us against the current, keeping us in place. Ryann kept her attention glued to the deep.

I was holding my breath, staring through the glass bottom, noticing nothing, but because of her intensity I felt as though I should be catching the glimmer of some mysterious holiness.

The bubbles streaming from the cave mouth grew larger. Soon

they were huge, like large and flimsy weather balloons. The spring's surface began to roil, as if the water were boiling. The underwater was white with air.

"Damn it!" said Ryanna.

"What is it?"

"This happened last week too. Had to cut a boat trip short and refund everyone their money. Some endless release of air, as if the caves sprang lungs. Maybe someone planted a machine that has coughing fits."

"Kind of weird then? Not normal?"

"Definitely."

Ryanna steered the boat slowly in a tight circles at the center of the spring, but the ferocious bubbling wouldn't let up.

She killed the stern's floodlight and headed back to the dock. It was becoming quite late; evening beckoned through the spring-fed jungle's trees.

Ryanna shook her head, clearly frustrated. A moment later she whistled a long sigh, seemingly releasing her tension. However, she'd stopped talking.

"That large cave at the spring's bottom," I said, "that was cool. Thanks for showing me that." We'd reached the launch, and I helped her tie the boat to the dock's pilings. She'd remained pensive and quiet as she steered us from Skull Spring's lake.

"Sorry about the clarity. I wanted you to see all that goes in and out of that tunnel at any given moment."

"Such as?"

"Can't really describe it. You just have to see it. It's never the same."

"Oh."

"And I don't know what's up with the flurry of air. More like a blizzard, a storm. Ruins the visibility, which is already getting tricky with all the other crap in the water."

"Like a giant alka-seltzer," I said.

Ryanna laughed. She opened her mouth and hesitated. "Don't

know what's going wrong in the aquifer caves, but something's out of kilter."

"Well, thanks for showing me. Both the Confluence and the springhead. Pretty cool. You're generous to give me a private tour."

Ryanna shrugged sheepishly, seeming to forget her musings on the aquifer.

Just before we slid into her car to leave, she surprised me again by giving me a fast, soft kiss on the cheek. She opened her Ford's creaky door.

"Hey, we're not that far from where I live. I'm down a dirt road a few miles away. Pretty view there too. You want to take a look?"

I glanced at her, and she was giving me the hugest smile she'd given me yet.

"O.K.," I said. "Sure."

Her dirt road was lined with overhanging oaks. Moss dripped in fuzzy icicles, or what I imagined icicles might look like if covered with bread mold.

We were soon careening down a narrow driveway. Overgrown azalea bushes stroked the sides of the car.

The Ford stopped in front of a cedar-siding shotgun house, and Ryanna leapt out. She stood tall beside the Toyota's radio antenna. She'd shown me so many oddities today, the disappearing stick at the confluence, the sights at Skull Springs, but I remained ready for anything. I cracked open the car door.

"What's next?" I asked, feeling unsure again and a bit dazed from the chilly air.

"Come on. There's something I have to show you in the backyard."

I climbed out and followed.

Wednesday, October 11, 2000

The second B-ball practice. Again Van Gear and I, a solo pair.

He cursed under his breath as we waited for the no-shows to no show. For the first half hour, we played around-the-world and horse, and Van Gear whipped me.

"What was with Jack the other night?" I asked.

"I don't think anybody knows. Something he keeps to himself. His wife probably doesn't even know."

I had no idea Jack was married. My directional senses suddenly felt askew.

"Invented?" I offered.

"No, seems real enough. He's not ready to let the cap off. Some other life, I suppose." Van Gear planted his feet and turned to face the rim. "Actually, I have no idea." He launched a shot from half court and drilled it. "Would like to know where the fuck he is, though."

For forty minutes we took turns firing jump shots. We shot the shit between dribbles, Van Gear growing more Zen-like.

My mind kept drifting to last night with Ryanna. In the backyard she showed me a large screened porch that overlooked a sinkhole. The water was dark in the dying sunlight. And beautiful. Then she offered another surprise. She pulled a manuscript from under an old typewriter and read a short story out loud. My Rad Sick ear for invisible voices kicked into gear, worked to hear a voice that should be heard. My ears opened wide. I'm good at this. I can tell *true voices* that spring to life in spoken and written words. As I'd tripped through my zoology degree, I'd known a kid who'd written poetry like mad (before I was interested in writing), and one night he'd murmured a piece called "Rabbit Time," and the lines made my skull crackle with tingles and jolts. I'd told him to send it to the English Department's big time lit mag, and a week later the journal accepted it. Ryanna's story was like that, as if it had been born whole and beautiful from the sinkhole.

When she finished, we sat in darkness.

"You need to send that to *the pacific* tomorrow; I'm not kidding," I said.

She laughed but could tell I was sincere, and she promised to mail it in the morning.

After that, things broke more wonderful. We crept through the darkness of her house, and we kissed and stripped and fell inside each other as if diving deep into the caverns that bled water to the sinkhole. We'd fallen.

The next morning, she drove me back to my car.

Van Gear and I exchanged bounce-passes, and he suddenly rocketed one, and the ball launched off the asphalt and smacked my face.

"Wake up," he said. He was smiling.

"I'm not so good at this sport," I said. I wiped my sore cheek, trying not to grimace.

"Yeah, if you're not paying attention," he replied.

He suddenly raced down the court at top speed and slam dunked the ball through the net. He knelt a second, as if catching his breath. The ball bounced beside his shoulder. He looked pale. I was about to say something, but he stood and kicked the ball to me, and I raced down the court to catch it on the fly with one hand.

"Nice," Van Gear said. I felt elated.

We sat on the sideline and stared at the stars.

"Kurt Mitchell is coming," Van Gear said.

"For sure?"

"Just confirmed it with Doc Primus today. He'll be here in December."

"Then we have plenty of time for practice."

"I suppose so," said Van Gear. He sounded a little wistful.

I'm not sure I've described Van Gear very well. The guy certainly could be cocky, arrogant, oddly intolerant, but these quirks only leaked out when he blew off steam at Wings or the basketball court. Otherwise, his German-Jesus look matched his saint-likeliness. The guy was kind, generous, giving rides to drunk kooks at late night English Department parties so that they would arrive home safe. He was compassionate; he listened. He'd sit in coffee shops and have long, soulful conversations with women who thirsted to be understood. He was recently divorced, and he used this as a shield to keep the women from getting too close (all females had a gigantic crush on the bastard; he was too good-looking for his own good). Willington, to ratify Van Gear's kindness, always brought up his and Van Gear's camping trip from last year. They'd been sleeping on tall dunes on a panhandle coastline, and a cold front had sneaked through, chilling the air. Their fire had died, and Willington woke up freezing. Van Gear, in his sleep, somehow sensed this, popped awake, and the pair scavenged driftwood and started a new blaze. Van Gear had done most of the work: that was the true Van Gear.

"If nothing else, it would be wonderful to spend tonight riding under the stars," Van Gear said. This track seemed a little out of the blue to me, but I didn't say anything. "Take a clay road into the woods, find a sinkhole and go for a swim with the full moon resting on the surface."

"That wouldn't be bad," I said. I thought about the bubbles popping on the surface of Skull Springs and imagined them as the racing images within a brain blown full with TallaTec. I remembered that Ryanna had never gotten around to telling me what we were trying to see beneath the glass-bottom boat.

"I know everyone thinks I'm too whacked on Kerouac, but I think people are missing something essential in *The Dharma Bums*."

"I haven't read it."

"But you know *On the Road*?"

"Not really."

Van Gear said nothing for a moment, kept staring into the star-pricked blackness.

"Within all the frantic energy, there's a pause for loveliness, a passion in the prose that's a breath, not just a rant. That's what people miss. All they hear is the rant. But they're missing the point. It's about the breath."

I wanted to make a dumb yoga joke, but Van Gear seemed serious so I kept my mouth shut.

Van Gear tried spinning the ball on the end of his finger, but surprisingly, he wasn't very good.

"Would just like to write something true," Van Gear said.

Before I could utter a response, he stood up and wrapped both arms around the ball.

"Let's go," he said.

Thursday, October 12, 2000

Nothing in the news about the U.S.S. Stonewall Jackson. The standoff has gone on too long. Usually in incidents like this, the *offenders* are quickly released. Even 1991's Great Lakes Incident ended in two weeks, the U.S. Coast Guard releasing the Russian sub's small crew to a Soviet battleship near Bermuda. Of course, the 1996 Tagalog Atoll Impasse lasted for months, with U.S. personnel keeping Soviet frogmen for questioning and shrugging at Russian demands to return them to their Piranha. Maybe the Russians are doing tit-for-tat, holding Taylor Velázquez for just as long. Or did they suspect the U.S. sailors held valuable information? Then again, did someone catch a glint in Taylor's eyes? And now were curious?

I need distraction. I call Ryanna again, see if she'll pick up.

Friday, October 13, 2000

Ryanna doesn't answer and that bums me out. Maybe I really blew it that night and didn't know it. Oh well. It's probably better. I'm not over my Ex as much as I'd like to think. She haunts me.

Last night we did do Wings. On Monday Van Gear reads at Ravensview. At Wings he didn't want to discuss his reading. Willington kidded him mercilessly, but Van Gear wouldn't take the bait.

Jack and Rand riffed about Raymond Carver, and Van Gear

weighed in heavily. The "Carver curve," as Jack called it, was bending us too much to the will of the minimal. We needed to jump the curve and U-turn back to fleshy prose. Rand and Van Gear disagreed. Van Gear had written a short article on Carver's use of the nonverbal. The essay had been published in a fancy university journal; he talked about the space between each story's beats that gifted the prose a glass-like sheen. Rand insisted Carver had reinvented the short story as poem. I, admittedly, didn't *get* Carver most of the time, but he did have work I admired.

Willington was full of a new news. He predicted the imminent end of the "Carver Era," the man's shadow of silence and alcoholism sinking into the mire; Willington named the new heir apparent as Cormac McCarthy, a writer we'd vaguely heard of but knew nothing about.

"You will know him," said Willington. "He'll be on the lips of every MFA kid north of the Panama Canal in ten years. I guarantee it."

"What makes you say that?" asked Ash.

"He's the next logical step after Carver. The no-stretch prose with a much darker bent."

"Sounds like you're talking Bukowski," said Van Gear.

"No, not that dark. I'm talking the true animal in the pinched white matter of every human brain. I'm talking the truly inhumane."

"You're talking Thomas Hobbes," said Ash.

"Hobbes and whoever," said Rand. "That's old school dressed up as new school with more blood. Big fucking deal."

"You read him?" asked Willington.

"I read enough of *Child of God* to know it's shit."

"You're wrong there, my friend. Just wait and see."

We scattered twenty minutes later. I got a flat tire on the way home and had to walk my bike the last mile. I patched the tube as soon as I walked in the door, though I had some trouble with the glue and suddenly wished I'd had a cigarette. I was relieved no one whipped out a TallaTec joint.

When the glue finally stuck and no air leaked from the patch's edge I sobbed. To double-check, I dipped the tube into a bucket of water. Unlike Skull Springs, no bubbles appeared; the tire tube was its own intact bubble.

My Rad Sick anxiety flattened. I caught my breath and wiped my eyes clear.

Sunday, October 15, 2000

Late this afternoon I took a break from my novel to leaf through Rand's notebook again. I don't understand why he tossed it. I keep finding interesting passages.

--The photos show children hovering in midair, arms splayed—arms as simply wings.
--Baby's feet grip onto limb and hands hold onto big brother's thick, limb-like legs. He grows out from the tree, his arms as seed bearing branches and his blond hair an overgrowth of leaves, his eyes, two knots in the wood.

I don't know why I keep forgetting to give this back to Rand. I'd like to talk about these lines. There's potential. And it's interesting how he pictures his unborn daughter as outside the womb, interacting with the world.

O.K. Going to bed. Tomorrow night's big: V.G. reads.

Monday, October 16, 2000

Getting ready to ride my bike to Ravensview to see Van Gear perform. I'm nervous and don't know why. Nervous for Van Gear? Why should I be? But I am. Despite the C-town front, the guy is sensitive. When he mentioned Thursday night that Kurt Mitchell was a sure thing, nobody said much. I could tell that deflated him. I hope his prose doesn't fall flat with the Raven crowd. Shouldn't. He's certainly got his fans. I, on the other hand, have no fans. Fuck. I want to read at Ravensview so badly—from my messy *Microwaves*—but I want the crowd to be awed as if my word-diamonds surfaced from literary atomic heat.

Blast-diamonds. That was the legend from *Incident '80*. Funny how the word *diamond* brings it up from the brain's carbon chaos. The radical heat melted carbon chunks into gems, so they said. As kids, we'd dig in the dirt, hoping to find the stones hidden in the sugar sand. Orange Bowl girders had been damaged by shockwaves, but the county had rebuilt it, churning up a lot of earth, and we always found ourselves with our mom's gardening tools raking and scratching the ground. We'd go any time we were bored, which was always. Didn't matter what was happening at the stadium. One New Year's night featured a game named the Atom Bowl to give a nod to the memory of the accident. Patrons stared at us as if we were glow-eyed rats escaped from the sewers, but we ignored them.

All right. Getting late. Time to hit Ravensview. I'm truly pumped. This will be the first Wing I will have heard read.

More later.

*   *   *

Back. Van Gear slayed 'em. Think he read the piece almost taken by *the pacific*. That's what Rand guessed. I sat with the whole Wings crew plus JAM plus Jack's wife Vicky plus Ash's latest gal Samantha. Van Gear was nervous, wanted to suck bourbon shots like a thirsty tick. Willington dissuaded him. And then Willington introduced him with good words and a little B-ball humor. Van Gear took it well. Climbed on stage with John Lennon glasses and his long hair in a ponytail.

Van Gear opened with some obscure quote by Henry Miller, then kidded the crowd with *Yeah, I don't know what that means either, but it fits me and the moment.* The people were on his side and laughed.

After that, he cruised and the audience soared with him. I was jealous.

I noticed beforehand that JAM was a radiant people-magnet. Not just the program-people, but all comers. Rand was a bit of a lodestone too, but in a more self-conscious way that intimidated. I think Rand might mean well, but it's easy to write him off as arrogant.

Mr. Orange Ski Cap and Ms. Ear Muffs—another chilly night so both sported headgear—paid tribute at the Wings table, and I finally remembered their names: Skate and Kate. I kept thinking, *Why in God's name is she dating him?* Kate talked to me while Skate, Jack and Vicky bantered. She asked me when my novel slice would make it to the fiction-class table. I shrugged. I can't recall anything I said. She was nice about my evasiveness, though.

Every few minutes I'd scan the room, looking for Ryanna. Never saw her. Willington kept asking me who I was looking for, and I said I was working out a crick in my neck. He laughed. He was the night's good humor man.

The first pitcher was served by the bartender with the mitochondria tattoos. Her vacuoles were empty, calm. Strangely, so was I.

The next round was plopped down by Elly. "Hi, Needlefish," she whispered into my ear as she poured my mug full. I lost my calm. Elly's smile put me on edge.

A good edge.

Her smile was sweet, nothing forward. Open. Generous. Why did my stomach flip?

"Be back, Needlefish."

Needlefish is not a word I like. Reminds me of my sister. She'd walk me home from school when we were kids, and we'd stroll by canals rife with the impossible-to-catch, translucent, string-thin, sharp-nosed critters. I'd throw rocks at them. Big Sis said I was being childish. And stupid. She said I hated them because they were just like me, invisible squirts. She'd even occasionally call me *Needle-brain.* Like a lot of older siblings, she could be mean. I'd threaten to toss stones at her, but she just laughed.

I hated Needlefish. They were the fish you could see but never catch. Always out of reach, like my hopes for normalcy. They'd eat your bait and leave your hook bereft. I got so frustrated, I'd fall to tears.

I never told Sis any of that.

I could tell her today, but she wouldn't care. She's obsessed with getting a job. Nothing else matters. I caught the business news on the radio last night. Recession dragging on. Jobless numbers climbing. Big Sis will never get hired.

Maybe I'll get hired at Ravensview, because I stayed for hours. I hung late and drank (the room is spinning as I write this) and chatted with Rand and JAM, Kate and Skate, Jack and Ricky, Ash and Sam, a spot of Willington here and there. Elly continued to serve us. At times I wanted to join Willington for a cigarette whenever he stepped outside, but I kept control.

I recall giving Van Gear a "congratulations" before he was swamped by fans, the program gang who swooned over his soulful vibe. I wanted to say more but didn't.

The crowd thinned. A singer/songwriter set up, and that drove out the literati. A gaggle of us clambered downstairs and snagged a booth. Jack and Vicky, Kate and Skate, and Van Gear (finally released from fans). Elly was working both floors, so she continued our tab.

Hours ticked, and somehow, I remained. Alone. Everyone had split. I hadn't noticed. I asked Elly for a shot of Jack, and when she brought it, she gave the slide-over hand wave and sat down beside me.

"What's up, Needlefish?" she asked.

I couldn't quite decide if I hated her or wanted to fuck her. Did I say she reminded me of my sister? Did I say Elly was pretty? Dark brown hair, tall, pale green-hazel eyes, cute, glasses, a sweet round face and a glorious smile.

I was fighting to convince myself I hated her, because I didn't like this *Needlefish* shit. Instead, I decided to make thoughtful conversation.

"I'm drunk," I told her.

"Save the Jack. For next time. I'll keep it in a sippy-cup for you, under the bar."

"Fuck you."

She stared at me, a bit slack-jawed. She looked shocked and hurt. But then a wide, kind brain behind the round, sweet face clicked through mysterious gears, and she reconsidered and pursed her lips.

"I didn't mean it sarcastically, Needlefish. I'm not mean."

I watched my shot, didn't touch it. I was thinking I should grab and gulp. Mucho on the macho. Instead, I stared.

No one spoke for a minute.

I turned my head and looked directly into her face.

"Sorry," I said.

Another ten seconds passed.

Then she spoke, her hand appearing on my shoulder as she cleared from the booth. (I, at that moment, thought it a big sisterly shove, that palm-butt on my clavicle, but now recognize the disguised affection.)

"Wait here, Needlefish. I'm cut in ten minutes."

And she was. And we were. In the backseat of her car just making-the-fuck-out without fucking, without even undressing. And God, it felt so good to kiss this girl. So very gorgeous. I'd convinced myself at this moment she was the most beautiful woman I'd ever kissed in my life; she was the most outstandingly lovely woman on the planet.

Each moment of kissing her was the absolutely new best moment on Earth.

You can accuse me of exaggeration. So what. She was cute, intensely pretty, intensely charming. I had an instant crush on her that got sweeter and more crushing each time my tongue edged her lip, her nose, her ear, her neck, her chin.

God, it felt great. I did start to feel a little guilty about Ryanna, but, you know, I couldn't get a fix on *nature woman*. We'd had one wonderful night, but she'd been incommunicado since. Maybe it'd just been a one night thing in her mind. Besides, I'd earned some much needed relief from me of Rad Sick loneliness.

How's that for a bullshit rationalization?

But after an hour of loving mouths and teeth and cheeks and

chins, for some screwy reason memories of my sister started seeping into my head, annihilating the moment. Why for God's sake hadn't I thrown those rocks at her back when we stood beside the filthy canal? She was ruining this splendid moment with Elly.

Oh Elly, I can only imagine the sweetness of licking your belly.

Yeah, I guess I'm still that drunk as I write this.

The sister memory:

She was giving me a ride home from school. As I'd slid into the passenger seat, Big Sis had given me a big kiss on the mouth, then the cheeks and chin, and slowly dragged her palm down my chest. It was disturbing. Almost like she was trying something out. She sighed and said, "I love you, kid." Started the car and said nothing all the way home. I don't think she had a boyfriend at the time, so in retrospect, maybe she was lonely or experimenting with the only boy she knew. As we climbed from the car, she had asked, "You wanna play checkers?"

Elly detected that I'd lost my momentum. She smiled gracefully and pulled a bottle of strong, clear liquid from her glove compartment. We took shots. Burned going down. It may have been pure grain she'd snagged from somewhere in Georgia.

Elly stretched a long arm from the backseat to the dashboard and flipped on the stereo.

"Oh yeah. I remember. You like music," I mumbled.

"Doesn't everyone?"

"No, I saw you that night Dirk Falter played. When Van Gear sat in."

"Where were you?"

"At a table," I said. The station hummed an old REM song. "You were sitting in the front. Your back to me."

"My old boyfriend was a musician," she said. She hummed along with Michael Stipe. "I play too."

"What you play?"

"Guitar."

"Acoustic?"

"Yeah, and I sing."

"Really? Let's hear you now."

"No, I'm not going to do that."

Between us hung a fermata of silence. The guitar on the radio jangled.

I asked, "What music you play?"

"Folk songs mostly. But different stuff. I wanted to teach music to kids. Still do."

"You're in school for that?"

"Not right now." She took a swig and handed the bottle to me. "I'm taking a break."

"Oh."

She looked squarely at me, sizing me up. I had a bad feeling she might say *You're a needlefish from Kendal, right?*

"You're in the writing program, right?" she asked instead. "What are you, a poet?"

"Not so much. Want to be a novelist."

"Hmmmmm. A novelist. You're too cute for a novelist."

I'm too cute? Elly was positioning herself onto my good side; maybe I could tolerate her calling me *Needlefish.*

"You'd be a cute singer," I said as a dumb but pleasant comeback. "And I'd really like to hear you."

"Not now. I'm too tired." She kissed me on the ear. When she leaned her head back and the streetlight glow struck her brown hair, it shone red. I exhaled. Tried to think up another compliment.

Elly sat up and cocked her ear towards the stereo.

"Listen to this chord change," she said. "The guitar's been strumming G and C, but listen how he switches up the voicings, and the bass suddenly gets melodic instead of plunking the roots."

I think the song was headed to the bridge. She counted off *one, two, three, four* on her fingers in time with the beat and pointed her fist at

67

the stereo as the guitar's chords became shrill.

I nodded. I'd understood most of her music-talk because I'd played bass in a garage band, but I didn't understand *everything* she'd said. Elly knew her stuff. She impressed me.

"I love that part," she said. "Makes the song for me." She smiled.

"You know your stuff."

She turned her head and stared out the window.

"My old boyfriend knew it better. He used to play here a lot."

"What happened?"

"He got married."

"To who?"

"His Ex."

"And now you're the Ex?"

"Ha-ha." She was annoyed now.

The radio was on the college rock station. They played a crazy variety. Mostly stuff I'd never heard before, which I like in some ways because you never hear the same song twice, but in other ways, the implied arrogance of this underground culture strikes a nerve. The D.J. gave a brief intro, and spun the next tune.

It sounded like upbeat synth-pop.

"It's the Magnetic Fields," said Elly. "These guys are pretty good. My Ex didn't like them. But he was wrong about that."

"And wrong about you too," I said on impulse, though I knew it was true. Elly projected a sly loveliness. Her Ex had to be a loser. Like my Ex.

Elly sighed. But she kissed my ear again, and I was happy.

A little while later, she offered to give me a ride home, so we stuck my bike in her trunk and tied the lid with twine. The back tire spun as it hung from the opening.

Now I'm still too wired to sleep. So I write these pages.

At this second I feel the grain alcohol fire trying to pull an Old Faithful trick.

I'm going to throw up now.

Tuesday, October 17, 2000

Can't explain, but there's something about Elly and my hangover that's made me decide I'm not going to miss another class this semester. Going to show up for everything. Even courses I'm not registered for. I am determined to learn.

And determined to stop *thinking* about smoking.

Starting tomorrow.

I'm still sick from last night. A Rad Sick stomach can feel like a 60 year old's. Need to force myself to gag again.

More later.

*   *   *

Ex called.

I shouldn't have picked up the phone—I had a premonition it was her. I answered anyway.

"Still smoking?" she asked. Arrgh! *She* was like a big sister. Sister of the Church of Our Annoyance.

"No. Instead, I'm going to stop playing hooky."

"You haven't been going to classes?"

I shouldn't have told her. I didn't want to reinforce why we'd broken up: I was stuck in neutral. Just because I'm sometimes aimless, doesn't mean I'll always be. She'd tell me I couldn't use radiation sickness as a crutch forever. But what did she know?

Yeah, she was right. Always a scold, but often spot-on.

"I've been going to classes. Just not every day. But now I'm making an extra effort."

She browbeat me with silence.

"Listen," she said, "I have a mind to do something, but I wanted to check with you first."

"It's about your editing gig in Kansas?"

"Missouri."

"The City."

"Your city."

"What's that supposed to mean?"

She paused in that weird way she does. The static on the line grew louder. I imagined her tongue as a drill.

"I want to see you."

My heart stopped, an ancient, leaky engine sputtering out its last drop of oil and coughing shut forever.

But then I thought about kissing her neck.

Next, Elly's face came to view, and I felt conflicted, annoyed, angry, guilty, dizzy. I grabbed a doorframe to steady myself. I'd hit Classic Rad Sick overload.

"Can I visit?" she asked.

Wednesday, October 18, 2000

Woke up with nightmares about Ex.

I desired to visit Elly at Ravensview, hoping to wash these premonitions away with kisses. But she didn't work the morning shifts, and I didn't know where she lived, so I didn't go anywhere.

I hadn't given my Ex a yes or no. But she is a tremendous browbeater when she wants something, and I have about as much spine as a spider thread when it comes to her.

No matter. Today I'd planned to get my shit together and head to the halls of academia.

But before I did that, I left a message at Ravensview for Elly to call. Super-server Kelt answered the phone, actually remembered me, and was gracious enough to jot a note.

I leapt on my bicycle and rolled to campus.

I'd decided to visit the short story seminar Doc Primus teaches in the mornings. But first I rode the elevator—something I usually avoid because I prefer stairs—but, sleep-deprived, I dizzily climbed aboard the box and regretted it. Like a Dr. Who inverse-TARDIS (with the space inside the box shrinking with every heartbeat), this thing had more panel buttons than south Florida sea anemone have eyes.

Each floor required two buttons—ten total, so I pushed every one and prayed I'd recognize the landing as the doors opened level by level.

Of course, I recognized nothing. Not a wall, not a door, not a tile. I jumped off the box near the top, located a leviathan stairwell and stumbled upon the classroom some insane architect had slipped beside an exit door. If the stairwell was Moby Dick's gut, this classroom would have been the whale's appendix.

For purely asinine reasons, I'd brought copies of the first chapter of my novel—still titled *Microwaves.* I'm not sure who I'd thought I'd share them with. I did think I might mark a copy while Doc Primus spewed wisdom, applying his words as appropriate.

Primus ignored me as I rolled into an empty desk jammed into a corner. A few people glanced back. Two hesitated. Kate and Skate. Skate gave a half-salute, and Kate smiled. I stared at their shoulder blades, kept hearing "I Saw Three Ships" wrecking the echo chamber within my skull. Weren't Kate and Skate in the other fiction seminar too? Did they have that much of a hard-on for it and Doc?

Everyone was staring at the third page of a ream of paper, the present manuscript on the hot-seat. Primus was nodding his head in a knowing way. He'd been standing at the chalkboard as I'd slipped seatward. He'd been drawing . . . what? Triangles? Then I got it.

Witch hats.

He was diagraming a rule. For "Whiches." Three witch hats on the board and one with a thick X.

"So a sentence that has three "Whiches" makes a coven. A coven is trouble. In sentences or at midnight, but especially in sentences. Avoid them," said Primus.

A girl in a blue sweater raised her hand. Primus nodded.

"So should sentences have no more than two dependent clauses?"

A couple of people in the back groaned under their breath.

"Well . . . it depends on the sentence," Primus said.

Skate looked back at me and grinned. I'm not sure what his grin meant, but I gave him a thumbs up. A woman beside me was clicking plastic sticks. No flip, she was knitting!

Primus minded none of it. The MFA prosers could have been staring at the ceiling, imagining daisies the size of Ferris wheels, and humming hymns. Or they could have been rapt (most of them were). Doc Primus took it in stride.

"Now," Doc Primus began, "this is quite a long story." He paused, glanced at the empty corner behind him, and nodded his head. "Kate, what would you suggest?"

Kate tensed. Primus was notorious for calling on people at random. You couldn't slip through without giving up a piece of yourself. I've never been a classroom talker. I realized I'd made a huge mistake tumbling in without having read a word. I crouched in the desk to make myself invisible.

But that wasn't possible. I suspect Primus knows I'm Rad Sick, knows my tendency towards paranoia and stupidity, knows I'm not 20 but 30 going on 60. I wonder if that's the only reason I got a rare fellowship, got into the program in the first place. He's waiting for me to sledgehammer my fourth wall so that I'll write about *Incident '80*.

No way, Jose!

Or he's expecting me to crack-up and exit.

"Wait Kate. Who is that behind you? Do we have a guest today?

Now I was tensing up.

"Just visiting," I said in the most pleasant voice I could muster.

"Good," Primus replied. We sat in silence as he scanned all the faces in the room.

"Good. Well, Kate?"

"I'd say let's get to where the tension starts. Where the story kinda jumps into gear."

"And where's that?"

"Hmmmmmmm. Where the guy is picking up the shovel. His boss bullies him at that point, and he grabs the shovel . . . *like a rifle* . . . I think it says."

"And what page are you quoting from, Kate?"

Kate started rifling through the ream. My fingers stung from imagined paper cuts.

"Page 21?"

"Page 21. And how long's the story?"

More page flipping. By everybody. I flipped through my own manuscript to fit in, to release the stress from Primus catching me in the corner.

"Pages. . . . ," said Kate. "I see 39 pages."

"Eighteen pages," said Primus.

"What?" said Kate. She started picking through the ream again with a puzzled look, a twinge of fear.

"No," Kate said. "Last page is 39. Unless they've been miss-numbered."

"But 39 minus 21 is 18, right?" Primus paused. "If the story, as you correctly said, starts on page 21, then, at most, we have 18 pages of true story. The rest . . ."

At this point, Primus started dropping, page by page, 1 through 20 on the floor. He returned to nodding.

"Now, I'm doing this for effect, of course," said Primus. "The first twenty pages got the writer to the story. But here's what we have to realize. Whatever got us to the story is *not* the story. That's whether it's 20 pages, 100 pages . . . or a thousand."

Kate sighed.

Class was soon over. I milled around talking with Kate and Skate. Then I raced home to see if Elly had left a message on my answering machine. I could imagine her sweet voice chiming grace notes of affection. If she'd simply said *Needlefish, Needlefish, Needlefish,* ad infinitum, I'd have been content.

But no. Nothing. The red eye of the machine had no wink for me, only its grim glare.

Thursday, October 19, 2000

Kate asked me after the workshop yesterday what was in my hand (my novel!) . . . and then asked me what my novel was about.

Why is that the hardest question in the universe?

Shouldn't be, right?

What is *Microwaves?*

A series of temp jobs during an undergrad's drift toward graduation.

A road trip to the Indy 500.

An isolationist's view of reality via a surreal TV signal.

A young man running in terror from a hornet's nest of responsibilities.

All these answers sucked.

What did I tell her?

A narrator believes his microwave talks to him, gives him clues to his lives, both real and imagined.

Her face fell blank, and then she smiled. Oh boy. She gave me the grin one gives to cross-eyed dogs and dirty toddlers. Or Rad Sicks. Thank God she doesn't know; I might have cracked with tears.

*   *   *

I attended Modern Poetry this evening. I was hoping the instructor would catch fire (metaphorically) and give me inspiration to write Elly a poem (and the courage to actually give it to her).

The professor knows my name (damn, I suddenly can't remember hers); in fact, she knows everybody's. As class begins she likes to point at each of us and slowly say each name. She loves to point out—over and over—how most Anglo-U.S. names are *trochees*, both first and last, and isn't it ironic since English, arguably, thrives on *iambs*.

Tonight, I bravely raised my hand and asked her if she'd heard the joke about the *iambic foot*?

She said she hadn't.

"Tell us," she said.

"Well, there's a guest lecturer in a middle school English class. Some guy from the local university, and he knows all about prosody. And he just loves to go on and on about the *iambic foot*. You know, iambic foot *this* and iambic foot *that*.

"Finally, a kid in the back wearing an oversized ball cap turned backwards raises his hand. He's a classic inner-city type.

"The professor calls on him and the kid says,

--You ain't.

Sorry. I'm not what?

--What you say.

I don't follow.

--What you keep saying. It's ridiculous.

About prosody?

--None of that. I'm saying you ain't. Shit, you ain't hairy enough. So why you keep saying it?

Am not what?

--Just stop saying it.

What?

--I . . . am . . . Big . . . Foot."

The joke got a few titters. The teacher gave me a blank look. She tapped the toe of her high-top sneaker. I noticed for the first time her feet were huge.

But she wasn't a Bigfoot. Nevertheless, at that moment, to me she became *Professor Bigfoot*. Professor Bigfoot will be my favorite teacher for the rest of the term.

Though I'd made a Big Ass of myself, Professor Bigfoot gave us the goods that night on Plath and then Poe. She talked about Poe's vile biographers. About the Baltimorean's big-footed, hairy-ass ape. She smiled at me as she referenced "The Murders in the Rue Morgue."

Van Gear, sitting near the front, gave me a friendly raised eyebrow.

I talked to the professor afterwards, and she mentioned a contemporary poets book club she'd started and thought I might consider joining. We discussed it, and I vigorously nodded my head, but her dialogue seemed to hint at what I'd already suspected: all the instructors in the program knew I was a "victim" of *Incident 80*, clued-in by all-knowing Doc Primus. None of the profs said this directly, but I could tell by their anxious glances, their careful smiles. I hated this. It felt too much like pity. "From your first paper on Walt Whitman and the Atom," she now said, "you seem drawn to . . . metaphysical territory. Such as, why do good but unlucky people suffer?" I steered the conversation back to Elizabethan prosody as fast as I could, and she let the subject drop.

Nevertheless, I'd made an impression on a professor. I'm not sure why that means so much. I've worked hard for a decade to say next to nothing in class; tonight's joke was my longest classroom monologue ever. I've stayed under the radar with teachers, with everyone, for so many years; Rad Sickness has played a big part in it.

Now, more than ever, I feel I belong. Dade was never home, but T-town truly is.

Friday, October 20, 2000

I'm considering calling my Ex today. Giving her an answer.

Or I should call Elly again, leave another message at Ravensview? But since Elly is avoiding me, maybe I should try Ryanna?

No. Calling Elly or Ryanna would be procrastination. I need to call Ex. Tell her, *No!*

A question to self: Would Ryanna or Elly like my Ex?

Of course not. Nobody liked my Ex.

So why did I?

She's unique. Let's say that. She's like a 1940s femme fetale but talks like Katherine Hepburn. She's head over heels about film noir classics and doesn't like the contemporary art cinema that I love. Like Brandelsonna, etc. We watched *A Clockwork Orange* at a revival house near the new Orange Bowl, and she sprang to the lobby like an adrenalized gazelle as soon as things got a teensy bit violent. I watched the movie solo while she played solitaire beside the concession counter and chatted with the popcorn manager. I finally gave up, because I felt guilty about her sitting alone in the lobby.

Yeah, I'm still mad at her. Still mad she broke up with me.

Am I? Didn't I break up with her?

Again. Why did I like her?

She threw a surprise birthday party for me. I was freaked at turning 19. A mid-youth crisis struck because my teens were kaput. Normally, I hate surprises, but it was sweet of her to do all that planning. And I *was* totally surprised! She was convinced I'd known all along, and I *swore* I hadn't. She thought I'd suspected, especially after she'd parked her car behind a dumpster at her apartment's lot, but I'd gotten used to her goofy stunts. *Surprise!* Perhaps the biggest shock had been the grim reaper balloons.

Was she too weird to like? No. But what did I *like* about her?

I liked her angular frame. I liked that she couldn't dance. I loved her laugh and smile. I loved it when she said, "You are so *nice!*" As if I was the only nice person on the planet—there *are* tons, right? Billions much nicer than I am.

She had no grace. She was all grace.

She mostly never mentioned my Rad Sickness. To me or anyone. Heck, she was the one and only real girlfriend I've ever had. I should have worshipped her more.

I have no grace.

But.

I need to call her and tell her not to come.

Saturday, October 21, 2000

Stopped by Ravens to see Elly, but she was slammed with patrons and couldn't talk. She at least smiled. I left a note with Kelt (he said she might get cut soon) asked her to drop by the B-ball court near McCombe Park where I shot hoops.

At McCombe, the late afternoon basketball session with Van Gear had a new number: 3.

Ash showed. And he was good. He brought out something new in Van Gear. The guy's fifth gear. I remember Ash had played football as undergrad, but a busted spleen during practice with the first string had meant he'd gone into retirement and philosophy. Nevertheless, he remained fit.

He had a sweet shot that annoyed Van Gear with each swish. We'd play two-on-one; I played the forward who never received a pass. Ash and Van G switched off as defender as soon as the other had the ball.

They were *way* too serious.

Elly appeared on the sidelines, but the on court action was so intense, I couldn't take a break. I'd suddenly been commanded to become double-team defender. I play solid defense, so I was glad.

Our two-on-one meant a full press on the ball handler. We were getting gassed.

"Let's take a break," I suggested. I badly wanted to greet Elly.

"No, we're playing the first to ten," said Van Gear.

"Since when? How'd I missed that?"

"Because you're an asleep-at-the-wheel defender. Come on. We're tied at seven. Only take another few minutes."

I couldn't say no to Van Gear. Elly gave small smiles from the sidelines. She still had her brown Ravensview apron wrapped around her waist. She looked as though she wanted to tell me something.

The battle took longer than V.G. had predicted. I was totally gassed when Ash hit a long jumper to win.

I looked toward the sidelines.

Elly was gone.

I felt massively depressed. Ash left soon after, and Van G and I took potshots from the top of the key. He actually let me win a game of Around-the-World, probably because he felt bad since Elly had vanished. He implied my win had been a gift. What a talented, arrogant bastard.

No, I love the guy. Maybe I just wish I were him.

Fifteen minutes after Ash left, Van G slid back into melancholy; he half-heartedly tossed the ball at the rim shot after shot, missing most.

"Kurt Mitchell will probably cancel," said Van Gear.

"Why do you say that?"

"He's the kinda guy, I bet, who can detect a low vibe. Or no vibe."

"Come on. We've got vibe. And look at Ravensview. You set the place ablaze the other night."

Van Gear jogged to midcourt and thrust a long range bomb that flew up and flew down like an ICBM fired from a submarine.

Nothing but net.

"If Ravensview is the best we've got, that Anti-H-bomb should have annihilated *this* town instead."

I was numbed. Dumbstruck. And hurt on many, many levels. But, of course, Van Gear didn't know I was a Rad Sick. Or did he?

And here in T-town, Ravensview was the best place on Earth. A Godsend.

Again, more bad karma from Van Gear. But I knew he was dead wrong. So what the fuck was eating Van Gear?

Sunday, October 22, 2000

Rand showed me what he called the best bookstore in town. I hadn't stumbled across it yet. It was called The Rack, and a curmudgeonly guy ran the place, but Rand said he was all right. His name was Paynen.

Since I felt terrible for leaving Elly stranded on the sidelines, I decided I'd buy her a gift, the perfect book!

"Hey, do you have any Wurlitzer?" I asked.

"Like the piano . . . ?" said Paynen.

"Yeah, I think he's from the same family. Rudolph Wurlitzer."

"Ruddy Wurlitzer?" Condescension rippled from Paynen's lips.

"Rudolph Wurlitzer. He wrote a novel called *Nog*."

"The only reason he got that published was because he was friends with Thomas Pynchon."

"Yeah. Pynchon read *Nog* and said *The novel of bullshit is dead!*"

"Only one problem with that."

"What's that?"

"*Nog* is bullshit."

Had this son-of-a-bitch just insulted my two favorite writers, each of whom warps the dimensions of time-space-reality-in-literature in such a way as to plow the canon into fodder? An Avant-garde minimalist (Wurlitzer) and maximalist (Pynchon) (Yes, . . . *Lot 49* is short, but look how much gets crammed into that Panini-Dagwood of a novel!), each of whom had stirred my ambitions into a chamber pot of rich, incoherent goo (*Microwaves*).

This cocksucker was insulting me! Slighting the core of my artistic soul!

I leaned over the counter and wound my fist back, and the cocky Paynen's face fell; his smirk vanished.

But before I launched my punch, Rand pulled my idiotic ass from the register.

Rand took Paynen aside and started talking to him in a rambling indecipherable whisper that I gave up trying to eavesdrop on. Instead I strafed the shelves with my fingers, stealing books.

I'm not sure why Rand defended me instead of freaking out. After this and Van Gear's *Incident 80* reference, I wonder if all Wings know I'm Rad Sick. How did they know? I'm too tired this second to give a fuck.

Here's what I stacked in the shop's back corner:

Writing the Almost Normal Novel by Bereft Brane.

Madame Bovary by Flaubert.

Igor Stravinsky: A Biography in Verse by Lawrence Zoo*cough*ski.

Ariel by Sylvia Plath (I had another copy back at Aluminum Village, but I didn't care. Plus, I thought Elly might like a near mint copy—a perfect gift!).

Invisible Man by Ralph Ellison.

Betty the Yeti, a play by Harry Xape.

Memoirs of a Survivor by Doris Lessing.

Homegirls & Handgrenades by Sonia Sanchez.

Howl by Ginsberg.

I made some tough choices and stuffed four down my pants; I stiff-legged out the exit while Rand calmed Paynen (the ass). I cut through an empty lot behind the strip mall and stopped in a wilderness of sandspurs to examine my stash, now stack.

Novels of bullshit were not dead, just rising from my britches.

1. *Ariel* (for Elly).

2. *Invisible Man* (for myself).

3. *Memoirs of a Survivor* (for Big Sis).

4. *Nog* (to someday show Paynen).

Paynen, the idiot, actually had an unthumbed copy on his shop's shelves, the psychedelic cover glowing in all its glory.

Yes, I stole *Nog* (even though I already own it)—just to prove that now and forever that **yes, *the novel of bullshit is <u>not</u> dead!***

No, I mean it is dead.

Or . . . *Nog* is not bullshit.

I think.

Whatever. I think Elly will really like *Ariel*. I'm going to wing it by Ravensview now.

Later, on Sunday, October 22, 2000

Again, Elly wasn't at Ravensview. Kelt said he thought she was coming in later. But I believe she was hiding in the kitchen, waiting for me to leave. Her favorite pink pen with purple stripes sat on the bar by Kelt's elbow. He didn't glance at it. But I knew the truth. She always took that pen home.

I left the book anyway.

The simple fact: Elly is avoiding me (probably because she knows I'm a Rad Sick—just like the faculty know, just like Rand and Van Gear have figured out).

But out of the blue a few seconds ago, as if all the Gods of Radiation felt sorry for me, Ryanna telephoned and asked if I'd like to see Big Dismal, a humongous sinkhole. I immediately said *yes!*

To hell with Elly.

My Ryanna-crush has rekindled. I am re-crazy about her. Though I know nothing about Big Dismal and it looks like it might rain, I would have said *Yes* to anything Ryanna suggested. If she'd asked me to study irradiated, albino fly larvae at the sewage treatment plant, I'd have arrived at Mach Speed.

*   *   *

By coincidence, the other night I overheard some scientist at Ravensview explaining sinkholes. I'd never heard of these holes. Apparently, North Florida is pockmarked with them; South Florida is not a "holy" place (ha ha). The scientist got technical, mentioned South Florida's thicker, less permeable earth, and all the sand (instead of clay) ready to fill in underground pocks as they pop, and cited the hundreds of feet of sticky sediments and bits of carbonate rock that are tough to melt. South Florida, well-protected from sinkholes. North Florida was apparently ground zero for sinks.

While waiting for Ryanna, I studied a regional map to find this sinkhole's site. A legend highlighted the area's natural wonders; Big Dismal is apparently one of the deepest holes in north Florida, plunging hundreds of feet. At the sink's bottom sits a tall, bright, red rock, a stalagmite, like the bull's-eye on a dartboard, red as the Communist star on a Russian ICBM. The huge stone is made of pink quartz and feldspar, and the minerals make the rock seem a bloodshot eye.

I'm reminded of a huge, red stone that sits beside the port's exhibition docks in Miami. My dad took me to see moored warships and submarines on a coastal tour. Two subs were there. The U.S.S. George Washington Carver, a nuclear-powered, missile-launching menace, and the U.S.S. Alligator, a Civil War vessel developed to attack southern ports. Blanco came along with us. He was particularly stoked that a military sub was named after a black guy.

The nuclear vessel was cramped and dark. Not what we expected. We'd been ruined by *Voyage to the Bottom of the Sea* reruns and images of James Mason plunging the Nautilus 20,000 leagues. Nevertheless, we were impressed with the spooky, claustrophobic vibe that echoed down the craft's corridors.

The Alligator was much tighter, meaner-looking. The nose looked like a hellacious drill, a giant spike, or the nose of a V2 rocket. Inside, eight mannequins sat on benches along the centerline: each sailor's hands would have spun the shaft of the propeller. Besides the eight human engines, squeezed into the 50 x 6 x 6 space were a captain, a helmsman, and two divers. When the craft was submerged near enemy ships, the two divers swam free with limpet mines in tow, the Alligator's teeth. But a small bite compared to the George Washington Carver's rows of ICBM fangs.

Blanco talked me into returning to the larger vessels, and we ran up and down the corridors like lunatics, ignoring the yells of the few annoyed Navy grunts onboard. The doorway openings were so small, we'd almost forget to duck as we dashed, nearly decapitating ourselves. One jerk sailor shut off the lights near the torpedo tubes as we played, and he gasped but then suddenly said, *Can't you Rad Sicks see in the dark?* Blanco screamed a few Dominican insults, then told the seamen to *Shove his honky-self up his own asshole.* The sailor laughed as we dashed up a spiral staircase.

My dad let us play on the huge red stone afterwards; it was like south Florida's only mountain, though it was merely 30 feet high and 50 feet wide at the base. Blanco kept claiming he was *King of the Submarines* as he stood at the summit and beat his chest. He said he could hear the vessel's engines chugging tomorrow as they puttered up the coast to their next stop in Jacksonville.

Despite Blanco's obsession with our supposed special skills, I began to suspect he didn't have, as he called it, the *invisible sixth sense.* Namely, because the subs didn't leave town until the next week.

*   *   *

Ryanna arrived just as I'd strolled outside to the Aluminum Village parking lot.

I maintained cool. Until I saw her smile, I didn't realize how much I wanted to make love to her again. I'm such a simple, stupid animal. I imagined us kissing to ultimate closeness at the edge of the crater. But I had a sinking feeling nothing would happen.

Like the selfish idiot I am, I decided to forget about Elly. She was probably permanently creeped out by *Ariel* I'd left. Probably never speak to me again. What a stupid gift to give a girl you like.

But Ryanna didn't seem interested either. In the car she was distant. Every time she moved her hand to adjust the radio, I reached out with a suggestion for more volume or another station, but as soon as my fingers got close to hers, her hand skated away like a skittish stingray. I remembered listening to the Magnetic Fields in Elly's backseat, and a twinge of guilt hit, but at the same time I wanted the brief magnetism between me and Ryanna to reenergize.

Or maybe she felt some charge bolting in electric Z's from my fingertips.

Or maybe she felt the bad vibe of my radiation.

Or maybe she could feel her uterus steaming with frizzing protons spitting from the membranes of her cervix's cells. All because of my glittering gametes.

No, no. Paranoia in my own head, born from radioactive glow. We pulled off the road next to a track of trees and rolled to a stop beside a heavily bolted and padlocked gate.

"This doesn't look too friendly," I said.

"Nah. Come on. People go here all the time."

Down in south Florida, padlocks and iron gates meant serious shit. The locked gates at Skull Springs had been one thing, because Ryanna worked there. This looked more foreboding. Nevertheless, I followed.

Ryanna and I plunged down a trail through the woods, the bare branches of dogwoods scratching our shoulders. A faint campfire smell cut the air. The day was warm for a T-town fall. Almost Indian Summer.

We walked a mile, then stopped. Beyond a perimeter of human-sized pines, the ground spread open, and hundreds of feet below bubbled the blue waters. This gouge opening into aquifer was ten times as large and deep as the sinkhole behind Ryanna's porch. If her sink was a lovely chapel, Big Dismal was a Cathedral's sanctuary.

She'd said nothing for twenty minutes as we hiked through pines, oaks, and magnolias. The silence felt awkward.

"Hey, something eating you?" I asked. "You were quiet on the ride over, and you've been silent on the hike."

"Yes, I was just thinking about what you might be."

"What I might be?" I asked. "Just a guy, I guess."

"If you might be haunted," she said. She looked at me with her luminous blue eyes, smiled a little.

"Haunted?" The word stabbed my head and heart. Damn, even Ryanna was on to me.

Why is it so easy to tell something ticks beneath *our* skin, that we're "haunted" by radiation, by the Accident? Miami newspapers had described ground zero of Incident '80 as *haunted by radiation*. Many buildings, not damaged by the blast since it happened near the upper atmosphere, stood empty and silent. People avoided the properties for years because of the atomic heat. Rad Sick babies were similarly haunted, like ghosts, the true living dead, everyone waiting for us to shrivel into corpses from the infection of misfiring protons and neutrons. *Haunted. Rad Sicker. By the orange of their eyes. See in the dark.* All these adjectives and phrases added to my defensiveness because I'd heard or read so much as a kid. And *here* I do not want to be found out, Dammit! I left Miami to escape the stigma!

"A good haunting, I believe. Spirits whispering the future to you," she said. She was backpedaling, could tell I'd tensed up. "That's what makes you . . . magic."

"OK. But what exactly are you getting at?" *Magic.* OK. Now things were sounding better.

Ryanna suddenly stopped, placed a hand on my shoulder, and gave me a quick but affectionate kiss on the cheek.

"You were right," she said. "*the pacific* took my story."

I stared at her; a stab of shockwaves tumbled through my backbone. Damn, that should have been the first thing I asked her. Instead, I over-focused on lust.

"Ryanna! That's great!"

"I wouldn't have sent it if you hadn't said anything."

"I'm glad I was right!"

We hugged at the edge of Big Dismal.

"I could just tell," I said.

"As long as it's not from a bad haunting," she said, and pulled back from me and beckoned. "There's a hidden stairs on the other side. Well, not a stairs really, but come on."

I was blown away that *the pacific* had snagged the work. Van Gear would be jealous. I wasn't sure what she meant by "a bad haunting," but I was glad my ear for invisible voices caught the tune of her story. I wish my ear worked better for my own prose. But it doesn't.

At this moment, I wanted her quick kiss to expand into love-exploding; I needed Ryanna to stop moving. Hidden stairs did not interest me. We needed to hold still, let a hug melt into more.

But she was only interested in sinkholes.

At the other edge of the sink Ryanna showed me stone outcrops that made for footholds. I hesitated but she cajoled me. The wall was as much red clay and overgrowth as it was rock. Halfway down we stopped our slow descent at a narrow ledge.

Cool air rose from the sinkhole. I shivered. The sky opened above us in a circle defined by pines.

Ryanna pointed down.

"See to the right there, just twenty feet below the surface?"

"A cave?"

"Yes, the mouth to the aquifer. Comes out in a gush. Creates eddies and whirls."

"Must be some *teeth* in that mouth." I recalled the mastodon tusks of Skull Springs, wanted to mention them but Ryanna distracted me.

"Hey, watch this!"

Ryanna pirouetted to face the wall. I held my breath, because her heels hung over the ledge as she searched the stones. We were still fifty feet from the bottom; the hole was huger than I'd realized.

"Ah," she whispered.

She stood on her toes and stretched an arm to a white silver dollar-sized bloom poking between rocks. Ryanna plucked it gently.

The flower crowned the tips of her fingers. She turned to me, as wide-eyed as she had been reading her poems at Ravensview. I wanted our lips to touch, but I was afraid I'd kiss her right off the cliff.

"Now. . . . ," she said.

She flicked the flower, and it spun as if a white helicopter. It aimlessly drifted for a moment then pecked the water near the mouth of the underwater cave.

After a moment, the flower charted slow, shrinking circles. Once it reached the middle of the original loop, the petals sank a foot below and popped back up ten seconds later. Then the circling began again.

"It's like they say, natural world wants to pull against itself in disorder in order to be reordered to the newer form," Ryanna said.

"What newer form?"

"As pure water."

I looked into her eyes; my brow furrowed. She was straight-faced, her irises two blue wondrous pools.

"See!" she said.

I glanced down.

The flower had disappeared.

In its place, a yard-wide ripple bounced and bobbed.

"Come on. Follow me back up."

I'd have followed her into the cave below if she'd only dove in first.

Monday, October 23, 2000

I waited until late morning to give Ryanna a call, of course she's not answering. Am I the over-anxious boy friend who's *not* a boyfriend?

I hate being infatuated with people. But I do feel I deserve a little more attention; after all, she got that story published because of me!

To stop thinking about Ryanna, I've been thinking about what I want to read if tapped to take the stage at Ravensview.

It's gotta happen, right? Because now I'm a Wing; and Willington, the Ravensview Readings ringmaster, is a Wing too! Of course, the group hasn't seen much of my work yet. That could be a problem.

OK. What from *Microwaves* would work at Ravensview?

Here's a passage that's not too bad:

My tub is full of sand that talks to me. I talk to it too. Miami sand dredged up from ocean bottom over a decade ago. Maybe two or three. I hear sto-

ries from the silicon in sand to the silicon in my microwave oven.

And here's another:

I can walk on the freshly-tarred asphalt road, dodge cars across A1A, and creep through the sea oats. The sign says, "Don't pick them!" and I don't. But the man with the binoculars and the green baseball cap keeps pointing his finger at me.

I'm standing on a precious little dune. South Florida coastal dunes don't find a lot of room to stretch: the waves and the road press from either side.

And another:

All things directed are directed to one thing: some variation of panic. Go the path of least resistance, or better yet, no resistance. Direction surfs best with no fin. My seven foot Nomad single fin surfboard has not one. I don't surf anymore anyway. The risk seems too great for direction.

But I'm supposed to be reading from a novel. A *novel! My* novel! What kind of dumbass reads randomly-chosen paragraphs from a book-length narrative? Who would be that stupid?

Me.

Because I can only find short passages I like.

Because I can't write a coherent story. Can't tell one either.

Because I'm into poetry, because I've stalled on *Microwaves*.

Because I'm an iconoclast.

Because I'm a moron.

The too easy answer: because I'm Rad Sick.

Tuesday, October 24, 2000

Funny thing happened today.

Not a funny thing.

Shocking. Unnerving.

A half-block from Ravensview, just across the street, I saw someone I knew.

From Miami.

A fellow Rad Sick.

Sure, sure, I've been assuring myself for the last few hours, *so what?* I'm a Rad Sick in T-town, so why wouldn't another one be here?

Well, it's because of our fucked-up brains: we're stuck in patterns. We're weirdly terrified of change, upheaval—since our genes got ripped by Anti-H rays that transformed our burgeoning pre-psyches, any other transformation is anathema! I got so fucking tired (we *all* did) of doctors and counselors saying *There's nothing all that wrong with you* as we fell into our ruts of listlessness. OK, yes, yes, on the surface, except for the drunken-lighthouse beam inside our eyes and some premature aging issues, we seem pretty normal, act pretty normal, behave pretty normal, even think pretty normal . . . but . . . how can I explain this? We are very much *not* normal. Our thinking, when we were most ourselves, becomes bumper cars inside a tea party madhouse spun along an igloo floor.

Our patterns of weird behavior made Haitian witch-mothers say we were invaded by the spirits of the hundred stillborns who passed that day (. . . in some cases, just weeks away from due dates). They were birthed after death, brought to the world of the living after entering the world of the dead—I start to cry whenever anyone mentions the stillborns from the Accident. Perhaps all those ghosts bounce inside our skulls, break our thoughts into fragments.

The truth is, *We*, each of us, especially when alone, are Rad Sick earthquake-prone islands. We're always on edge; thus, all change is terror.

Of course, there are exceptions to any rule. Look at Taylor Morgan Velázquez!

And look at me!

I overcame my colossal inertia simply to apply to nine grad schools. . . . and then to actually come to T-town—it's a big part of the reason—as I look through earlier journal entries—that I felt so negative.

But here's another Rad Sick. Another like me. I know him. His name is Sombre. He's Cuban. For a time in middle school, we were good friends. I loved his mom's rice pudding. I raved about it; so much so that every time I dropped by, she'd have a fresh batch and I'd greedily dig in to the custard and cinnamon suffused rice. But when his dad suffered colon cancer in early high school, Sombre and I lost touch. His mom blamed the cancer on the radiation from Incident '80, and I tired of her rants about the Anti-H; poor Sombre must have been even more weary of it. I became too anxious as I listened, so I stopped visiting. But Sombre and I remained friendly throughout high school, even as he started hanging with the grunge rockers and suicide-sheiks, and I mixed with surfers, footballers, and musicians.

Today Sombre's *ojos* didn't glow. He must have got his hands (his *eyes!*) on a pair of contacts. Like me, he must have saved up. And, like me, he must have been willing to put up with pain. Before I'd left Dade, I'd heard of only one other Rad Sick who'd had the lenses installed, some rich kid I didn't know who'd gone to a prep school overlooking Biscayne Bay. And now here was good ol' Sombre, wearing the contact lenses too. No glow haunted his eyes.

He looked homeless; he always looked homeless because of his love for grunge, but this getup of black skully and torn overcoat was over-the-top. Of course, all homeless look worse than usual because the economy is belly-up. The jobless were cashing their last unemployment checks and scattering to the streets in droves because they had no place else to go (I wonder if Big Sis has more interviews?)

As I stood and stared, Sombre disappeared around the corner heading north.

I dashed across the six lanes of Highway 90, T-town's Death Race 2000—nearly getting my hip shattered by the fender of a massive pick-up. But when I got across, the motherfucker had vanished.

Was it really Sombre?

Wednesday, October 25, 2000

After classes today, I've returned to my Alum Village pad to ponder and puzzle. Had it been Sombre? The possibilities spin endlessly in my

Rad Sick mind. I keep rereading Eliot's *The Wasteland* for Bigfoot's class, but none of it sticks. To find better distraction from my *black* thoughts (about *Sombre*--ha ha), I snatched Rand's spiral notebook from underneath a pile of *Big Yorker*s and flipped pages. I scanned for lines that caught my eye, snagged my ear for invisible voices.

Rand's got some good stuff here and there. Here are some more passages that I like:

The young boy and tiny girl danced round-leaf circles as we leafed through the pages of our books. The words felt heavy and dull against the pull of high voices and laughter.

Her brown eyes caught the color of wild flowers.

Outside the owls and foxes gathered at the windows. They hid in the shadows and watched the shadows inside they feared.

Reading all this poetry made me turn to my own work: what will now be a three-part poem about bridges. The work (yes, a terrible distraction from *Microwaves*) was originally about two bridges: Puente de los Patriarches in Spain and a rope contraption stretching across the Mekong in Vietnam, but now I've stumbled across an important one near here—The Natural Bridge. And a Civil War battle. Here's another thing about North Florida, the War between the States was waged here. South Florida might have had a few forts to bully Seminoles (thus, Fort Lauderdale, Fort Myers, Fort Pierce), some minor clashes, but Dade had no major battles, no strong connection to that war. So I've searched and found a website that gives the skinny on the Battle of Natural Bridge.

Turns out, the Confederates were mostly teenagers from the Florida Military and Collegiate Institute (which has somehow become the Big State U I now attend), and the Union soldiers were mainly of the 2nd and 99th U.S. Colored Infantry. On that day in 1865, Union Brigadier General

John Newton was determined to combine army and navel forces to start an advance from the St. Marks Lighthouse towards T-town, 25 miles away. Rebel encampments had been spied just north of the Confluence, so Newton wanted naval support. The U.S.S. Alligator—the same one as a kid I'd seen down in Dade—was one of the vessels the general had at his disposal. To surprise the enemy, he ordered an approach by the submarine up the St. Marks River to the Natural Bridge just before dawn. The Alligator headed upstream filled to capacity with Union troops. Just a half mile behind it, the two infantry divisions crept along the banks. The teen Rebels were fast asleep.

But things fell apart. The Alligator, according to an accompanying platoon that slinked along beside it, ran into something below (a mysterious quartz stone formation?)—or at least that's what the loud *clang* made them think. A roiling of air fizzed the water beside the riverbank, and the submarine and its soldiers never surfaced. The platoon waited until the 2nd and 99th divisions caught up, and then delivered the bad news to Newton. The general decided, despite the setback, to attack, and thus the Battle of Natural Bridge was fought, with the advancing Union troops forced to return to the coast after three unsuccessful charges.

I think this poem is falling into place. I will drop by Doc Primus' office and show him, though he's mostly a fictionist. I trust his words. He can help me tweak it.

Fuck. Reading about these troops advancing to T'ville is not helping me forget about *Sombre*.

Poem be damned!

Thursday, October 26, 2000

Last night and early this afternoon I started scouting the alleys and dumpsters of the Ravensview block, searching for signs of Sombre. While milling around the bar's kitchen entrance, the door swung open, and a woman walked out with an unlit cigarette: Elly!

She didn't see me as she tried to make her lighter work. I figured that after leafing through Sylvia Plath's book, she'd choose to ignore me for eternity. Anyway, I was too obsessed with finding Sombre to be hurt. I peeked into a nearby trash barrel, tried to act casual.

"What you doing, Needlefish? Where you been?"

I realized we'd hardly spoken since Van Gear's reading over a week ago. Oddly, I'd felt like we'd talked all week because I'd been having miles of imaginary conversations inside my head. I'd dreamed of more night's like our midnight make-out in her car.

But wait a second. Was she talking to me? For real?

"Nothing really," I said. "Thought I saw a friend of mine from down south."

"In the garbage?"

"Not exactly."

I wanted to explain a lot to her, but I couldn't. Wanted to explicate the reasons for:

1. Skulking around the parking lot and rummaging through dumpsters;

2. Fearing a visit to T-town from my Ex;

3. Fighting off a pointless crush on Ryanna.

But mainly, I wanted to explain my overall confusion, and how I felt convinced that she, Elly, now disliked me, so I'd been scarce.

Also, I was especially dreading telling her about my Rad Sickness, because that would finally seal the deal, kill the love.

And I love Elly, despite my reservations:

1. What's with calling me *Needlefish?*

2. Why had she taken such a deep look into my eyes when we'd first met?

3. How'd she known I was from Dade?

Nevertheless, huge swaths of me loved her. She seemed so go-to sweet and as beautiful as the taste of berries.

"So this guy, he's from Kendall?" she asked.

"I'm not from Kendall."

"Not you. Him."

"No."

She sighed. Glanced around behind her, as if to check if the coast was clear.

"Needlefish, I got something to admit."

"What?" My stomach fell. What disaster would she unleash?

My eyes neared tears.

"It's about you." She looked down at her tennis shoes, pink-smeared by floor sludge but laces bright-white, fresh-new. "And me."

My stomach boiled. I wanted to throw up and then hide inside a dumpster.

"I think we're related."

I squinted at her chin. She did not have my sister's. Her chin was cleft; Elly's was round, a baby face. She was not my sister come to play an elaborate joke on me.

"What!?!?"

"Distantly."

"I have no cousins."

"That's not what I mean."

We both waited. She crammed the unlit cigarette she'd been holding into a front pocket. She knelt down and tied her shoe, looked up at me.

"We're the exact same age, I'm betting," she said.

She stood. Now taller than before. Her brunette hair with its traces of red decorated her shoulders as if stripes on a uniform. She wasn't wearing her glasses. She was suddenly a Viking princess.

"We were born on The Accident."

And I almost believed her.

But her eyes didn't have the glow. Had she managed to nab the eye contacts too, the same ones I wore, Sombre wore?

"You searched my eyes . . . and I remember nothing in yours," I said.

"Here, look more closely."

Elly made her fingers into circles and pressed them to her eyes as if a comic's pantomime of glasses. She looked upwards as if at the foot of Jesus on the cross. She held her breath and made her eyes bulge.

"Look," she said. "Get right up against me."

And so I did. We were nose to nose. Her warm breath was slightly starchy but in a yummy way that made me want to kiss her. She trembled.

I peered deeply into her lovely green orbs.

Clouds covered the sun.

And that's when I noticed. The speck of what I thought was sun-reflection in the back of her eyes was a pin-prick of glow, the same orange ember as in my own.

"I've never seen it so soft before. It's barely there."

"I know," she said. "I was born at home. Just on the edge of the radiation plume."

I stepped back, Elly dropped her hands to her waist.

"I don't look it," she said. "But I'm Rad Sick too."

Friday, October 27, 2000

Reuters: An F-1 navy helicopter from the aircraft carrier U.S.S. Dwight D. Eisenhower flew over the three vessels involved in the Arctic Ocean Standoff: the Soviet cruiser Marshal Ustinov , the Losos-class Russian submarine Piranha, and the U.S. submarine Stonewall Jackson. The Soviet cruiser fired a warning shot off the bow, and the U.S. helicopter immediately evacuated. However, the Russians have accused the U.S. of unprovoked aggression. The Kremlin now warns of imminent countermeasures.

Meanwhile, Lieutenant Taylor Velázquez was spotted being escorted into the Russian Piranha submarine an hour after sunset.

This latest news vibrates through my radio this morning and makes me realize something about myself, Taylor Velázquez, Elly . . . and maybe even Sombre: we are the only Rad Sicks who've left Dade. Taylor is the most impressive. She joined the Navy before the special eye contacts; she had the full-glow, like me and Sombre, unlike Elly.

Taylor was tougher than the rest of us. She marched into the recruitment offices near the port's red, mountainous rock, and stared down the officers, daring them to dissuade her because she was Rad Sick. Her eyes must have glowed brightly, two hot charcoals burning her ambitions into their brains. They signed her without protest.

What sets us apart? I can only speak for myself. Getting pigeon-holed and condescended to for so long is crippling, and despite the outsized anxiety that comes with Rad Sickness, I had to make a break. But let's hope we don't get broken, especially Taylor Velázquez.

Saturday, October 28, 2000

Ex calls and will need a ride from the airport in seven days.

What the fuck?

I couldn't dissuade her. I made up excuses about a 25 page paper on Samuel Beckett due a week after Halloween; oral presentations on the narratology of Berryman's *The Dream Songs*; novel chapters due in a fortnight; a group reaction paper centered around Kathy Acker's postmodern take on the sub-continental post-colonial diaspora!

All true!

She'd have none of it.

What can I do to keep her from visiting me?

I love this place, and I know she's coming to ruin it.

And since now I know Elly is a Rad Sick too, I plan to fall massively in love. If Ex is here, she will eradicate Elly from my radar.

O.K. She cared about me once.

I just don't want her here.

We're over.

Right?

Monday, October 30, 2000

Back from another Wings night. Expansive. Full of portents.

We sat around the table in a sea of beer and mountains of wings and curly fries.

Ash promised the "bottled" TallaTec for later, so there was giddy anticipation all around, even from normally uptight Rand. Jack's accent was clear Serbo-Croatian, and his beard glowed redder. Willington glanced at the light fixtures as he charted the course of readers at Ravensview. Van Gear stayed steadfast on his praise of the Beats, specifically Kerouac novels none of us had read.

"Kerouac makes me think of Brockberry's first book," Rand said. He paused. Everyone fell quiet. "But Brockberry's not back yet," Rand lamented.

"I told you that," said Van Gear.

"Don't rub it in," said Willington.

"He's just one more great string in T-town's good vibe," said Rand.

"Don't worry. Bernice Jann and Tay Shields are back from England," said Jack. "So we *do* have returning heroes." He scratched his beard as he spoke.

"Heroines," said Ash.

"Did Jann really just invite Shields for writing," asked Van Gear, "or are they turning Lesbian?"

"What's it matter?" asked Rand.

"Just wondering, that's all," said Van Gear.

"Don't worry, it ain't catching," said Willington. "And what's important is we'll have our dialogue-specialist back."

"Teaching you *what*?" asked Van Gear.

"I just said. Dialogue. Real dialogue. Make your tough characters actually sound tough, not like 18th century philosophers," said Willington. He stared at Van Gear. "Her playwriting classes kick ass."

"You *would* need that," said Van Gear.

"And what the fuck is that supposed to mean?" asked Willington.

"Mean? Where the fuck have you been? Fuck you and tough dialogue. We've been needing on-court toughness. Why haven't you shown up?" This marked the first time at Wings Van Gear had mentioned B-ball practices.

"You're serious about that shit?" asked Willington.

"These two have made it!" He pointed at me and Ash. "The new guy has more dedication than all you assholes put together." Van Gear reached across the table and slapped me on the shoulder.

I felt knighted!

"Van Gear," said Willington, "Kurt Mitchell does not give a shit one way or another if we play basketball. He wants good writing."

Willington and Van Gear had a unique bond. And rivalry. They'd motorcycle tour on occasional Sundays, exploring highways along nearby forgotten coastlines. But they were quite different too. While Willington had wife and two kids, Van Gear flew solo. And Willington, the family man, very much needed a fulltime job in the near future. Thus, a tension hovered between the two.

"You need every break you can get," said Van Gear. "Willington, you are a total asshole!"

The table melted into hush.

Ash read his cue. Smartly.

"Let's break this up and grab the check," said Ash. "I've got TallaTec waiting for us in the parking lot."

"I may be cynical about basketball," said Willington, "But I'm not cynical about TallaTec."

Van Gear said nothing. I didn't realize how much the Wings guys' lack of B-ball stoke broke his heart, though I suppose it should have been obvious.

Wings' indifference to hoop-play was torqueing him into depression. No wonder he'd been so moody the last few times at the court.

We settled with the server and slipped outside to the high corner of the parking lot. We always closed the place, so only our cars remained.

"I think they keep improving this shit," said Ash. He pulled the pre-fab joint from a jacket pocket and dug for a lighter.

The air was both chilly and humid, and we all exhaled vapor clouds as if already smoking. A misty sprinkle started. The sour smell of fermented wings drifted from a roof vent.

"Who's improving it?" I asked.

"Not sure," said Ash. "Someone around here."

"And it's only from around here?"

"Have you heard of it before? I sure as hell haven't; and I know just about everything grown, mixed, or burned from here to Tampa."

"I heard someone say it's from the university," said Jack. "They're hoping to juice the undergrads for more cash by getting 'em so glazed the kids'll tackle extra minors they don't need."

"Now that's complete bullshit," said Willington. "Where the hell you hear that?" Willington had worked briefly as a journalist, so he was cynical about conspiracy theories.

"Just a word from someone," said Jack, not interested in pressing the matter. He wiped his hand over his mist-wet hair.

"Well let's get the word straight from the source," said Ash. He'd managed to light the TallaTec spliff, and now hit it. An orange coal grew at the tip.

I was uncertain about inhaling. The chemical had twisted my sub-conscious into my consciousness with such ferocity, that I half-remembered not wholly enjoying the trips.

The joint went around the circle. Rand breathed in deeply as if he'd been born on a Venusian landscape that offered an atmosphere thick with TallaTec fog. Jack hit quick. Van Gear and Willington took long drags.

Then it was between my fingers. What to do? I was all hesitancy on the brink of the mindscape's abyss. The mist became a sprinkle. I shivered.

"What you waitin' on, guy?" asked Willington. "Don't worry.

You're not an undergrad, so you're resistant to the craving for more aca-
deme."

"No way," said Jack. "He's in grad school, so he clearly can't get
enough."

I sighed and put my mouth around the son-of-a-bitch.

And then I was under.

*   *   *

Why did we return to the house with the computer boxes and
tubes?

Van Gear, Willington, and Ash plugged into one black box, and
Jack, Rand, and I sucked on another. I became fascinated with the ceiling,
which was splintered like the deck of a movie pirate ship.

And then Sombre entered. There he was—the S.O.B. hadn't just
vanished into spilt beer and vomit behind Ravensview!

For some reason, the box's tubes had been strapped tightly around
my face with medical tape, so as I stood to confront Sombre, I was jerked
back like a catfish on a snag-hook. Another hook caught on my shoulder,
but I realized it was Rand's hand, and he was reeling me in.

"You had enough? You want me to unwind you?" asked Rand. All
six of us, even Rand, had the IV tubes taped onto our faces. We were TallaTec mummies.

I coughed into my tube. Rand had been hard to understand, as
if he'd plugged his voice through a vintage Herbie Hancock vocoder. My
mouth was dry, but I tried to huddle vowels and consonants around each
other.

"I see somebody I know."

"No, you don't," said Jack.

"For real. Somebody I know from down south."

"TallaTec can do that to you," said Jack. "Last time I was here, I
thought I saw my wife. And then her whole family burst through the door.
Fucking lucky it was all hallucination."

"No, this is for real." But was I sure?

I stared Sombre down as he sat solo by a box and plugged in a yellow cartridge.

He wore a trench coat, but at other moments it appeared a robe of canaries. This was probably the TallaTec talking.

Sombre swiveled his head, and we locked eyes, but I don't think he saw me. He was seeing conquistador ghosts inside the walls dancing with Apalachee tribal spirits.

I'd had enough. I needed to know. I dug my fingernails into the edges of the medical tape, and I ripped the strips in one fell swoop. I stood.

My Wings men ignored me. I glided to Sombre.

I twisted my mouth as my face itched where the tape had been, and then my vision faded. I stumbled across the dirty hardwood floor; the tape's glue made canyons of uncomfortableness in my cheeks.

Somehow, despite the darkness, I swam through the house's irritating atmosphere. My thoughts itched, and I scratched my head. And every time I scratched, I thought of Elly.

Lovely, lovely Elly. She was a Rad Sick too!

It'd been four days since Elly had manifested her true affliction and confessed her bond with the bomb. I've a fiercer bond, but it's nothing to brag about. Why hadn't I asked her for a date? I didn't want the make-out in her car to become *oh, you know, one of those things.*

Elly was such a lovely world of loveliness! Her inner self had to be pure heaven!

*   *   *

As I re-read passages above, it sounds like a clichéd acid trip; but I can 100% guarantee that it wasn't. Yes, TallaTec has hallucinatory qualities, but TallaTec . . . how can I explain this? O.K., if acid picks you up like a chip and dips you into a thin sauce of surreal, then TallaTec grabs you by the scruff of the neck, and like the Ghost of Xmas past, flies you over what's visceral and real, what are the true (yes, at times, metaphorical) landscapes of past/present/future. Acid gives you thin similes; TallaTec gives you so much metaphor, that like metaphor, you *are* the thing the TallaTec has made you become.

Maybe I should give up explaining.

*   *   *

The itching finally stopped.

And there I was. Sitting beside Sombre, both of us cross-legged on the floor, shoulders touching.

"Sombre, what are you doing here?"

He stared, didn't recognize me. I looked deeply into his orbs, not catching the glow, convinced he'd bought the contacts down in Dade.

"Sombre, come on. Bro, look!"

His forehead scrunched into moon-valley ridges.

"Remember the Atom Bowl!" I said.

He'd been one of the neighborhood kids digging in the dirt outside the rebuilt Orange Bowl. Sombre always used a plastic shovel he'd stolen from his little sister's sandbox. The shovel's handle had a plastic ruby on the handle. He swore the tool brought him luck looking for the "blast-diamonds" we never found. He'd go on and on about how the bigger gems were closest to the surface, some theory of his about how Incident 80 had randomly melted Miami carbon into perfect diamonds. He was nutty. He was there that night of the Atom Bowl, when Nebraska dropkicked Notre Dame. He insisted this would be our night to strike a mother-lode. He dug through earth like a human steam shovel, and ignored the shouts of Midwestern fans in goofy gear hooting fight songs from the 19th century. That night Sombre found a golf ball-sized quartz nugget he insisted for weeks was cousin to the Hope Diamond; he crowned the non-gem *the Atom Stone.*

"What did you do with the Atom Stone?" I asked him.

"Stoned?" he mumbled. He pulled the tube from his mouth.

"What are you doing here? In T-town?" I asked.

"Oh." Sombre paused, scratched the ridges in his forehead with a pinkie. "They told me to come for the Thing. Said I needed it." He smirked as if he'd just told a joke to himself and thought it brilliant. "So I'm doing it."

"The TallaTec?"

My vision became hazy, distorted.

"Huh?" Sombre asked.

Grips grabbed me. Suction cups pawed my hands, arms, shoulders. A TallaTec octopus or kraken laced its appendages through me to pull me into its mouth!

No, Wings was dragging me out the door, laughing, scolding, eye-rolling, gnashing terrible teeth, smiling like fools. We apparently had places to go and no time for Sombre. Since TallaTec was floating me, I went along for the ride. My vision cleared.

We flew to the Lake Jackson pier, the swamp thick with alligator-stink. I recognized it from the night Jack had taken a dip and freaked.

"Don't harass people in the shack," Ash told me, scolding me for hassling Sombre. I could only shrug my shoulders. I didn't want to explain the whole Rad Sick thing to these guys. They were cool, but I had no guarantee they wouldn't start treating me differently.

We had a giant stack of two-thirty 9-packs we'd snagged at a Meridian Road convenience store right before the turn off. We drank.

Rand stacked the empties up to his waist at the muddy entrance to the boardwalk. And the next thing you knew, we crowded together at the far end of the pier, the water lapping behind us, taking turns tossing pebbles at the beer can tower and making bets on each throw. Your heels had to hang off the edge for the pitch to be legal. We kept missing, even Van Gear.

"Maybe we should get closer," I suggested.

"What? Not let the prep basketball star show off his long range jumper?" said Willington.

Van Gear growled. As his arm whipped across his body, he released a rocket, as if a fast-ball specialist pulled from the bullpen to cinch the final strike. Van G. had been a prep baseball star in C-town too.

He missed.

"Let me show you," said Jack. His accent blended Aussie/Slovaki-an.

Jack was especially toasted. He was on the wrong side of stagger-ish. He hadn't taken a throw yet.

"This is the way," Jack said. Rand handed him a stone, but Jack shook his head. "Need a pocketful for luck."

Rand smirked, then shrugged and handed the man a handful.

"More, more," Jack said, waving his arms, palms up, like a holy orchestra conductor. Everyone got into the spirit and dropped stray stones until Jack's hands and pockets overflowed.

Jack walked a few feet toward the middle of the dock, back to-wards land.

"You can't do that, Jack," said Willington. "Starting line's at the edge." We were all playfully scolding him.

Jack shook his head.

"No, this is the way we did it in Serbia," Jack said.

He stumbled forward and rained meteors at the stacked cans, peb-bles strafing aluminum, sloshing backwashed beer.

The cans clattered down, as the hailstorm pecked the ground and water.

"You cheated," said Rand, but he was grinning.

Then Jack was sprinting back up the dock toward us, dashing like a spooked gazelle.

"Out the way, out the way!" Jack yelled.

We cleared. He spilled—into Lake Jackson. Splashed around like a kid on holiday.

We were really laughing now. Just howling.

"Gets deep in here!" Jack hollered.

"No shit, dumbass," snickered Willington.

We were all bunched at the end of the dock, watching Jack swim and splash as if trying to attract sharks. He was yelling phrases from famous poems, and one of us would take up the cause and finish the stanza. Which made him swim more frenetically.

The game tripped along for several minutes.

"Come on back in," said Van Gear after a brief pause in the poetic palaver.

"I can't! I can't," yelled Jack.

My neck tensed up.

Was he drowning?

"I let him go," said Jack. "But only for a moment. A moment. They could strafe us. I wanted him underwater where they wouldn't hear him crying."

"What's he talking about?" I whispered. Willington looked at me and frowned.

"Oh, God! Where could he have gone?!? My son?!?" screamed Jack.

"Jack, it's all right," said Rand.

We all stood silent, paralyzed.

Van Gear swiveled off his shirt, slipped from his shoes and jeans— all in a micro-second flash. He dove in and swam out to Jack.

Van Gear's voice was a low mumble, a calm of words we couldn't decipher. Jack slowly settled. The lake's surface grew placid.

The pair treaded water, then drifted to the end of the dock where we waited, clustered at the edge. Willington and Rand clutched the right elbow, Ash and I grabbed the left shoulder. We wrapped our appendages around Jack and pulled him onto land.

The TallaTec had drained from us; we each tugged off our shirts and wiped the water from Jack's skin. We all shivered in the fall air, but Jack trembled, his wet hair spitting muddy droplets.

As Van Gear dragged himself onto the dock, Willington reached down a hand. Van Gear looked up and hesitated, but then he clasped Willington's fingers, and soon we were driving at a funeral pace from the parking lot.

Yes. Wings night. Expansive. Full of portents.

I am witness.

Tuesday, October 31, 2000

I had to find Sombre! I was determined to psych myself up to head to what Ash calls The House that Tec Built. I'd only been there in the company of Wings, so I felt scared and paranoid and completely out-of-sorts—but I was resolute!

Why was Sombre in T-town? What the hell had he been talking about? Who was this *They* who'd said he'd needed *the Thing*?

I hadn't received direct messages to aim for T-town, had I?

Or were they indirect?

T-town's university had been the only place to offer a fellowship! Have I been set up too, set up for *the Thing*, set up for TallaTec?

I paced. My apartment's dust spiders clung to my worn sneakers. I was working up my courage. I grabbed a bottle of beer from my fridge, slapping two motherfucking German cockroaches that scurried from the seal's cracks, and slammed Tears for Fears into my old boom box.

I would dance my way to decision. In spiffy new socks, *Shout. Shout. Let it all out* cranked loud, I slid atop the ancient linoleum. My neighbors' Chinese delicacies were wafting their smelly tentacles from one kitchen window to another. I felt underwater.

The House that Tec Built. I had to recreate the map in my head. I'd pedal my one-speed there, weaving my way to the dilapidated structure where the black boxes spit invisible smoke. I had no idea if Sombre would be there, but if he wasn't, I would grill the occupants for info.

Did Elly know about the House that Tec Built? I wanted to see her, start with her. The truth: I was afraid of facing the House, afraid of facing Sombre in ways I couldn't explain.

But might Elly U-turn with talk of TallaTec? I didn't want to scare her away.

I had to go solo to the House. This was *my* quest.

The weather had gotten chillier since last night's adventure at Lake Jackson. As I pulled on an old ski jacket, a bulky relic mom had purchased from Sears, I worried about Jack. Did he really have a son? Was he truly from Serbia? No Winger said anything; no one, seemingly, knew anything. It was a conundrum. Like Sombre.

After I oiled my bike, I was out, wheeling down hills, taking the Lake Bradford Road straightaway to the grand football church. I turned right, veering onto campus proper.

Traffic was light but freaks were heavy. Zombies. Vampires. Ghouls.

Halloween!

I'd hated Halloween in Dade. There was always a small cadre of assholes who "dressed" as Rad Sicks. They'd wear glasses with florescent-orange eyes attached. When they stumbled across one of us, they'd yell, "Imposter!" and claim our "title." As a ten-year-old, I'd taken a swing at a teen wearing fake peepers that popped from his sockets on springs. I knocked the wind out of him. My sister glared at this motherfucker. I adored her in these rare moments when she defended and not teased. Perhaps her teasing had been the kidding kind, but it always hurt. I know she'd had to tolerate peoples' razzing about her Sick sibling, and she had to take out her frustrations on somebody (mostly me), so I worshipped these uncommon instances of solidarity. The teen's fake eyes flashed like an out-of-sync late night traffic light. Once he caught his breath, he cocked his fist. But Big Sis gave him such a look, that he skulked away. She was ready to clock him. I loved my sister but still hated Halloween.

I slid by a Gaines Street warehouse where costumed students queued to enter T-town's most gruesome haunted house. Would the House that Tec Built be decorated too? Would I find spider webs stretched over black boxes, rubber bats glued to tubes?

I slowed to study the sillier of the Halloween get-ups. Thankfully, T-town was so far from the realm of the Accident that dressing as a Rad Sick wasn't on anyone's radar, not even freshmen from Miami.

In line stood a stand-out Betty Boop, a lovely Guinevere, a mus-cled Conan, and a dingy abominable snowman. A motley crew of Hallow-een clichés.

Some idiot stood barefooted with a C-Sox ball cap. The ware-house district was littered with broken bottles; shoelessness meant bloody feet. His gal dressed prim and held a book. A minister's daughter? An 18th century writer? Emily Dickinson, maybe?

Oh fuck, I know them. It was Rand and JAM!

Rand waved me over. I braked my bike and walked it through the gravel. JAM gave me a friendly hug and Rand shook my hand. He seemed embarrassed to be caught in costume.

"What are you doing for Halloween?" Rand asked.

"Nothing," I said. Of course, part of me wanted to ask directions to the House that Tec Built, but I didn't want to unfold my paranoid quest. I tried my best to look *above* all the holiday chicanery.

"You should slip into the haunted house with us!" said JAM. She *was* Emily Dickinson—the book was the Complete Poems of ... none other. She was showing, the baby expanding into a horizontal hill beneath the skin. Did Emily Dickinson ever have kids?

"Nah, I'm on a ride. Just going to pedal around and check the scene," I said.

"Well, don't get tricked," said Rand.

"I'm careful."

The line moved, so Rand and JAM waved, and I backed away.

The house filled, and then the line stopped again. Rand and JAM disappeared inside.

I noticed a guy with bandages wrapped around his head, but he wasn't a mummy. Something else. Literary. His face was wrapped so tight I found it hard to believe he could see or even breathe. Atop his nose sat dark, goggle-like, round-rim glasses.

A wintery fedora crowned his head, and a thick scarf strangled his neck. He wore a heavy trench coat. The Invisible Man!

Then, as if he knew I was staring, he began to unravel, unpeel, his chin, his lips, his nose. The skin was chocolate icing. He smiled—the teeth perfect except for a missing bicuspid.

Next: brown eyes (glasses now in coat pocket) and creased forehead and tight fro. He was fully revealed, sparkling and good-looking, but then he quickly rewrapped himself.

As he re-bandaged his forehead, something suddenly struck.

Oh fuck, I know him. It was Blanco. My Dominican friend from Miami.

A Rad Sick!

Another Rad Sick!

The Invisible Man had completely re-covered, his black goggles snug on his nose.

"Blanco!" I yelled, and pedaled like a madman and skidded a half-arc beside him. Dust clouded people's shoes. Three Klingons gave me a dirty look.

"Watch it," said a Kirk, his phaser set to stun.

"Blanco, man. Is that you?"

The Invisible Man turned his dark glasses in my direction.

"Blanco! What the hell you doing in T-town?"

The Invisible Man stepped out of line.

"Hey, did you know Sombre's here too?" I asked.

The Invisible Man gave me his hand.

I shook the hell out of it. His gloves were grey suede. He leaned to my ear and mumbled.

"A'ight. Can't talk 'cause my mouth's wrapped in gauze."

"Yeah, sorry. Damn. I can't believe it's you."

He took a step back and gave me the up-down.

"You the one with the hot sister, no? Didn't she call you, *Needle? Needle-face?* Something like that?"

"Yeah, that's me," I said. I'm sure I sounded defeated. Yes, yes, I was a rail-thin kid. You could have broken me off at the knee and used my femur as a toothpick.

Needle, he had said.

I'm here to escape *Needle*, no? Forget my sister. (I keep forgetting to ask Elly why she calls me *Needlefish*.)

"What you doing for Halloween, man?" asked Blanco the Invisible Man.

"Me? Nothing."

"You want to make some money?"

"Tonight? On Halloween?"

He suddenly leaned to the left as he lifted a gloved hand. His fingers splayed bandages from his mouth, and he started to whisper.

"No. Serious stuff. Psychology study. Professor had no idea it was a holiday tonight, so he needs subjects. Paying gig. Like 20 bucks an hour."

"You're full of shit."

"You wanna miss out on being *full of cash*?"

"What's the study?"

"They expose you to different atmospheric conditions, and then you take a survey."

"What conditions?"

"Fuck if I know. Some study on atmospheric effects on cognitive functioning."

"Blanco, you a psych major? Invisible man head-shrinker?"

"This is serious shit. I'm pre-med, so I'm interested."

I doubted Blanco was pre-med. He'd always been more interested in low-key graphic novels than hands-on graphic gore. But things change.

"It's on campus, this study?"

"Yeah, come on, man. I was headed there."

"Thought you were in line for the haunted house."

"Didn't realize how late it'd got. Line's slow as dirt."

"Huh.... O.K." I was noncommittal, but wavering. My quest for the House that Tec Built was getting sidetracked, because bumping into Blanco was freaking me out.

"So, let's go. Let me sit on the handle bars, and we'll cruise to Technology Hall."

I gave in.

We launched down Gaines, cut over on Woodward. I rode with the Invisible Man on the handlebars, his tape unravelling from around the ears and streaming past my eyes.

Technology Hall marked the center of campus. It sat by the campus green, beside the library and near the underground swimming pool.

I locked my bike and we entered Tech Hall's southwest corner through tall, glass doors. Blanco led us through a door into a barely lit stairwell.

"What about the elevator?" I asked.

"Takes too long in this building. Slow and creaky. Don't want to scare folks."

"Scare who?"

"You," he said. He turned and pulled his wrap completely off his mouth so he could flash a grin. The missing bicuspid was a black hole into the Invisible Man's cagey brain. "They pay you up front, man. Don't worry. We'll get back to the haunted house before they close."

I wasn't worried about getting paid. I was worried that Blanco was fucking with me, had no idea where he was going, and had half-baked plans for a wild goose chase.

As we circled upward, we passed transparent doors leading to dim hallways. At the top floor, the halls were brightly lit.

"Come on," Blanco beckoned. "We got to register with the registrar. No first register, no fast dollar."

"Quit talking like a goof, Blanco," I said. I'd forgotten what a joker the guy was. He'd used his Rad Sick eye-glow to peak into older girls' bedroom windows and scare the shit out of them. There was a whole posse of us teens that waited below, cheering him on. His bare feet had gripped my shoulders as he spied through high windows, and after the scream, I'd laughed as hardily as all the other goons scattering into suburban stillness.

On the 10th floor of Tech Hall we reached a water-stained wooden door and my Invisible Man opened it, revealing a small waiting room where an undergrad woman sat behind a red card table. We were the only ones waiting. She pointed to a set of blue plastic chairs and we sat.

She wore a white polo shirt and jeans. Her hair was auburn except for one blue streak that outlined her face. She had bangs, so the blue streak literally *framed* her face. Her eyes were green. She was cute. I was anxious.

She handed us pink vouchers that looked like $20 bills and asked us to fill out generic forms.

"This only takes an hour?" I asked after reading the form's first paragraph. I'd been hoping for more cash.

"Usually," she said. "But if it takes longer, the university will fully reimburse you. I'm giving you the pink slip to guarantee you get 20 bucks even if they decline to survey you."

The room had two grey love seats against the same wall, and after filling out the documents Blanco and I each claimed one.

The undergrad said it would be a minute, and she disappeared through a mirrored door.

"What are we doing again?" I asked. I was getting nervous. The place seemed too quiet. And I was completely off-track. A classic Rad Sick behavior. Idiot! My quest for Sombre now knocked way off course.

"Cognitive functioning in various atmospheric conditions," said Blanco.

"Sure, but what atmospheric conditions?"

"Smog, I think. Or smoke. Second hand smoke."

"Well, of course that's gonna fuck up your thinking."

"Nah, man. It's more nuanced than that. Wait till you hear the survey questions; they're crazy-hard."

"How many times you've done this before?"

"Once."

113

"And what was it like?"

The Invisible Man hesitated, sat completely frozen. He was silent for so long I began to wonder if he'd actually disappeared inside his gauze and his dried sweat had turned the bandages into papier-mâché.

The silence made the room feel cold. I glanced around for a thermostat.

"Well?" I said.

"I don't remember."

The girl shot quickly from the mirrored door and gestured to Blanco in a *hurry up* way, and within a split second I was in the room alone.

A minute later the same girl waved at me. I suddenly felt dread.

I was shown into a room with a recliner in the middle. The girl closed the door. From a cabinet she removed a colossal fishbowl and placed it over my head. It looked like the sort of thing as a kid you'd snag from a junk heap to use as a space helmet.

The bowl's opening around my neck was wide enough to fit her hand.

"Here," she said. "Open up. Please chew on this. It will create the experiment's atmospheric conditions."

I blinked, wrinkled my brow.

"And it's perfectly safe," she added.

She pressed a stick of gum against my bottom lip.

"What's in the gum?" I asked.

"Compounds calibrated to release microns of oxygen and other purified gasses."

She smiled now. Her extreme prettiness, which I'd overlooked up to this point, was pricking pins and needles in my chest. She kissed the bottom of the fishbowl, the veritable top of my helmet.

To hell with my search for Sombre!

Or no, I jerked, and her mouth softly, but accidentally, brushed against the glass. The blue streak in her auburn hair, the aqua frame, fell out of place and zig-zagged across the bowl.

My incisors grabbed the pink gob, and I gave it a soft bite.

All was lost!!!

*   *   *

Was any of this real?

I was gassed inside the fishbowl. Out cold. Gum and spit equaled vapors.

When I awoke, Blanco and I sat in a room. I felt monstrously groggy. He'd unraveled. Other Invisible Men and Women sat around a long table.

My eyes adjusted to the room's weird green lighting. No one was invisible. In fact, I recognized several faces! I saw more Rad Sicks, all looking pale, frozen in the swivel seats of this seminar room—we were like ghosts from a mediocre magical realism novel.

There was Sombre. There was Tay Chillieri. There was Bea Miller. And Tuck Zeedo. And for a frightful second, I thought I made out the silhouette of Elly in the room's shadowed far corner.

Who hosted this unscheduled Rad Sick reunion?

We were Halloween Invisible People, unmoving, awaiting tricks. Some had shoulders and necks wrapped with gauze, as if they'd caught the disease from Blanco after a gang-read of H.G. Wells.

We were astronauts with our fishbowl helmets.

A tall, bearded man stood at a chalkboard. Was the man in front lecturing with a pointer or waving a rifle? Did he wear a Captain's uniform or tweed jacket with elbow patches? Were those horned rimmed glasses or military issue night-vision goggles?

On reflection, his questions—post atmospheric-exposure—were absurd. The most impossible quiz of all time. The words I could understand, but the meanings slipped through my thin neurons like alcohol through cell membranes.

First Question: *What feels prickly in Afghanistan tomorrow? A question for you, Ms. Miller.* The voice browbeat her into calculating the tactile of tomorrow's Kabul. A figure appeared behind Bea as she brooded. Bea said nothing. The figure reached around and slapped her. She began to cry but remained silent.

Second Question: *What does a collapsing CDO from Credit Suisse Bank smell like that matures on September 11, 2001?* I thought, yes, do the dollars that rot in the filth of such greed stink like rotting cabbage leaves? Could a lucky few compose compost of those rotten CDO's and make them grow into a nest egg?

The man at the chalkboard pointed at Tay. Tay's eyes glassed over. The man continued to point the white stick. Tay mumbled nonsense, indecipherable syllables. The pointer whipped the air in a flash, a lightning strike, cracking him in the forehead near the temple. My friend stayed quiet and composed, but a line of blood appeared and seeped into his eye. I was now terrified, but the atmospheric conditions kept me paralyzed.

I heard Blanco whisper into my ear, "We're underwater in the prescient classroom of this neglectful university, as if trying to hear a submarine's Morse code from a Russian Geiger counter. Forgetful college stands as our benefactor, savior, keeping us alive with coins called *stipend.*"

I glanced around the room. No Rad Sick glow. Everyone owned the contacts.

Third Question: *What does the future of Chernobyl taste like, Mr. Zeedo? How many will ultimately survive?* Neither Bea nor Tay had answered their questions, and now Tuck kept up the silence.

Two dons then approached the chalkboard. How many professors does it take to lead a Psych Department experiment? When would my question come? With what would I be hit?

In the shadows someone was honing metal, something sharp. The scraping echoed in my skull.

Sombre snorted but appeared to sleep. Blanco quietly rocked forwards and backwards. Tay bled. Bea stopped crying.

Tuck suddenly spit a tooth on the table.

Blanco whispered, "You-all have the gift. I've been cursed and left bereft. Oh, how I've longed for mine to arrive, prayed, but instead I could only witness yours appear one by one while mine festered and drowned. Why don't I have my own?"

I pray I dreamt all this shit up. I think they'd fed me some industrial-grade TallaTec. That or something worse. Of course, our heads hovered in fishbowls, so it was hard to accurately know what the fuck was going on.

I doubt myself.

*   *   *

I have started packing my suitcases because I want to go home. Being Rad Sick in Dade was maybe not all that bad. Here, it's too clear I'm being fucked with by The-Great-All-Over, and I have no idea who or what that includes.

Wednesday, November 1, 2000

Ex called and said she'd changed her flight and was showing up tomorrow. I promised to meet her at the airport.

I would be glad to have her perspective.

Though I'd changed my mind about leaving and unpacked, hundreds of questions lingered.

What was going on in T-town and at the colossal college? I recalled Jack's comment from the other night: he'd said TallaTec was university-made. And he was right in some way, yes? At least the university *had* the stuff. The experiment at Tech Hall was definitely a casting-net to snag bottom-feeders—but what the hell were the staff trying to learn from us? Learn from *me?*

Why was the room stuffed with Rad Sicks?

One thing for sure: I was not getting near TallaTec again.

*   *   *

Last night's events both scare and intrigue me. This is another Rad Sick quirk. Complexity makes us curious, especially labyrinthian connections within connections that float at the edge of comprehension. However, Halloween has made me terrified as well. It's weird.

Nevertheless, *I love this place. Love Wings, Ravensview, even the classes, the workshops.*

And O.K., so I really, really, really love Wings.

And I'm hoping something blossoms between me and Elly.

And I want to, need to, read at Ravensview.

But also, I want to get to the bottom of this TallaTec bullshit.

I need to connect the dots. I need to satisfy myself about this strangeness.

So, the dots: Sombre; Elly; the House that Tec Built; Blanco; the experiment at Tech Hall. If I connect these what will take shape?

Something isn't right.

I'm headed to Tech Hall tomorrow. Today I'm too wound up, my focus too scattered.

Also tomorrow: meet Ex at the airport.

Thursday, November 2, 2000

Ex is asleep in my bed as I write this. I had to meet her at the terminal before sunrise, 5 a.m.

She's the only person I know who gets jet lag flying across a single time zone.

Presently, I'm recollecting all traces of my morning's investigation of Tech Hall.

Here goes.

First, Ex and I returned to Alum Village in the dark, and she fell asleep. I stared at the ceiling while Ex snored beside me. I felt super-restless. I threw on clothes, downed neither donuts nor coffee, scrambled onto my one-speed, and made a beeline for campus.

At Tech Hall, everything had been swept clean during All Saints Day. No exam results flapped from office doors. No M.A. program flyers hung from corkboards. The walls were spotless. The floors so polished, the Stanley Cup Finals could have been played wearing socks instead of skates. The ceilings contained no flickering bulbs.

I scoured every floor, tried every doorknob and found all locked tight. Wasn't it a school day? There were no faculty, students, staff anywhere. Tech Hall had been abandoned. The clean-up made everything hard to recognize, but I finally found the experiment's waiting room door. Again, no signs. Not even a stray form crumpled on the linoleum.

Yes, it was dawn, before even the 8am classes groaned to life, but the place was too dead.

I spewed a stream of curses in every language I could think of—why hadn't I gone yesterday to check? Why had I waited 24 hours? What Rad Sick stupidity!

In a daze, I slid to a restroom to take a piss. It took a while because my bladder's slow; my Rad Sick prostate got middle-aged this year. Afterwards, I sidled up to a sink to wash my hands, and lo and behold there sat beneath the faucet of the deep basin . . . a fishbowl.

And one solitary goldfish making circles into infinity.

Ah ha! Proof of Halloween's shenanigans!

But it also felt like a taunt. I grabbed the bowl. Part of me believed janitors had forgotten it, as they unknowingly returned things to pre-experiment normality. But what did I know? Like a Rad Sick goof, I scrambled downstairs, fishbowl in hand, like a nine-year-old who'd just won a carnival prize tossing a ping pong ball into the mouth of a mechanical gator.

But as I exited Tech Hall and walked to my bike, I realized I'd have a tough time riding with fish in hand.

I decided to walk; my Ex could help me get the bike later. Thus, I made my super-slow way back to Alum Hall, both arms wrapped around the fishbowl.

When I returned, I found my Ex still asleep. I lowered the fish bowl on the nightstand's corner, the fish circling near her head, stirring her dreams as she now snoozed, and I pondered the mysterious depths of T-town.

Friday, November 3, 2000

Ex woke up feeling well this morning, a big cat-like yawn to greet the day, and she smiled, and I almost wanted to like her again.

Almost.

"Why are you here?" I asked pouring a cup of coffee.

She sprinkled rainbow-colored flakes into the fishbowl; she'd insisted yesterday evening we buy high-end fish food from a nearby pet store. I half-wanted the gold dot to starve, but I acquiesced to humor her. We'd rescued my bike too. I'd noticed a strip of gauze in my spokes; I'd pulled it out and trashed it. She'd asked my about it, and I'd shrugged.

At this moment she looked away and shrugged.

"I missed you," she said.

I sighed. Did I miss her too? Of course. Was I going to admit it now?

No.

What to do about her?

"I quit my job," she mumbled.

Oh no.

"And put all my stuff in storage."

Please, no.

"You're saying you want to crash *here*, in T-town? What the hell for? There are no fulltime editing jobs here," I said.

"Well, I was thinking about doing some writing."

Every inch of me wanted to murder her. She was here trying to kill my life!

I took a breath, calmed myself. Because, yes, she could help me. Eventually. I needed to work up the nerve to describe everything about TallaTec, Tech Hall, and the sudden appearance of Rad Sicks, because I desperately desired an objective perspective.

Of course, I was afraid if I spilled the details too soon, she would give me that *oh you poor Rad Sick* look. So, I decided to wait.

Instead, I offered to take her to the English Department and show her around. She could meet some professors, meet my cohort. And what the hell, maybe we'd bump into a Wing or two.

*   *   *

Ex and I stumbled through the ground floor entrance near the multiple-personality-disorder elevator and literally bumped into Doc Primus. Ex has always been A-1 in making good, if goofy, first impressions, and Primus listened carefully with a knowing nod as she expertly slalomed through topics related to her K.C. editing gig. I'd asininely panicked at first, thinking she would embarrass me, but her smooth talk impressed, and I got the impression that Doc Primus was thinking I wasn't a complete disaster after all.

And then the elevator doors opened and out splashed Dirk Falter, my itinerant theory professor, guitar case in hand, ready to barge past.

He did a full-halt when he saw Doc Primus.

"Dirk, where are you off too in such a bluster?" asked Doc Primus. He loved to spout such *Winnie-the-Pooh* vocabulary as *blustery, heffalumps, honey pot,* and *woozles.* An ironic intent? Maybe, but it went over my head.

"Me?" asked Dirk, actually pointing at his own head with one hand and lifting the guitar case with the other. "I'm going to go make a radically sick record."

Had he glanced at me as he'd said this? I tried to catch Ex's eye, but she was staring at Falter expectantly. *Radically sick*? Had I actually heard him say that? Yes, it's an old slang phrase . . . but?

The elevator clanged again and belched out Van Gear!

Weirdly, even though two top profs stood before him along with my beaming Ex, Van Gear's eyes bore into me only, as if I were the only worthwhile fragment of personality recently released by the demented elevator.

"Practice at 7 p.m.," Van Gear grunted.

"What are you practicing?" asked Doc Primus.

"He," said Van Gear, giving a nod and smirk in Falter's direction, "is practicing his guitar, so he can learn how to play it."

Falter mirrored Van Gear's fake smile.

"Been practicing your poetry?" asked Falter.

Van Gear ignored him. Falter half-turned.

"Got to get working on the rad record," said Falter. "Good day, people." He truculently slammed through the exit to the great outdoors.

Doc Primus was nodding again, in his knowing way.

"And what are you practicing?" Primus looked back and forth between Van Gear and me. Ex stepped back and shrugged her shoulders, admitting to no part in these unknown schemes.

"Basketball," I squeaked.

"For Kurt Mitchell," said the German-Jesus. "I think I told you he's a B-ball buff."

"Very good," said Primus. "And I hope he'll talk about writing too. Unless we'll workshop at half court?"

"He's here for writing," said Van Gear. "Just like the rest of us."

There was an odd silence, and then Doc Primus slid into gracious goodbyes and darted into the dust of Dirk Falter's exit.

"Hey!" I exclaimed to Van Gear, because he suddenly looked ready to bolt through a different doorway. "I want you to meet my Ex. She's here visiting."

"Or maybe doing a little more than visiting," she said, as she offered Van Gear her hand in a manly way to match his manliness. I was beginning to think I'd made a serious mistake dragging her to campus.

"Oh? What are your plans?" asked Van Gear, as they shook hands.

The schizoid machine again clanged open and out hopped our blond-haired philosopher and TallaTec expert Ash. What was he doing in the English Building? Slumming?

"Practice at 7," Van Gear blurted, interrupting Ex's meandering description of her ex-job in K.C.

"I will try to be there," said Ash. He stopped in his tracks and smiled big at the gal. Oh boy. One could always tell when Ash was enamored by the way his laidback persona instantly shifted to charismatic charm. He subtly leaned toward Ex and touched her lightly on the shoulder.

"And who's this new writer in town?" asked Ash. Ex lit up. I think partly because Ash was saying what she wanted to hear—validation for her shift from editor to proser. Or was it poser?

Before I could add my spiel and be proud of my lost love (now becoming lovelier in my bitter eyes), the lady jumped in and made her usual strong first impression. Well, unusually strong.

Did she like Ash back?

And then. A voice. From somewhere.

Needlefish!

What? I looked around, startled. The others kept talking, not noticing my disorientation.

What was going on? Had I become unhinged, psychotic? Or was the fishbowl still over my head, and was I the only one not to notice?

On an inhale, I caught a whiff of spliff from Ash's collar, and then—oh shit!—I recognized the barely detectable smell of the House that Tec Built. Was he now splicing together weed and TallaTec in his spliffs? Did it now take only a whiff to make me tumble into the TallaTec tunnel?

Needlefish!

The voice was Elly's. But where (and when?) was it? Was I hearing an invisible voice from tomorrow, an echo inside my head of simple memory, a word spoken somewhere at this very moment? Why did the voice sound worried? Almost . . . panicked!

I had to dash to Ravensview.

But what about Ex? I couldn't ditch her. I'd feel like shit.

"Do you-all want to grab a coffee at Yak's Tea Shop?" asked Ash.

Van Gear had already managed to say a quick goodbye and exit.

"Yes!" said Ex. She was Ms. Maximus Enthusiasmus.

"Well. . . let's see . . . we were planning," I stuttered. I could not get trapped philosophizing with Ash and Ex over a cup of Earl Grey; I had to see Elly!

"Can't we meet your Contemporary Poetry professor tomorrow?" asked Ex. I'd completely forgotten that I'd promised to introduce her to Bigfoot. That was my ticket-out of tea time!

"No, I've actually got to ask her something about class, about an upcoming paper. Gotta differentiate New Historicism from New Criticism from Old Historians to hysterectomy and hysteria. She's an intense feminist. That's why I thought you'd like her."

"Yes, but can't we meet her later?"

Now I had my escape hatch.

"No, I really should see her today. Need to start that paper. But hey, why don't you and Ash head over to Yak's, and I'll catch up."

Ash grinned. His smile annoyed the hell out of me; but what right did I have to be jealous? I was running off to find Elly!

Ex accepted my suggestion with a nod. She seemed pleased.

"Sounds good, man," said Ash

They left through the main exit, as I pretended to board the elevator.

As soon as they vanished, I took the door Van Gear had exited.

Outside, I cut a diagonal line between brick towers, heading directly to the dark but welcoming door of Ravensview.

I banged through the street side entrance, and glanced over at the bar to see the woman with the mitochondria tattoo standing glumly beside the cash register. She turned to squint at me.

"Is Elly on?"

She pointed straight down.

Elly was working downstairs! My heart soared. Suddenly, I was almost happy to be called *Needlefish!*

I slipped downstairs and looked around. A third of the tables were stacked with late-lunchers. The bar was empty.

I didn't see any servers.

Not knowing what else to do, I sat at the round booth where Elly and I had conversed after Van Gear's reading. I suddenly recalled her kiss, the endless kissing bliss in the backseat of her beat-up Mustang.

"Hey, Needlefish!" She stood there smiling, as if genuinely pleased that I'd appeared from nowhere. Plath's *Ariel* hadn't scared her off. She whipped out her pad, ready to take my order. I, of course, wanted *her* on a platter, wanted to pour myself into her glasses-framed green eyes. "What you want?"

"I'm here to talk to you. To see you, I mean." I was talking way too loudly.

"Sure. But I'm on shift till late. And then I'll be too tired. But why don't you order some stuff, and we can talk between courses and re-fills?"

I shook my head.

"Elly, I thought I heard you calling me for!" I sounded psychotic, delusional, a 'roided-up romantic.

"Calm down, OK?" She looked serious. She raised an eyebrow. "What do you mean?" She dropped the pad on the table and waved me over so she could sit beside me.

"On Halloween did you get paid for a study at Tech Hall?" I asked in a half-whisper.

Elly looked at me, then stared at the center of the table.

"Things got weird for me on Halloween. I just. . . ." She drifted off. She grabbed her pad and started doodling overlapping circles.

"What happened?"

"I was just hanging-out on campus that afternoon—you know I'm thinking about going back to school—and I saw this flyer tacked to a bulletin board by the library. It'd said FREE MONEY! Get paid to do a survey! As I stared at the page, some guy dressed as a mummy wearing hat and glasses tapped my shoulder—he spooked me until I remembered, *My God!, it's Halloween!*—so I kidded him, because of his horn-rimmed glasses, about being a *smart* mummy. Well, this guy said the survey was at

Tech Hall, and it'd be easy cash, and he'd just done it, and he'd take me over there, and it'd be quick, and I thought, *OK, I've got some time to kill.*"

Elly stopped talking and doodled furiously, nearly flattening the tip of her ballpoint pen.

"I was there too," I said. "Damn, I swore I saw you, but I thought the shadows played tricks."

"You saw me at Tech Hall?" asked Elly.

"Yeah, at the experiment. The place the Invisible Man took you. He was trolling for volunteers. He caught me too. I saw you there."

"I don't think so. And what's the Invisible Man?" She paused. "Oh, you mean the *smart mummy*." She looked puzzled, her brow wrinkled. She stopped scratching circles on the pad and stared across the bar at a row of vodka bottles. "No, I never made it to Tech Hall. Never got paid."

"But what do you mean? You just said that night was weird. You seem surprised I asked about Tech Hall. What else happened?"

Elly said nothing. Sighed. A dude at a nearby table signaled to her for the check, but she didn't see him. The jukebox got louder, murmuring Yes's "I've Seen All Good People." Or was it "The Gates of Delirium?"

"Needlefish, I'm just not sure. I'm scared. I'm worried to death that the smart mummy injected me with a date-rape drug when he shook my hand and said, "I'm Blanco," because I don't remember much after that except walking at dusk alone near the Business College and heading here for a drink to clear my head."

"That doesn't sound good, Elly." My gut boiled. I was sick with anxiety. Had Blanco messed with her? I would kill that nut-brained Dominican sonofabitch.

She paused and looked me in the eyes.

"So what was the experiment?"

And I spilled, told what I remembered from the blur that was Halloween night. She listened, her face neutral, her pen making unfocused Venn diagrams. I told her about TallaTec, the House that Tec Built, sightings of other Rad Sicks. Several customers waved their hands to get her attention, but they were not on her radar. The jukebox played Renaissance's "Can You Understand?"—the live version from the 70s.

"That," she said, "sounds like an acid trip. Did you just make that up? Didn't you tell me you're in the fiction program?"

"I didn't make it up. Some of it may have been hallucination, but not all."

I cleared my throat.

"I can show you *the goldfish*!" I said.

Elly eyed me skeptically.

"Hey, how have you been?" said a voice from across the table.

Ryanna stood at the edge of the booth.

Ravensview was just that kind of place: the spot where progressive and arts folks gravitated. This made the place even more magnetic. In South Florida you could only count on bitter know-it-all drunks consistently haunting the same dives, but here in T-town Ravensview offered conversation with all wild-minded types.

"Hi. Have you met Elly?" I asked.

"I know I've seen you before," said Ryanna.

"Yeah, I work here," said Elly. Her voice fell neutral. She seemed to be losing interest in me and this moment. She almost smiled, then stood up. "I gotta get back to work. Good talking to you, Needlefish."

She brushed hips with Ryanna as she pushed out of the booth, her hand grazing Ryanna's jeans, but neither seemed to notice.

Was Elly jealous? Or just bored? Did I want her to be jealous? Could she detect Ryanna's too friendly *hey-we've-made-love-before-and-it-wasn't-too-bad* vibe?

And I'd finally spilled my guts about TallaTec to somebody, an Earth-rattling revelation, and it seemed to barely make a dent on Elly. *Did she think I was making it up?*

I was not *that* good of a fiction writer!

"What have you been doing lately?" asked Ryanna.

Elly passed by (oddly closely) holding a platter full of empties

127

with one hand, and I thought I caught a glimpse of her slipping something into Ryanna's back pocket, but Ryanna didn't notice. I figured it was more of my chronic mis-seeing.

"Hey, there's another place I'd like to take you," she said.

"Where's that?"

And I could have sworn that whatever I thought Elly had slipped into her jeans was now what Ryanna was unfolding in front me.

A map. The paper was full of green and blue creases that met at bends in a waterway. The map plotted the Apalachicola River and surrounding state park.

"There are some awesome hiking spots here. Bluffs overlooking the water. And the Torreya tree is there, nearly extinct."

I studied the map.

"We should go soon," she said.

I suddenly wished I sat sipping Early Grey with Ash and Ex at Yak's. That seemed a lot less messy. With Elly doubting my story though she'd been at Tech Hall, Ryanna offering me a new trek to water, and the pair passing notes, sitting for tea sounded wonderfully straightforward, even if it included winks and moon-eyes.

But wasn't Elly on my side? I was in love with Elly. I wanted to rescue her from the Tech Hall hangover she wasn't sure she suffered from, and make her fall for me and stop calling me *Needlefish*. Of course, I held half-a-candle for Ryanna, even though she'd made it clear she wasn't interested; she simply wanted to show me wonders of the Big Bend wilderness.

Moron! Elly and Ryanna were somehow conspiring against me! Like, wake up, dude!

Where the hell could I turn?

"In thirty minutes," said a deep, commanding voice from another side of the table.

Van Gear stood there in shorts, tank top, and headband.

"You're going to practice, right?" he said.

Ryanna stepped back from the table, smiling her soft, warm smile.

"Sorry," said Van Gear, suddenly scraping together a modicum of manners. "I interrupted."

"That's OK.," said Ryanna. "Heard you gave a nice reading the other night. Sorry to have missed it." She turned to me. "Keep the map. I'll call you. We'll go soon." And then Ryanna wandered to the stairwell and headed up.

"Where's your ex-girlfriend? She in the bathroom? And you setting up dates with other women?" He stared blankly at me, as if seeing me in a new light. I couldn't tell if it was a good or bad light.

"She and Ash are over at Yak's."

"And you're here. Doing a rendezvous."

"Not really."

"Well, now you're with me. You going to ask me for a date?"

"No."

"Yeah, you don't need to. We already have one. At the court. At 7. In a heartbeat. Come on. I'll drive you."

We exited.

*　　　　*　　　　*

Once we got to the court, Van Gear scouted out the park's bathrooms to take a piss, and I unfolded the map of the Apalachicola River and what Ryanna called The Bluffs. I considered "bluffs" a silly word in hilly but not mountainous north Florida. A gust flipped the map across the back of my left hand, and that's when I saw the Post-It note.

The scrawl was tiny, barely legible:

Needlefish, I can't talk here. I keep seeing faces from that night at Tech Hall. They sit at the bar and order never-ending platters of raw oysters. I can't help but think they're keeping an eye on me. Or maybe they're new marine biology professors? We need to talk. I'm off at midnight. Meet me at my car and we'll go for a drive? --Elly

My brain spun. She *had* remembered that night. And she was as confused and scared as I was.

I needed to devise a way to meet her.

So much raced through my mind: a date tonight with Elly; another at a river with Ryanna; and my damn Ex sharing my bed? My life was a crazy mess. How would I sneak out and rendezvous with Elly without Ex noticing?

At least Elly and Ryanna weren't in cahoots. Elly had pick-pocketed the map, stuck the note in, and slipped it back to Ryanna without her noticing.

Maybe she'd hoped nature-girl would hand me the document without seeing the yellow square.

Maybe Elly had *smelled-out* that future with her own undeclared Rad Sick super-sense.

Van Gear powerwalked from the john as Ex pulled up with Ash. Ex drove. Damn, she was good, talking a perfect stranger into driving his vehicle. She loved to drive. No matter what.

Ex stepped from the truck snd lit a cigarette. Van Gear gave me a disapproving look. Hey, I'd quit smoking! I couldn't help that she'd faltered! Besides, Van Gear had been into smoking TallaTec.

Ex's cigarette immediately went out, and Ash angled around the front bumper like a wide receiver on a buttonhook (his Gator gridiron days still sturdy in his bones) and pulled out his lighter. She smiled and he put his hand gently on her shoulder and grinned.

Were they flirting? Ugh. It felt weird.

Van Gear practiced foul shots, ignoring the rest of us.

I centered the Post-It note on the map, folded the pages, and jammed it into a pocket before anyone noticed.

Ash shuffled to midcourt to stretch.

Ex strolled up beside me and leaned her head against my shoulder.

"We waited for you. But Ash said we should head here." She yawned. "Did you get the answers you were looking for?"

"What?"

"From the feminism professor."

The pieces of my jumbled brain stumbled into place.

"Yes—she wants me to go New Historicism all the way."

Ex looked at me and smirked, lifted herself on tip-toe and gave me a solid kiss on the cheek.

Now *we* flirted?

I'm lying to her, and I bet she suspects; nevertheless, she's obviously got some sort of crush on Ash, and he on her. So why the kiss as if we'd stepped back into love. The kiss lingered and made me worry about her interests later.

And then this ridiculous concern: Was that goldfish hungry?

Before I drowned in dread, in pulled a station wagon, and out popped Willington and Rand. Van Gear kept arcing foul shots as if this were routine. I freaked in a good way because it looked like we had the entire Wings contingent.

"Is Jack coming?" I asked.

"Haven't heard from his Slavic ass," said Willington.

"He called and said probably not," said Rand.

I introduced the newcomers to Ex, and soon we guys jogged across the court and shot hoops. Ex stood beside the post. Smoking. Silent.

Willington and Rand were having an intense conversation about parenthood. Willington gave golden words. The man had a terrible-2 and a lucky 7. Rand's newborn with JAM would arrive soon, and he was becoming fast pals with JAM's son. Nevertheless, Rand was all nerves. Tonight he edged up against tears.

To fight my own anxiety, I practiced my unskilled jump shots as we warmed up. I was improving, shooting damn near 50%. The practicing was working! Even *I* might impress Kurt Mitchell! Van Gear was coaching genius.

"Let's run some plays," said Van Gear. "We'll go three on 2-D. Rand, Willington, you guys guard the hole. We three will take it to your lazy butts."

Van Gear and Ash crashed the basket against the rusty Rand and

Willington. I stayed in the background, occasionally got a pass so I could take an open jumper. We worked up a sweat in the November evening chill.

Ex looked bored. She lit another cigarette. Everyone ignored her. I had a strong desire to stand beneath the post and puff away.

Some guy rode up on a bicycle from the opposite side. Black dude. He leaned against the post at the other end.

We ignored him. He watched, sized us up from across the blacktop.

At one point, Van Gear seemed overly winded, so we took a break. He looked a bit pink in the gills (like a hungry goldfish!). One too many Wild Turkeys the night before.

I stood at the top of the key and turned to face the half court circle.

The guy on the bike wore a fedora and super-weird sunglasses. Glasses as think as goggles.

Shit! It was Blanco, the Invisible Man without his wraps. Motherfucker!

"We're back on, man," shouted Van Gear.

I felt the ball but never saw it. I was too busy staring at Blanco.

The ball popped my crown, I tilted but kept my balance.

My ears rang.

"What'd you do that for?" I snapped.

"Sorry," said Van Gear. "What? Is that guy in the department or something?"

I was pissed about the sucker-pass, and I was damn determined to confront Blanco, so I rocketed a pass to Van Gear (which he caught with one hand, no sweat) and headed up court.

"Play without me. I'll be back," I said.

I marched up the court. Blanco sat on his bicycle and didn't flinch. He waited. His hat made him look like a private detective. Sam Spade on a BMX. The glasses made him look like an ass.

I stopped a foot from him.

"What was that shit on Halloween?" I asked.

"Trick or Treat?"

"I should punch you."

"What? You didn't get paid?" Blanco dug around in his back pocket and offered a $100 bill.

I ignored it. He continued to hold out his hand. The bill sat on his palm, as if a lettuce leaf waiting for an entre of bullshit.

"I don't want money. I want to know what that was. And I don't want any more of your doubletalk."

Blanco looked hurt. He reached a hand underneath this hat and scratched his afro.

"The money's good, Needle-man."

I took a swing. Connected on the spot he'd just scratched. His hat flew off. His glasses tilted on his nose.

I missed the second swing and was in mid third-swing when I felt tentacles from the Four Wings-men pull me away.

"Quit it!" I shouted. "I need to beat some information out of this bastard!"

Blanco righted his glasses, picked up his hat.

"You don't want more money?" asked Blanco.

I was pinned by Wings. An easy target for Blanco's Benjamin. He stuffed the bill down the front of my shirt.

"I just want answers, asshole!" I yelled.

Blanco lifted onto his bike and pedaled a slow circle around us. The Wings were oddly silent. Their hands felt sea salt sticky. Maybe they had transmogrified into an octopus.

"A'ight. Just letting you know. The next study is at the underground pool on Veteran's Day. High noon."

The Invisible Man rolled into the evening.

"What was that about?" asked Ash.

I didn't know what to say. Should I give Wings the story? The full story? Even now, I didn't think they'd realized I was a Rad Sick. Probably

133

they wouldn't care. They weren't from Dade.

But I'd have so much to spill. Would take hours to unfold.

"Fucker owed me money," I mumbled.

"Well, looks like you scared it out of him," said Van Gear. He pulled the bill that half hung out of my collar and handed it to me. "Now let's get back to work."

"Hey, when we left the Haunted House, we saw you ride off with a mummy wearing a fedora like that dude," said Rand.

"He was the Invisible Man," I whispered.

"No, I could see him," said Rand.

Ex still stood at the post, smoking, staring to her left. She hated violence.

She picked up the ball that now sat beneath the basket and rolled it down court.

That cinched it. Back to practice. I'd have to tell "the story" later.

"We've got miles to go before we sleep, brothers," said Van Gear.

Saturday, November 4, 2000

I really should date this November 3 ½ because it's 4:30 a.m. and my Ex is sound asleep in the other room, completely out of it, and I've been up all night dealing with more strangeness. It started with the B-ball practice wrap-up of two-thirty 9-packs provided by V. G. we drank beneath the rim. The new brew, Atomic Lager, sported a carbon atom on the can—the corporate dumbasses didn't know carbon is a stable atom. Willington made reference to a Brandelsonna film—one V. G. hadn't seen—about radiation-eating rats gnawing pencil leads. Then I took Ex home despite protest from Ash who suggested we head back to Yak's. But then I got brow-beaten by Ex who said she found Yak's "absolutely charming"—so we spun off with Ash, even though we boys were sweaty. We hung at the tea shop, where I could barely focus on the conversation because I was trying to rig a way to meet Elly behind Ravensview at midnight. Then I got the most brilliant idea: Ex was absolutely susceptible to Sleepytime tea.

So much so, after one full cup she'd sleep eight hours straight (normally she was a rather light sleeper—unless jet-lagged). We finished a pot, and I stood up and said I'd grab the next round. When I ordered, I asked for an entire box of Sleepytime, which was a rip-off at $12 bucks (these bastards should know we're all broke from the recession!). I ripped open every package, stuffed the teabags into the steaming water and forced the pot's lid shut. I arrived tableside with a big grin. Half a cup later, Ex started yawning, asked to be taken home. Ash looked crestfallen (ha! the bastard would have to wait till tomorrow to continue his lothario shuffle). Ex and I slammed back into Alum Village, and she fell dead asleep as soon as she slid beneath the covers.

Lights out! I snuck out to find Elly.

I pulled next to Elly's car in Ravensview's lot and waited. After ten minutes I got out and sat on the hood of her Mustang.

After another ten, she appeared.

"Needlefish, thank God."

"What took you so long?"

"I had to serve the Smart Mummy. Except he had no gauze."

"The Invisible Man? Blanco is in there?"

"Was," sighed Elly. "He left up the stairs. I went up to check a moment later, and he'd definitely dipped. I checked both restrooms to be sure."

"You had to wait his table?"

"He somehow knew my zone." Elly nervously glanced behind her. "He was making me paranoid."

"What did the bastard do? I saw the fucker today at the basketball court."

"He ordered oysters. Like the marine biologists."

"That's it?"

"No, he said I could make easy cash at the underground pool next to the library. On Veteran's Day. At high noon."

"That's the same bullshit he told me."

"I do not want to go to the underground pool."

I suddenly pictured the sinkhole Ryanna had showed me, the mysterious whirlpool effect. Could that pool of natural energy reverse the black energy of Tech Hall's crew and their underground campus pool?

"I read your note on the back of the map," I said.

"I just wanted to tell you. I didn't remember anything about Halloween. Like I said. But as you started describing all that shit, I could picture it, you know? And I was picturing it so vividly that I knew I wasn't just imagining it!"

"What do you remember?" I asked.

"All those weird questions. About smells. Tastes. Sounds. Textures. It was like they were talking around a subject they didn't understand."

"Yeah, all those other Rad Sicks got questioned. Some mumbled. The interrogators never spoke to me. Not that I remember. Did they ask you anything?"

"Time?"

"What? It's after 12:30. Why?"

"No. That's it. There was something about time involved in all this."

"What?"

"Like they were somehow trying to predict things."

"Sure. But predict what?"

We stood silent for a full minute. We were both sitting on the hood now.

Then Elly leaned into me and wrapped an arm around my shoulders. I reciprocated. We were netted in a sideways hug.

*   *   *

Later this morning, Ex still inside her Sleepytime doze. I wrote her a note, stuck it on the night table and took off for campus. Wanted to catch a special guest writer Doc Primus had invited.

I think I'd convinced Elly to sneak in early on Veteran's Day to

136

scout-out the underground pool. Blanco had told her to go the *observed* day, the 10th, not the traditional 11th, so we needed to decide soon.

I pedaled to campus and thought about Halloween, the experiment, Blanco on my handle bars. I wish I'd hit a curb and sent him sprawling. Of course, if he was a Rad Sick, why did they make him a lackey? Why hadn't they been draining his brain? He'd sat near me, but he seemed aloof, not part of the interrogated, neither victim nor foe. But they'd enlisted him. How? Why? Why'd he sign up? Was it true what he'd whispered on Halloween, that he lacked a skill and was jealous?

I locked my bike, barged into the building, and found a safe stairwell to the lecture hall. Doc Primus had said this writer was well-known for blending literary and science fiction. I hadn't heard of her. He said we'd probably workshop afterwards; Doc was a serious taskmaster. His words would help me forget all this mess. At least temporarily. And I was still interested in improving my prose, despite my obsessions with Tech Hall and all.

The lecture hadn't started yet, and there was an empty seat next to Kate, so I plopped down and said *Hey!* She nodded and smiled.

"Where's Skate?" I asked.

"Late," she said.

Doc Primus strolled in and stopped beside me.

"Where's your young lady friend?" he asked.

"Asleep," I said.

"On such a blustery morning? She's a good sleeper, indeed." He was right. It had been damn windy. And cold too. Since I was from South Florida and didn't own gloves, my hands had turned pink as I biked to campus. With near freezing temps in early November, I couldn't believe T-town was in Florida.

"Who's up for workshop today? After the lecture," I asked Kate after Doc strolled away.

"You didn't read them?" said Kate.

Actually, I had read them, but with all the chaos since Halloween,

I wasn't sure what was what.

"I read "Blue," "The Mother Scarecrow," "Moon Source." Does that sound right?" I asked.

Kate laughed. Her snow cap's tassel bounced from front to back.

"You are right on track."

Doc Primus asked someone to close the door.

"Well, apparently our guest writer cannot make it this morning. No matter. Let's get to work. Even though it's Saturday."

He chalked on the board three words in a column: *blue, mother, moon*. He stood at the front and stared back at us, giving us an impish smirk.

"What do these words share?" Doc asked.

We were all quiet. The knitter stopped knitting and raised her hand.

"They're elemental words, so to speak. Powerful words," she said.

"Yes, yes. Go on."

The knitter paused a moment, looked up at the ceiling.

"They're simple but very evocative."

"Good, good." Doc's tone was encouraging, generous.

Skate burst through the door that'd been left slightly ajar, his winter weather skully emblazoned with a West Ham United logo. He slapped his palm against it as if he'd just remembered something.

"How 'bout *blur* and *whir*?" he stuttered. Expectorant flew from his mouth.

Kate gave him a puzzled, questioning look.

"Those are good words too," said Doc, not skipping a beat, as if Skate's entrance had been prearranged.

Skate looked incredibly pleased with himself as he stumbled into the room. His Spitfire Wheels hoodie had super-baggie sleeves, and as he slid by me the smoky smelling fabric slapped my face. He sat in an empty desk in front of Kate who glared at him.

Next, the chalkboard began to expand and the word *blue* became both *sky* and *ocean*. The breeze was slightly humid, but mild. I squinted because of the sun rising over the sea. I rubbed the hell out of my eyes.

The knitter was damn right about maximum evocation!

Or no. My brain was taking literally the *blur* and *whir* Skate had serendipitously introduced to our discussion.

Doc Primus wrote *whir* and *blur* below the blue. The board leaked unsteady, unfocused tears.

As he chalked the letters *B* and *L* in super-long, slow-flowing, precision-lined script, two strange figures appeared beside him. To his left trumpeted a proud heffalump. To his right stood a defiant woozle.

Oh fuck! The smell from Skate's hoodie! He'd been toking TallaTec. I was getting another contact high and hating it!

I closed my eyes and could hear all the voices of T-town creep into my soundscape. These were the near-future voices. These were the hearts of T-town's culture that contained the glue that pulled like-minded people together. The peoples' voices clattered in joyful noise because the titles in The Rack danced along their spines and flapped paper wings; because Vinyl River was the grooving soundtrack of this trip; because Video Planet offered intelligent dialogue.

What had Elly realized? That Tech Hall's experiments were for deciphering the future? As I thought about this, I envisioned (no, the TallaTec forced me to *hear*!) the sea-changes soon to hit T-town. The Rack would drown under the weight of unbought books; Vinyl River would evaporate, drained by computers, each song spit singingly to individual ears; Video Planet would implode as the timbre of Hepburn and Bogart became fiber optic cable bits.

What else would alter? What about this very ground we talked and workshopped upon? A tidal wave would build of criticism, about *telling* and not *showing*, about a character's *wants*, about too little *yearning* or a lack of *vividness* or too little *dialogue* or too much *dialogue* or too little *tension* or too little *character development*. The wave would wash these words from state to state, from college-town to college-town, as every academic tower would house an MFA in the art of prose and poetry. And thus would be born the Age of the Ubiquitous MFA, which should be a beautiful thing (to create more good words and legions of readers demanding better words), but somehow MBA norms would leak in, and competition would reign and the sanctity of the creative community would be lost, splintered—dying voices suffocating in the egocentric cage of individual success. Only the *awards*, the names of *publishers*, the *titles* of the prestigious journals would matter. These words would dance tantalizingly out of reach of the plebian but competent new proletarian writing class. And the towers' programs would bloom in the millions and millions, regurgitating *Writers* in the billions and billions, each seeing a spiraling death dance of loneliness and despair. Oh God! All these terrible and sobbing voices from the future, when T-town's school would be bloated with writers producing a dearth of meaningless words no one would hear. Oh Hark! what frightful future this fucking TallaTec rings aloud within my ear canal!

Fade, oh blessed fade, the TallaTec contact high diminished. Doc Primus lost his sidekicks: the heffalump drifted into an eraser; the woozle lost his shirt and slipped through a floor crack. The chalkboard's five words rested plainly upon the slate. Skate kept slapping his West Ham patch, but everyone ignored him.

On to fiction!

"Blue" got whitewashed; "Mother Scarecrow" got unstuffed; "Moon Source" got cratered. Maybe a bad mood dominated because it was Saturday morning after a Friday evening of boozing, something Rand called *hangover hate*.

It wasn't that bad. And Doc Primus kept praising the titles! But it made me fearful of the reaction to *Microwaves*. I'd been crafting sections of the novel into a short story called "Surf-boy," named after a tangential pseudo-mythical character I invented. It's more of a rambling prose-poem than true narrative.

Ex is still asleep as I've returned from school now and plan to end this entry and start working on "Surf-boy."

Sunday, November 5, 2000

I called Ryanna yesterday and set up today's trek to the Apalachicola River bluffs. Need to keep Ex occupied.

Weirdly, I was enjoying having Ex around, appreciated our quiet talks about Elizabeth Bishop (Bigfoot's favorite) and Edna St. Vincent Millay (Ex's favorite) and Sylvia Plath (my favorite) as we sat around my sorry Alum Village apartment and cooked pancakes; Ex at one point made an interesting assertion that Carolyn See had predicted the nuclear fall-out future; I agreed and disagreed and also grew anxious. Ex steered the topic elsewhere once I unconsciously leaked a "You're picking on a Rad Sick" look; I didn't mind the reference and found it sweet that she still worried about upsetting me—she'd always been careful.

I told her I was feeling inspired and needed to carve around on "Surf-boy" for an upcoming workshop, so I suggested maybe Ash wouldn't mind taking her for coffee.

Her smile lit up, which deflated me—but again, as Van Gear inferred: what a totally hypocritical asshole I was being!

I called Ash, and he was more than happy to do it; his paper on Derrida was getting to him. Why did I begrudge the son-of-a-bitch when he was doing me a favor?

I met Ryanna at a gas station where Highway 20 crossed the truck route, got into her car, and started the hour drive.

We passed through lonely, hilly countryside. A similar drive on south Florida backroads would offer mangrove jungles, sawgrass swaths, and flat landscapes.

We bobbled through a state park entrance and made an immediate left turn, parked. Ryanna had her usual grin.

"Hope you brought your walking shoes," she said. "It's a distance."

We ambled down a wide path and said nothing for five minutes.

"Your friend seems nice," said Ryanna, turning to me. Were her eyes green in the forest-dimmness . . . or grey or hazel?

"Who?"

"The woman at Ravensview. The one who works there."

"Oh. You mean Elly. Yes, she's a friend."

"I think she's a good one to have. I like her."

Our conversation was stranger than usual.

"What do you mean?"

"You know what I mean."

I didn't say anything. I was annoyed. Was she pointing out my potential girlfriends, like Big Sis had once done? Big Sis liked to pick Rad Sick girls for me; when we Rads were eight, she thought Taylor Morgan Velázquez and I would make a great couple. What a bunch of crap. I prayed Ryanna wouldn't play matchmaker. I loved Elly, but I didn't need pushing.

"You are going to love this view!" she said. "If you think hard enough, you can believe you're in the Appalachian Mountains."

"But instead we're in the Apalachee Mountains," I said a little sarcasticaly. "We've lost a P."

"A what?" she asked, "a P?"

"Think about the spelling. Two P's must mean mountains. One must mean hills."

"Hmmmmmm. I kind of like that."

Two deer strolled across our path. We stood statue-still and said nothing. The deer gave us a casual glance and proceeded to leisurely pick their way through the woods.

Ryanna and I were not two deer and no longer dear to each other. At least, we were no longer dear to each other in the way I'd hoped after glass bottom boating on Skull Springs. Again, hypocritically, I felt hurt and saddened. I could no longer handle anything that felt like *loss*. Wasn't this why I'd headed north, to escape my Rad Sick sadness, to escape the pity? I wanted release, a fresh start.

We walked another 20 minutes.

"We're close," Ryanna said. "Listen, you can almost hear the river."

She seemed to be full of shit. I heard nothing.

But I did detect an uptick in humidity. I smelled the ghost of a campfire.

We hiked up a steep incline to a fire pit at a flat spot. A tiny A-frame structure was hidden in a clump of trees, apparently a state-certified outhouse.

The A-frame's door popped open. Out popped a tall bearded guy with an oversized backpack, a backpack so large one would assume he was hiking the Appalachian Trail not the Apalachicola River.

"Good morning," Ryanna said.

The guy nodded. He wore a goofy hat, one of those floppy hats you might see a fisherman wear except this one was full of fish-shaped lures from the 1950s. Emblazoned across the front of his hat: STATE U.

"You *teach* at State?" I asked. Why did I make this assumption? Well, he certainly looked professorial.

"Yes," he said. I realized he seemed startled, shocked to see other humans afoot. Did he think he'd have the park to himself?

"Are you in environmental sciences?" Ryanna asked.

"Marine biology actually," he said. He paused. "But enjoy hiking."

"We too," she said.

He nodded again and turned and trotted up the path.

Marine biology?

"Look through this break in the trees," Ryanna said. "Down through this long crevice of branches."

She was standing on the highest spot on the campsite plateau. I shuffled beside her and stared where her finger pointed. A steep drop-off angled to the north, a forest landscape dotted with outcrops of stone and lichen-furred gullies. Several hundred yards below, I saw water.

The Apalachicola River! My God! She was right! It was as if we stood on a mountain bluff in the lower half of the Smokey Mountains!

"Look at that!" I exclaimed.

"Let's check the river," she said. "I have something else to show you."

We got off the path and wound our way between rocks and trees, working hard to not break our ankles on the steep incline. The ground was soft, and our feet sank into piles of leaves like quicksand. The sound of the river grew steadily. At one point Ryanna pointed out a bald eagle in a nearby treetop. A bald eagle! I had no idea they nested in Florida; Dade suburbia was the home of crows, pigeons, and mockingbirds.

We meandered to a stone outcropping that hung over the Apalachicola, about ten feet above the surface. The water murmured. The sun glinted across a few ripples in the center. Tree reflections wavered.

Ryanna was a magician of nature, a wizard of pines and water. I felt more and more amazed in her presence. She was making me forget TallaTec and all my troubles. Of course, it was as much her as it was the river, the mighty span of water humming downstream.

"Now, look out at the middle. Where the water gets deep," she said.

There was another whirlpool, like the one at the Confluence near St. Marks. This one, though, was considerably more visible.

"Watch," she said. There was a pile of pine and hardwood branches, and she kept grabbing one at a time, inspecting each, as if searching for the perfect throwing stick.

"Is this another case of order and the natural world, etcetera, etcetera?" I asked.

"It's like they say: Natural world wants to pull against itself in disorder in order to be reordered to the newer form."

She found the branch she wanted and tossed it a dozen yards upriver from the whirlpool. It hit the water with a terrific splash.

The forest behind us quieted. The chatter and chirping of squirrels and birds faded.

The branch drifted to the turning pool, then glided right through.

"That's strange," said Ryanna.

She grabbed another stick and swung it whirl-ward. The stick inched its way to the river's quicksand circle, but again, nothing happened; the tree branch kept heading downstream.

"Don't understand," said Ryanna. "I've never seen this before." She was puzzled.

A third thrown stick offered the same result. Ryanna turned and stared at the pile of tree branches.

Something caught my eye on the other bank. It was the marine biologist. How the hell had he gotten across? A kayak? Canoe? His hat was askew. He was dipping a black box into the water. I recognized the box. It was one from the House that Tec Built.

Before I could point him out to Ryanna, he slipped back into the overgrowth, the black box spilling a torrent on his shoes.

"Something somewhere must be completely out of sync," said Ryanna. She stared into my eyes, but she wasn't seeing me; she was completely lost in thought. She looked worried.

On the other side of the river two silent vultures circled.

Monday, November 6, 2000

Associated Press: Reports have surfaced that the submarine U.S.S. Stonewall Jackson's chief navigator, Lieutenant Taylor Morgan Velázquez, a captive on the Russian's Piranha mini-sub, has been tortured by the Soviets. This action has made more contentious the boarding of the U.S. vessel by the Russians during the two-month standoff in the Arctic. According to accounts, Velázquez's right eye was completely removed during interrogation. She was escorted from the Soviet sub to the U.S.S. Stonewall Jackson's medical facilities to receive emergency surgery to stem the bleeding from the empty socket. Moscow claims it was an accident, but Velázquez, despite the pain and shock, has indicated that the Russians had switched to enhanced questioning techniques to gain intelligence.

Taylor, oh, Taylor. We have let you down. Me, we, the entire U.S.

of A.

The only reason they'd gouge out your eye is if they saw *the glow*. Oh, you should have simply come clean and admitted what it was, just a defect, a flaw created by stupidity in 1980. Why didn't you confess? I would have.

I'd never want to lose an eye! (or any part of me for that matter)

And so there it is. This wrenches my gut, rattles my core. This bends me to decision. I'm tired of hiding. I will now confess, unlike our brave Lt. Velázquez; I'm not as intrepid. I must unburden. I must tell everyone here in T-town *I too am a Rad Sick*, just like our tortured hero Taylor Morgan Velázquez. I don't want to lose an eye, even a metaphorical one.

And I want to swear my allegiance to my fellow Rad Sick, a pledge of solidarity. Why hasn't the news mentioned she's a victim of *Incident '80*? We Rad Sicks must declare ourselves and speak with one voice!

Wednesday, November 8, 2000

Last night, November 7th, I'd planned as confession night at Wings. I was planning to spill my guts about Rad Sickness, connect all the possible dots to TallaTec, confess details about Tech Hall's Halloween experiment and Veteran's Day's gambit, announce all aspects of my conspiracy theory, and decry the torture of Taylor Velázquez.

She was my main motivation to confess. The news of her mutilation had rattled me even more than all the other crazy shit that had been shocking-my-world since I'd arrived in T-town.

I could no longer stay mum. No longer remain contained. On the night of the 7th, I would be truth teller.

I arrived late. Wings and beer had been ordered. Voices were buoyant. Celebration danced atop the table.

Had they not heard the news of the navigator of the U.S.S. Stonewall Jackson butchered during a pointless and failed interrogation? Why weren't they somberly discussing it? Could the population's Cold War ennui hit such a level that even this atrocity could be ignored? What was wrong with people? What was wrong with this country?

"Van Gear just published a story!" shouted Rand. He seemed much woozier than usual—was he a Doc Primus *woozle?* Perhaps he'd started boozing early.

"In *the pacific?*" I asked.

"No," said Van Gear.

"Where?"

"In *Bikers Bizarre*," said Willington and raised his glass to the German-Jesus.

"It's an OK enough place," said Van Gear, sounding oddly deflated.

"Hey! They actually pay you something," cried Jack, sounding even woozier than Rand. "Unlike all those bloody literary journals. God . . . fuck 'em!"

"Jack got two rejections in the mail today. Both from hotshot journals," said Willington.

"Yeah, fuck 'em!" said Jack.

"What about you?" asked Rand. "You sending anything out?" This question sent me reeling. Made my mind swerve off course. Sending my own work out terrified me. *What? Face more rejection!?!?*

That's all it took: the question triggered my warped Rad Sick numbskull paranoia. I was thrown off my game. Did they know my *tell-all* disposition? Did they suspect I was an on-the-verge ranter of atrocities suffered not only by Taylor Morgan Velázquez but by me?

"And how's your Ex?" blurted Ash.

Oh God. More fuel for the fire. This celebration, these questions, were all throwing off the careful wording I'd practiced in the car. It would be so much easier if they just asked about Rad Sickness. Didn't they suspect? Did they know I'd been fried? Were they taking it for granted? Were they anticipating my confession and, thus, heading me off, keeping me from spilling, saving me from shame?

Someone simply could imply the Rad, and then I could just straightforwardly confess: *yes!* Weren't they suspicious because of my weirdness? Well, maybe not. All writers are weird, if not radically sick.

Ha, ha.

At present, these questions and this conversation were making me lose my thread on TallaTec too. How would I be able to have my monologue connect all the pieces. Why didn't they ever ask me how I liked TallaTec? Didn't they note how the black boxes left me plastered?

Oh, blessed rage for order to escape this pointless, distracting, banal palaver from my best friends in T-town! Were they innocent? Or complicit in raking me into TallaTec?

Before I could answer Ash about Ex, Rand pulled his legs from beneath the table and oddly crouched on his seat on the booth, topped his mug with beer, and then stood tall. (Later, I did found out he and Jack had arrived an hour earlier and gained a head start on earning their tippler merit badges.)

"A toast to Van Gear and *Bikers Bizarre!*" shouted Rand. The few other patrons in the joint glanced at Rand and turned away.

"We need more than beer to truly toast our man Van Gear," piped Ash.

"What then?" I asked. Oh shit, were they going to drop the latest, greatest TallaTec on me?

If so, I was going to walk out, hop into my Toyota, and scram. Fuck TallaTec. And fuck these guys.

Ash squeezed out of the booth and passed through the doorway between rooms. I stood up too. Where Ash went, I refused to travel. But instead of bursting out the nearby exit (to pull his stash from his glove box), he turned in the direction of the bar and disappeared from view.

I sat down. So did Rand. No one said anything about Ash. The Bosnian started in again on lit journals and idiot editors.

"What did you send them?" asked Van Gear.

"My latest and greatest stuff."

"Not the story about the two bank robbers on roller blades," said Willington.

"Yep. You guys didn't get it."

Rand sighed.

"That story is shit," said Van Gear.

"No, it's not!"

What fiction were they talking about? Had it shown up in a class on campus? We'd occasionally brought in ours (well, theirs, not mine) work to share and repair, but I didn't remember the roller blades.

Ash reappeared with a grin and banged two bottles of Jack on the table.

"I think this is just the thing," Ash said. Our server Celine, her long dirty-blonde hair, as always, braided intricately and hanging past her knees, stood behind him with a tray of shot glasses.

Ash was not much of a liquor drinker, but his sense of occasion must have broken him from his norms. He grabbed a shot glass from Celine's tray, popped it on the table, and poured it to the brim with Jack Daniels. He slid it to Rand. The next skated to Willington. Around the table he went. With great ceremony, he handed the last glass carefully to Van Gear.

Celine smiled and bounded away. Rand raised his glass. Ash followed. We all glanced at each other (except Van Gear who stared at the ceiling).

"To Van Gear and *Bikers Bizarre!*" we shouted in unison.

And thus began The Night that Jack Built.

*   *   *

I lost track of the toasts. We were the only patrons left. Celine didn't mind that we hung-tight. She swept the floor and refilled the ketchups.

I lost track of the hours. How late was it?

One bottle of Jack was empty, and the other sat half full.

I was wasted.

I was glad it was liquor and not TallaTec. But I was shit-faced. Truly hammered (the hammering in my head at this moment is magnified by each clack and click on the keyboard).

Van Gear riffed on Brandelsonna's film about the samurai and the three-legged child in the city with the golden, bell-shaped umbrellas. We all mumbled how we loved it, though I doubt any of us had seen it.

Willington soared on notes about writers whose first names (or last) started with C.

Rand shouted that his newborn's name should start with A.

Ash hummed the guitar solo to "Stairway to Heaven."

Jack banged on about tambourines in Serbia.

I remember going on a riff about drinking a shot of Jack Daniels. The purity of it. The table attentively listened! I said, *Start with the initial sniff. The odor of forest wood and bitter sugars. The anticipation of the body as the gut boils and the mouth salivates. Bumps on the tongue grow into mountains of anticipation. The lips hunger for burning. The mouth cracks like a crater but wants to swallow the magma instead of spew it. The liquid in the mouth, heavy like pudding, light like juice, but hot and strong. Join the burn! Join the burn! And the throat opens for Jack, a cave of winds waiting for God's angry flood. Fiery flood. The brown liquor heats the throat, warms the stomach, cleanses the body and mind. The taste lingers in the mouth like a bitter lime. The heat from the body goes straight to the brain. Soon, though sight is blurred, clarity lines the consciousness from synapse to synapse, cell to cell. And the cell is escaped—freedom, yes, to pour the next Jack in the glass!*

Yes! Yes! The talk would only continue! We had slurred conversations about prelim exams, GRE scores (the Wings were shocked that my Quantitative beat my Verbal), bad poems written, great poets loved, acid trips, bad sex, great sex . . . the night splintered into dialogue tributaries.

Ash explained how shot number infinity + infinity = infinity; how theorists were now talking subsets of infinity within infinity and how these subsets could be moved between universes on a formulaic level; how infinity is the only number summed with itself that equals itself, except zero (Ash's GRE score was probably near infinity!).

Contemplation! Infinity created a lull.

Van Gear turned to Jack who'd been taking small sips from his latest shot.

"So what's with your freak-outs at the lake?"

The table, which had been ready to return to boisterous, fell straight to hush.

"What?" mumbled Jack.

"Did you and Vicky have a son?"

"My son?" stuttered Jack.

"At the lake. When you're panicking, flashbacking," said Van Gear. He was giving Jack his most intense stare. "You always mention a son. Like you're looking for him. In the water."

"My son," said Jack.

"Your son."

I felt some weird mojo spread its dark wings over the table, acting as an odd bell-shaped umbrella, a soundproof booth, a time machine. I had thought they'd already known what he didn't want to talk about, but it seemed they were clueless too.

"I'm Bosnian!" declared Jack.

We knew that, despite the goofy wavering of his accent.

"I'm Bosnian! I didn't abandon my country. We had heart! Morals! Abandoned nothing!"

"Nobody said you abandoned anything," said Rand. He looked particularly distressed.

"I fought for my country. Did my service. And now it's done."

We'd all had inklings he was an ex-military man, but we also thought it might be one of his many personas. Perhaps he'd been a Bosnian sharpshooter. Those marksmen had been well-known during Yugoslavia's break from the Communist Curtain, during its split into several regionally-ethnic nations that eschewed Russia's dictates. However, the deconstruction of Yugoslavia had been bloody and terrible. Stupid media critics would mumble on and on about how *despite the Berlin Wall's contin-ued strength, and the steadfastness of most of Europe's Iron Curtain, the break-up of the former Yugoslav Republic . . .* marked a *strange period.* Instead, the media should have focused on the war's atrocities. The world ignored them from 1992-1995.

"And for country . . ." Jack stared at some invisible demon. "And for country, I gave everything."

"Of course," said Van Gear.

"No! No! No! I.... Gave.... Everything!"

"We get it."

"No! No! I . . . ." Jack reached his hand into the miasma steam-ing from his drink. The rising molecules reinvented the time-space con-tinuum; Ryanna's voice splashed my memory, *Natural world wants to pull against itself in disorder in order to be reordered to the newer form.* What new-er form had Jack made for himself? What had been in the disorder of his former life; what forces had taken him under? His faced tightened. "I . . . lost! Lost! Lost everything!"

We sat silent.

"What happened?" Van Gear whispered. There was an edge of compassion in his voice that he rarely let slip at Wings.

"I was an officer!" said Jack. He took another sip from his shot glass. He kept his eyes glued to the invisible whorl at table's center.

We all leaned forward a notch.

"They knew I was an officer!"

"In the Bosnian military," said Van Gear gently.

"Bosnian special forces. Black Swans. A Zastavnik, a Master Ser-geant. A platoon leader. Assigned to keep our Muslim neighbors safe. Damn Serbs wanted to kill them all," Jack slurred.

Jack held his shot glass in front of his eyes and stared deeply into the brown, sugary cloud.

"They knew," he whispered.

"Who?" asked Willington.

"Serbian bastards."

"Serbian Separatists?" two voices asked.

"So called Patriots," replied Jack. "Wanted to keep the old ways, by . . . cleansing." He coughed. "I'd been on patrol. On the border. Between the two."

"The two?" asked Willington.

"The new Bosnia, the new Serbia. We were keeping the bastards at bay."

Jack suddenly bolted down the rest of his drink, and it was as if the heat of the bourbon kicked him back to consciousness, forced him to a coherency he hadn't shown in the last hour. He sat up, ramrod straight.

"I was the commanding officer. Recently promoted. We patrolled just beyond the border. Inside the new Serbia." He paused. Stared at his empty glass. "I actually worked hard to avoid enemy operatives. Looked for the signs, and headed the opposite way. My unit was green. They didn't know better. And if they did, well, they were so damn scared they were glad I wasn't doing my job."

"No, that was your job," said Van Gear. "To keep them alive."

Jack paused.

"The lot of us, Special Bosnian division, they embedded us in a local platoon. One unit. But it was kept secret. I don't know why. Politics." Jack closed his eyes for a full ten seconds and then opened them. "But to protect our Muslim neighbors, they wanted the Special division to move closer to the Islamic villages. I decided to move my family. Thought it would be better to keep us close. So I could see the kids. We felt safe about it . . . so stupid!—I moved my family *closer* to the new Serbia."

"Vicky was with you?" Willington asked.

"This was before Vicky," said Jack.

"Didn't know you were married before," said Van Gear.

"Now you do," said Jack. He poured himself another shot. No one said anything. "All these countries . . . not really countries, despite old allegiance to Russia, the Soviet Union. They're all tribal. Borders are irrelevant, tentative at best, flexible, always changing. Especially the early years of the Yugoslav break-up."

Jack paused, stared at a notch on his thumbnail.

"People talked. Not all Bosnians loved Muslims. It was easy for word to travel. Too easy."

Jack glugged half his glass and set it gently on the table. "They knew where all the officers lived. They bloody knew where we lived! Knew where I lived! Me!"

Jack sipped his Jack, held the glass an inch from his nose and stared. A moment later, he snatched a bottle and poured us each a fresh shot.

I think we were all holding our breaths. The noise of Celine's sweeping melted away.

"I was home after week-long patrol. This village we lived, a place on the outskirts, a more rural spot. We had a few acres. A large pond behind the house. I'd taken a truck back to headquarters that night and decided to walk home. I'd cut through the vacant fields and woods, come through the backyard to surprise the little ones."

Jack picked up his glass and downed it. He nodded to us. We all did in kind.

"It was horror. I knew soon as I saw it." Jack paused.

"What?" asked Ash.

"An ambush."

He poured himself another glass.

"There was four of them. They had Kalashnikovs. Each creeping toward a wall of the house. Bent low. I froze. What could I do? I was 100 feet away. I'd left my CZ-99 in its holster at the base. Rarely took it home. Had an old Zastava M70 I kept in the attic, but. . . ." Jack stuck his thumb in his drink, then finger-painted the center of the table with bourbon, drawing disappearing circles in the invisible whirlpool that continued to turn.

Jack dropped his head. Closed his eyes.

"And there he was. My boy. Creeping out from overgrowth at the pond's edge. The pond water somehow swallowed up the light. "He pulled at my belt, and he was about to ask me something, so I slapped my hand over his mouth. Hard. I shook my head. Even in the darkness, I could sense he was holding back tears."

Jack opened his eyes and glanced around the table, then went back to scratching his nail into wood, attempting tabletop graffiti.

"Then there was light. Fire. I don't know what they used, but all sides of the house were lit. The roof too. Sheets of flame. And I heard screams. I froze. I heard my daughter's high pitch terror. My wife's shouts, full of anger. She must have seen them. She was cursing them."

Rand's face creased in grief; he released a half-swallowed gasp.

I was freaking. It was like a TallaTec trip but real. As if TallaTec had grown wings and flown into the hole that brought nightmares to life. As if the past instead of the future had transmogrified into the present. But this had nothing to do with TallaTec. This was Jack's dark past, made alive through Jack's words.

"I froze. My hand still on my son's mouth. I couldn't move. I could do nothing. But I should have done something, yes? No, they'd have mowed us down with their machine guns. And my son. I had to save my son. We were crouched, balled-up with fear."

His thumb stirred the drink. He stopped but left his nail on the rim.

"My hand had slipped from my boy's face, and he let out a yell. The Serb closest to us thought he'd heard something and turned to point his Kalashnikov in our direction. The house was all in flames. One of the men was laughing. The other two kept throwing something on the walls that made the fire leap higher. The harsh smoke bit at my nose and throat, but I wouldn't let myself cough.

"The soldier who'd heard us stepped in our direction. I put my hand tightly over my boy's lips and I backed him into the big pond, one silent footstep at a time. My heel hit the water, and I crouched down lower, and we stopped moving. The soldier hesitated. But he continued to peer in our direction. I didn't think he could see us, but I'm sure he could sense us.

"I held my boy tight, my palm still across his little mouth, and we backed into the water quietly, slowing every fiber of muscle so to be seamless, noiseless. We crept backwards into deeper water. It was damn cold. It smelled of algae. I was treading in place and holding my boy against my chest, keeping his head above water. The back of his head scraped my chin. I could smell his mother's shampoo in his hair.

"I stopped staring at the fire ball that had been our house, despite the burning's noise. All I could do was watch the man with the gun. His three companions ignored him. One had started doing a dance near the western corner of the house. But our Serb kept staring into the pond. I was hoping to swim backwards, tread water to the far edge, then maybe me and my boy had a chance.

"But then my boy started murmuring. Trying to say something. Blurred words. And the soldier seemed to hear because he marched to the pond's edge, holding his gun in front of him. My boy wouldn't stop his mumble. He wouldn't stop. What could I do? What could I do? I used all my strength and wrapped my hand around his face like a tentacle. I heard the soldier's gun click. I took my boy under. Deep. We sunk deep. Deep into the black.

"And what would happen when we ran out of air? What? He wouldn't know how to take a desperate but silent microsecond gasp of air at the surface, would he? I opened my mouth at the surface to breathe, just for a heartbeat, my mouth like a whale's blowhole. I sucked as much air as I could; I would breathe some of it into my boy's mouth to give him what he needed.

"I'd thought he'd been gripping me tightly. We were back down deep; I'd plunged us to the bottom. I let go of his face and tried to feel for his shoulders in the darkness so that I could turn him to face me, and my hands clutched nothing.

"I reached again, shocked. Could he have drifted off that quickly?

I scratched around desperately. Nothing.

"*He must be sinking*, I thought, so I swam frog-style straight down to the muck. With my ribs brushing the muddy bottom, I moved in circles. I stabbed arms and legs in all directions, hoping to bump him.

"What had happened? Where had he gone? I was so damn cold, shivering while swimming, but I couldn't stop, could I?

"I must have been underwater for minutes; it was as though I'd forgotten that my body needed air.

"I had to find my boy!

"I cut through the water, stroked deep, desperate stabs; I spread my fingers as wide as they'd go, hoping a fingernail would graze his hair, and then I'd think with great relief—*Thank God!*—But it wasn't happening. I wasn't finding him. He'd disappeared."

Jack had a single fist on the table. He brought his head down to his hand and rested there for a moment. Then he sprang up, his eyes glassy.

"I was the one rescuer, unable to make a simple rescue—of my own child! What was wrong with me? How could I have failed so miserably?"

Jack slammed his fist. Our shot glasses rattled against the tabletop.

"I wanted to be a shark! A good shark. Smell blood of my son to find him. But I couldn't, didn't find him. The pond wasn't that big, but on that night it was a fucking ocean. And I was not a shark.

"Why couldn't God for that one night have made my boy spring gills! He could have been breathing silently at the bottom, waiting for me." Jack closed his eyes, squeezed them shut, then opened them wide. He coughed, stared at the edge of the table.

We sat silently, all too transfixed and devastated to utter a word; we barely breathed.

I pictured Jack's pond. The pond had been the Earth's one evil mouth that had opened deep below him and his son, a sudden sinkhole, a spring that led to the freezing waters of the underworld; it was as if that invisible gaping mouth had swallowed him into the Devil's gullet. I wanted to imagine myself there, kicking out the Devil's teeth as I swam, as if the evil son-of-a-bitch had shown himself whole and in the flesh. But that night, it was only too clear, the only devils were the bastards dancing around the house, shooting Kalashnikovs into the air. If I'd been there, I'd wished for a flame thrower and melted each of them to cinders.

Jack looked up. He was crying but forcing the tears to stop.

"I had to surface to see if he was there. My lungs were screaming for air.

"The one soldier had returned to the flames. He was laughing with his comrades.

"I treaded water in circle after circle after circle, thinking my son would rise to the surface, and I would grab him before he made too much noise. Mud and algae racked my mouth, slid in and out of my nostrils. I thought I saw something in the water plants and darted over but found nothing, so I swam along the edges of the pool, seeing if maybe he'd drifted near shore.

"But I couldn't find my boy. He wasn't there. He wasn't there!

"He was gone."

That was The Night that Jack Built.

Thursday, November 9, 2000

Ex is taking a nap. Supper time nap. I should be too. As I read over my notes on The Night that Jack Built, I wonder how I could have written so half-way coherently. We were all so drunk. Van Gear, as drunk as any of us, refused to let anyone drive home, so we all had to pile in his antique Ford, and he took us from house to house. Willington insisted that he had to buy a gallon of milk or his wife would be pissed, but I think we were more pissed at him than he realized as we sat outside the Suwannee Swifty while he stumbled through the aisles in search of dairy. We were all wasted and exhausted and nauseous. At Rand's, the guy climbed out, puked, then insisted we all walk him to the door so that pregnant

JAM wouldn't kill him, and then he threw up again, projectile vomiting from the porch steps. Ash got out of the truck several blocks from home, mumbling he needed to walk to clear his head and then proceeded to light the fattest TallaTec spliff we'd ever seen him roll. When we dropped Jack at his bungalow, Vicky was waiting at the doorway with a sad look on her face, as if she knew this was the night that Jack had let it spill.

Van Gear drove me to Alum Village. We were silent.

As he pulled in the parking lot, I said, "How long has he been keeping that in, I wonder?"

Van Gear shook his head. He leaked tears, but I don't think he realized I could see him in the dark.

I'm musing on this irony: *on the night I'd fully planned to reveal my Rad Sick self, Jack jumps ahead and confesses first.* My little troubles pale in comparison; I have no real need to unburden myself. Compared to Jack's trauma's—*who cares* what I've been through! And Taylor's troubles are not my own. Not really. Despite my desire to shout my solidarity. She's *true* news (though hidden beside the papers' chess and bridge columns), and I'm *not* news.

My current news: Ex is snoring. I should be sleeping beside her. I've felt ill all day and missed my poetry lit class and a prose workshop. Dismal. Alcohol poisoning. The worst. Except, of course, for radiation poisoning.

With evening here, I am feeling a little better. Ex, just before she fell asleep, was so sweet, fixing me herbal tea and feeding me Melba toast—when she's generous, I feel crushed we broke up.

*   *   *

I realized there'd been a long hum echoing inside my skull since noon. It wasn't the noise of the hangover; instead, it was the sound of re-alization, of the clear notes from an invisible voice that had launched itself to light at Wings. Of course, Jack had sprung a demon that required an attack by words, a beating by prose, transformed into a first draft: readers needed to hear this story, to see the horrible demons in all their glory, to feel every inch of this tragedy.

I called Jack a few moments ago, and Vicky put him on the phone, and I insisted the night's confessions become the new and steady heartbeat of everything he wrote. All else should be buried, forgotten. He argued with me, but I was insistent. I knew my Rad Sick ear was never wrong. I told him to mail the first piece pulled from the material to the *Mönchengladbach Review* in New York.

*   *   *

Midnight. My Ex finally woke. I should promptly fall asleep. But I finally feel normal, the alcohol completely drained from my veins. Times of drunk-sick make you swear off booze for the rest of your life. Temporarily.

I munch crackers and sip water from a plastic cup, and my stomach feels steady like municipal bonds in a prerecession portfolio.

Here's what's popped into my head: *connections*; I'm looking for glue between TallaTec and Recession, quartermaster Velázquez and her torturer, *an eye for an eye*, novels and readings, love and friendship, basketball and writing. And for what keeps my mind super-busy: the link between Rad Sicks and Tech Hall.

Between TallaTec and me.

Friday, November 10, 2000 (Veteran's Day, observed)

Yesterday, Ex was annoyed with Ash because they'd planned to go to tea, and he failed to show. He was on the Ex shit-list. But this morning he called full of apologies and invited us to breakfast at the groovy Nut-Cheer's Way. I declined because I needed to work on "Surf Boy" (and of course, hatch plans with Elly), but Ex was only too pleased to eat granola with the king of TallaTec. He said nothing about Jack's confession, maybe because he was wrestling with a paper on Derrida he had to deliver soon at the Southeast Philosophy Annual.

Anyway, their great journey to Nut-Cheer was perfectly timed, because I'd promised Elly we were headed to the underground pool beside Tech Hall to get to the bottom of today's experiment that Blanco had pushed.

On my way, I saw a few ROTC undergrads shuffle past campus on their way to the day's downtown parade festivities. Would these young soldiers disappear into the Cold War? The parade itself might have one ICMB-shaped float, but all other Cold War references would remain muted, despite the Arctic standoff. The culture is tired of the Cold War, bored with it, wants it off everyone's radar to help quiet the angst.

Elly and I met at 9 a.m. outside the closed library. A homeless guy milled around. Since the Recession began, the homeless now flocked to public places, including State U's library.

We sat on a bench in the small courtyard across from the library's doors. The campus was empty. Elly looked as distressed as I felt. We were both hyper-drive Rad Sick anxious.

"What's your vision for this?" Elly asked. Her brownish hair was in a bun, and she wore jeans and a sweatshirt that said RAVENSVIEW. Her glasses were slightly askew. The shirt had a blackbird in profile with an X for an eye and a lit cigarette in its beak. I wore a t-shirt with a big X on the front; the X represented nothing.

"We're going to sneak into the underground pool. See what's up before the experiment starts."

"Yeah, but how? I know nothing about the building. Do you?"

Extraordinarily enough, I actually had a plan.

"I was looking at maps in the registration catalogue, and the Hillevi Gym layout shows an old locker room in the basement. I heard it's unused because of remodeling. We could start there."

"Doesn't anyone use the pool?"

"I don't think so. Unless this next experiment happens underwater." I coughed and watched the homeless guy try to enter the library, but it was locked tight. "Look, we can spy on them as they set things up, see how they get all those fishbowls in there." I realized I'd forgotten to feed the fish this morning; usually Ex would've remembered, but she was so energized to meet Ash she'd forgotten too.

Elly seemed doubtful about spying. She looked at me askance.

It was at this point we fell into typical Rad Sick stasis. We didn't move and said nothing for five minutes.

"I've always wanted to believe I wasn't a Rad Sick, you know?" Elly said, breaking the silence. "I rarely had the signs. I wanted to blame those rare eye-aches on allergies." She pulled the bun out of her brown hair and swept it back over her shoulders. The henna highlights had a plum color in the autumn sunshine. She removed her glasses and wiped her eyes. Her hazel *ojos* registered no glow.

"I couldn't do that," I said. "It was always too obvious. Until I got these contact lenses."

Elly was lost in thought.

"I'd been doing so well until the spring term." Elly paused, took a breath. "I had an internship at a local school. Loved teaching the kids music, ukulele and recorder playing. I tutored math, science. Basic music theory."

"Music education was your major?"

"Yeah." She hesitated. Stared at the library's door. "This boy, Jamal, maybe six years old, I tutored him in science. On deep ocean fishes. We'd been sitting at a table, looking at a book about oceans. We found a page with deep sea fishes, all terrifying giant mouths and ferocious teeth. As we read a page out loud, we learned the monstrous beasts were actually quite small. Jamal pointed at one critter with an orange glowing tear-shape that hung above the fish's mouth. Of course, this was a lure for other fish that'd end up a meal for these cruel-mouthed munchkins. And that's when this darling little boy became a cruel-mouthed munchkin himself. He looked up, studied me and said, *You got a fish glow in your eyes.* How on earth could he have seen it? I froze for a few seconds, then sat upright. *You got allergies? My sister's got 'em,* he said. This made me feel a little better, and I was glad that he assumed I wasn't a deep sea fish. But, I was thrown off. I could not stop thinking about it, even on campus. I started wondering, when random people glanced over their shoulders at me in class, if they knew I was Rad Sick. I got more and more depressed. I barely finished my internship; I avoided Jamal the last three visits." Elly paused and looked up at the sky. "So I decided to take a break from school."

I didn't know what to say.

Elly sighed.

"So what's this about *starting in the old basement?*" she asked.

"The lockers?"

"Do you know how to get to these lockers?"

"Sure. Follow me."

I am good with maps, and I'd been combing over this particular map for long stretches while Ex took her naps. I had the blueprints memorized.

I headed west, and Elly followed.

Beside Hillevi Gym's main stairs, a skinny sidewalk hugged the stone banister and led to a wall with a disguised doorway, half the normal width. The sidewalk angled down.

"Shit, I'd never noticed this before. It's almost like they don't want you to see it," said Elly.

"Exactly," I said. "It's a maintenance entrance, for certain people— like Rad Sicks—who should remain unnoticed."

Elly looked at me as if I'd lost my mind.

"O.K. O.K. Just thinking about this TallaTec bullshit is making me ultra-paranoid. Sorry." I said.

"TallaTec?"

"From the Tech Hall experiment. The hallucinogen."

"Where'd you hear that name?"

"You haven't?"

She shook her head.

"That's what some friends of mine call it."

Elly sighed. She tried the door.

"It's locked," she said, her voice thick with annoyance.

"Weird." Of course, I hadn't tested the door before. Why *should* it open?

I grabbed the handle and started shaking it like a lunatic.

"You're going to make a scene," she said.

I continued to rattle the door as if I were a desperate soul trying to escape hell.

"Nah," I said. "Look around. The campus is dead. It's Veteran's Day."

"Veteran's Day is actually tomorrow, you know."

"But I'm pretty sure . . . fairly sure, Blanco said Friday." I wasn't sure at all.

Elly sighed again.

I grabbed the handle with both hands and pulled. I gave the bottom of the door two solid kicks.

Magic!

The door clanged from the inside. I stopped pulling but kept my grip. Another clank echoed from within, and the vibration went through my hands and tickled my carpal tunnels.

The thin door opened. I let go.

A maintenance woman stuck her head out. She looked 60-ish, with stern but not unsympathetic night-colored eyes. Her dark, round face projected friendliness though her mouth was a frown.

"What you want?" she asked. Her neatly pressed, blue uniform had the university's sparkling insignia and looked brand new except for a fresh mascara stain on her shoulder just below her right ear.

"Ah, ah," I stuttered. "We wanted to use the pool. Change in the locker room."

She stared at us quizzically. She paused and looked around behind us. Then she nodded and almost smiled.

"Well, no one ever uses that pool hardly," she said. "About time someone took advantage of it. I've thought of it myself. Yes, you-all come on in then."

She opened the door wider, and Elly and I slipped through.

"Do you two know how to get to the locker?"

"Yes, Ma'am," we chimed. She nodded and leaned a push broom against the wall.

As we walked past her and her cleaning supplies cart—a six-wheeled contraption with a grey cloth exterior that covered the top—I glanced down and could have sworn I saw two partially visible fish bowls.

I grabbed Elly's shoulder and full-stopped, turning to get a second glance, but the woman in uniform gave me a dirty look that made my heart sink into my bladder, and I knew we needed to plow forward. Hell, we were lucky she let us in.

We made our way down a series of narrow stairwells that might have been the university's original stairwells from the 1800s, back when people were smaller, before boys and girls started regularly feasting on steroid-stoked chicken and growing as tall as hybrid corn stalks.

We reached a shower curtain. And paused.

"What now?" asked Elly.

"Onward," I whispered moving the curtain aside.

We entered a cavernous locker room shower. A dozen nozzles protruded from the walls. The place appeared unused. Nevertheless, the stench of bleach netted the air; the woman with the mascara stain must have recently mopped.

A brightly lit opening beckoned from the far wall. We treaded forward.

Voices murmured from somewhere beyond the opening.

Elly and I froze.

Two voices. A conversation.

Elly and I stood on either side of the doorway and peaked into the dim abyss.

A traditional locker room. Garnet-colored lockers without locks. Gold-painted benches. Flickering fluorescent lights.

Two men sat side by side, talking, getting dressed. Had they been swimming? Showering? The shower area looked completely dry except for a thin glaze of bleach on a few tiles.

One guy pulled on a sock—it was the marine biologist Ryanna and I spotted, the man who dipped the black box in the Apalachicola River. He still wore his goofy fishing hat.

Elly waved me over to her side of the doorway. Their backs faced us, so I darted across and leaned my ear to Elly's mouth.

"I served those guys at Ravensview the other night. They were part of that marine biologists group," Elly whispered.

We spied.

"Think they'll get rid of that quarterback?" said Dr. Fish Hat.

"He's slow out of the gates, that's for sure," said Professor Other Guy.

"He's dumb."

"No argument there. Reminds me of the kid who was the control last week."

"Which one was that? I didn't know you'd assigned a control?"

"One of the women. I think she had brown hair. Dorky glasses. Cute girl. I think she works that hippie bar."

"No, not that one. Tell me you didn't use the subject I'm thinking of."

"I'm drawing a blank on her name. I know I've seen her somewhere recently. Maybe she's a bartender?"

"No, no. That's who I thought you were talking about. You can't use her as the control. That's a complete mistake."

"Why not?"

"She's from Dade."

"She is?" asked Professor Other Guy. "Well, so what?"

"You didn't look at her eyes?"

"Her eyes? What are you talking about?"

"You mean you haven't been checking all their eyes?"

"Yes, the hidden dark-lights show the contact lenses."

"No, you don't get it. She wouldn't be wearing lenses. She doesn't need to. Her glow's dim. You have to look carefully . . . as you should be doing for all subjects. She was born at the blast's rim. The circumference. She's only halfway, but she's still there." He shook his head. "Damn, you're as dumb as she is."

Elly slumped down and folded into herself. Her eyes were wet. I wasn't sure what to say.

"They're talking about me," she whispered. Tears fell. Their voices in the locker room were now an undistinguishable mumble.

I wanted to cry too. Why were they fucking with us? And if they were so smart, why couldn't they see that Elly was far from dumb! We both frowned. It was that friggin' condescension that had been hammering us Rad Sicks all our lives. Why did they think the blast had fried us stupid? And if we were such idiots, why were they trying so hard to get something out of us with these screwy Tech Hall TallaTec experiments?

I wondered how many times Elly'd been punched with condescension. Her Rad Sickness was basically invisible, only half-there. I suppose the first mean-spirited sucker punch is always the worst, the one that catches you the most off-guard. Had this been it?

We were sitting beneath a showerhead that had been bent to face the ceiling. My arm wrapped around her shoulders, and she leaned her head in the crux beneath my shoulder. We stared at the floor drain. Both of us got sad-eyed.

She trembled. My gut instinct was to get Elly out of here. She became enormously precious at this moment; she shrank in size and metamorphosed into an eight-year-old. I could see the child in her. Maybe her pupil-glow had been more obvious as a kid, but maybe as a teen she'd gotten lucky and "grown out of it" because she'd only been partially irradiated. I'd heard rumors but never stumbled across an actual case of Rad Sick eyes spiraling to normal.

The men's voices became louder, as if they'd stood and were now facing our direction.

"I'm really thinking Subject A is our best bet."

"You sure? Halloween didn't go so well. I think we've made him super skittish."

"I think we need to try Plan X."

"Oh, come on. That is the most ridiculous thing I've heard."

"No, no, you've got to play to these kids' paranoid imaginations. If it's elaborate and weird enough, they'll bite. They won't run away."

"You're nuts."

"Well, let's set up today's experiment first and see how it goes."

"Right. But Plan X is a nonstarter. Honestly, it's just silly."

"We'll see. Believe it or not, ever since our AxeAll hit the market, I've reminded administration they owe me a favor or two. I've got a few strings I can pull."

"Sure. Pull it. Let it topple on top of you."

The voices in the locker room drifted away.

"Let's go," I said, feeling very strongly that "Subject A" was *me*. "We've heard enough."

Elly stood and rubbed the tears from her face.

"No, we gotta find out what they're doing. We've gotta see what they're setting up at the swimming pool," she said.

"You sure?"

She nodded.

We tip-toed into the locker area and looked for the best exit. The room's lights were dim and made the benches glow a dirty gold.

Many doors. We tried them all, slowly opening each, searching for the smell of chlorine.

Elly stopped at a green-painted square near the locker room's far corner. She tapped on what we thought had been drywall. I tapped too. Ah ha. Wood, not drywall. We put our hands on the surface and gently shook. The wall moved. The green paint was slightly sticky. The wood panel was a sliding door. Elly and I spread our palms on the surface and slipped it into the wall's empty gut.

The green slid away to reveal the blue water of the underground swimming pool. The rest of the room was barely lit.

Above us, a huge balcony surrounded the perimeter. Underwater, bulbs made the pool shimmer as if sunlight had been stored beneath the deep end's huge filtration grate. The light reflected upwards and created creepy shadows above. The cavernous room's ceiling lamps hung unlit.

A stack of head-sized globes glistened in a balcony's corner.

Elly pointed.

We crept to a spiral staircase that wound around a golden pole. We climbed.

When we reached the pile of fish bowls and Elly's brow creased with suspicion, I became more enamored with her. Despite her doubting nature, Elly was open and beautiful, and I loved how in this moment I did not feel alone in my paranoia. She knew too that the experiment would begin anew. Where? In the deep end? The water looked especially deep from 15 feet above the surface. Would the bowls not only trap the TallaTec gas for the brain but also allow each subject, as if a Tarpon Springs sponge diver, to tread the bottom of the underground pool?

We heard voices below and stepped back from the waist-high wall at the balcony's edge. We ducked into shadow.

Dr. Fish Hat and Professor Other Guy appeared, dragging some multi-armed gizmo towards the deep end. The thing looked as big and heavy as an oak dining table. Initially, I thought it was the latest, new-fangled, automatic pool-sweeper. But when I studied it more carefully, doubt hit.

"I've got this fucking thing working. I've tweaked it," said Dr. Fish Hat.

"Too many bugs in this octopus."

"O.K., smart guy, at least help me set it up?"

They dumped the giant disk into the pool and let half the arms plunge in too. The four remaining arms snaked around the men's legs. The machine sank past the underwater light fixture making a huge black circle appear on the ceiling, at first expanding and then contracting.

"I'm telling you, once I get this fine-tuned, this delivery system will be much more efficient," said Dr. Fish Hat.

"I think your ambitions have got the best of you."

"Help me plug it in and set the hoses."

First they stretched four tentacles out of view. Then Fish Hat re-appeared, gripping a coil of orange cord plugged to the gizmo, and as Other Guy helped him unwind the line, the two disappeared on the hunt for a wall socket.

A moment later, a mass of tooth-sized bubbles fizzled to the surface, and a gentle hum emanated from the disk lurking near the deep end's humungous filtration grate.

Elly grabbed my elbow and squeezed. I gave her a reassuring glance, but she was hawk-eyed on the pool's crab-like invader.

A whirlpool formed on the surface, about a yard wide, directly above the disk.

Laughter echoed as the two returned to view.

The whirl was a perfect circle, a whirlpool made by protractor; its circumference absorbed and broke the light into reds and greens. I heard Ryanna's voice inside my head, *Natural world wants to pull against itself in disorder in order to be reordered to the newer form.* But this had nothing to do with the natural world. This effect was manmade.

"And what?" said Professor Other Guy. "We'll offer it to subjects to see if it can be delivered as a liquid?"

"And why not?"

"Come on. Even if it has some effect, we have no idea the necessary dosages in aqueous form. That could take years. The gas we know. We have the gas figured out."

"Today we'll set aside another test group. We'll tell them it's jello shots. They'll lap it up."

Other Guy sighed. "Well, if it works, it certainly will be much easier to deliver. The gas is . . . a pain in the *ass* in some ways."

Fish Hat chuckled. "And if it works also as a liquid, think of the implications!"

"Yes?"

"We can pump it directly into the water supply!"

"What would be the point of that?"

"To prove my other theory! That there are others beyond the irradiated subset who can break the code, others who can do it more efficiently. And more coherently!"

"You really have let that Eminent Scholar title go to your head."

"Be serious! You know it too! These Rad Sick morons are a complete waste of time!"

I couldn't take it. I snatched a fishbowl from behind me and beamed it below with as much ferocity as I could muster in my Rad Sick heart. The bowl's rim snapped from my fingers like a hard-slung Frisbee. My follow through was spot on.

But where had the fates aligned themselves this morning? Had the whirl declared its mysterious energies? Because the moment the bowl left my hands, the cavern's dim light disappeared. Only half the filaments in the pool shone, giving the whirlpool a ghostly glimmer, like a dancing skeleton with slices of water for bones.

My aim sucked.

The bowl completely missed the two professors and landed with a plop in the deep end.

The glass glowed weakly in the underwhelming light.

The profs must have looked up, but since the balcony was completely dark, a jet-black nothingness, there was zero to see, so their eyes—and ours—returned to the fish bowl bobbing on the pool's surface.

The semi-sphere steamed directly towards the whirlpool, dead on for its dead-center. The bowl sat evenly on the surface, like a top hat on a table. An echo of splash bounced from ceiling to walls. The fishbowl neared the whirring eye.

And then it skated right through, as if there were no whirl at all.

"I'll be damned," said Professor Other Guy.

"I have a theory," said Dr. Fish Hat. "Those heavy metals we've added to keep the reagent from releasing too quickly have some undefined electro-magnetic chemical reaction with specific oxygen and hydrogen atoms in the water. And it does something to the laws of physics...."

"The laws of nature...."

"Yes, at least the laws as we know them."

"The molecules have abstracted their patterns."

"Or left no pattern. At least none recognizable to us."

Elly's fingers locked around my elbow, and I almost yelped in pain. Her beautiful lips popped against my ear, registering panic, terror, a desire to leave immediately.

We found a hallway in the balcony's darkness that led straight to the far side of the building and to an orange, softly glowing sign that read *EXIT.*

Sunday, November 12, 2000

Four days had passed since the Night that Jack Built, and, except for Ash, I hadn't had any face-to-face with the Wingsters. Maybe after a night like that, a bit of hibernation was appropriate. So it felt out of the blue when Van Gear showed up at my apartment with the gang nestled in his truck. Maybe TallaTec had leaked into the drinking supply from Fish Hat's dipping the black box in the Apalachicola River; perhaps he'd polluted the entire Big Bend aquifer, forcing all the laws of physics and reality to flow contrary. I wanted to walk backwards to Van Gear's truck in robotic slow-motion.

I squeezed between Willington and Jack in the cab's backseat. Rand rode shotgun. Ash was sleeping in the pick-up's bed.

"Where we headed?" I asked.

"Apparently, Mr. Van Gear has a big surprise," said Willington.

Van Gear said nothing and started the truck. He steered onto the street, and we angled toward Lake Bradford Road.

"I think we're on a rescue mission," said Rand. "That's the best I could get out of him."

I noticed a socket wrench on the dashboard.

"Help someone swap out a spark plug?" I asked.

Van Gear shook his head.

The truck's ashtray was stuffed with guitar picks instead of quarters. I decided it was a sign.

Meanwhile, we quietly and aimlessly talked. Rand described feeling the baby kick against JAM's tummy. Willington mentioned he might have an interview at Northwestern Central Georgia State, and he felt good about it. That made me think of Ex, who, like Big Sis, needed a job. I rambled about Ex borrowing my car to shop for interview clothes; she'd spotted an ad for an editing position at the State Health Agency. Jack mentioned the latest TallaTec rumor, about scoring the stuff from a circus-staffed mini-submarine spotted in a campus pool during a sorority gig. Willington snickered. I mentioned "Surf Boy," but no one listened.

Van Gear was silent.

I remained silent about the machinations Elly and I had witnessed at the underground swimming pool. They equaled something dangerous: the college scientist as Machiavelli-in-miniature. We didn't know what to do after leaving Hillevi Gym. We'd headed for Ravenview's parking lot and sat on the hood of Elly's car in the dead quiet, midmorning, pre-lunch slump of Veteran's Day's Observed. The conversation circled back to this: *What "code" did they hope to break and why?* For the two brainiacs at the pool, TallaTec seemed a truth-serum, designed to make Rad Sicks spill their guts about abstract bullshit. What Truth did they want? And why? Elly and I debated about spying on the experiment at noon and witnessing what transpired, but we worried about getting caught, and in the end, we both chickened-out. Elly seemed especially stressed and talked of going home to her mom in Dade even though the two didn't get along. My full-

Rad half-Sick gal might sail from T-town, leave me stranded with the details. Her anxiety went molecular and made the autumn air so jagged that when I inhaled, I became just as anxious.

And now I was back in denial-mode, hoping to plunge into course work and writing and Wings and let Tech Hall crap drift off my horizon. Elly and I had had two, brief phone conversations since our "mission," but we'd said little about the pool's weird scene (I'd called during Ex's naps). We were both keeping it close to the chest. That being the case, though surprised, I was pleased to find Van Gear pounding at my door on a Sunday, sending us on some unknown but likely resolvable undertaking.

We pulled into the parking lot behind Ravensview. A very light drizzle started.

"Are we going to do Wings here?" asked Willington good-naturedly.

"Everyone out, and then I'll explain," said Van Gear. He climbed out of the truck, and we followed. Ash rolled himself out of the bed. Jack bumped into me as we stumbled from the cab, and, when no one was looking, handed me a manuscript. I was wearing a trench coat, so I slipped the pages into one of the deep inner pockets.

"Here's what happened yesterday," began Van Gear.

"Starting with back-story?" asked Willington.

"Yeah, that's risky," said Rand. "Especially since we're presently immersed in the immediate timeline."

"Hey, but at least the guy's narrative seems fairly linear for a change," said Jack.

"Are you jerks going to workshop my explanation?" asked Van G.

"We're just fucking with you," said Willington. Everyone laughed, and Van Gear leaked a brief smile but then became serious.

"I dropped by Ravensview yesterday for a quick beer after lunch time, and the entire upstairs bar was shut tight. I know they keep the Makers Mark up there . . ."

"For a *beer*?" asked Jack.

". . . the best whiskey's up there, and I wasn't interested in the well brand downstairs, and when I insisted . . . they said they needed to check with Dirk."

"Dirk Falter?" asked Rand.

"One and the same," said Van G. "He's paid the owner for exclusive use of the top floor in the afternoons."

"For what?" asked Willington. "To write his next book?"

"To record his rad record," said Van G.

"You've gotta be kidding me," said Ash.

"And we're going to help him," declared Van G.

"Have you lost your mind? Wasting our time with this?!?" asked Rand. "JAM already wants to kill me for running off on this secret adventure. She could birth a preemie, if bad luck strikes, at any minute." He wiped the misty rain from his hair.

"You hate Dirk Falter," said Ash to V.G., clearly annoyed too. "And he, I recall, hates you."

"I know, I know. But when I walked up there with the bartender—that guy Kelt—we stopped at the door at the top of the stairwell, and just before Kelt knocked, I made him pause. Falter had just started a tune, and it wasn't half bad. Nice chord changes. An interesting melody. Decent enough lyrics. His songs are actually good. It's that he's a shitty musician. And that's where we're going to help."

Jaws dropped.

"I'm dead serious. We are going to save Dirk Falter's rad sick record!"

      *   *   *

And so we began to make Falter's rad sick record better. And I wasn't going to let myself get paranoid or pissed about the Rad Sick reference—I was going to let it go.

Instead, I focused on something more important: Wings had musical talent! (I'm trying to think of a Paul McCartney joke, but it ain't coming.)

Ash strummed acoustic and sang with a decent voice; Jack played banjo and lute and vocalized sea-shanty harmonies; Rand could plunk keys and sort of sing; Willington tapped drums; and Van Gear sang well and knew his way around a fret board. I'd played bass in a garage band in undergrad years, so we were ready to go.

Dirk Falter was not happy to see us as we barged into his gypsy studio. He'd chaotically fangled together equipment in Ravensview's upstairs, but the stage had topnotch instruments. He sat at the exact spot where poets read, his back rigid. He was pure confrontation, especially with Van Gear.

But Van G. put up no tough front; he was almost embarrassingly earnest (like he was about the Beats most nights around the Wings table), and Falter's usual jerk-self melted.

Falter wanted help. Knew he needed it.

And then a rattling came from behind the door, making Falter look put out again, as if thinking, *who could it be now?* He marched to the door, swung it open, and in popped, to my ebullient surprise, Elly with a beautiful Guild acoustic guitar. Had Van Gear tapped her too? Or had that night back in September, when Falter and V.G. had their standoff as she'd sat at the front table, inspired her to help the tune-smith poet as well. Perhaps on Elly's Saturday shift she'd done some clandestine listening at the door herself. She was full music-hearted and, like Van Gear, must have had the same impulse. So here she stood. Her brown hair lit with the henna streaks shaped like treble clefs, her glasses framing her eyes like whole notes. I could have not been more pleased.

Everyone knew Elly, superficially, because everyone knew all the bartenders and servers at Ravensview. All Wings greeted her with friendly smiles and waves; she scooted up to me, and we awkwardly hugged. She was acting a little distant, as if only acquainted with me, and that made me insecure, but I did my best to make my smile sincere. I don't think anyone in Wings (well, maybe Van Gear) knew that Elly and I had a romance going, but I was too unsure and embarrassed about how to present this, so instead I took the guitar from her and cleared my throat.

"Hey, guys, Elly's damn good with this thing."

"Damn good singer too," said Van Gear. "Didn't you play with Brent Evans?"

"Yeah, a while ago," Elly said. "So Dirk? Spell-out a song for us." Falter had expensive recording equipment. He'd been playing all the tracks himself, without much success. Despite the nice gear, his limited talents were producing limited results.

So we started to talk about songs and tracks. Falter would play a tune for us with his rough electric chord strumming and crackly off-center voice, and we'd learn it. Then we recorded tracks. The first was Willington setting the drums, laying down some decent rhythms.

Then we figured out what would work next. A real collaborative effort. And this was a much needed reminder of what I loved about T-town and the energy of this community, how we spun ideas and inspired each other and gave each other gentle criticism but mostly encouragement, the reinforcing words to keep working and pushing forward in the great creation of the next humming and drumming of language, art, and sound. I imagined this powerful sense of community protecting me from the shenanigans within Tech Hall. However, despite the motivation from Taylor Velázquez's eyelessness, I still couldn't tell Wings about TallaTec, Tech Hall, and my permanent radiation sickness. Even though Elly and my spy mission had definitely confirmed Tech Hall's rottenness, I remained mired in self-consciousness. Rad Sickness had won again.

Instead of mentioning my Rad Sick woes, I stole a glance at Elly, and we grinned at each other. My heart sang!

Yes, that's how I'd confess to Wings, I'd do it as song. Plot a bass line, then murmur matching lyrics; lace Falter's tunes with the great Saga of the Rad Sick Kid; let the gang know they had to gather with me to lead a siege of Tech Hall. (I'm remembering a teenage D&D campaign in Goblins Deep. I played with norms and always got stuck playing a half-orc. A half-orc was the perfect spy to penetrate goblin walls.) I'd finally release my story, the story I'd been dreading to tell—that Damn Rad Sick Song.

Or not.

Falter's music called instead. The next tune we arranged, "Grapevine of the Holy Sin and Sacrament in Bagdad, Florida," had been envisioned as folk meets country meets gospel, but we heard it as rock n roll. The truth is, with all Falter's work, I could understand Van Gear's point about the dumb prof having some songwriting talent, but at the same time, my ear for invisible voices could hear how, even with our help, these songs were going to come up short. Not way-off short, but, nevertheless, short.

But that didn't matter. What was important—as with my *Microwaves* and "Surf Boy"—was that we moved through and bowed to the process, that the bread of creative life got eaten, that we made our way through this ritual to continue the right and holy way of wordsmithing and occasional genius.

I tried to thump a funky bass line, and Willington got into the spirit and cracked danceable action on the drum-kit's high-hat. Ash plugged in one of Falter's electrics and started working the wah-wah to give the groove up-stroke boogey, and before you knew it, Falter was singing his melody in a new and breathy way, better than he'd done a moment earlier, and Van G. began to fill the other vocal channel with harmony that made the over-all vocals striking and edgy. Elly came in with some clean and perfectly fretted acoustic chords and added her own (Wow!) rich voice to the harmonies.

Jack added a broken chord banjo part, and when I glanced at the bearded, red-headed wonder, he winked. Willington was smiling big and nodding at the two of us. Ash, grounded in his stoner-world, was wandering the stage and playfully elbowing us as he strummed. Elly meandered by my bass amp and studied the ceiling before briefly resting her cheek on my shoulder. Van Gear concentrated on making his harmonies match Falter's rough vocals. Though his eyes were closed, the German-Jesus clearly recognized the interconnectedness of this improvised Wings session. Elly, though not a Wing, fit well too.

Only Falter wasn't "plugged-in." His forehead crinkled, his entire soul giving every bit of himself toward the oomph of his song. And that was OK. It was his music. We were just there to help.

During a short break between takes, Elly and I stood on the stairwell balcony outback for some fresh air. She explained how Falter's hidden gentleness reminded her of her father, reminded her of a childhood game when she'd lean her tummy against his bare feet as he lay on the floor, eyes closed, and he'd lift her into the air, encourage her to spread her arms wide as if she flew; he'd say, *You're high-flying above the radiation clouds, Elly.* And this struck a chord because Big Sis had played a similar game with me when we were young, and had whisper *You're the final ICBM zeroing in on your target.* Elly and I grew animated as we shared these memories; but then Van Gear appeared and impatiently gestured us inside. We fell straight into music and forgot our conversation.

Elly left suddenly at 7 (very disappointing), giving me a brief wave, but Wings stayed till 9 p.m. recording two more songs. We played the recordings back as Kelt appeared with a plate full of bacon that we appreciatively devoured. The tracks sounded pretty good. An especially arrogant aficionado might say, *At best, polished demos.* But to me, to us, they sounded heart-perfect and true.

"Van Gear," Falter said, "I knew all along that I might have totally misjudged you."

"O.K.," said V.G. "Thanks."

"And your poetry's O.K. Keep working on it."

For Falter, it was at least a start. To give an almost-compliment marked a sea-change for the madman.

Rand broke the moment with jokey anxiety.

"Gentlemen, it's nearly 9:30, and I may be dead before my daughter is even born because JAM is going to kill me when I get home."

"We'll vouch for you," said Jack.

Soon enough we were back in the truck, now reliving the rhythm (but not the drunkenness) of *The Night that Jack Built*, our returns home via Van Gear's able steering, the infinite repeat of our infinite Wings voyage.

Monday, November 13, 2000

I called and reached Elly at Ravensview this afternoon where she was working the noon shift, freaking out about random marine biologists strolling in for lunch. I'd always thought of marine biologists as the good-guy scientists; why did these Tech Hall jerks stain the moniker of ocean-ographer-types?

I always call Elly, because even though Elly has my number, she never calls. I don't know why, but it's just as well, because Ex might pick up, and I'd have to give an awkward explanation. Would any woman believe if only one bed existed in an apartment . . . that ex-lovers would sleep together literally and not figuratively?

Elly and I spoke (Ex had been out buying cigarettes) for a bit about the wonders of the recording sessions with Wings and Dirk, but mostly we ranted about the craziness at the underground pool; she wasn't quite as anxious as she'd been on Friday, but she was still edgy. Thankfully, she'd stopped planning a move back south. The music sessions had calmed her. For a heartbeat, I wanted to tell her Ex was staying with me to reorient after a move, but I didn't want to rekindle Elly's tension. And, I have to admit, I didn't want to risk anything that might kill the spark between us.

We set a date for Friday. She didn't have to work, and I would be able to take a break from the reading and papers and work Doc Primus, Bigfoot, et al., had assigned.

Hey, I finally have a real date!

Tuesday, November 14, 2000

I called Jack first thing in the morning to tell him the manuscript he'd handed me on Sunday, his essay about that night in Bosnia, was ready to fly; I told him to send it posthaste, as I'd mentioned before, to the big-time *Mönchengladbach Review* in New York. Jack admitted he'd dug through some old diaries recently, and had been madly rewriting, even cancelling (secretly) the composition classes he taught. He was pleased to know my ear heard his words' music.

And then, moments later, Jack called back.

Rand and JAM were having the baby! All hands to the hospital! All Wings on deck!

We were like mad sperm cells—each in our separate vehicles—racing to reach the egg/hospital first. But the hospital meant the place where the Rand/JAM zygote would finally release itself from its fishbowl of nearly breathable blood. Maybe mother's blood is the true TallaTec of the universe, and Tech Hall's TallaTec, the anti-universe's poisonous plasma. The unborn inside breathes the exhilarating fluid of life in the continuous present . . . while the Rad Sicks, warped in the womb, must breathe destabilizing TallaTec within Tech Hall's wet womb (the underground pool!) to "glimpse" fragments of the unstable and unreliable future.

My mind, over-excited, riffed like crazy.

I pulled my Toyota into visitors' parking; Ex was with me, riding shotgun. She fluctuated between giddy excitement and existential dread: a baby!?!?

A baby!

We climbed stairs to the delivery rooms' waiting area. *Everybody* had arrived for the most-sacred ritual and prime reason for being alive: to fight the Second Law of Thermodynamics! If all closed systems must run down, then, *By God*, we life forms were going to do our damnedest to spit out replacements.

Everyone stirred. Kate and Skate paced the hall. Willington was there with his two kids who got bored quickly and headed outside to toss a football. Van Gear stood with his back to the mute television. CNN was reviewing old news about the Arctic stand-off, but I was too freaked about the baby to think about Taylor. Van Gear's motorcycle helmet nestled in one arm reminded me of a fish bowl. Ash sat with his arms crossed, waved at us but mostly at Ex. Jack and Vicky stood near a water cooler, and Jack nodded as we made eye contact.

Even Falter was there, though aloof, with the mitochondria tattoo woman sitting beside him.

The scene made Ex nervous. She headed downstairs to grab a cigarette, watch the kids play catch, settle her nerves.

Rand had his head in hands on an uncomfortable love seat with JAM's boy sitting next to him playing with a Super Hero action figure.

After a minute, Rand took a Super Villain out of a backpack and the boy and Rand allowed the figures to clobber each other in an intense, escapist, other-world pretend.

Jack had brought cigars. He passed one to me, then paused and turned.

"Hey, you're the father," said Jack to Rand. "You should be handing these around."

"You know you can't smoke in here," said a nurse at the waiting room's reception window.

We all nodded and waved. The nurse eyed us. Yes, we were a ragtag bunch. After all, we were graduate students. But we weren't stupid enough to spark cigars in a hospital. After all, we were smart; we were graduate students!

So Rand gave half to his boy Dill, and the two of them got to work. First, to the English Department gang, and then the extra sticks to anyone else.

Jack popped a cigar in his mouth and chewed the end. Vicky glared at him.

Following Jack's cue, Willington did the same. Ash stuck his behind an ear. Skate and Kate slipped theirs into coat pockets. Rand and

Dill forgot to leave a couple for themselves.

Van Gear had his in his mouth as if it were a cutlass. The man was quieter than usual. He, at moments, looked as lost as Rand.

"Sir! Put that out immediately!" The nurse at the reception window shook her finger.

Falter and his gal were sitting side by side, their heads tilted back, blowing perfect smoke rings. The room smelled richly of tobacco. The phrase *What does the future smell like?* popped into my brain.

And what would it? For Rand and Jam, obviously, pails and pails of dirty diapers and milk vomit. In the near future, we'd all wreak of cigar smoke. What about me? Would the mildew smell of my apartment stick to me for the next few years, the vanilla scent of Ex soon disappearing as she found her own place or possibly shacked-up with Ash? (Which was OK. I liked Ash. He was brilliant. And Ex seemed much happier around him than she ever had with me.)

I teared up; I wanted nothing more than all of us to smell like happiness.

Rand was crying.

The nurse clambered through a half-door, her face belligerent and red.

"Out! Out! Before I call security!"

"Settle down," said Falter. He and his girlfriend stood up. "We were headed outside anyway. Don't be so prissy."

I could tell the nurse wanted to rant, but she held her tongue. The uncooperative pair shuffled to the elevators.

Rand wiped his eyes and tried to fight the tears. Dill gripped both the Hero and the Villain, and the clash of these titans filled the room with clacks and clicks.

Jack sat down beside Rand, put a hand on his shoulder.

"It'll be O.K.," said Jack quietly. "JAM and the baby will both be fine."

"I know," Rand said. "I just had no idea how stirred up I'd get. I don't even understand why."

"It's scary," said Jack. "Maybe when *life* comes, it's much scarier than even death."

Rand nodded. He wiped his eyes dry.

A nurse with a red hat burst into the waiting area.

"Mr. Rand Salt?"

Rand stood up.

"Mr. Salt?"

Rand nodded.

"She's about to deliver. Come quickly!"

Rand and the nurse dashed through double doors, down a hallway splicing together a maze of delivery rooms, each room holding happy zygotes now full-formed in their temporary skin of blood and afterbirth.

We all shouted variations on *Congratulations!* and *Good luck!* as Rand disappeared into the hall.

Van Gear sat down, looking pale and exhausted. He still hadn't said much.

"You doing all right, Van Gear?" asked Willington. "You look as worried as Rand."

"Got coffee-stomach, burning my chest," said Van Gear. He paused a moment. Then glanced around the room as he realized everyone was staring at him. "It's nothing. I'm fine. I'm thinking about my prelim exams. That's all." He gripped his cigar tightly in his right hand.

"You did notice Rand and JAM are having a baby?" said Willington.

Everyone laughed.

"Of course," said Van G. He placed the cigar between his teeth and bit down on it like Jack and Willington. "Should we join Falter outside and smoke these, or should we wait for Rand to return with babe in arms?"

I sat beside Dill and offered to play the role of Super Villain. He handed me the figure, and soon we were doing hand to hand combat as two powerful plastic beings clanged and clattered but refused to create a zygote. The amalgamation of these two was not within the realm of our universe, not even in Dill's imagination.

Rand suddenly popped from the doorway.

"Oh, OK. You've got Dill. Thanks."

He disappeared again, and we were all jittery from thinking he was about to yell news.

I couldn't help thinking of my own improbable birth. How as a zygote I'd been perfect and beautiful, cells splitting until I formed a pristine embryo and fetus, but when those radioactive rays hit as I struggled through the birth canal, they scarred my genetic code, making my double helixes a rat's nest. And what if I'd been a zygote or embryo or early-stage fetus when the blast plume spread above the city? The rate of miscarriages shot through the roof the week after the cloud formed and rained radiation. A sad and terrible bleeding from so many bodies, feelings of undefinable loss. Whenever I considered this as a kid while moping alone in my room, it brought me to tears. I can't explain why. I was lucky. I was not a loss, just inside-my head lost.

"How long before babies can talk?" asked Dill.

"Takes some time," I said. "A year or two. What makes you ask?"

"We need another D&D player. Another character. Like an elf. Rand has been teaching me the game."

"What character are you?"

"Me? I'm a paladin. I use a two-handed sword."

"You kill any half-orcs lately?"

"No, but I cut in half some whole ones."

I laughed.

Ash strolled from his spot by a window and squatted beside me and Dill.

"Quite a collection," said Ash. He picked up a Super Hero whose head happened to be protruding from the backpack and examined it carefully. The hero had a human face but a turtle-like body. She also had a tail with spikes and wore a tiara made of teeth.

He glanced up at me. "Hey, where did your Ex go?"

"Downstairs," I said. "For a smoke. Or two. Watching Willington's kids. Maybe she's chatting with Falter. Maybe you should bring her a cigar? Here, she can have mine." I handed him my cigar.

"O.K.," said Ash. "I'll go check on her."

He slid toward the elevators.

I didn't resent him so much now. Maybe he was just right for Ex. Ex was difficult but had a ton of good-sides. Ash could use his philosophy to manifest her good-sided-ness.

We watched the clock in the waiting room for the next 30 minutes. Dill and I kept bashing the plastic figures; Willington and Van Gear chatted, still chomping their cigars; Jack and Vicky whispered affectionate palaver; Kate and Skate joked about some something. The minutes ticked, and even though we each ignored our individual anxieties, the growing pressure of the unknown made us jittery. Time was a tiny but sharp needle jabbing us at each second.

We heard a surfer's hoot.

Rand burst through the doors with the tiniest creature I'd ever seen. Up to this moment, I'd never realized how I'd either never been exposed or subconsciously avoided any contact with infants. My God! What a terrifying tiny lump of proto-human she was!

Rand was all smiles and shock. He exuded the astonished happiness of a high-stakes lottery winner. The infant was red with a few dashes of black hair.

"JAM is great, everybody!" shouted Rand. "I gotta bring the little one back to her because she's got to be with her mama, but I wanted to be sure you-all gotta look."

Everyone crowded around. Even me. Dill pushed to the front, snatched a quick glance, grew instantly bored, and went back to the plastic people wars.

I could have sworn the baby homed in on me. Her tiny unfocused eyes must have had a radiation-seeking radar, because her off-center vision kept returning to my face. She knew I'd been a Rad Sick baby, and she, as a baby, fully living within the reality of her baby-self, acknowledged what a tough infancy I must have had. Rand and JAM's babe was pristine; I'd been expected to die, to not survive a second sunrise. I wanted to hug her with well-wishes, to congratulate her on her healthy bones, to kiss this full-grown zygote created by the ultimate creativity of Rand and JAM. I suddenly felt very sad.

I'd been told I'd never have my own baby.

Wednesday, November 15, 2000

The invitation! I can't believe it! And I'm nowhere near ready.

Because I have nothing to read!

But yes! To read at Ravensview!

Me!

Willington called this morning and asked me to read for the English Department's Ravensview Series because someone had canceled. The show is the 16th, one night away, *tomorrow*!

I said, definitively, *yes!*

Ex was happy for me. I was glad for the change of subject. She'd been on a rant against Ash because after a Monday evening tea-house session, he'd tricked her into something he claimed was pot (which she hated anyway) but was obviously much stronger (probably TallaTec). She railed against his slickness with a surprising vehemence. She said she never wanted to see him again. I was flabbergasted and confused. I was just getting over the jealousy, getting ready in my selfish hypocritical heart to let Ex go, and now she was acting more affectionately towards me, calling me *Babe* and leaning her head against my shoulder when we sat on the apartment's tiny couch. I was freaking out. Probably less so than when Rand and JAM's baby was born, but this was making me squirrely. I had been looking forward to Ex moving out. Now what? Plus, I was feeling guilty about what Elly might think if she dropped by while Ex wallowed.

However, I needed to totally backburner these anxieties, because I had to decide what to read. Obviously: passages from *Microwaves* and maybe "Surf-Boy" (which, too, was passages from *Microwaves*). I would be Mr. Fragments. I prayed the audience would piece it together.

I grabbed my clumsy manuscripts and searched for anything salvageable. Ex helped. She flew from compliments to sarcasm . . . then back again. My hopes ebbed and flowed on Ex's words.

Did all my sentences suck?

Would the audience appreciate a prose reading that had no narrative?

A prose reading that was really an excuse for a poetry reading?

As I scanned pages, I found spots where I'd at least picked some pretty good words.

That's it! I would just go uber-postmodern and read a random word-hoard chosen from my manuscript. It would be like composing music on a twelve tone scale, the words picked at random.

What coolness!

No—what shit!

Ah ha! Why not read pages of *automatic* writing, sentences off the top of my head?

Yes, fresh, brand new writing!

So I told Ex to stop talking. I sat at the word processor and processed words in earnest.

But first, refreshments. I brewed tea; Ex boiled water for instant coffee; I uncapped a bottle of beer; she uncorked some chardonnay. Now I had options, just to the right of my keyboard. But more than drink, I needed sustenance. Ex really got into this. We prepared a gigantic platter of Hors d'oeuvres. We piled cheese-slick nacho-Ritzes, stacked PB&J saltine sandwiches, made finger foods with bread, mayo, and cucumber. A smorgasbord for a fiction king.

And thus, word-sparks popped:

Sidewalk-less T-town breaks my skateboard heart with its no-bike-path infidelities.

Seawall-less river-lands give birth and go south to the brackish sub-tropical canals walled with concrete and dead oysters.

Ex sat in the corner and read Edna St. Vincent Millay.

I fell flush with flashes of great typing:

North hits south in the oak and pine forest of palm hearts.

Inside the noise of the barred owl rests the bark of gators, the whisper of pygmy rattlers, the hoofed drum-beats of dashing white-tailed deer.

And then, for some unknown reason, I was tempted to write about TallaTec. I'd been trying hard to not think about it—but the fact that Ash had tricked Ex into imbibing made the news of chemical gruel groan loudly in my brain.

I typed: *What is TallaTec's story?*

More than likely, State U scientists had developed a drug to beat the tar out of some disease.

No duh, huh?

I doubted TallaTec's first batch had been made to bully Rad Sicks into childhood confessions. Perhaps it was a psycho-tropic drug—creating hallucinations in Norms (as speed makes Norms race and pace) but calming the suicidal, schizophrenic, and psychotic (as speed calms the autistic and ADDs). Here's my guess: when a Rad Sick accidentally got tested, strange effects arose: he/she mumbled about the 4-Senses of the Future, about the taste, sound, feel, and smell of tomorrow. But what would this tell these knucklehead "marine biologists?"

Ugh. I don't want to write about this. I am as tired of it as I am of my radiation sickness. Who wants to write about what one is sick of, what has made one sick? They say, *Write what you know. Write what scares you.* Well, screw them. Why would I want to write about the condescension and pity directed at me for 20 years? I am so weary of it. If they let me into this program on the hope I might write about Rad Sickness, well fuck them not once but *twice*, because I find a million other topics more interesting. The Writing Profs are wrong. Do they know I'm Rad Sick? Yeah, probably—just a few too many out-of-place pitying looks give it away. Well, I will *not* write about my condition for these professors, these workshops, these lit mags, these whoevers. And I'm not writing about TallaTec!

I broke off the fugue on radiation and drugs, because *fresh writing* about TallaTec was a distraction. I had to get down to business: I required *real* fresh writing for the reading!

More bursts:

Parking meters that eat pennies are the saints of the Big Bend; a Dade meter greets copper with a jeer and demands quarters.

Lantana blooms forever in Lauderdale, freezes back in T-town to reveal its twisted, gnarly arms.

I glanced over at Ex to get her opinion, but she'd fallen asleep reading over my shoulder.

Why was *fresh writing* so hard?

Van Gear rattled on and on about his favorite flavor of *fresh writing*: the Beats. Kerouac was the original master, rolling out high-energy sentences that fired fast along superheated synapses. All his brilliance lit by the rockets of Benzedrine and then launched, blazing away from the debris of the era's counterfeit culture. And hell, maybe we're on the tip of a new age with TallaTec, *the Thing* as new Benzedrine leading writers to the new form. But it's not working for me. Maybe I've inhaled just enough to totally waste my ass, all my *fresh ideas* are freezer burned. I'm not neo-Kerouac plunging word-nerves across the page, not singing the new hard-bop.

I'm in trouble. They will laugh at me, boo me off the stage. Or worse, they will go so silent with boredom.

In they're view: I'm talentless too.

Oh, Ravensview! I may not survive you. I'm through!

Thursday, November 16, 2000

I survived!

I want to sing, *I rule Ravensview!*

Tonight I read "Surf-boy," which actually worked better than I thought.

Ex and I arrived 30 minutes early, so I could get settled, but of course Ash was there, and he and Ex started flirting as if the TallaTec tiff had never happened.

They were into each other, so I searched for others. Wasn't Elly working tonight (Damn, I needed to tell Ex about Elly . . . and vice-versa.)? Would Ryanna appear? Where were Wings?

For five minutes I nervously stared at the ceiling and waited. Not even Willington, the king of the readings, stood stage-side with notes in hand.

But—ho, ho! Skate and Kate appeared. Huge smiles.

"Watcha gonna read?" asked Kate.

"Not that *Surf-boy* shit, I hope," said Skate.

I eyed him in disbelief.

"No, I'm just kidding you. I actually like those pages. You are going to read it then? Far out! Reminds me of tripping," said Skate.

"I'm not big on tripping," I said. I hate acid. A Rad Sick on acid only burns and dissolves; it's worse than TallaTec.

"Yeah, I hear you," said Skate.

"Will be a big crowd," Kate said. She adjusted her pink ear muffs. "I think I saw Doc Primus chatting with Willington outside. And I heard Dirk Falter's coming. He never comes. Is it true you guys helped him record an album? And Professor K-Facto and Bella are sure to arrive fashionably late and sit up front."

I'd totally forgotten my Profs might appear. What if I finally revealed to them what they'd always suspected: *This Dade kid's a dud!*

To hell with that. Me and "Surf-boy" were going to rock their worlds.

The Wings finally showed. Ash and Ex joined them. JAM and Vicky mingled.

Elly trudged up the stairs with a gigantic tray of drinks; I tried to catch her eye, but she didn't notice.

I needed positive vibes, so I surfed through tables and people, and shuffled to Rand's back and gave him a big *Boo!* that made him jump out of his skin. JAM laughed but kept rocking the baby in her arms. They'd named the child Ariel. She was quiet, sweet as a long haiku maybe written by Sylvia Plath or Shakespeare.

How had it gotten so crowded so quickly? The place was packed, making it impossible to swing to the bar to ask for a beer. I caught a glimpse of Elly, but again she was swamped with delivering pitchers.

My thoughts bobbed. At one moment I'd work to attain the perfect performance state of mind. The next I planned for instant exit. If the damn place hadn't been so crowded, I'd have slinked to the door.

I tried to listen to the palaver of Wings and wives and other folks, but my focus kept wandering, and I looked around the room, trying to recognize faces. Damn, there was Professor Bigfoot with the *Norton Anthology of Postmodern American Poetry* in one hand. She was busily annotating as she stood in the corner, prepping for tomorrow's class. And Ryanna stood near the far side exit, probably waiting to bolt if I embarrassed myself. And—son-of-a-bitch—I could swear marine biologist Dr. Fish Hat (minus the hat) stood near her, staring up at the ceiling as if smoke clouds were algae blooms.

And suddenly Willington appeared behind the mic, glaring at the audience in his bemused manner. The crowd ignored him. I hoped they'd ignore him until the joint closed. My nervousness boiled. I had no desire to board the stage. I was too seasick with fear. Why couldn't I be strong like Taylor Morgan Velázquez suffering on the high seas?

And then I double-taked, because in the shadows of the stage's back wall, just behind a drum kit . . . kneeled Sombre and Blanco (did Willington even know they were there?). The pair smiled like idiots—Sombre's blue eyes flashed orange (he'd apparently forgotten his contacts), and Blanco was wearing a fake grey mustache on his black, beautiful face that made his teeth hard to see.

But instead of panicking, I got pissed. How dare these assholes, Fish Hat, Sombre, and Blanco, come to ruin my reading. How many positive moments had I had in life so far?

Zero!

These fuckers were not going to fuck up my night. I'd spout angry words, loud as alligator coughs, and drive those dolts through the back exit.

Willington began to talk and my thinking clicked back on track. Willington gave greetings, cracked jokes. The crowded settled. Quieted. Willington took his time, knowing he'd wear them down with his earnestness, his heartfelt guff that turned the listeners to dumbstruck awe, waiting for what would unfold.

Sombre and Blanco slipped from behind the stage into the crowd, and I lost sight of them, but I thought I could spot Blanco's *Invisible Man* spectacles between others' shoulders and elbows. Willington didn't notice. He started in on matters at hand: how'd there been a last minute cancellation, and tonight's first reader would be *making his Ravenview's debut, a writer and poet from the subtropical lands of Dade.* I felt queasy. "Surf-boy" sentences were swimming on the pages that shook in my hand. I quaked. I would not survive, not the night, not this minute.

I thirsted for a shot of Jack (Jack had just whispered into my ear, "The *Mönchengladbach Review* took it!"), anything to steady my nerves, and I stared at the bar hoping to spot Elly, but instead I saw the girl with the mitochondria tattoo smiling at Dirk Falter. If he'd brought his guitar, we'd have had music! This audience, all these heads, like the dots of a plethora of sixteenth notes, could have sung like a Greek chorus.

But no.

I would have to spill without bourbon or tunes.

" . . . so now please welcome to the stage . . ."

Rain. A hundred drums. A cacophony that launched me to my feet. The blood beat in every capillary in my cheeks in time with the applause. I felt hot and faint.

They were clapping for me! I'd never had a crowded room of a hundred people applaud for me. I was stunned, overwhelmed. My eyes were wet, and I wanted to shake my head *No, No, No,* and I didn't understand how I was getting what I never deserved. I tip-toed my way through a gigantic duck-duck-goose gaggle of floor-sitters clustered around the foot of the stage, and Willington offered me a hand and pulled me from floor to mic . . . and there I was before the sea that had grown calm.

"Surf-boy wasn't whole human. Things inside him quickened the crack between man and sea, split the critical point until he made himself two equals that quaked in his belly like plasti-cast jellyfish poured from the same genetic mold.

"Surf-boy knew the loneliness of living half and half."

I read, and the words tumbled. I stumbled at times, but by slowing down, I'd recover. Ex had helped me rehearse; otherwise, I'd have bulleted through the pages. The piece was a love story really, lonely Surf-boy's search for love—found then lost. Typical boy meets girl stuff.

For the first minute I trembled. But as I glanced at the audience, I could see the attention in their eyes. The entire room cared about my words. *My* words! I felt overwhelmed, astounded.

Though my eyes flooded, I stopped shaking. My confidence spread from toe to nose. My voice rang strong. I spoke with a confidence that had never leaked from my lips, not even in conversation with those who were close to me. I launched myself into the stratosphere of pure language, becoming a noble soul striving to deliver to an audience of open ears. My vocal chords became an entire symphony, the words—*the syllables!*—were the largest orchestra in the world, an infinite symphonic landscape. "Surf-boy" was my song, and I was singing!

The narrative drove me forward.

To, of course, after 20 minutes, the end.

"In the water, Surf-boy rolled off his surfboard," I read.

I paused.

"I watched and waited, but Surf-boy never came up for air."

I thanked the crowd.

Super-sonic applause ripped my eardrums. The sound of one hundred, one million, an infinite number of hands clapping is not only massively better than one hand clapping, it blows the frigging doors off that one hand. The sheets of white noise permeated every cell in my body. I felt vibrations run through every nerve, every bone and nail, my tongue and toes, and the pure positive energy of this sound lifted the Rad Sickness from my body as if I were born a norm and every molecule of radioactivity drifted to the ionosphere never to return. The feeling didn't last, but I still felt so elated, I didn't care. I was smiling like an idiot, the happiest idiot on this half-assed, half-baked planet.

Weirdly, I felt whole.

Ex embraced me. Elly, with a lovely smile, handed me a beer and said it was "On the house." (She hadn't noticed, luckily, Ex's a little too affectionate hug.) Willington slapped the hell out of my back. Rand shook my hand. Van Gear nodded. Jack grinned. Ash clasped my shoulder. It was all Love and Wings (another great name for a band!).

From behind me and over my shoulder, someone reached out and offered a gift-wrapped present. My brain, though full-throttle adrenalized, paused.

Sure, my reading was great—but I didn't deserve to be showered with gifts. People were tightly packed around me, many well-wishers I recognized from campus coming to smile and nod; I couldn't see behind. I strained my neck to glimpse the gift giver. It was Blanco (Sombre stood beside him) now dropping the present on my clavicle; I caught it with my left hand. Instantly, he and Sombre churned powerfully against the current of the crowd. I lost sight of them within the packed bar.

The box was wrapped with Santa Claus paper. Hand-written on the tag: *Open Before Xmas!*

Everyone continued to be enchanted by me, so no one asked about the present, or even seemed to notice. Maybe they didn't want to embarrass me with innuendo about a secret admirer.

Ex did ask me about it at one point. I shrugged, and she didn't press.

When we got back to Aluminium Village, my gut instinct was to toss the present in the trash. I haven't yet.

It rests now beside this very page as I snap down this sentence's final word.

Sunday, November 19, 2000

I can write about nothing else: Elly ran into Ex.

Literally.

I'm not sure what to make of it. I can't tell if there's a tornado of turmoil that's been created or if the turmoil is inside my head.

Ex and I were leaving Yak's this morning after a tea-session with Ash. We were rambling down the sidewalk, when a lone figure appeared on the horizon, a woman with dark hair and glasses. I barely noticed because Ex was expounding on Ash's latest philosophical riff about Nietzsche and the current Cold War. Ex and I were so engrossed in our conversation and—at that point—the glasses-wearing woman was so engrossed in her own thoughts that. . . .

Ka-phlump!

The pair knocked shoulders. With energy! The impact made Ex bump me, and I teetered at the edge of the sidewalk as a giant truck whistled past.

"Oh, I'm *so* sorry," apologized Ex. She was so good at *sorries*, I sometimes wondered if she was more *English* than English major.

"That's all right," mumbled Elly, glancing up and recognizing me.

Elly and I locked eyes. We had a date late this afternoon at a park downtown. I was planning to pawn Ex on Ash to make this happen.

"Hey," Elly said. She sounded tentative.

I fell into automatic pilot and made awkward introductions, not clearly indicating that Ex was an ex and Elly was dear, so a weird tension immediately punctured our sidewalk chat. Ex oddly mentioned her employment search.

"You're looking for a job? If you need cash quick, there's always serving. I work at Ravensview. Just down the street. I'm there so much, it's practically home."

"Oh. I was there last night," Ex said as she pointed at me, "for his reading."

"Yes, I thought I saw you. I'm not sure I've seen you there before."

"No? You know, I think it was my first time despite the way he keeps telling me Ravensview is so wonderful."

"I hope he would say that." Elly squinted at me. "Funny that he'd be keeping you away."

"It wasn't intentional," I said, clueless to what to say next. I was desperate to change the subject or kill the conversation clean so each party could say goodbye.

"She helped record Dirk Falter's record with us," I said. "She's a great guitarist and singer."

Elly stood taller as I spoke; my words gave her lift, and I was glad.

"Oh. You know Professor Falter well then?" Ex asked.

"Not really. He knew my ex pretty well."

I started to sweat.

"Your ex a professor too?"

"No, just a musician."

"You should hear Elly sing harmony; she's got an angelic voice," I said.

"Enough about me," Elly said. "What do you do?"

"Edit," said Ex.

"Books?"

"Anything."

"She worked for a publisher in Kansas City," I added.

"What brings you here?" Elly pointed at me. "Him?"

"Well, he'd been saying such great things about the place, you know."

"Had he," Elly said. She paused. "Well, I've got to head off. Nice to meet you," she said to Ex. Elly gave me a scowl.

She paused.

"Oh. By the way. Can't make it today. *Sorry*."

I was sunk.

Monday, November 20, 2000

Bummed majorly about missing a moment with Elly. Of course, yesterday Ex was asking about what *Can't make it today* meant coming from Elly's lips. Since Ex seemed only platonically curious (which both relieved and hurt), I admitted I kind of liked Elly, but things were moving slowly. Ex could tell I was uncomfortable about the subject so she mercifully broke it off and became obsessed with carefully feeding the goldfish a flake at a time.

Truth is, I've got so much academic work to obsess over that I can't afford to lose time obsessing about the broken date. Ex peppered me again with questions as we got out of bed this morning, but I ignored her.

So now that I've written about this, gotten it off the proverbial chest, I need to work on everything else but *this*.

As I try to break off this entry, Ex is mumbling about travel plans and inside my unfocused Rad Sick brain, I make myself believe it's about her returning to the great town of Kansas City.

I will write a poem to solidify it: "The Return of the K.C. Kid: So Long to the South Forever."

Wednesday, November 22, 2000

Thanksgiving. I'd forgotten about it. Classes cancelled for half a week.

Ex flew home to see her folks, and I decided to drive to Dade to see mine and Big Sis. Haven't had much contact with family except the occasional phone call to Mom and Dad, maybe about once a month. Zero communication with my sister, except for Trivial Trial back in September. I'm kinda looking forward to seeing her. Or maybe I'm happy to be doing something other than writing papers, crafting fiction, prepping for midterms, doing massive amounts of reading—and feeling massively depressed about screwing up with Elly. Or for that matter, worrying about TallaTec and Tech Hall. I've been so swamped these past few days. I've been so in over my head, I've been ignoring my journal, and hopelessly trying to ignore my heartbreak.

Since Ex and Elly "met" on Sunday, and my date with Elly evaporated. I've only been able to visit Ravensview twice to find her, to explain. And it hasn't gone well. She will serve me at least, but she's monosyllabic and aloof. I need to find the guts to grab her by the apron . . . and tell her everything about Ex....

But no. I've blown it. I was confident that she truly liked me. I had been feeling my chest expanding with . . . call it LOVE! But now that's gone. Honestly, the real reason I haven't been journaling is because I've been too depressed; it's clear I've torpedoed my chances with Elly.

Dishonesty. Lies of omission.

I'm sunk.

O.K. To stop moping on my loss, I will refocus on my gain: my reading of "Surf-boy" and all the upbeat vibes my peers gave me. The great gush of good feeling lingers—I can shout *I'm the King of the Mountain*, and still believe it.

King, double king, Big Sis once said.

But she can't find a throne.

She still has no job.

She's a piece of unemployment data.

Big Sis is crowned *loser* by the Recession.

*　　　　　*　　　　　*

Before I'd left for home, I'd stashed the X-mas present on the upper shelf in my closet, buried the package under a pile of t-shirts. I wanted to forget it.

I should have thrown that garbage from Sombre and Blanco into the landfill, next to a pile of ancient Fall-out Shelter signs that have been replaced by the newer ones. I should have set the package on fire, watch the pretty red bow go up in toxic fumes.

The damn package.

What could it be?

TallaTec. No duh.

Prolly mixed into eggnog schnapps. Happy hallucinatory Hanukah! If I finally open the package, I will summarily dump that drivel down the drain. If Elly still cared, I know she'd tell me to do that.

Though I'm trying not to, I've been massively obsessing about Elly today. I keep sketching her face on the backside of pages within this journal. Part of me hopes, since she waited on me at Ravensview, though monosyllabically, she still likes me. A bigger part of me wishes I'd been forthright and grabbed Elly by the wrist and explained, apologized, invited her down to my parent's house for cranberries and pumpkin. Of course, since she's originally from Dade too, I've convinced myself we'll serendipitously run into each other, like in the All-Dade Mall on Black Friday, but that is one of my usual asinine expectations.

OK. So here I am. Home at last. In my old room. Sad.

Knock on the door. Big Sis standing there, smiling, holding a stack of Trivial Trial cards. Oh shit.

*　　　　　*　　　　　*

Big Sis just left. I think we've played the best game ever.

Because I won!

Sort of.

When she first stepped into the room, she gave me a huge embrace that puzzled me, as if she'd actually missed my Rad Sick ass. My parents had hugged me pretty good when I stumbled through the door, but Sis had one-upped them on the *abrazos* front. My eyes got a little wet, but she didn't notice and instead plopped down on the floor and asked me to sit also. In one hand she clutched the game cards, ignoring them.

"How are you doing? We haven't talked in forever," she said.

"Getting through grad school," I said.

"You're not going to drop out?"

I gave her a funny look.

"No, I don't mean like that. I mean, one time I almost dropped out of accounting grad school at Owl-U."

"Really?" I hadn't heard this before.

"Yeah, I had a bit of a crisis. Like, I had a feeling a MAc. wasn't going to matter: I still wasn't going to get a job."

"Recession will end soon. You'll see. Don't worry."

"Feels like it won't. Feels like no one will ever work again."

She started to cry, but just as suddenly stopped.

"Hey, we've got to play round two this fall of our favorite game," she said.

"Your favorite, not mine."

"That would be checkers, silly. Come on. You'll have a good chance this time. An easy category. What are you studying? English?"

"Right. Mostly 20th century literature."

"Oh my. That does sound intimidating." She shuffled rapidly through the cards. "OK, I'm looking through the *Lit* cards on 20th century writers. Should be all homeruns for you."

"We'll see. Hurry up and hit me."

"Hmmmmm. Here's a good one." She held the card close to her face and squinted.

"Who wrote these lines?" Big Sis began. "'Hard Times' . . . *"Trust me. The world is run on a shoestring. / They have not time to return the calls in hell . . . And now every day / Will have to dispel the notion of being like all the others."*

This sounded familiar. Familiar as hell. As if it had trickled through my eyes over the course of the past ten days via the thin but heavy pages of some Anthology. Wait. . . . Ah ha! Professor Bigfoot's class! New York School poets!"

"I know this one," I said.

"No way." Big Sis looked doubtful.

"John Ashbery."

"You bastard," she said. "You're actually learning something in school?"

"Lucky guess."

"All right, Mister. Not going easy on you now."

She grabbed a trio of cards and shuffled through them, grimacing with her glance at each scrim of text.

"Here you go. From the Charles North poem 'A Note to Tony Towle (After WS)', fill in this blank: *even the . . . BLANK! . . . / for all the enigmas concerning who is trading what to whom, / and while deracination is fast qualifying as essence / rather than attribute . . .*"

Charles North? Who the hell was that? Someone, obviously, as contemporary-as-hell. Hmmmm. . . . Bigfoot had been sneaking in some newer poems here and there. . . . Yet at this moment, nothing sprang to mind. Why did the image of the accidental internship in the Boca Boiler Room pop into my head? Oh yeah! The *"who is trading what to whom."*

"I got it! The World Trade Center!"

Big Sis looked pissed.

She sighed and reread the question to herself.

"Well, maybe that one was a bit obvious. Fair enough. You're ahead, 2 to zero."

"You mean I might actually win?"

"No."

She intensely studied a dozen or more cards. I waited.

Then a wicked grin crossed her face. A comeback was in the works.

"OK, literary boy, who wrote the following lines?"

She paused. Cleared her throat. Pretended to adjust invisible reading glasses.

"Bomb then, bomb now—doing the breathing arsenic job, we want / *mouth-sized suburbs; yale locks running hot round-robin stillbirths. . . ."*

It was an impossible question.

No. More than that, it was a low blow. My Big Sis, the total un-kind bitch. Why was she being so mean? She knew how it got to me, the stillbirths, the unbirths, those who died instead of being born during those horrible weeks…. Yes, yes, she'd ordinarily make jokes related to Rad Sickness and whatever, but I couldn't tolerate the unbirth jokes. They were cruel. Even for her. Why was she being so heartless? When I was little she'd tell unbirth stories she'd invent (how the hell would she have known?), and I would run to mom balling, my eyes not only orange but blood-red from crying.

And now she was being an asshole just because she couldn't find a job.

I wanted to tell her to fuck-off, but I held my tongue. Stared at the carpet instead.

And then she was sobbing. She was tearing the card into tiny shreds, small as atoms. She leaned into me, wrapped her arms around my chest, and gave me a billion megaton hug that took the breath out of me, the longest and mightiest hug she'd ever given in her life.

I felt hurt, sad, but also happy, loved. Awkward as hell.

"What was the answer?" I asked.

She tried to hold back her crying.

"I can't remember. I don't care," she said. She took a humungous gulp of air, made brief eye contact with me. "It doesn't matter, because you won!"

Ha-ha. No I didn't. Not really.

She held me . . . we held each other . . . for another ten minutes.

It may have been the best ten minutes of my life.

Sunday, November 26, 2000 (Sunday after Thanksgiving)

Van Gear called everyone to schedule a final basketball practice before Kurt Mitchell's arrival. Van Gear was geared up. He'd stayed around town for Thanksgiving. Rand and JAM had invited him over for pumpkin pie, but he'd passed. He'd practiced his jump shots all weekend. Funny, he was the only guy who didn't need practice.

As soon as I'd pulled in from Dade on Saturday night and opened the door to my apartment, the phone was chirping.

"Tomorrow night. No excuses. This is your last chance to polish your game," said Van Gear.

"Can we just spray my game with a hose? I'll never be polished," I said.

"Hilarious," said Van Gear. "Just be there."

I immediately called Ravensview. Kelt answered and said Elly didn't work until Monday. My heart sank. I forced my thoughts solely onto basketball.

All Wings arrived at the court on Sunday evening within minutes of one another. It was freezing. I couldn't feel my fingers. Everyone complained about the cold, but Van Gear ignored us. He wore a Chicago Bull's beanie and a University of Chicago jacket. He'd said he'd found them both at Goodwill near the homeless shelter, but I doubted it; I think they were keepsakes from his C-Town youth.

Before the drills began, we had to kick the leaves off the court. The surface was a freaky fall wonderland. Down in Dade, the subtropics kept things steady warm—nothing ever changed—but here in T-town, this was storybook autumn. Pear trees sported bright red leaves like huge torches blazing above parking lot medians. Yellows, golds, and oranges blistered the branches of oaks and sweet gums. We swept away a patchwork quilt of brightly colored leaves.

Van Gear whipped us into action.

As he shouted directions, we became quiet. Shivered. The cold had caught up with us. None of us, except Van Gear, wore warm enough clothes. My clothes were warm, but too bulky for basketball. My ancient Sears ski parka with rainbow stripes on the sleeves cramped my shoulders. My gloves were made for digging snow forts. But once I was down to t-shirt and shorts, I felt icy. Van Gear had thrown his jacket in his car, but he didn't seem cold.

I ran around like a madman getting my body heat into action, but a breeze gusted over the asphalt and kept me shivering. My feet were numb, even after sprinting nonstop. Crazy, damn cold! Made me think of half-blind Taylor Velázquez still stuck in the Arctic Stand-off; few reports had been in the news lately.

I took off one glove and blew warm air into it, hoping to help my right hand thaw. Damn, was it below freezing? Rand had mentioned *a hard freeze after midnight*, whatever that meant.

When we started a charity stripe drill, Van Gear noticed me trembling.

"Put that coat back on," he said. "You're no good to me if you're frozen stiff."

My body had tightened more, because we'd stopped drills and now stood and shot foul shots. The wind was a knife. I had a stiff gait as I ran to the sideline to nab my coat.

With my coat on, my underarms began to sweat. I couldn't win.

Next we ran layup drills. Van Gear schooled us. His layups were effortless, either hand, any angle.

He became a layup showboat. He'd sprint to the hoop, leap, and twist his body in circles.

"Let me show you something special," he said.

Van Gear made a mad dash from midcourt, sprang from just past the foul line and pirouetted in midair as if a ballerina, but as he extended his front leg to the space beneath the rim, his foot turned and landed sideways, rolling his ankle. He fell hard.

Ash and Willington told the superstar, "Get up already," but Rand and Jack shuffled over to check on him. I stood nearby.

Van Gear stared at the court, grimaced. The man was in pain. Van Gear in pain wasn't pretty. He was the fallen hero, a true Achilles, nipped near the heel and down like an axe-slit pine.

"I just tweaked it," said Van Gear. But he wasn't getting up. He looked pale.

"You want us to help you stand?" asked Jack.

"Give me a minute."

Now Ash and Willington stumbled over.

Van Gear, for the first time, looked cold.

"You want my jacket?" I asked.

He hesitated for a moment, and then, without looking at us, he sighed and said, "Yeah."

I ripped it off my body as if I were lending a blanket to a child in a war zone. Willington and Ash helped him slip it on.

"I'm OK," he said. He tried to stand up, but he was obviously in pain. We grabbed his arms, and he stood up, gingerly putting weight on the weak ankle. We guided him to a bench near the court's edge.

"Need to rest it a minute," said Van Gear, "just a minor sprain." We were all pretty doubtful about his diagnosis.

The sun was dropping near the horizon, and with each notch it traveled downward, we could feel the temperature fall. We were all cold as hell as we stood around Van Gear. He pulled off his shoe and sock and studied his ankle.

He did look ridiculous wearing my puffy, blue ski jacket. The rainbow stripes around his broad shoulders gave him a super-hero look from a 1970s TV cartoon, which greatly contrasted with his bearded face and long hair. Elly would have laughed had she been there. Damn it, I miss Elly.

Van Gear's ankle was not swollen. But it was obviously stiff, because every time he moved his foot in a circle, he frowned.

"Doesn't look too bad," said Ash.

"But it's painful," said Rand. "You want to end practice?"

"Just give me another minute," said Van Gear. He feverishly rubbed his foot and ankle. He was the shaman restoring his own dead joint, the German-Jesus as miracle worker, healing himself.

We were silent, as if in prayer, the court our cathedral, the backboard our cross.

"If nothing else," said Van Gear, "I can practice foul shots on one leg."

Willington shrugged. Ash rolled his eyes.

"You sure that's a good idea?" asked Rand.

"What are you, his mother?" asked Jack. He was kidding.

"Didn't you know?" said Van Gear. "He's our Ma. Ma Rand."

Willington and Ash laughed.

Van Gear suddenly stood on one leg and held his arm up to Rand.

"Here, Ma Rand, give me a hand."

Van Gear hobbled to the foul line with Rand's help. We all stood there, watched in silence. I'm not sure if we were in awe or dumbfounded by his macho stupidity.

"Give me the ball," said Van Gear.

Ash tossed it to him.

"Watch the technique, boys. And learn."

Balancing on one leg, the guy took a one-handed shot. The arc was perfect. The ball made no contact with the rim. Swish.

At the moment Willington fetched the ball, Van Gear became pale again, as if his good ankle were collapsing, but then he beckoned for the sphere and sank another foul shot.

"O.K., you were watching, right? I want each of you to use the same technique."

As if robots, mindless automatons with Van Gear's tough-guy programing now in our brains, we lined up and tried to imitate Van Gear's form. Ash came nearest. The rest of us were pathetic. Rand made his (a lucky bounce off the backboard), but then Jack, Willington, and I all missed.

I didn't even hit the rim.

Van Gear had his back now against the post beneath the basket, and he was shaking his head.

"No way with only half my legs I shoot better than half of you."

We were silent. Van Gear grimaced. We weren't sure if it was our shooting or the twisted ankle.

"Maybe you should give us another lesson, Hop-a-long," said Willington. He was kidding, but he said it as a challenge, his favorite tack with Van G.

"I think we should take you home, man," said Rand. "Seriously, you don't look well."

"Go shoot another round," said Van Gear. "And all of you, flex your knees as you shoot. Don't forget the follow-through, especially you, Rand."

We obeyed. But when one of us missed, he'd make us take another shot. He kept giving us advice, encouragement. Serendipitously, his advice seemed to charm each shooter, because each person sank it after Van Gear's tips.

I even swooshed my shot.

We practiced another few rounds. Our fingers were numb.

The temperature had dropped another five degrees.

Van G. leaned against the post with closed eyes, whispering unheard syllables in time with the b-ball's beats on the backboard, rim, pavement.

His one leg gave out and he slid down the pole, dropped to his ass like a rock.

We all stopped and ran over. We were adrenalized, a multi-headed animal locked on panic-mode. Our eyes all huge and round.

Van Gear cracked his lids and locked eyes, one by one, with each of us.

"O.K., gentlemen. Time to go home. We nailed it tonight."

I got my ski jacket back, and then Rand and Willington helped

Van Gear to his truck. I said good night to Jack. Ash had already driven off into the evening in his small pickup. Rand waved as he got into Willington's station wagon (they'd car-pooled—"family-guys" sticking together), and they zoomed off, Van Gear right behind them.

For no particular reason, I was still standing beside my Toyota, fiddling with the pockets of my ski jacket. I was, for whatever reason, afraid to put it on, even though I was freezing. I had my gloves on. I was shivering. The collar of the coat smelled of German-Jesus.

I thought of slipping into Ravensview, maybe catching Elly back early from Thanksgiving, but then I remembered she wasn't working until Monday. A gust came through. A strange mist of freezing rain sleeted my face.

I sighed. I slipped on my coat and drove back to Alum Village.

Monday, November 27, 2000

This afternoon while returning from a Doc Primus workshop, I wondered about Ex. I hadn't heard from her since I'd returned. I hadn't spoken to Ex over Thanksgiving either. But lo and behold, as I wheeled my bicycle through the front door, Ex and Ash were loading up boxes.

Of course, I'd been expecting this, but when I pushed open the door and saw the pair standing at the table, loading clothes and stacks of books, I gasped. Ex glanced up with a guilty look, and Ash gave me his usual stoner-placid stare and grin. My stomach crashed straight past my feet.

"Hey," she said gently.

"Didn't know you were planning to move out," I said.

"Well, yes. I guess I made the decision recently."

Ash wrapped his long arms around a heavy box and lugged it past me, through the open door (the weather had suddenly warmed up considerably, and rain clouds hovered). He meandered out to his tiny truck.

"Oh. Well, that's O.K. I mean . . . ."

"I'm sorry. I really am. I should have told you," she said. She sighed. "About me and Ash."

"Well, the attraction was there. Hard not to notice."

"Yes, yes . . . but . . . did you have a nice Thanksgiving?"

"Yeah, I was going to call you, but got caught up with family and everything. You know, my sister and all," I said.

"Yes, how's she doing? Any luck with the job market?"

"She's going to an interview tomorrow."

"That's great." She sighed again, paused. "Hey . . . listen. I love you. And you've done so much for me, letting me stay here. I . . . should have called you. Explained. I certainly wanted to . . ."

"Really, it's O.K."

". . . but then I would have had to tell you where I was calling from."

"Oh? You didn't go to Dade?"

"No. . . . I flew to Tampa to be with Ash. I'd planned it . . . earlier."

Why in the hell were my eyes tearing up?

"I lied to you. I'm sorry."

"What's to worry about? I mean, it wasn't like we'd made specific plans to hang-out."

I was crying. I couldn't control it. I was just on the edge of starting to sob, and I was fighting to keep sad gulps from springing into a tidal wave of broken-heartedness. I'd lost Elly. And now, even though I'd known we were over, I was losing what remained of me and Ex.

"I'm so sorry," she said.

Ash walked through the door and put his hand on my shoulder. At first, I bristled, angry, but when I looked into his eyes, I could see he felt bad, and my anger sloughed away. Ash cared. Ex was breaking my heart (Yes, I know. We were totally broken up already! What gives?), but she genuinely cared too.

Here I was, immersed in one of the weirdest and saddest moments in my life, yet I had never felt more loved.

Ex had finished packing a box moments before. I lifted it from the table and took it outside to Ash's truck.

A little later, Ex made a pot of tea, and we sat around quietly and drank it.

Tuesday, November 28th, 2000

They were trying to set a record at Ravensview. A few of the crazier poets had decided to make their mark on the literary universe. They'd gotten permission to keep the upstairs open 24-7, and they were attempting the longest poetry reading known to humankind!

O, the great idiocy of graduate students!

Ravensview had already let Dirk Falter have all night recording sessions, so they had no problem with a poetry marathon.

Kate and Skate had brainstormed this word-festival while maxing out on coffee at Yak's (though I suspected TallaTec might have been involved), and were now continuing the black coffee bacchanal as they hosted the world's longest poetry reading.

I'd woken up at 4 a.m. because I couldn't keep loneliness from brazenly burying itself in my brain. Yesterday's event with Ex and Ash still haunted.

More pertinently, on Monday I'd called and left three messages for Elly at Ravensview, but I hadn't heard back. I was getting my glum-Gus sleepless-mojo on. I thought about simply heading over to the joint and confronting Elly, but, no, I was, as usual, too scared!

But it was my only chance to get Elly back. I knew I had to face the demons and sell Elly on my *redeemability*. Damn it, I knew I was a decent guy. How does one get past Rad Sick inarticulateness to express the heart?

As soon as I heard about the marathon reading, I knew I had an excuse to limp back to Ravensview. I had something to push me past my fear.

I pedaled over to T-town's holy land. Even if Elly wasn't there, I'd get to witness poetry awake and kicking in the predawn. I entered and found two dozen listeners near the stage, including two homeless guys, lots of my cohort, and some moody, death-obsessed undergrads clutching reams of skull-laced riffs.

A kid ranting about subway tunnels kept everyone rapt. Kate spotted me. She was wearing her tiger-eared snow cap, and she looked thrilled to see me.

"Are you going to read?" she asked.

Damn. Why didn't I think of that? I could have shoved something in my pocket and been ready to shoot off syllables.

"Could improvise something," I said, not really meaning it.

"That would be wonderful!" She was way too emphatic. But I knew she meant well. Kate was smart. Sharp! I would argue her work was as good as JAM's, K-facto's, Bella's or Ryanna's. Socially though, she seemed such a space cadet, as if the world had been put together backwards, and she was the only person in the room slowly sliding it back into place. Or, shit, maybe that's what intelligence really is. And man, I just don't got it.

A dozen people milled up the stairs from below and strolled past. The reading was growing in numbers. Heads nodded to words about guitars in tunnels, subways. The woman with the mitochondria tattoo was working late, serving coffee.

Was Elly here?

Kate leaned into my ear: "We'll be doing this through Christmas, and then at some point after New Years, we'll have set one rad sick record."

I gave her a look that she didn't register. Was she drunk or caffeinated into hallucination or trudging her synapses through TallaTec minefields? Rad sick record. *Rad Sick Record.* I remember the Dade skateboard gangs doing their rad sick tricks, their 580s spinning top-like above the rims of drained swimming pools, and they'd shout to one another *That's rad sick!* --partly in celebration of the maneuver, but also with the deep irony of the Rad Sick's plight. We were all lousy skateboarders. Balance was never our strong point. And somehow this *rad sick* as modifying phrase, as off balance adjective, leaked its way into Dade culture at large; thus, *rad sick* was used from time to time as a barb. I have to admit, my blood roiled over the years as the phrase was spat from numbskull lips, but now . . . at this exact moment . . . it has stopped stinging, as if the phrase has lost its punch. I almost want to laugh. Anyway, Kate's use of the modifier didn't modify my mood. I quickly gave her a smile.

Kate skipped to the stage to intro the next reader, and I looked around the room and spotted Elly sitting by herself at a tiny table in the back corner. She wore on-duty clothes, but she didn't seem to be working. She was stirring a drink that was not coffee.

My blood vessels fired with fear, relief, exhilaration, abject terror. But, I told myself, *no Rad Sick self-immolation allowed—approach Elly! Now!*

I shuffled in her direction, and she turned and nodded but didn't seem happy to see me.

I stood at the far end of the table with my best feel-sorry-for-me face, but she unwaveringly stared at the stage.

What to say to quell the fire of an angry girl?

"Why don't you climb up there so they can hear you sing? Your voice is better than a thousand poems."

Elly acted as though she didn't hear me. My brained whirled and whirred.

"Hey. I'm sorry I didn't tell you about my ex. That was stupid of me. I wish she wasn't trying to settle here. Really."

Elly as statue: rigid; glasses of stone; hair of brownish and henna rock; eyes locked in place.

"She's dating Ash now," I said. "Ever since she got here." I was staring at the stage too. Kate was wrapping up a very long intro. The next reader was a student in her composition class. Kate stood proud.

"I want to date you," I softly mumbled to Elly. "That's all. Sorry I'm so slow."

Elly sighed and swiveled her head. Looked glum but almost agree-able.

"What's up, Needlefish?" she whispered. Kate's student was on stage, an undergrad with a booming voice.

"Just thought I'd pop by for this marathon. You working? How've you been?" I whispered back. "Did you get any of my messages. I left, maybe, *a dozen?!?*"

"More like *three*." She sighed again. "I'm not sleeping. That why you're here?"

"But you're dressed for work."

"Force of habit. A mistake."

"Oh," I muttered. "Yeah, can't sleep either."

The undergrad bellowed big words.

Elly took a long swig from her drink.

"You know, that scene at Hillevi Gym . . . that was super freaky. Keeps me up nights thinking."

I didn't reply. I was feeling like the super-freak, because I'd ne-glected her. Elly—with dark circles bruising her eyes—did not seem her-self, and I blamed myself.

I'd abandoned Elly (no wonder Hillevi haunted her). I should have kept her firmly on my radar.

Instead, I'd been distracted by babies and basketball, Ex and Ash, papers and poetry, my reading and Ravensview. I'd been an idiot, a jerk. I should have camped in the bar's kitchen and held her for hours in the walk-in freezer. My love had been lacking.

Elly's radar waves projected kindness and concern. Mine, not so much. I had to improve. Drastically. After all, we are fellow Rad Sicks, and I'd neglected our bond.

I also feel bad about how I've stopped thinking about one-eye-less Taylor Velázquez too, how much she's sacrificed in the face of endless Cold War. She's my favorite chica from childhood; at the very least, she needs keeping in my Rad Sick thoughts.

There's so much I've not done, so much I need to do.

For starters, I decided, I needed to give Elly a big apology.

But how to begin?

Well, awkwardly.

"Did you go home for Thanksgiving?" I asked.

"To Dade?"

I shrugged.

"My parents moved to Vero last month. I didn't go any further south than Hobe Sound."

"Oh. I was hoping to run into you in Dade. Invite you over for cranberry pie. Turkey potatoes. Pumpkin dressing. A rad sick Thanksgiving."

Elly stifled a laugh.

"You're idiotic, ridiculous, and silly." Elly sighed, then smirked. Her posture relaxed. She exhaled.

"So how are you doing?" she asked. "The other night, I think you looked more scared than I felt at Hillevi Gym. During your reading, I mean."

"I was all right. I'd been so swamped with papers and other academic bullshit, but the reading was good. A relief. People liked it, I think. I've just been missing you. Really wanted to serve you that pie. I help make it sometimes. At home. Once before at least. Sometimes Christmas. Or Thanksgiving."

Elly put her hand over her mouth and stifled another laugh.

"You, sometimes, make absolutely no sense. But yes, your reading was good." She was smiling. The gym-fears had disappeared. But maybe these fears had caused her semi-Rad Sick focus to careen.

The undergrad kept booming poems of false-bravado. At least one dozen people listened attentively.

She kicked the table's empty chair to signal me to sit. I did.

She leaned over and whispered, "I thought I saw the Invisible Man give you a Christmas present."

I frowned.

"Don't remind me. I'd forgotten about it. I should burn it."

"You kept it? We should see what's inside."

"I think I *will* burn it."

"Seriously. We should see what's in it. I want to see it opened."

"No you don't."

"Suit yourself. Go bury it."

I sighed. She was still smiling. I wanted to kiss her. It had been a long time since I'd felt like kissing, even though I'd been all in love with Elly . . . and then Ryanna before Elly . . . and Ex a little bit . . . all in my own hypocritical way; but the love-impulse had been of anxiety not action.

"I thought you were scared of this Tech Hall stuff," I whispered.

The undergrad continued word-roaring.

"I am. But . . . can't help wondering what's in the package," she said.

"I think that's the point. Kill us with curiosity."

"I know . . . but . . . what if we open it someplace safe?" She blinked. "It won't be so dangerous because we can control what happens."

I'd now gone from super freak to super confused. But at the same time, just like Elly, something made me want to tear open that package and see what hid beneath. The unhinged machinations of the Rad Sick mind had made this pretty package an obsession.

Suddenly Elly slid her chair around the table, wrapped me in her arms, and put her tongue around the rim of my ear.

Parts of me stiffened and tingled.

"O. K.," I said, "Let's make a date. At my place." I could not believe I was saying this. So brave, so unpassive. Maybe when she arrived I'd just tell her I'd lost the present, and then we could fall into each other's arms instead.

"Really. You'd let me watch you open the present?"

"Yes."

"What time tomorrow?"

"*Today* tomorrow or *tomorrow* tomorrow?"

A new poet had taken the stage. Kate didn't introduce her. She hummed her first piece.

Elly beamed. "Six at night! *Tomorrow* tomorrow."

Elly's five words were my new favorite one-line haiku.

Wednesday, November 29, 2000

Tonight we opened the package.

Elly arrived at my doorstep promptly and surprised me with a bottle of red wine. I had, goofily, purchased a half gallon of eggnog but forgotten to buy the liquor to spike it.

Elly's hair was browner than usual; the henna had faded. She'd left her glasses at home.

I used the corkscrew in my Swiss Army knife to pull the cork. I found a few cups. Elly was all smiles, greeted me with a big hug, and the joyous feeling of her squeeze sang in my bones.

We sipped wine, Elly from my one wine glass, I from a freshly-washed tumbler.

"Are the poets still reading at Ravensview?" I asked.

"I think they're planning to read until after New Years," said Elly.

"That'd be them," I said.

She topped off her wine glass.

"So where is it?"

"What?"

"The Christmas present, you goof."

"Oh, you're serious about that thing." I don't know if she could tell I was disappointed. Was she just here to see the surprise package? But then why bring wine?

I had to keep my confidence.

But I also had to please her.

"I'll go dig it out of my closet."

I scurried into the bedroom and dug through my summer clothes on the top shelf of the closet. I didn't own much in the way of winter clothing, so I found myself too often wearing a State U sweatshirt Big Sis had given me years ago. I was wearing it now.

I'd buried the present somewhere in the stacks of shorts and t-shirts: ratty old tops with surfing images; Billy Joel concert t-shirts; cargo shorts; a polo with a cat-face; a Dade Book Fair freebie; a newer shirt with Emily Dickinson's profile. Dig, dig, dig.

My stomach began to hurt. I knew Sombre and Blanco's gift was bad news. I wanted nothing more to do with TallaTec and Tech Hall. I was through with that shit.

"What's taking so long?" shouted Elly from the main room.

I couldn't find it. I was feeling elated. Maybe someone had stolen it! Wonderful! I'd never loved a thief so much in my life.

I lifted up some futbol cleats I hadn't used since I'd arrived in T-town and the package tumbled out, as if the boots had kick it from the shelf.

I caught the box with one hand. I admired the tight wrapping, the kitsch of the Santa Claus paper. I studied again the hand-written tag: *Open Before Xmas!*

My gut instinct was to toss it in the Dumpster.

"You find it?" she asked.

I walked out of the bedroom and sat beside Elly at the table and dropped the box next to the peppershaker.

Elly grabbed the present and studied it.

"Wrapping job looks too good for a couple of dudes."

"I'm sure they didn't do it. It's probably *Part Three* of those Tech Hall assholes' experiments. They probably paid sorority girls to wrap it."

"Don't be sexist."

"I say we burn it," I said.

Elly was quiet, considering.

"Will you let me open it?"

"I don't get it, Elly. You were scared as hell of this shit at the underground pool."

"But nothing really happened there."

"What are you talking about?"

"To us."

"But you said Tuesday we were lucky to have escaped with our lives."

"Exaggeration. I was trying to make conversation. I still wasn't sure how I felt about you after meeting your ex. I was coming up with an excuse for why I couldn't talk to you, but I lost track of it. What can I say, I like you too much."

We stared into each other's eyes. I could see a flash of the deep, deep, barely perceptible glow of her semi-Rad Sickness. As her flame blinked, I thought of Taylor Velázquez, her eyes with a full glow. Would a spark at the end of her severed optic nerve still project Rad light from her empty socket? At this moment Elly's incredible irises *willed* me . . . to act, to please her curiosity, to recognize I made her feel safe (Really? Was I dreaming? *Me?*). She implied a lot with this look: first, trust, a tunnel to the vulnerable place in the heart that only I could protect, and second, a wet kiss.

"I'll open it," I said, somewhat begrudgingly.

I pulled the bow and removed the red ribbon. Elly wrapped it around her ponytail. I used my fingernails to tear into the Santa Claus wrap.

A shoe box hid beneath the paper. Orange twine tied the lid shut. I looked around for something sharp. My keys. Where'd I tossed them? Elly began to work the twine with a fingernail, to see if she could nick it to the breaking point, but the string was resilient.

I finally grabbed the box and used my teeth. Gnawed. Gave the strands a scrape with my incisors. Elly laughed. I gave her a fiendish look.

This was ridiculous. I couldn't even get the Xmas gift *open*. Yes, I should have thrown it in the trash!

But a bicuspid-made notch finally cut a clean path across the grain of the twine's strands, and the string snapped.

The lid was ready to lift.

Open Sesame.

I raised the lid and tossed it like a Frisbee into the kitchen.

Swaddled in tissue paper lay five items:

A skeleton key.

A toy submarine.

Two generic-brand cold capsules.

An index card-sized envelope sealed with Scotch tape.

Inside my head, I breathed a sigh of relief. This didn't seem so bad. I'd been expecting worse. What? Well, easily: rat-motored TallaTec delivery systems; the Invisible Man's visible eyeballs; a photograph of me and Elly being tortured inside a ginormous-fishbowl (damn, Ex had taken the fish with her; I hope she remembers to feed it!); a deadly cloud of TallaTec gas taking us straight to hallucinogenic hell.

Elly picked up the submarine, studied it.

"This is for kids," she said.

I shrugged.

"What's with the old school cold capsules?" she asked. I was suspicious of those too. Pills looked too much like specialized TallaTec delivery systems. They'd crafted TallaTec to smoke (Ash's revelation), and perhaps the time release capsule was stage two. Those tiny rounded cylinders could be the shoebox's ticking time bomb, if we swallowed them.

"You know," she said. "My cousin had one of these." She turned the toy from side to side. "You put capsules in a tiny compartment, and the sub goes up and down underwater. Drifts to the bottom, then floats back up."

Bells rang inside my head. She was right! I'd played with one in the tub when I was little. Big Sis supervised. Had taken the caper quite seriously and been super-nice (she was much younger then, much sweeter, like all humans before their teens). We had pretended it was a nuclear-powered submarine stuffed with ICBMs, churning the great bathtub ocean, working hard to make sure the shores of the faucet were safe. A wet washcloth was a plume of radioactive gas the sub had released to prevent an explosion inside the engine room. A floating bar of soap had been Earth's last iceberg.

"Let's give it a try," I said.

Elly and I strolled into the bathroom and began filling my tub. Alum Village's tubs were on the small-side. On the rare occasion when I decided to take a bath (instead of a shower), I squeezed into the basin with my knees near my chin, as if I'd been plopped into an aluminum wash bucket.

"I've seen bigger sinks," said Elly.

I turned the faucets, let the water roar.

We studied the surface of the toy sub, searching for the tiny compartment to snap inside the cold capsules—*the up/down pills,* as we started calling them.

She dug her fingernail into a tiny notch near the prop.

Presto! A lid hinged open and revealed a spot for two pills, two pretend plutonium pellets to power the sub.

I handed the pills to Elly, and she tapped them into place.

The tub had filled, so I turned off the faucets.

Elly handed me the sub, and I gently . . . ceremoniously . . . placed it on the water's surface.

We watched in silence. Elly put her hands on the tub's rim and leaned over the water, lining her nose up with the submarine's nose. I sat on the toilet lid with my hands folded over my chest. I suddenly felt exhausted.

"I think it's sinking," said Elly.

"No, your mouth's so close, you are blowing it underwater."

She gave me an annoyed look.

"Bubbles are streaming from the propeller. Seriously, it's starting to go down. Come look!"

I stood, my hands on the tub's rim beside hers, my head over the water. Our ears touched.

She was right. It was sinking.

The toy submarine sank like a dead body, a human expelling a last gasp of air. The thing sank an inch every 10 seconds. It was as enthralling as watching ice melt.

Elly and I simultaneously turned our heads towards one another and our chins collided. We laughed. Elly was still the bright sunshine I had kissed in the Ravensview parking lot those months earlier. God, she was gorgeous. She smelled of jasmine and licorice.

I kissed her. She tasted slightly of cherry; her lip gloss glowed.

We started making out while watching the submarine sink.

We must have had our lips glued for minutes, because we laughed and looked down and noted that the sub had touched down and now headed to surface. Slow-blooming, larger air bubbles rose from the toy's nose as the submarine made its ascent. Each grew in size like a kid expanding a gumball bubble, but then it would pop and disappear inside the tub's sea. Quickly, the next air-sphere would form. No part of this process affected the ascent.

Elly and I stood up. We hugged and kissed, forgetting the toy. I edged Elly toward the bathroom door, and we made a slow and careful dance to the bedroom. My heart was banging against my ribs with anxiety and joy. I was all alive. Sinking into her. Elly's fingers sank into my neck and shoulders. Sue me if I no longer gave a shit about *anything*: the submarine, Sombre & Blanco, Tech Hall shenanigans, TallaTec, the Wings Group, my papers, my classes, my professors, my poems, my novel, my fiction, my Rad Sickness. *Our* Rad Sickness!

I pulled Elly on top of me as we fell bed-ward. She was a delicious weight, and I instantly loved how her belt buckle bit into my stomach.

We lay side-by-side, passionately clutching each other, and continuing our kisses as if we thirsted for the radioactive heat at the center of each other's Rad Sick soul.

Here's the point where I think that sonofabitch submarine belched a toxic TallaTec blend. I should have been more suspicious of those bubbles that grew from the sub's nose as the vessel rose. I should have taken heed of the Technicolor hue that rimmed the top surface of each balloon that birthed from below; no, instead, I was too seduced by my seduction of Elly to pay attention to the poison coughing from the unholy machine.

Was Elly affected too? I'm not sure. I think we were both convinced that it was *love* making us see/hear/feel/taste/smell the weird cacophony of twisted everythingness. And, well, I'd definitely *like* to think it was love.

But I'm sure it wasn't. Those Tech Hall bastards were way too slick.

At some point, a darkness folded inside the sounds within my room. This wasn't the full drug-immersion, more like trickles, drops of light, a stop-action film machine projecting micro-second blitzes of TallaTec reality. And all I could hear was the noise—at first I thought *avalanche* (or blood rushing loudly in my ears because I was inside Elly, and I felt as though the world had been reborn, and I was no longer afraid to die), but then the sound was of demolition, of collapse, of steel and concrete and glass melting and shattering and twisting. But all before that, I remember street noise sliced by a dollop of Doppler whir, the long crescendo from airliner engines streaking over the loud cityscape of a humongous, island neighborhood. And when the engines stopped, all exploded. Screaming and falling, screaming and falling. Terror . . . but, again, it was at the edge of my reality; I could only equate it with the monstrous fear I felt making love with anyone for the first time. These screams and explosions were muffled; it's only now in reflection, going over each sound from those moments that I recognized the ignored cacophony: a devastation occurring at some time and place in the future. It signaled an ultimate collapse, as if World Trade Center skyscrapers rumbled into pieces, as if one after another the buildings shook their bricks into dust.

How could have Tech-Hall gotten any data from this little scam with the *up/down pills* whistling in the bathtub? No, I couldn't see the future, but I knew I was hearing it, hearing a Godforsaken catastrophe tapping the Morse code of tomorrow in my ears-drums.

And now I remember something odd about that night. I had the weird sensation that a data collector had hung above us. What springs to mind is Blanco's heavy breathing behind his shadow-colored bandages, his rasping breath so near he must have hung feet first from the corner of the ceiling, as if he were vampire or bat. And his endless moaning about *markets on Monday, markets on Monday* as if it were a pop song lyric. Then Gotham returned in soundscape, but normal this time, as if in the much nearer future, practically tomorrow, with nothing more than cabs honking, tires squealing, pedestrians shouting, basketball's bouncing, newscasters yammering, stockbrokers yelling. Voices mumbling numbers in the thousands. Thousands in the S&P, the NASDAQ, the Dow. Incredible first-of-the-week numbers! The cheering! The laughter! The backs slapped! The hoots of joy!

I was mumbling all that I heard, unintelligibly, but Elly didn't seem to mind, and neither did I.

Because in the forefront of the *all*, all I was experiencing *was Elly*. I would have cried enormous tears of happiness if our night together could have lasted a millennium.

*   *   *

She's just left, and she's all I want to think about—except for the night's background noises, Blanco's words.

I found two strands of Elly's dark brown hair wrapped around the sub in the bottom of the drained tub. She forgot about the rest of the Xmas box's junk; I'm planning on improvising a Yule log and burning what's left.

Sunday, December 3, 2000

United Press International: As a gesture of goodwill, Russian sailors have placed a bouquet of roses on a table atop the U.S. submarine Stonewall Jackson. Taylor Velázquez's surgery has been reported as successful, and though she has lost an eye, there are no other complications. The reasons behind the violent incident between the American navigator and Russian interrogators are still unclear. The Soviets still claim it was an accident, and Lt. Velázquez, after initially implying she was tortured, now remembers nothing. Medical officials attribute her memory loss to complications involving anesthesia.

At this point in the months-long stand-off, tensions have settled between the two nations, but both remain on high alert. Nevertheless, diplomats seem hopeful for eventual resolution.

Taylor, oh, Taylor, without your eye, what can your tongue do? Has your uncanny sense of taste been hurt? Or strengthened?

As kids, we hunted the Bomba-Pop Helado Truck that patrolled the neighborhoods. As a child she was obsessed with all things frozen, from icicles to popsicles. We'd buy our ice cream, sit on spongey St. Augustine grass, and make predictions. She'd try new flavors, asserting correctly, just by the taste, which ones would be discontinued, even when they were popular and delicious. Those days linger in memory: chasing down the Bomba-Pop Trucks, ignoring their side panels painted with a red, white, and blue ICBM-shaped popsicle, pulling out our coins. Sometimes as a treat the Bomba-Pop man gave Taylor a rose-shaped candy, told her she had beautiful eyes. Won't she be just as beautiful with only one?

Monday, December 4, 2000

Facing Finals Week next week. A paper or a creative project due for every class. Friday the 15th, Bigfoot's final.

Yesterday, Elly finally had a day off, so we picnicked in the crabgrass field beside Alum Village; the weather changed to Indian Summer.

For our meal, Elly wanted roast beef, so I made the best Swiss and beef on pumpernickel possible. We laughed and talked beaches and football and landscapes and stockings and trees; we purposely avoided mentioning the Xmas present and the submarine; hopeful we were through with Tech Hall. We kissed and rolled about on a blanket she'd brought. Each of the blanket's patches had stitched guitars or saxophones. We took turns putting a hand on a patch and imitating that instrument with joyful noise.

After she left in the early evening, I got back to studying poetry for Bigfoot's exam. Poems, poems, poems. A phrase reminded me of a line I'd recently read, and I walked away from my anthology and spotted Rand's spiral notebook on the floor. I grabbed it and started skimming. So strange how Rand wrote about the baby in present tense before the girl was even born. But this strangeness and other surprises kept coming. Some of my favorite passages include:

--*We aren't the heroes in our own lives. We are the ones that things happen to, tragic or comic or melodramatic or simple or stupid.*

--*My children tear at my ears and eyes, demand attention always. The demand grows more constant with each growing cell in their bodies reproducing more and more living tissue by the second in order to become larger and longer and louder and more and more full of life. They spring out of control.*

And then I went on a tangential riff and collected all my favorite passages from Rand's notebook and charted them on a blank sheet of paper, arranging and rearranging. And after thirty minutes, as I read lines out loud, the words *fit*! They fit to birth a magnificent poem. I was stoked. Rand's lines had great energy, and my Rad Sick ear had pieced them together. I was Pound to his T. S. Eliot, just as Bigfoot had been describing this term (well, I'm no Pound and Rand's not Tough Shit, but fuck it, we're close enough.).

I called Rand and asked if we could meet because I had something to show him. He suggested a Monday "baby's naptime" coffee at Yak's. I told him I looked forward to tomorrow. Which is now today. I'm off to Yak's.

Just back from Yak's.

Rand at first freaked but then became amazed that I had and had been reading his spiral notebook he'd abandoned in August. He'd felt those pages had been failures. I showed him what I'd found and cobbled together. He nodded and didn't think it was so bad.

"No, better than that!" I said. "I've got a good feeling about this. I can hear the voice here that must be heard by others. You need to put it in the mail to the *Cambridge American*."

"You're kidding. They'd use it to wrap spoiled mullet."

"No! You must send it! Promise me you will send it!"

After a lot of cajoling, Rand promised. We left Yak's an hour later. It was a little after rush hour. Rand took his journal with him; I hope he keeps writing in it. Wild, gorgeous phrases.

In my car, the news blared from the radio. More paranoia about the Soviets building underground missile silos in Afghanistan, but nothing about the Arctic Standoff. Fear because an alligator swallowed two twenty-foot pythons in the Everglades. And celebration for a great day for the markets! The Dow up 3.1%, the NASDAQ up 3.5 %, the S&P up 2.9%. Maybe the Recession would be over soon! Just in time for Christmas!

Waiting at a traffic light, I stared at a row of pear trees, all lit red because of fall's cold, their leaves on fire with pre-winter color, soon to be bare. *Bare. Blank. Blanco.* What had he asked as he'd hung in the corner like a bat?

Markets on Monday?

Thursday, December 7, 2000

Reuters: The first significant action in a month has occurred above the U.S.S. Stonewall Jackson, but no one is sure what it means. KGB operative Egor Volkov set a table and chairs, a bottle of champagne, and a bouquet of roses on the American submarine's deck on Wednesday morning. The table apparently

sat on deck for 24 hours. Neither party acknowledged it. The Americans tossed it
overboard before noon on Thursday.

I dozed and dreamt I heard leather snap against skin. Lt. and First Navigator Taylor Velázquez had donned a khaki eyepatch and a winter formal uniform. On the deck of her submarine she circled a table beneath a moonless sky in the brutal cold and choppy seas. She stopped and examined the flowers one by one.

Who had she been waiting for? The man with the scalpel? Can he reattach her eye?

I can't hear if she shivered or sobbed.

Did she await an apology? One she can taste as she repeats?

I think a lost eye can launch a nuclear holocaust.

I picture that eye floating in a jar, bouncing in boiling fluid, still glowing as if a fluorescent guppy. I can imagine them experimenting, sticking it with syringes to make the orange light leak. I don't know what they'll expect, but they'll surely note the loud clicks of their Geiger counters.

Stay inside your submarine's warm shell, Taylor Velázquez. Let this moment be forgotten, the same as every other Cold War episode.

Friday, December 8, 2000

And then Kurt Mitchell's day was upon us, the hour when Van Gear's basketball boot camp would come to fruition.

Because I'm a dumbass who'd been obsessing about Elly and drowning in term deadlines, I did not anticipate the scale of the event. I'd imagined we'd play HORSE with the big-shot editor and talk craft. But no. We had faculty members decked to play full court.

Doc Primus arrived with Air Jordan high tops. Bigfoot, who'd apparently been a point guard in college, appeared in a John Stockton Utah Jazz jersey. Dirk Falter stepped out without his guitar; instead, he wore

All-Star ABA-style red, white, and blue socks. K-Facto looked set to play center; black sweatbands with Laker emblems adorned his wrists; he practiced his skyhooks from the top of the key.

You could easily have forgotten that Kurt Mitchell was here for an academic gig. A talk and tea and Q&A. That's why Van Gear had brought him here? Yes?

No.

Other faculty and many grad students loitered, perhaps hoping to force a workshop beneath the backboard.

Kurt Mitchell had arrived with Doc Primus, and Mitchell dressed unassumingly. He wore blue Converse, tennis shorts, and a dingy polo with the silhouette of the World Trade Center on the front.

Van Gear ambled from the other side of the court, ignoring Doc Primus; he shook hands with *the pacific*'s Editor.

The V.G. grip was tight; Mitchell winced; Van Gear didn't notice. He wanted his handshake to signal, *Yes, I'm the guy sending manuscripts from Tallahassee who needs you to accept just one,* but also, *I'm the youthful upstart, ready to play ball.*

The pair talked quietly. This was as close as I'd ever seen Van Gear to fawning, but of course the German-Jesus kept it cool.

The air was cold again. A frosty front had swept southward, the kind that never made it down to Dade. My icy fingers twiddled with something in my coat pocket. I yanked it out.

An envelope.

Fuck! I recognized it! The envelope from Blanco's Xmas gift! How on earth had it gotten into my pocket?

I crumpled the thing and jammed it back in. My B-ball game required distraction-free environments.

But I thirsted for distractions. I glanced across the parking lot, searching the cars. I'd invited Elly, but I hoped she wouldn't show. I didn't want to embarrass myself. Plus, Ex was there to root for Ash. The thought of Ex and Elly facing off again terrified me.

With so many faculty, the court felt like an open-air lecture hall. The vibe was weird, and I wasn't sure if intellectualism could hold court—would scholars describe the hoop as the edge of the moon or simply the hole attached to a backboard? Would professors profess or rain field goals? I could do neither. I was sorely out of place.

Doc Primus pulled on a jersey with black and white vertical stripes. He clearly planned to be referee. I suppose this was apt, since he acted as ref in workshops, making sure no one got too sarcastic during discussion. Primus grabbed a loose ball and blew a whistle.

"O. K.," shouted Primus. "Let's choose teams."

Van Gear stepped to the center circle.

"Our guest should be first captain," said Van Gear. He pointed at Kurt Mitchell. "And I will be the other."

There was some grumbling amongst the faculty, but Van Gear stared them down, and the older men fell silent.

"Go head," said Van Gear, gesturing with his chin to Mitchell. "Choose first."

The Great Editor was no fool. He recognized solid athleticism.

He chose Ash.

Van Gear picked Professor K-facto, probably because of his height, hoping the guy could play post and snag rebounds. However, we Wings were hurt; we'd expected one of us chosen next. Willington rolled his eyes.

Mitchell nodded to Dirk Falter—he'd been sinking plenty of shots during warm-ups. Van Gear put a hand on Rand's shoulder.

And the line-ups took shape. Professor Bigfoot was particular-ly annoyed that she was one of the last picks (Van Gear chose her), but the German-Jesus, in his advanced wisdom, made her the starting point guard.

I'd been the last one picked, but I was very pleased to be "6th Man" and ride the pine. Elly hadn't arrived, and I was sad because we could have chatted.

Nearby chimney smoke cut the air as the adjacent neighborhood fools (mostly humanities grad students) burned downed-limbs in their meant-for-lumps-of-coal fireplaces, smoking the sky and their living rooms. The air was bitter. I could feel it in my prematurely old bones; my thumb knuckles throbbed. Gusts ripped across the blacktop.

Doc Primus blew the whistle again. K-facto and Skate stood at center for tip-off. Yes, tall, lazy Skate could play basketball. And so could Kate, who assigned her best two undergrads to maintain the Endless Poetry Reading. She was Mitchell's substitute. Mitchell and Ash were the guards, Jack and Falter were the forwards. Van Gear had Rand and Willington as forwards. He and Bigfoot would play the backcourt.

Skate won the tip. Jack snagged it and tossed it to Mitchell. The Great Editor dribbled as if wedded to the ball. Bigfoot covered him, defending tightly. She was giving no slack. From the onset, it was clear this was no friendly match: the game would be a battle for Creative Writing Supremacy!

Mitchell tossed it to a breaking Jack, but Rand had him covered, so Jack sent it back to Mitchell who rifled it across court to a breaking Ash . . . but Van Gear, the B-ball sage, read it perfectly, intercepted the pass, and raced down court.

Van Gear's ankle injury had miraculously healed. He headed to the rim at full-sprint, faster than I'd ever seen him gallop.

Boom: lay-up!

He backpedaled quickly as he returned to defense, rejuvenated. I could see the years melting off the ol' German-Jesus.

Mitchell dribbled up court, concentration scrunching his face. He wanted to take control. He charged down the lane towards the rim, faked a pass to Skate, pulled up short, and sank a ten-footer. Mitchell held up a fist.

Tie game. The faculty on the sideline clapped. They politely rooted for the Guest Speaker.

After that burst of applause, we and Van G. became the grad student's de facto team to cheer.

Bigfoot glided to the center circle with the ball, tossed it to Van Gear, and he tossed it right back. Ash was giving her way too much space. She suddenly stepped back and launched an arching bomb that clipped nothing but net.

The grad students, the sideline's majority, shouted and hooted.

Mitchell and Falter were agitated. The game's intensity upped a notch.

Things got rough. At one point, Willington deliberately fouled Falter, and within heartbeats Falter slammed into Rand.

Doc Primus blew his whistle.

"That's a technical foul," he said, and pointed to Willington.

The crowd roared, a mix of cheers and dismay.

Van Gear lost his shit.

"What about Dirk's plowing into Rand Salt?!? That's what deserved the technical!"

Doc Primus shook his head in his knowing way, made a brief comment about the hour's *blusteriness*, and pointed at Mitchell to take two free throws.

The Great Editor sank them.

The game was tied at 15 when Doc Primus called a long timeout. I'm not sure if he was keeping careful track of the match's half. The players were antsy; no one wanted a breather.

Almost no one. Rand leaned forward, hands on knees, straining to catch his breath. I asked if he wanted me to spell him, but he said no. JAM walked over with their lovely baby in her arms and kissed Rand. Rand kissed JAM and then the infant. The child stared into the night sky. Dill gave his stepdad a high-five. Rand's breathing calmed.

I fumbled with the crumpled letter in my pocket, having forgotten it, now wondering why I didn't throw it in the trash. I wanted Elly here to help me, because a big part of me felt tempted to split the envelope open and read it.

232

As always, heavy Rad Sick retardation leaned heavily on my decision-making apparatus. Instead of acting, I scanned the setting.

Willington talked to Professors K-facto and Bigfoot, and they debated strategy, or maybe they argued a post-modern take on T. S. Eliot. Kate and Skate hugged to keep warm. Kurt Mitchell, Van Gear, and Doc Primus had a serious center-court discussion, either about inconsistent foul calls, or dirty realism in short fiction. Jack and Ash shared a cigarette that I hoped packed nothing more potent than tobacco.

An orange, black-lined moon floated in the sky. The moon hung above Orion's Belt, a three-point shot ready to swish.

I tore a thin strip from the envelope's edge, further tempting myself. The envelope now hung open, luring me into Tech Hall's TallaTec trap. I fought my impulses, glanced across the blacktop.

The court's sidelines were now a party. The grad students talked and joked, as if it were a break between readers at Ravensview. Someone passed around spiked punch in a milk jug. A faculty member hoisted the thermos of wassail. The professors joined degree candidates to make holiday jokes. I caught a glimpse of JAM, Vicky, and Ex having a cheery chat. The scene felt joyous!

Skate and Kate walked over to say *Hello! Happy Christmas!*

"Yo, what'cha got in the envelope?" asked Skate.

"A Christmas card," I said.

"Who from?" asked Kate.

Why did they care? They were so weird sometimes. Weirdly nosey.

"Don't know exactly," I said.

"Considering the score, maybe it's a new game plan from the Spirit of Christmas Future," quipped Kate.

"I suspect it's mostly bullshit," I said.

"Bullshit for Christmas? Have you been naughty? Got on Santa's shit list?" asked Kate.

"Bet your game's gone to shit, freezing your ass off on the side-

233

lines," said Skate.

Since when had this pair been so competitive? Were they that rare breed of grad student who wasted weekends shouting fight-songs around the gridiron green?

"Game is tied," I said, apropos of nothing, hoping to change the subject.

"Yo, bro," said Skate. "I'm jonsing to see what's in the envelope. Break that shit open."

Skate's obnoxious surf-talk made me want to punch him. His fiction in the workshops leaned heavy on a California clang.

But he was right. The friggin envelope. What the Hell. I jammed my finger into the slit and ripped open my universe once again. The basketball moon was halfway through the three-star rim. The wind gusted hard; as it died, smoke from nearby chimneys drifted over the court with a pine-smoke fog. The backboards wavered in and out of focus.

The Xmas card had the university logo plastered over a generic holiday tree. A blue star stood at its top.

"What's it say?" asked Kate. "Let's see."

Skate, being his usual annoying self, snatched the card and read the handwritten inscription aloud.

"Christmas Day Invitation: Come to the "Hillevi Gym" for a reception at the Indoor Pool for those graduate students who will remain in town for the holidays."

Oh my God. Such an obvious trap. Did they really think I was that stupid?

"Festivities begin at noon on December 25th. Bring a gift for the Secret Santa Exchange, if you wish. Nonalcoholic beverages and holiday snacks will be served. Each invitee may bring one guest."

"Bring me!" shouted Kate.

Skate shot her a dirty look, but then returned to his oration.

"All invitees should RSVP by noon on December 23rd. Please dress business casual or Holiday Formal (Ho, Ho, Ho!). And don't forget to bring your key

for the Christmas Raffle."

"Why can't I go?" said Kate to Skate.

He handed the card back to me.

"Because we're going to your folk's for Christmas."

"Oh yeah," said Kate with odd disappointment. Maybe she was stoned, had caught a contact high from Skate's TallaTec habit.

"And I wouldn't let you go to no *key party*. Come on, 1975 called and wants its shindig back."

I ignored the pair and scrunched the envelope and card into my jacket pocket.

Doc Primus blew his whistle. The second half began.

For now I'd squelch Xmas pool party nightmares.

On the first possession Mitchell drove down the lane and scored on a reverse layup. Van Gear cursed because he'd been defending shoulder to shoulder. At the restart he sent the ball to Bigfoot but immediately signaled for a pass back. He caught the ball one handed and casually drifted past the center circle, studying the defense.

Van Gear dribbled down the sideline, and Rand swept past him, taking the guard role. Mitchell followed Van Gear. Ash leaned towards Rand, but it was a feint. He closed in on V.G. like a Venus flytrap.

Van Gear was trapped, meat in a Mitchell and Ash sandwich. Tall Ash tenaciously positioned for a steal.

Bitter gusts swept the court clear of fog. The smoke smell vanished.

The crowd was going crazy. More grad students trickled in, lining every inch of court perimeter. I stood with the wall of bodies, my heels on the boundary line. The knitting woman from Doc Primus' Wednesday workshop stood nearby, sewing a colorful quilt that I hoped she'd offer; after all, I was, as Skate noted, the *freezing* benchwarmer.

Van Gear's teammates sprinted into openings, but he couldn't find space to pass. Jack, Skate, and Falter played a zone defense hardier than the Berlin Wall.

The double team swamped Van Gear. Ash readied for a steal, but V.G. swung his body to land an elbow directly to Ash's sternum, and then he dropped the ball and tilted ground-ward like a tree clipped at its roots, as if he'd been the one roughed up.

Doc Primus' whistle screamed. The crowded roared; emotions mixed; spectators bellowed in confusion. Wassail and punch were spilled!

"That's a *technical*," shouted Doc Primus.

"Sorry," said Van Gear to Ash. The anger left the philosopher's eyes, but he bore the hurt look of the betrayed.

V.G. didn't argue the call. He bounced the ball to Mitchell.

"Take your shots," said the German-Jesus.

"Air ball! Air ball! Aiiiiiirrrrrrrrr baaaaaaaaaaaaaaalllllllllll! Aiiiiiiiiiiiirrrrrr baaaaaaaalllllllll!" came the chant from the sidelines.

The game's tension rose higher than the basketball moon.

Mitchell nailed both shots. The crowd quieted.

Then the tone changed again. Bigfoot stole the ball from a gasping Dirk Falter after the inbound pass, and she sailed a bomb to Rand who streaked down the court. Ash raced at his heels.

Rand's legs awkwardly tangled on a misstep and his left foot twisted. He groaned as he collided with Ash. The ball rolled out of bounds. The two fell hard, Ash's head landing on Rand's stomach.

Primus blew his whistle.

Ash pulled Rand from the asphalt, but it was clear that Rand's left foot hurt. He gritted his teeth.

He'd mangled his instep.

"I'm done," said Rand. And he limped to the sidelines; his family greeted him, JAM, Dill, and baby.

Rand slapped me on the shoulder as he hobbled past.

"You're in," he told me.

And so I was.

Bigfoot directed me to cover Jack. I smiled at him, but he stared right through me.

Jack received a pass from Mitchell and dribbled aggressively, lumbered toward me as if an angry Quasimodo. A good act. But I was determined to appear strong; I'd not let Jack score an easy bucket.

Mitchell raced past hoping to give Jack an outlet pass, but Van Gear stuck tight on the Great Editor, as if a shadow, a ghost.

Van Gear, breathing hard, looked pale, seemingly worried that we were on the precipice of falling further behind.

Jack shuffled left and right, still dribbling.

The crowd noise grew. I worked to keep my concentration, but I was realizing we had as many people packed around the court as we had inside Ravensview. We were "reading" the great poetry of basketball and they were listening. What's that Houseman poem about the athlete dying young? Were we all here to experience some sort of human sacrifice? The sacrifice of the spirit to sport? Each bounce of the ball like a ticking clock, the slow rhythm of a poem read, the sound speaking to us like Homer spoke to the stoned worshippers at his feet (hmmm, what was the ancient Greek's TallaTec?). Homer was blind in the same way that I am blind to the future, but unlike him, I can *hear* the future, can't I? But why hadn't I heard within Jack's dribble the sound of his next move.

Jack sprang his body around, looking to fire a pass to Falter across court who'd given Willington the slip. Jack launched the ball hard.

I timed my jump perfectly. The ball stung my right palm as if one hundred bee stings. The bones and tendons in my elbow popped. My shoulder creaked. My old-before-their-time joints throbbed. The ball had stopping spinning as it fountained above me. I pivoted on a heel and snagged it. The leather felt amazingly smooth.

"Here!" shouted Van Gear.

I looked up, and V. G. sprinted down the court, alone, no defender within 50 feet. He was making a beeline for the post.

I launched the ball with both hands, sending it full force, hoping to time my throw so he'd not break stride.

Maybe I threw it a touch too hard.

Van Gear's pale face grew whiter as he watched the ball leave my fingers; his eyes widened. He knew he'd have to give chase, put on the proverbial afterburners to catch the errant throw.

The crowd's voice swelled. They awaited an electrifying Van Gear catch and dunk.

His legs pumped as if pistons bordering on the redline of a tachometer.

Why did it seem as though the chimney smoke on the court settled just above his head? Why did the wind go silent? The far side's backboard blurred in the reformed fog.

Van Gear stretched both his hands high into the air, hoping to save the ball from the boundary. He leapt, just in front of the rim, straight up. He became taller, super-sized.

Up he went. The ball landed on his palms. He grimaced as he pushed his hands together.

But the ball sprang loose, as if it were a stunned bird, and tumbled downward.

And Van Gear fell simultaneously, splayed, as if sucker punched. The two hit the asphalt at the same instant, but the ball leapt up and Van Gear did not.

On the sidelines, silence. We held our breaths. He didn't move.

He'd landed hard on his ribs and shoulder.

He made no sound. He did not roll onto his back or chest. His skin was pale, his eyes shut.

And then people rushed in. Rand and Willington got to Van Gear first and kneeled beside him. Doc Primus and Kurt Mitchell came up quickly, followed by Jack and Ash and the rest.

I hung back a bit. I feared the worst. Why hadn't I heard this coming?

But then I realized I had.

Just as I'd released the ball, I'd suddenly had a premonition of absolute silence, the whole universe going still. One heartbeat, disappeared.

We were at the hospital again. But there was no joy. We Wings stood outside the ER's doors waiting to hear the inevitable. JAM was crying. Jack had his head in his hands. The rest of us milled around aimlessly. Gloom darkened our faces.

The docs appeared, gave the news in hushed voices.

Van Gear was dead. A heart attack.

We were stunned. How could a 39-year-old have a heart attack?

A congenital disease.

No one said anything. K-facto and his wife, the poet Bella, were the first to leave, looking devastated. Bella was in tears. I hadn't known they'd known Van Gear that well.

A naive thought. After all, we were all in tears, or at least glassy-eyed in the solemn way of the stoic mourner. My gut burned. Kurt Mitchell sat on a chair staring at the floor, shaking his head.

And, too, *we all* knew Van Gear that well. He was a main constant in the T-town writing community, a stalwart guy, kind to everyone, respectful of all, only breaking form at Wings, on the B-ball court, or around Falter or Primus. The shockwave of Van Gear's death would shake the foundation of our community for months. And for Wings, the scar would last forever.

Wednesday, December 13, 2000

<u>Associated Press</u>: Observers report the suspected Soviet torturer of Lt. Velázquez, identified as KGB officer Egor Volkov, has appeared alone atop the U.S.S. Stonewall Jackson. He had set the table and chairs upon the detained U.S. submarine's deck on December 3rd and 7th.

In contrast to Lt. Velázquez's formal uniform from Thursday, the Russian captain, who's been the most apologetic of the Soviet spokespeople, wore a ragged, heavy, black wool coat and maroon hat. Some sources claim he held a single rose.

After initially being spotted at sunset near the U.S. sub's conning tower, the Russian officer returned to his own ship an hour later.

I make nothing of this report. Van Gear is dead. Taylor, though eyeless by one, still lives. I want to wish the Russian bastard ill, but I haven't the heart to hate. I'm swamped in finals week, and I'm having a hard enough time getting everything done while not letting Van Gear's death overwhelm me.

Sunday, December 17, 2000

Lately, I've been spending a lot of time alone, sometimes at Alum Village but mostly at Elly's. I try to finish the books I didn't quite finish for classes, but more often than not, I fall asleep. My mind is a blank. I'm so exhausted from finals: the papers, the rewrites, the fiction, the essay exams, and all other distractions. I can't get going on *Microwaves* or even tweak "Surf-boy." Of course, the main weight is Van Gear. Memories of him keep me in half-waking moments like a fierce wave continuously breaking on my spirit and I'm pummeled to depths where I cannot breathe. In dreams his face hides beneath a reef's ledge; though trapped, he looks determined, as when he read that night at Ravensview. I'm kicking and kicking to force myself downward, but instead I'm drifting up and away; the sea's depths become blurry. I awake with an aching chest and ankle.

I did visit Rand and JAM one afternoon recently while Elly worked the lunch shift. They were showing me computers they'd just got as gifts from family, explaining the bells and whistles of the new word processing software. Rand kept saying, *Well, they're just glorified typewriters, aren't they?* But he was obsessed with the templates, that and the latest version of a popular ICBM-warfare game. JAM was searching with the latest web browser, *FrugalGate.*

Within this wired thing called The Internet, JAM says good journalism boils up. In something called Gerry's Guide to Underground World News, JAM has found interesting reports. Rand say it's all conspiracy theories. But JAM shows me articles related to the Arctic standoff. How did she know I might be interested? Maybe she's intrigued, having caught the headline on page 16 in Sunday's *Times* noting the story of unopened champagne atop the U.S.S. Stonewall Jackson.

Perhaps a lovers' quarrel on the icy sea? she asks rhetorically. She pauses, hearing from another room the napping baby's murmur, but then quiet returns. *This is better than the intrigues in classic fiction, don't you think?* I'm not sure Taylor Velázquez would agree.

Maybe this story has stirred JAM's creativity, launched a haiku or villanelle.

I read over her shoulder and note speculation about others attempting power plays. What other possible actors, forgotten in this strange moment in history, could sneak into view? Somewhere on the globe, as the naval stand-off in the Arctic drips and drips, countries with chips on their shoulders are polishing their own artillery, their own jets, their own bombs. Could China attack? Or Pakistan? Chechen rebels in the North Caucasus make a play? North Korea or India? Covert groups hiding in sands of the desert?

I was intrigued for a moment, but then I could absorb none of it. I'm glad Elly and I are together and solid; having her shoulder to lean on has really helped in recovering from the autumn's shocks, from Van Gear's death to Bigfoot's final, from Taylor's missing eye to Tech Hall's traps.

Gerry's Guide to Underground World News: Anonymous CIA sources hint at something afoot within subversive agents from outside the U.S. and Russia, including possible terrorist attacks. Though officials have denied it, intelligence leaks indicate "intercepted chatter" referencing the current Arctic standoff. The intercepted communications indicate a tie to stories from 1999 in Moscowistan concerning missing aircraft, a Tupolev Tu-160 White Swan, and other military devices. At that time Moscowistani generals had claimed these reports were unfounded. However, U.S. Intelligence disagreed.

Would Taylor and her crewmates have been briefed on subversives? The Russians too? Is it relevant? Or simply distraction? I want to picture Taylor rolling her one eye on this reported intelligence. I imagine her smiling. One eye, gleeful.

Wednesday, December 20, 2000

I spent this afternoon at Ravensview, keeping Elly company as she worked. I've been doing this regularly since the term ended, usually for about two hours. Today I stayed from noon to nine. Elly and I had long chats when things got slow.

Business was light but steady. The lunch crowd swelled and disappeared, followed by the supper throng, and then the drinkers trickled in around eight.

Willington, by happenstance, appeared. He had a folded newspaper under his arm. He needed a drink. He'd just returned from an interview in Georgia. He wasn't sure how it'd gone. It was with Southeastern Central University. He was anxious as hell; he really needed a job. He had interviews lined up at a convention in late December, but wanted the search finished, a job in hand. The pressure ate at him; his wife was tired of supporting the family on the modest salary of an engineering firm's executive assistant. Sweat beaded over Willington's eyebrows as he drank his gin and tonic. He fidgeted with the paper on the table.

I offered encouragement. I sounded lame, clichéd, but he appreciated my listening. We talked about Van Gear a little, what a damn shame it was he'd died so young, just when he'd hit his stride.

Elly checked on us. She was cheerful, but measured. Though T-town bustled through the holiday, Ravensview did not feel festive. Students comprised too much of its core crowd, so the atmosphere flattened in December.

After bringing Willington a second gin, Elly chatted for a minute, then hurried off to seat a large party. Willington stared at his drink.

"Can't help thinking about Van Gear's argument: writer or teacher? Not both."

I shrugged my shoulders. What'd I know? I'd never taught.

"I always argued he was wrong, but now," said Willington, ". . . I'm not so sure." He pulled at his scruffy beard. "Why can't I just sit behind a typewriter and write? What's wrong with that?"

"You've got a wife and kids. Responsibility."

"Should go back to journalism. Because that's what I did, *sat behind a typewriter and wrote!*"

"Why'd you quit?"

"Wanted to write a novel. That romantic, artistic bullshit."

"Regrets?"

"I don't know."

I sipped my beer while Willington swirled his drink.

"I think that's what Van Gear held in high esteem, that romantic bull," I said.

"I know, I know. But sometimes I miss reporting." He opened the newspaper and flipped to the back pages. "Getting tips from contacts, wondering if it's crap, but then following your gut to see where it leads." He folded the newspaper in half and turned it to a short article on the bottom of page 10. "What do you make of this? Bullshit? Or the glimmer of something bigger?"

United Press International: U.S. surveillance radar spotted a decommissioned Russian bomber flying over the edge of Siberia, according to sources. The plane had no national designation, but apparently had clearance to fly over Soviet airspace. However, no one seems certain of the bomber's purpose or allegiance. Neither the U.S. nor the Soviet governments acknowledge the plane's existence.

"See how's it's buried on this page, because it may become *nada*, and they hope nobody notices if that's the case? But if it's got validity, this could be tomorrow's headline," said Willington.

"You follow the Cold War?"

"Can't help it. I'm an ex-journalist."

"Me too."

"A journalist?"

"No, just follow the Cold War."

Willington nodded and rolled up the paper. He left soon after. Made me feel less lonely to realize other people paid attention to the ever unfolding Cold War.

After an hour I gave Elly a quick kiss goodbye and headed into a chilly, rainy evening.

Saturday, December 23, 2000

United Press International: *A high-altitude airplane of unknown origin dropped an atomic device on the Arctic standoff between the U.S. and the U.S.S.R today, sources said. However, the bomb's explosion was contained by an Anti-H launched from the U.S.S. Stonewall Jackson.*

Neither government will confirm nor deny the incident.

Observers claim that at noon U.S. officer Lt. Taylor Velázquez appeared on the sub's deck. A Soviet sailor boarded the submarine from the Russian Piranha. After ten minutes of conversation, the U.S. sailor pulled a six foot device from a hidden compartment on the sub's conning tower. Velázquez aimed the object at the horizon with the Russian's help, and a shoulder-launched missile sprang skyward.

Sources confirm that two fireballs from approximately 5.2 megaton explosions lit the high atmosphere for two minutes early Saturday morning, accompanied by rising mushroom clouds. While some sources say Egor Volkov was the Russian, others only report Velázquez and the Russian are missing. However, neither government has confirmed nor denied the fireballs, and neither military has acknowledged either sailor's whereabouts, except to say they're performing assigned duties.

If this is true, O, the ironies. Taylor launching expertly, unerringly, the life-saving Anti-H, unlike the poor idiot who shot his too low and for no reason in 1980, creating our Rad Sickness. But if not for the Rad Sick condition, she would have never tasted the charged air molecules of the future, would never have sprung for an Anti-H.

No officials have confirmed witnesses' statements.

No surprise there.

And they've said nothing about the *USA Today*'s blurry snow-dotted photo on page one showing a figure propping a rocket launcher on a shoulder, and a large, red-hatted soul kneeling beside.

From the photograph, I can imagine what transpired before the two blasts lit a volcano of Northern Lights.

First, happenstance played a part, as the two simultaneously stepped outside on the eve of Christmas Eve as flurries fell.

When they saw one another, so much must have swam through their minds. The horrible act. The gift of roses. Apology. Forgiveness.

As they faced each other, feeling the arctic cold tighten the cells in their bones, phrases would have been exchanged. Each word within the frozen air slowing time to a standstill.

And after a few minutes, something must have latched itself to Taylor's tongue, first a prick, like a dot of pepper, and then a slithering snake of bitterness, a spit of bile, a film that wasn't there but soon would be.

When she fully recognized this taste from the future, she'd have known it was neither pepper nor bile, but metal. She'd have had the sensation of aluminum foil wrapped around her tongue, the clear taste of a radiation plume.

She'd have made him stop talking. Forced herself, despite the shock, to carefully think through this scenario-to-come. From where would the blast originate? An explosion from an engine room? A triggered torpedo or rocket? Then within seconds another flavor offered a clue: the charred gasoline and formaldehyde taste of jet fuel!

A leaky bomber soared high above, minutes from its target.

Next, she'd have commanded action, words that convinced the Russian of the moment's gravity. She'd have pulled the man to the conning tower, made him close his eyes as she unlocked the Anti-H.

Positioning the rocket launcher would have been hard with the thickening flurry, whitecaps rocking the deck. She'd have needed his help.

In this case, such sweet irony to know the future just minutes before it becomes the now. The Rad Sick curse fully a Rad Sick blessing. Taylor knew what needed done; her prescience told her the exact moment to pull the trigger.

Taylor Velázquez and her Soviet torturer, aimed the Anti-H perfectly, a launch that prevented annihilation, that stopped countless deaths.

But this evening's TV news gives a different official story. Both governments claim a secret joint U.S./Russia space venture, the NASA-Soyuz Project, suffered a nearby accident. Two booster engines failed consecutively on the orbiter vehicle, creating two explosions in the Arctic sky. This disaster cost the lives of two Cosmonauts and one Astronaut. Additionally, several crew members at the U.S./Soviet standoff are unaccounted for.

But I know the truth. I can hear it in Taylor's impatient foot-tapping on deck as her rocket pierces the sky, my ear now recalling the sound from last night's dreams. There's no secret space venture. Both nations will race to solve the secret of the bomber pilot's origins, but details will never come to light.

In the meantime, the Arctic Standoff is officially over.

And wherever Taylor Velázquez is, she who has sacrificed all for us, bless her.

Bless her.

Sunday, December 24th, 2000

I had nowhere to go for Christmas, because Big Sis landed a job in New York. Near the World Trade Center.

She needed an affordable apartment. Immediately! Time to search Brooklyn with Mom and Dad. Get her settled before January.

My parents half-heartedly suggested I go along, but the arrangement didn't look too jolly. I was happy for Big Sis and would have liked to celebrate, but the four of us trapped in a car and a cramped hotel room didn't sound joyous.

So here I was. Stuck in T-town for the holidays. Almost as if Tech Hall had planned it.

The invitation from the University had sat on my dining room table all month. The card's blue Xmas star hadn't faded.

Though I'd been in Elly's orbit 24-7, I'd failed to mention the invitation until recently. She was staying in town because she had to work, didn't want to lose her job. That made me lucky because I could surround myself with her smiling face. Nevertheless, I'd kept the card hidden from her, which was stupid, because if I was going to ask anyone to go, it would be Elly. But after the underground pool's weirdness, I was sure she'd be terrified to return, despite how she'd been so damn curious about Blanco's Xmas present.

It was bizarre and absurd and against all logical impulses, but for some idiotic reason, I obsessed about the Xmas reception. Rad Sicks have many stupid-streaks, including obsessive curiosity about the ridiculous. A group of us in our eleventh year had dug an eight-foot deep hole searching for blast-diamonds, because a damaged, tilted, and forgotten hotel's neon Peter Pan pointed at the spot. Obviously, we thought Pan's finger directed us. We worked a fortnight and found nothing. It may be this same curiosity-streak, Taylor's obsession with all things frozen, ice cream and snow, that led her outside on the 23rd , an obsession that has apparently resolved the Arctic Standoff, despite the mysterious shenanigans. Whatever the case, I should be more attuned to the cliché of curiosity and dead cats. But

I'm not.

Also, because I loved Elly so, I felt sure her all-encompassing love would shield us, like the layers of reinforced steel surrounding a nuclear reactor's core. In other words, together we'd be safe. Didn't she often imply as much?

All the same, I'd only go to the reception if Elly joined me.

Truth was, Elly and I had become inseparable. Ever since Van Gear's death I was relieved to spend swaths of time with Elly. It was weird; for so much of my life I'd been a guy who'd thrived solo. But now, the lingering sadness of Van Gear's passing made me feel broken.

When I'd left the hospital that day, I'd gone to Ravensview to tell Elly, and I found her at a table folding napkins. She teared up when she heard the news. She'd probably had a crush on Van Gear like every other female in T-town. But I wasn't jealous. I started crying too. Big gushing sobs. I loved Van Gear. I loved all the Wings, but especially him.

As soon as I'd broken the news, she'd gone on break, and as we'd stood together in the parking lot, she'd rambled about an uncle she missed, who'd died young, her dad's brother. He'd actually been the one who had first propped her on his feet and made her spread her arms as if an eagle as he tilted legs to the left and then the right. He was the one who bought her an acoustic guitar and taught her chords and blues scales. They played folk and rock songs together. She adored him. Maybe he looked a little like Van Gear. At least he had long hair too. His name was Uncle Michael. And he taught her how to play "Norwegian Wood," and they sang it together when she was eleven. "Norwegian Wood" was the Beatles song Van Gear played that night back in September.

After ten minutes she'd returned to work, and I'd stood there holding a cigarette in my hand that I refused to light.

Since the day of the basketball game, Elly and I had either been hanging out at in her tiny house on Sharkey Street, within the cinderblocks of Alum Village, or at Ravensview. As she worked, I sat in a booth ordering water after water, and occasionally a draft beer and a plate of carrots.

I'd bring my journal, but I couldn't write. Too much had deflated me earlier in the month, including a wall-to-wall rewrite of "Surf-boy" for the fiction workshop; a long paper on Vonnegut, Walker Percy, and Monasticism for Falter; a short paper on the kite in Beckett's *Murphy*; the endless studying for Bigfoot's poetry final—and, of course, Van Gear's death.

Most recently the 23rd's weird events, that may or may not involve Taylor Velázquez launching an Anti-H into the frozen north and preventing catastrophe and ending stalemate, had me briefly writing again, mostly about Rad Sickness and its potentiality. But the topic grated on me quickly. In my mind, she's made us significant again, and that's enough. Instead, I will write my *now* in T-town.

Now includes last week when I mentioned the invite to Elly. During a particularly slow Ravensview Thursday night, I sat at a booth nibbling a plate of steamed vegetables and sipping a glass of water. On impulse, I finally popped the question.

About the Xmas gig.

The evening was slow. I was Elly's only table. She sat beside me while bartender Kelt leaned on a stool and stared at the Netscam Neutron Bowl on TV.

She was doing some prep-work: wrapping paper napkins around spotted silverware.

"How are those veggies?" she asked. "The cauliflowers came out looking like brain coral seared by lava."

"That's original," I said.

"Been hanging around writer types too much." She smiled. "So, when are you going to let me read *Microwaves*?"

"That? I need to burn that with the Yule log. We can light it in your tiny fireplace."

"As long as the log's the size of a hotdog. I'm not up for another smoke-out." We'd burned too much wood two nights before in Elly's fireplace-meant-for-coal—the house filled with smoke. The moment reminded me so much of the basketball game, I teared up; Elly had thought the smoke made me cry.

"About the holidays. I've actually got an invite for Christmas Day."

"Really?" She seemed genuinely surprised. And curious. "Who from?"

"The big U."

"You're kidding."

"No, it's actually signed by the President and everything."

"You're pulling my leg. What are you really talking about?"

"It was part of the Xmas present shit. One of the things we didn't look at."

"The envelope?"

"Exactly."

"It wasn't instructions for the toy submarine?"

"No. It was an official-looking invitation to go to a holiday reception on campus for grad students stuck in town."

"Right! Like us! Well, you anyway."

"Yes."

"Where's the party?"

I hesitated. Glanced up at the ceiling.

"Well?" Elly asked.

"The Gym. At the underground pool."

"That's very weird."

"I know."

"You're not going, are you?"

"Well. . . ."

Elly looked at me with intense incredulity. She stood, dropped three spoons on the table (they clattered like breaking glass), and walked away. Kelt looked up from his football game, glanced at us, then lost interest. Elly stalked into the kitchen, came back seconds later with a huge stack of paper napkins, slammed herself back into the booth across from me, and started wrapping the silverware at a higher gear.

She was angrier than she had been about Ex.

"Are you crazy?" she asked.

"But you're the one who'd wanted to open the Xmas present in the first place."

"That's totally different, and you know it."

 I did?

"But what if you go with me?" I asked.

"What? Me go too? Are you totally fucking crazy?"

"I know. I know. But. . . ."

"But what? You're a lunatic. You should leave."

"But they want me to bring the key."

"Key?"

"From the package. The skeleton key. Remember?"

"For what reason?"

"I think it's for Secret Santa or something like that."

"You are *not* going to that reception."

She was right. I was being stupid. Crazy stupid. Inside my skull a bulb flashed red and told me DANGER! DANGER! DANGER!

What was wrong with me? Could this Rad Sick stupid-streak, this asinine curiosity about labyrinthine silliness, be so intensely fixed? Of course, at the moment, it didn't seem to be affecting Elly. But she was only half-Rad.

"And what brings you two here on such a blustery night?" said a voice. I turned.

Doc Primus stood there, doing his usual head nod, observing us with his impish smile.

I was still a little mad at his iffy calls as basketball referee. He did, though, appear crestfallen when he'd realized how bad-off Van Gear was—maybe even regreted the uneven relationship they'd had. He'd arranged an impromptu memorial service in the English Department lounge the day after the tragedy to ensure that Kurt Mitchell could attend. We'd all been so somber. Food had sat untouched.

I turned in the booth to face Doc Primus and tried to smile.

"Elly works here fulltime, and I'm here hanging out for the holidays."

"Inside Ravensview? Is the World's Longest Poetry Reading still going on upstairs?"

"No, I think they're taking a break. I think they're allowed to take an eight day hiatus for religious reasons, according to the Guinness Book of World Records."

"Splendid," said Doc Primus. He nodded knowingly, and then, oddly, he slipped into the booth, squeezed next to Elly, and faced me with an unnerving stare. Elly slid over a foot.

"So you're still in town." said Doc Primus.

"Family's away for a trip to New York, and I didn't want to go."

"So you're in town through Christmas?"

"And probably through New Year's too."

Again, the knowing nod.

"There's a holiday reception for grad students on Christmas; have you heard? They've designed it specifically for the lonely souls who can't leave town for one reason or another." Primus looked at me, then Elly, then back to me. He shrugged.

"I was planning to go," said Primus. "They've requested that I attend, actually. Do you two need a ride? I can certainly give you a lift."

"I might have to work that night," said Elly.

"It's in the early afternoon, I believe," said Primus.

"I always have prep work to do."

"Oh," Primus paused, then turned to me. "How about you? Would you like to go?"

"I'm not 100% sure," I said.

"You can't spend the entire holiday season folded into a booth," he said.

"Maybe," I said.

"Where do you live? Alum Village? I can pick you up there."

Elly and I were silent, as if both hit by a stun gun Doc Primus had kept stashed in his overcoat.

Doc Primus snatched a napkin from the table's dispenser and whipped a pen from his shirt pocket.

"What's your apartment number?" he asked.

I gave it to him.

Elly shot me enough stink-eye to fill a sinkhole. Her irises blasted me with anger, and I deserved it.

Moreover, paranoia crept in. I was 99% sure Primus knew I was Rad Sick. That being the case, could it mean he was in on Tech Hall's plots? Could I trust this sage of prose? Doubts bounced between my ears.

But wasn't Doc Primus just being nice? If he was going, maybe the event was actually legit, and Tech Hall had nothing to do with it.

Who knows. So anyway, that's where things stand.

Tonight is Christmas Eve. Tomorrow is the day. Elly and I have said nothing about the university's holiday reception. Instead, we've been spending a quiet night at my place. At eleven we sipped plain egg nog and hummed carols around a star-shaped candle.

All's been mild.

Silent.

Monday, December 25th, 2000

This morning, Elly and I dressed for the Holiday Reception. As the invitation requested we dressed business casual, not in suit or high heels, but more formal than everyday.

Elly decided to go as safeguard, maybe we'd somehow safeguard each other. She wasn't scheduled for work anyway; plus, she didn't want to be alone Christmas Day.

Doc Primus picked us up in his creaky, Volvo station wagon that had recently been painted a bright red to hide layers of rust and scratches.

As we pulled away from Alum Village, I leaned forward to whisper into Elly's ear, *You're brilliant and beautiful.* She was, always. She'd decided not to wear her glasses and to wear her brown hair in a bun, as she'd done Xmas Eve. She'd been my apartment's bright star all night.

Doc Primus chit-chatted with us as he drove. He asked if we'd seen the new Brandelsonna film. I hadn't known it was playing.

As Primus and Elly talked about movies, I recalled a conversation that we Wings had had outside the hospital doors after Van Gear's death. Willington was in an understandably sad, contemplative state, and he started to make a comparison to what we'd just experienced to a Brandelsonna classic.

"Guys. Damn. It's like the Brandelsonna film with the tiger, the five princes, and. . . ." He trailed off. No one said anything.

"You know what?" Willington started up again. "I've never liked Brandelsonna films."

"Me neither," said Ash.

"They suck," said Rand.

We'd all laughed. It was true. We hated the pretension. The group confession was cathartic, even if those films were Van Gear's favorites. Or maybe he'd been bullshitting too.

As Doc Primus drove us to campus, he was slow and careful. He turned a ten minute drive into fifteen. But that was OK. Primus could tell we young-ones felt nervous. He was working to put us at ease, as he told jokes and one-liners. Primus came across within the confines of his car as a sweet and vulnerable man. We all three were laughing at our wit as Primus pulled into the gym's parking lot.

Holiday lights draped the perimeters of the building's windows. The gym, usually gloomy, had gone happy and gay. A wreath decorated the door with the university symbol flashing in the center.

A few other cars sat parked in open spots around the building, so the place wasn't as dead as on Veteran's Day. But no one milled around the entrance, not even a smoker. The steps were quiet.

"I think we're a little early," chimed Doc Primus.

He led us into the gym's large, high-ceilinged foyer (quite a spectacular entrance, unlike the side door into the labyrinthine halls we'd explored in November). The walls were laced with silver and gold garland, all intertwined with colored lights. The room smelled of cedar and pine. Small wreaths decorated the foyer's many doors. The main portal closed behind us.

A woman dressed as St. Nick and wearing bulky beatnik glasses stood by the open door to a wide stairwell which led to the underground pool. Beside her on a small card table stood a giant fishbowl filled with presents wrapped with colorful paper and bows.

The young lady wore heavy make-up. She rang a little bell as we approached. Her other hand gestured to the fishbowl.

"Did you bring a gift for the Secret Santa exchange?"

Elly and I were bereft. I'd totally forgotten that line on the invitation. However, I had stashed the skeleton key in a pocket, just in case.

"Yes, certainly," said Doc Primus. He pulled from his overcoat a book-sized box tied with a crimson bow. Ms. St. Nick took the gift and added it to the stack within the fishbowl. She made the Professor write his name on a legal pad. He smiled.

She swung her arm to an open doorway as if a game show host.

"Enjoy," she said.

We plunged downward. Elly held my hand. Doc Primus led the way. The handrails were lit with dim lights shaped like Stars of Bethlehem, Stars of David, and Star-shaped Kwanza caps.

We arrived at a floor with a fireplace directly across from us, raging with flaming logs. The heat was intense. My skin felt dry, crispy, scaly. Elly gripped my hand tighter.

The sound of voices echoed from behind us. We wound around the stairwell's base, pushed through a door and found ourselves at the pool.

"Or maybe we're *just* late," said Doc Primus.

People packed the room. A 15-foot Christmas tree stood at one end of the pool at the exact spot where the Marine Biologists had manhandled their octopus-contraption. Punchbowl and snack tables lined the pool's edges.

Grad-students stood near the food and drink, making up for a semester of starvation. The other folks, faculty and administrators, filled all other available spaces. The room was loud with talk, good cheer, the smell of roasted turkey and gingerbread. The ceiling lights lit the room as if suns on wires. Holiday songs drifted through the air, piped in via hidden speakers. Elly let go of my hand.

Doc Primus saw a colleague from another department and drifted in that direction.

"Looks like this is for real," said Elly.

"Yeah, just keep an eye out for Marine Biologists."

We approached a table covered with thumb-sized roast beef sandwiches and dug into the grub.

I noted the pool looked different. The surface had been prepared for the holidays. A plastic cover the shape of a Xmas tree stretched across it. Since the cover was essentially a long, skinny triangle, the uncovered corners of the pool's deeper end glimmered. Spruce-green colored the plastic. Hand-painted garlands and ornaments made the triangle festive. The State U.'s logo was plastered at center.

Elly and I nibbled snacks and sipped punch. We didn't recognize any students or faculty, but we didn't try to mingle either. We felt uneasy.

Five minutes later, someone tinkled a bell. Ms. St. Nick appeared on a makeshift stage we hadn't noticed. She stood on the balcony where Elly and I had observed the octopus gizmo. The woman now wore a huge red cape that completely covered her. She'd lost her glasses. Everyone stopped talking. The music faded. Ms. St. Nick bent down and lifted a huge red sack onto the stage. Her red and white cap tilted but remained fast on her head.

"Let's keep up the yuletide cheer with the presentation of our lucky Secret Santa receivers."

Everyone stared up at the balcony. It felt weird, as if we were waiting to hear a political speech. Ms. St. Nick unhooked her cape to reveal a red and green full body wet suit.

"That's an ugly suit," Elly whispered into my ear. "Do you think she'll dive from there into the pool?" I shrugged. She smirked.

Ms. St. Nick dug into the sack and pulled a small box from the pile. The box might have held a pendant or earrings. She held the box high, then bent down, grabbed a clipboard, and checked a list.

"Associate Dean of Undergraduate Studies, Michael Stanley Fernando Harper. This one's for you. Where are you, Dean Harper? You haven't been naughty, you've been nice."

A middle aged man on the other side of the pool raised his hand and several people in his group laughed and applauded. Soon everyone was clapping.

Ms. St. Nick rang her bell, and the crowd noise subsided.

"Here you are, our sweet Dean."

She expertly tossed the box, and it spun close to him, and his wife made a one-handed catch. More applause.

The sack was stuffed, so this went on for a while. Name read. Applause. Gift thrown and caught. More applause. Elly and I felt quite pleased we'd forgotten to bring a gift for this weird ritual.

"This is kind of . . . off balance," I whispered to Elly.

"Yeah, but kind of nice too."

"Where's Professor Primus? *Professor?*" said Ms. St. Nick.

I scanned the room, wondering where he'd meandered.

He raised both hands. He stood directly below her balcony.

"Lovely, lovely Professor. Here's your present."

What was with all this gift giving? I'd always thought that universities were primarily in the business of giving the gift of education (which students generally paid for handsomely), but the last few months had been such a homage to gifting, from my mysterious Xmas package to the birth of Rand and JAM's baby, from Primus' ride to this reception to Blanco's $100 bill. I thought about having a gift and receiving a gift. How, in utero, we Dade babies were normal but not gifted, then the bomb gave us Rad Sickness, glowing eyes, and "useless gifts." And then there were the Tech Hall experiments where I was convinced scientists were trying to tap our "gifts" for some unpleasant purpose.

Now people were showering each other with more.

I'd become tired of gifts, in all shapes and forms. An odd prayer came to me, *Please, please, Tech Hall bastards hidden in this throng, let my only gift be for you to bring our dear friend back from the dead.* No, no, no. This was a season of birth, not death or resurrection (had the baby Jesus been a variation on a Rad Sick?—*that* would be truly mind-blowing!). Of course, at this point, I was happy to have the gift of standing beside Elly and sipping warm wassail.

Doc Primus caught his package.

Though the Santa Claus sack looked quite a bit lighter, we all stared up at Ms. St. Nick with anticipation.

"And now," she said, "it's time for the key party."

People hooted and applauded. Elly and I glanced at each other and held our breaths. Had Skate been right? Really? A key party?

"Test your keys on the Christmas Seas," Ms. St. Nick said. "All who received a key with their invitation may now approach the Holiday Sea-craft." She gestured at the pool.

What the hell was she talking about?

I leaned way over a snack table, my sweater's cuff dipping into a mustard dish, to see where she pointed.

In the deeper end of the pool, in one of the uncovered spots near the pool cover's Xmas star, floated a small, strange, intricate boat. This vessel reflected the lights from the nearby 15-foot tree. How had I missed this thing? Where had they hid it?

The craft was the size of a narrow skiff. But I found its top confusing in two ways: One, the top was decked with holiday lights, as if it were the smallest entrant in a South Florida boat parade—those long trains of yachts and pleasure cruisers idling up and down the Intracoastal Waterway, each entwined with enough bulbs to light a skyscraper. Two, the actual surface of the vessel resembled a miniature military submarine.

Mainly, I was wondering where in the hell it had come from. It must have been obscured near the shallow end beneath the wide part of the pool cover.

The sea craft floated near the pool's edge. A group of broad-shouldered, sweater-wearing, undergraduate men and women muscled a few of the food tables away from the pool so everyone could see. People stepped back, as if slightly unnerved. But after a moment, the crowd tittered and *aaaaaahhhhhhhhed:* the lights on the vessel suddenly blinked in various and unexpected patterns. A fat, red bulb dimmed and glowed on its nose. Were we all being hypnotized? I did not like this. But, damn, it *was* mesmerizing.

Two new guys in garnet sports coats moved the snack tables further from the pool's side, so people could easily make their way to the boat.

Ms. St. Nick strolled down the spiral staircase. When she reached the floor, the crowd parted. Her Santa cap bobbed as she marched. She stopped at the boat and snatched a soapbox-sized podium from the deck, plopped it at the pool's edge, and stepped up.

"Who has a key?" asked Ms. St. Nick. "Would the person standing closest to our *holiday special* please approach and try the keyhole?"

A grad student gal (or was she a young professor?) with a stretch of long red hair held hers in the air, and everyone cheered. She stood five feet away.

"Wonderful!" said Ms. St. Nick. "Take your chance!"

The woman walked to the pool's edge and leaned over the vessel's . . . what might one call it? *The conning tower on an ICBM carrying nuclear-powered submarine!*

She leaned over the waist-high conning tower as if searching for a door.

"Dear, that's right," said Ms. St. Nick. "You're very close. Look on the top surface of that little tower in the middle there. You'll see the key-hole."

The woman swept her long, red hair from her face, bent down and placed her palm on the submarine, and then looked back and nodded her head.

"Try it!" exclaimed Ms. St. Nick.

She carefully stuck her key into the lock and jiggled it. Nothing happened. She clutched the key tighter and torqued it back and forth. She let go and stood up, clearly disappointed.

"Oh, I'm so sorry, dear. You're not the one this Christmas. Let's let another try? Take your key with you, please."

The woman grabbed her key and shuffled from the pool's edge.

"Who's our next lucky little Christmas elf?" asked Ms. St. Nick; she pulled at the collar of her wet suit, as if it itched.

A plump gentleman wearing a purple houndstooth jacket made his way through the crowd, splitting the ocean of party-goers.

He waddled to the submarine, dug inside his coat, and pulled his bright white skeleton key from a pocket. Mine was not bright white. I thought he might have the lucky winner, and that would be that. I would be so very glad. The weirdness would end, and we'd return to Xmas un-scathed.

The gentleman leaned over the conning tower, slid on a pair of glasses, and studied the key hole. A hush swept over the crowd.

"Did you bring your key?" whispered Elly. I didn't say anything for a moment.

"Maybe," I said.

He stood fully erect, peeled off his purple coat and handed it to a colleague.

A few folks applauded. Some chuckled.

He bent over the submarine, jammed his key into the top, then positioned his body as if readying to grapple with an outsized opponent.

He aggressively jiggled the key. I imagined him yanking Excalibur from the Stone or twisting open the world's largest can of tuna.

Minutes ticked.

"Well, I just don't think you're lucky today," said Ms. St. Nick. "You may stop."

The large man ignored her. His efforts intensified. The sub rocked, making the Xmas tree cover undulate like a yuletide hula dancer.

"Yes, you can please stop, sir," said Ms. St. Nick. "You just don't have the right key, do you?"

"Damn it!" he shouted.

He tossed his key in the pool, grabbed his jacket from the acquaintance, and stalked through the crowd toward the exit.

"Well, well, well," Ms. St. Nick chanted. "I know we have one winner out there. Please! Let's have the next key holder approach the sea craft."

The remaining unlucky one's lined up. A half-dozen folks, a mix of grad students, professors, executive assistants. One by one they tried the skeleton keys in the sub's conning tower, and one by one they couldn't get the lock to budge. Some folks were intense and determined like the angry man, others gave up quickly and shrugged. The reception's revelers cheered and applauded for each key holder; everyone seemed giddy with anticipation.

No one's key worked.

"Tell me. Now. Did you bring it?" whispered Elly, this time pinching my arm.

"This has got to be a trap," I whispered back, jerking my elbow from her pinchers.

"What trap? Would could happen? There's hundreds of people here. And I've seen no sign of the Marine Biologists."

"It doesn't smell right." At this point, I suddenly wished I could have smelled the future instead of hear it.

And why could I *hear* nothing of this future? I was tone deaf to this skeleton key, and deaf to what the gift would sound like, what it might reveal.

"Oh, I know, I know," said Ms. St. Nick, "there has to be other keys out there. At least one more?"

People looked around, but no one approached the submarine. A mumble rippled through the crowd.

"Let's get to the *bottom* of this," whispered Elly. "Try the key! Run afterwards, if you want, but try the key!"

I was getting pissed. *Bottom* of what? Voyage to the *bottom* of the sea? Ms. St. Nick's bottom? Elly's bottom? My ass? Wasn't Elly on my side? Hadn't she been scared shitless when we'd snuck through the gym's showers to arrive at the pool's balcony, when the plots of the Marine Biologists unfolded. She was the one who'd said I was crazy if I attended the Xmas reception!

"Leave me alone," I said, forgetting to whisper.

I suddenly felt the eyes of Christmas Future burn into my skull.

"Oh, you! You!" said the voice from on high. "Do *you* have a key?"

I turned. Ms. St. Nick was staring, pointing. Her wetsuit seemed to fit her more tightly than ever.

"Oh, if you have a key," she said, "you must, must, must try it." There was pleading in her voice, as if the "non-opening" of the submarine would spoil the Xmas cheer, ruin the party, chop the event at the knees.

Everyone examined me. The hundreds watched my rib cage expand and contract. I coughed; the stink of fresh chlorine and muriatic acid assaulted my lungs.

The eyes of all these bastards, these frigging *ojos* wriggled under my skin, willing me to pull the key from my pocket, rub the silver surface with my palms, and slot it in the hole atop the conning tower of the world's smallest submarine.

What could I do? Deny this groundswell of eyes?

But why couldn't I *hear* anything? Why could I not see through this Ghost of Xmas Future and see directly into this can of worms, this sub of shit? Yes, see through my ears! My ears were so goddamn blind at this moment!

Was the submarine made of some substance that blocked my Rad Sick ear? (Of course, I wasn't doused with TallaTec, was I?)

But on another level, this submarine was intriguing me, tapping into my paranoid but gullible imagination. This was all so elaborate and weird. I had to know what was on the other end of this fascinating complexity.

I approached the vessel. The crowd split wider than it had for the others. Elly followed me for ten feet, then stopped. She now looked worried. I felt abandoned. But she weakly smiled. She whispered, "Let's just see."

I continued and halted when I reached the pool's edge. The strange craft floated steadily against the tile rim.

"Oh, I'm so happy we have at least one more key to try," said Ms. St. Nick from her podium. "This is *wonderful!*"

Everyone quietly murmured.

I studied the submarine. The conning tower actually had a periscope tube, a ready tool to help torpedo and obliterate. A palm-sized version of the State U's logo decorated the tower's side. Circular indentions near the sub's nose and stern hinted at the possibility of miniature ICBMs springing from the vessel's innards, probably a nuclear missile about the size of the anti-nuke that incompetent nut launched in Dade in 1980, or the same model that Taylor V. shot from the deck of the U.S.S. Stonewall Jackson. The machine was highly polished, gleaming. Next to the periscope on the conning tower the keyhole awaited, the shape and size you might expect for an old school skeleton key, as if we were all in a TV After School Special originally broadcasted on Halloween, and mistakenly shown on Christmas. I leaned over to study the hole. My back strained, my prematurely aging body catching up with me.

The key weighed heavily in my pocket. A tightness climbed from my stomach to the muscles in my neck and shoulders. I wanted this over with. People were murmuring; they too were tired of the overdone drama.

I revealed the key, and all fell silent.

Nonchalantly, I popped the thing into the hole and turned. A loud click echoed throughout the cavernous room, and everyone cheered.

"Did you hear it?!? Now you must see! Go see! Go see!" The voice of Ms. St. Nick was in my ear. She stood beside me.

Up close, I could see that her red and green full body wetsuit fitted tightly around her throat. She must have found it hard to breathe. Beneath her jolly red cap, the makeup caking her face was a thick as mud in a brackish swamp. She squinted; what'd happened to her glasses. I felt sorry for her. Who'd bullied her into doing this? Was she getting paid? Perspiration spotted her skin like a pox. Oddly, her smile seemed genuine.

I glanced over Ms. St. Nick's shoulder to Elly, but I couldn't spot her.

A creaking emanated from the submarine. A manhole cover-size hatch was lifting on a hinge directly behind the conning tower.

More cheering! Someone with a saxophone began to play the State U's fight song. The sound rang and expanded in the room. The sub's lights continued to blink.

"Step aboard," said Ms. St. Nick. I looked at her as if she were crazy. The craft did not appear stable; the vessel had a canoe-vibe. I imagined a footstep seesawing it into chaos.

"It's perfectly safe," she said. And with that, she gently leapt onto the deck, one foot at a time like a ballerina; she stopped in first position beside the deck's circular door.

The crowd applauded. The saxophone kept blaring.

"You're wearing a wetsuit," I said. "If you fall in, it's no great loss. You're prepared."

"Trust me," she said. She reached out her hand.

I turned again to look for Elly, but now the audience had closed in on the docking area, gathering around me in a tightly knit fabric of humans. I couldn't see her.

"Please," said Ms. St. Nick. "You're almost there."

"Where?"

"To the key's prize!"

She reached out both arms, curled the fingers of both hands, a flutter of beckoning, like a game show host.

I lay my hands on her palms, lifted a foot, and she seamlessly pulled me aboard. The craft didn't rock an inch.

The witnesses talked loudly amongst themselves.

"Look inside," she whispered near my ear, still holding my wrists. "Look!"

I peered into the belly of the submarine. The cramped chamber was well lit. A seat—a bucket seat fashioned after an old 280Z sports car—sat among control panels of lights, switches, and dials. Resting in the seat sat a turkey-sized white box wrapped with red ribbons. A festive bow topped the present. The gift's shiny paper glimmered.

"And there's your prize, that and the 3-D television" said Ms. St. Nick. She was urging me into climbing beneath the conning tower. I had misgivings. Applause rained.

"Our lucky key holder has just won the 64 inch SONY X-D 317 widescreen television with 3-D performance settings; it's the latest in TV technology."

When had Ms. St. Nick become the host of *Wheel of Fortune*?

More importantly, where was Elly? I scanned the perimeter of the pool. People stood at the edges, clapping furiously. I imagined a slight push from behind—by a gigantic invisible hand—sending the entire wall of humanity thrashing into the pool, a human waterfall, lemmings launching off the cliff into a chlorinated canyon.

I could not spot Elly. She was not a lemming, but she'd vanished.

"Go down and get your prizes," said Ms. St. Nick.

"Where's the TV? And what's in the package?" I asked.

"You can't know until you go down and bring it up; the TV's there too; you'll just have to look for it." I could barely hear her because of the applause; nevertheless, I heard her.

"Why don't you go in and grab them for me?" I asked.

Ms. St. Nick gave me a look. Wasn't it the same look all Rad Sicks got as kids? *What's wrong with you—are you a baby, a wimp? Can't you act normal? Can't you do normal things?*

"Trust me. You can do it," she said. Her eyes were full of scorn.

I was beginning to crack. I started to rationalize: what was the worst that could happen? A submarine in a swimming pool can go no further than the darkest spot in the deep end. There were no sharks or reptiles. No Marine Biologists either. But I was fighting a sense of dread, my brain's demand to back out and ignore Ms. St. Nick's browbeating and cuteness, flout the persuasiveness of her tone. Scorn was such a great tormentor's tool. Bullies made sure we Rad Sicks did what was absolutely the worst for us. Our childhoods of idiocy were often spurred on by cretins. Ms. St. Nick struck me as neither bully nor cretin, but her voice contained such impatience and pleading. What was she so worried about? That my obstinacy would kill the party? She looked particularly sad, and I have to admit sad-faced women have always masterfully manipulated me. Big Sis was particularly good, her dejected face tricking me into stupid pranks that got me in trouble, or allowed her to get out of trouble because she made me feel so sorry for her, even though I'd been the injured party. I love my sister. At that crazy second, I may have even decided to love Ms. St. Nick.

"O.K.," I said.

The crowd cheered as I lowered myself onto the ladder that knifed into the belly of the sub.

"You're almost there," she said.

I reached the floor of the sub's interior and glanced up at Ms. St. Nick. I hadn't noticed how much she'd been sweating. Her foundation and mascara were melting; her face reconstituted, reconfigured, reshaped.

Her Santa hat slipped off her head.

I recognized her. The shape of her green eyes. A weird, blue, face-framing streak became visible in her auburn hair as dye wept onto her brow. She'd been the woman in the white polo and jeans at Tech Hall, the one who'd plopped the fishbowl over my head.

"Sorry," she whispered. She'd must have noted the look on my face.

Then with a kick she slammed the sub deck's door shut.

*   *   *

If the submarine were nothing else, it was clearly a perfect human-sized fishbowl. Except, I don't think anyone could see in. At the sub's bow stretched a viewing window that reminded me of Skull Spring's glass bottom boats. Though it extended across much of the vessel's pointy nose, all I could see was the swimming pool's wall. Attached to the ceiling was a widescreen television.

TallaTec vapor steamed from the glimmering, red-bowed Xmas package.

The bastards had me.

Again, I verge on a description of the clichéd acid trip; but with TallaTec that's not it. Not for me. Ash once described TallaTec as the ultimate heroin-like hallucinatory buzz, but TallaTec . . . *for me* . . . it . . . what?

This: made reality *squared*, bigger as in hellacious, more visceral like plunging inside a moment's molecules to witness all potential realities. We're talking *real* reality. Realities I can *make* real. I know it's true. If some drugs made me sputter with spins, then TallaTec sprang my world to life with clarity inside clarity, and like a Dickens' Xmas ghost, it made me soar headlong into a wormhole version of the possible, where, if I could just learn to control it, what would happen in the TallaTec world would become real in the actual world.

On this day, I finally had control.

At that moment, I wondered where had the motherfucking Marine Biologists been hiding? Those smug bastards! I wanted to suffocate them with gallons of pool water, choke each with a chlorine cloud.

And what would happen next? Would they interrogate me via radio, voices piped through speakers in the bow and stern?

The reception forgot about me; must have figured I was inside enjoying my gift. What in the hell could Ms. St. Nick have told them? She was being naughty, not nice.

What did Elly do when she saw the wet suited gal kick the sub's door shut? Oh, they must have escorted Elly up the stairs and fed her bullshit. But wouldn't Elly be freaking? Demanding action?

The gas thickened; the smoke had tentacles.

Yes, like an idiot, I held my breath. I hated and feared this stuff. And it looked like I was going to be inhaling a pure TallaTec atmosphere for hours, more intense than Halloween's fishbowl headgear.

A minute passed. My lungs ached. I grimaced. Within the next 20 seconds, I would have to breathe. The television screen above filled with snow. An electronic hiss leaked from the ceiling. The white gas filled the sub's interior. I was inside a cloud inside a submarine. My eyes stung from the vapors. I squeezed my eyes shut, began to cry.

And then I inhaled.

Devastation.

As always, all was lost.

Part of me wonders if the submarine actually took me to the places I now recall. Or was the dose of gas *that* strong that I did not lose my mind but became *all* mind, and my imagination (manipulated by Marine Biologists and whoever else) took over my consciousness for torturous, lost hours?

No, there are too many after-signs; I know what happened next *happened*.

First, the white cloud got brighter as if wallpaper. A flash! Total whiteout.

The submarine dove, dove, dove! Violently. A fury of bubbles appeared beyond the viewing window. Maroon light flashed from the TV, bloodying the thick London fog of TallaTec. The gas hissed a furious whisper.

And then the vessel shot upward, but not nose first. We flew upward like a high-speed elevator, as if zooming to a penthouse. The television's red light became brighter, blinding. My ears popped from the pressure. The television screen came to life. Either that or the sub's interior
widened and lengthened.

Why? Because the sub sat in the midst of a campus seminar room.
Arms pulled me from the hole above and slid me to the dry floor. The craft
folded itself into the shape of an oval seminar table. I blinked and found
myself tied to a chair at one end of the oval. Despite what you might be
thinking, know this: *I would have bled if cut!*

This was real.

There were clouds in the room—more TallaTec. The TV screen
hung above us in a nearly invisible ceiling.

A man slid from the cloud but remained shrouded in mist. He
stood at the opposite end of the table. I wanted to believe I stared-down
one of the two Marine Biologists (most likely Dr. Fish hat), but I had my
doubts. Nevertheless, the one seemed multitudes. At times he was the
calm professor in tweed jacket, elbow patches, and glasses. Other moments he was the Army Captain with night-vision goggles. The next second, he was dressed in a Brooks Brothers suit and had the cocky air of a
Goldman Sachs investment banker.

I wanted to murder all three.

But instead, he held a knife-like laser pointer, a pistol, a rolled up
contract explaining a Collateralized Debt Obligation. He held the power.

I was stuck to a chair. I was the perfect student. Powerless, except
to listen.

I wanted to see Sombre, Blanco, Tay Chillieri, Bea Miller, and
Tuck Zeedo. I wanted my Rad Sick friends at the table to help me discern
the soon-to-be interrogator's bullshit. We'd all been together on Halloween. But now at Christmas I sat alone. I felt heavy tired. I wanted to rant
and curse, but the fingers of TallaTec, for the moment, laced my vocal
chords with ice.

269

I was alone with the man in the cloud.

"We want you to *hear* into the future for us."

The more I thought about it, the more I thought . . . what shit! I couldn't hear into the future. Not the way they wanted me to. I could hear the voice in written works and know if the voice was true, and from that truth, gain a true sense of a work's potential, it's final fruitful resting place (so to speak) in journal *X* or *Y*. But beyond that, I could not hear the words and noises of tomorrow like a psychic at a séance might know the voices from all yesterdays. I could not hear the scream of the future dead, did not know the sound of my own last breath and hear the hour of that ultimate clock tick, the universe then burning off into its fiery eternity of exhaustion and perhaps then violent return from the Big Bang sequel, the rebirth, retry.

But what had I heard that night with Elly when we'd launched the toy submarine? How had I sensed the bull that bucked—Monday's stock market boom?

Truly, I wanted to hear a future without these Marine Biologists.

"Can you hear the next war? Where will the first bullet or bomb shatter the silence—on what street, in what desert, beside which cave, near which ocean? In what language will the shooter swear as she pulls the trigger? As he pokes the bomb to life?"

I knew nothing of war.

But the TallaTec reentered me like an infantry, boring into my cerebral cortex and taking over my temporal lobe, torqueing my medulla oblongata, setting up camp in my internal carotid artery. A fleet of new-fangled destroyers sailed across my feet and hands, moored in my heart. A squadron of super-bombers flew their loads of atomic vomit into my cerebellum and cerebrum, into every spare nerve ending, every speck of white and grey matter.

And then I was war.

I could hear sandstorms. Screams of anguish in languages I did not know. If I guessed? I might say, *Farsi? Arabic? Urdu?* Mosques shattered like old men's teeth hitting stone steps. I might shout cities, but not understand the syllables, might understand the lapping language of seas, but not know their shores. Was it much use to hear future wars? All meant incessant nightmare.

My mouth took over me, and I sputtered vowels and consonants of what I'd heard from this future.

"Name the sound of each place struck dumb and charred by the flash-landing of each ICBM!"

More mumblings spurted from my now TallaTec-heated vocal cords, words I couldn't control, grunts the cloud-man understood.

"What we must, must, must hear is the sound of the next economic crash, the near and far stock market plummets . . . from where will these come and go? When will the sound of clicking computer keys give clues to flimsy bonds and credit default swaps? *We must be smarter! We must have bellies full of safe treasury bills.*"

I wanted these scientists burned to cinders, made chum.

Bankers too.

And Generals.

Did a throat clear? Was that an avalanche? The noise of an endless stream of bills spit from an off-its-rocker ATM?

"When will the *Next Big One* happen? You must hear it. Press your ear to the wall of that future!

"Where do the moans of the jobless groan? From which Exchanges do the traders' voices go shrill and vulgar? Tell me where oil wells pump air instead of fuel, hiss instead of gurgle."

I wanted these people literally to drown in their research.

"Give me the sound of numbers! The tiny pinpricks of bits and bytes tapped onto silicon to create line graphs. Listen to the sound of suit jackets swishing! What's those fabrics' quality? And those shoes! What's the leather sound like as a broker's toe nervously taps from panic's spikes?"

And it happened again. I heard something. And my TallaTec-lassoed mouth growled and gnashed, echoing explosions of pitches and volumes that made the cloud-man write furiously on a clipboard.

He paused as if struck by a new thought.

"And Lt. Taylor Morgan Velázquez? Where has she gone? Can you hear her voice? Is she speaking Russian or English or Mandarin or Urdu? What engine grumbles in the background—ship, sub, or jet?"

No.

I was not going to betray my fellow Rad Sick.

These final queries created a tidal wave of resistance that stretched from toe cell to scalp cell, as if all Rad Sicks had psychically bonded with me in this moment. The psychic wave soaked every square inch of my body, even, I now believe, every square inch of my soul. I now understood how this latest strain of TallaTec was fidgeting with my mitochondria, juicing my brain and vocal cords. And most importantly, this huge wave wiped me free of helplessness.

I was left with a clear path. *I* could *use* TallaTec, bend the drug to my will.

I pulled back into myself through a TallaTec tunnel only I could dig. I muffled the mumblings worming though my vocal cords. I controlled the words. Squelched the grunts.

The cloud-man fumed. I'd found my lid.

After that, TallaTec was simply *the* universe, and my own new universe birthed from it.

*   *   *

Rereading this years from now, I know what I will suspect, but I can guarantee what happened next was *not* an upping the ante of outsized hallucination. Know this: my mind engulfed in TallaTec made any possibility within our infinite universe possible. Like I said, TallaTec can spring a new world to life, make you carve out a wormhole version of past/present/future, where, if you know what you're doing, what happens in the TallaTec world becomes manifest in the real world.

On this day, I finally knew what I was doing. Here's what happened.

My vision returned, and I listened more carefully than ever before. This is what I saw, but it's the soundscape that keeps ringing inside my skull.

After I'd clammed up about Lt. Velázquez, the interrogator began a new set of questions. Within seconds, I made my mind kick an opening through the vapor, a gap in the gas where I could focus and find these motherfuckers' vulnerabilities. I searched like an avenging angel knifing past ice and lightning. I found a *door*. A *backdoor* out of the interrogation chamber and into a plane of existence I could manipulate and use to counterpunch these Tech Hall bastards.

I was out the *door* and back inside the submarine. But I'd made the vessel *move*.

A TallaTec sea change!

Ryanna crouched beside me at the control panel. Her breathing was raspy. I knelt down beside her. The cloud had cleared. The ceiling's television hummed and projected wrinkles of light in crystal clear water. We were no longer in the pool. We were in a cavern, the earth's arteries of ground water bleeding somewhere above in sun-kissed sinkholes. The sub swooshed past limestone walls. Dim lights dotted the cavern's ceiling. We were deep. Way deep. We were on a mission.

She stood and walked to the control panel, then calmly steered the craft past 10 foot alligators and ragged columns of stalagmites growing from the cave floor. The sub's nose swooshed through darkness. The control panel reminded me of Skull Spring's boats, a row of levers and softly lit buttons. Ryanna flipped a blue switch. She was silent, her blue eyes determined. The sub's viewing window now grew. The entire nose was a glass cone. I could see such detail! The jagged teeth of gators haphazardly poked from the reptiles' grim smiles. I could hear them hiss as their jaws opened.

The craft slipped from the mouth of the cavern.

Ryanna pointed at me and then the front of the sub. A gator-shaped, old-school torpedo, three feet long, rested near the vessel's viewing glass.

What was I to do?

And then it filtered true into my ear. I would hear the compression of explosives within our missile, a sound like snoring coming from the sleeping TNT, a sound like a giant reptile's grinding growl. I looked forward to the big bang to follow. I heard the sounds of *what's next*, and I was ready! *Ready*, for the first time ever!

The water suddenly became streaked with sunlight.

An underwater tornado of tiny flower blossoms spun like a genie escaped from a lamp. The tornado hovered a yard below the surface.

We were in Big Dismal sink, where Ryanna had showed me the whirlpool below the narrow ledge, where the white petals had spun, floated, vanished.

Ryanna was rushing to head something off—and I knew exactly what it was!

In the sinkhole's weird light, a barely perceptible nimbus glowed around everything.

Ryanna guided the craft to the bottom of the sink, and slowly circled the perimeter.

We waited. The sub's motor hummed.

Eclipse! A dark circle appeared above, making an enormous shadow. As the circle sank, the black disk grew. Someone on the surface was adding a pupil to the Big Dismal iris, like my contact lenses that hid my Rad Sick glow.

The disk was the dark octopus, the black crab, the Marine Biologists' contraption they'd tested on Veteran's Day. The machine sprang to life, its eight arms shaking as if trying to jumpstart blood flow.

The bottom of the gizmo was transparent glass; inside I saw two huge cold capsules, one white, one red, shaped like the tiny ones Elly and I had jammed into the toy submarine. Each capsule was the size of our vessel's gator-shaped torpedo. The capsules bubbled furiously.

Within the bubbling, I could hear the future bursting of the capsules, the "catalystic" noise of two chemicals bonding and creating gallons and gallons of TallaTec pollution, but I also heard the sound of their failure, brought about if the capsule's contents were melted by the heat of our torpedo's explosion.

Ryanna pointed desperately at the torpedo and then to the back of the sub.

I knew what I had to do.

A Plexiglas cylinder stood at the craft's tail, spanning from floor to ceiling. The outline of a door appeared on the cylinder's surface.

I grasped the torpedo at the nose and tail and lifted the missile from the floor with a grunt. My shoulders and spine popped, my Rad Sick agedness flaring up. The metal was freezing cold. The thing was monstrously heavy. An oil and sulfur odor leaked from the torpedo's surface; a bitter chlorine taste covered my tongue. I coughed. Hesitated. Somehow the Marine Biologists were reaching through the *backdoor* I'd created and were punching back, screwing with my brain.

But I reached into my TallaTec laced mind . . . and slammed the *door* shut!

Ryanna steered the craft directly below the descending disk. The octopus arms slithered like serpents.

As the *backdoor* had hung open, I'd spied the scientists' plan. When the machine landed at the mouth of the sinkhole's cave, the TallaTec would gush from the eight tubes, polluting the freshwater aquifer for hundreds and hundreds of square miles.

Ryanna gestured with the intensity of a hotheaded basketball coach speeding her players on a fast break.

She wanted me to jam the torpedo into the Plexiglas cylinder. Hesitations be damned!

But *was* this a traditional torpedo? After all, it was in the Marine Biologist's submarine. Perhaps this was all a trick. The torpedo was simply the detonator. Or perhaps it had as much TallaTec as the mechanical crab. But maybe . . . just maybe . . . Ryanna, as stowaway, had smuggled the torpedo aboard; thus, the Tech Hall scientists knew nothing.

I crossed my fingers.

Then again, what if it were an anti-bomb H-Bomb like the one the dumb spy had launched above Dade all those years ago? Was I about to blast the north Florida aquifer with enough radiation to wipeout everything for the next century?

Ryanna couldn't be real, no? After all, she didn't speak!

"Launch it!," shouted Ryanna.

Damn, she sounded real enough.

The disk was nearing. The submarine's glass nose darkened with shadow. I lumbered to the Plexiglas launch tube. The torpedo's ends were cold on my palms.

The tube projected bright yellow light. Its door hung slightly ajar. I pictured the missile striking the black circle above, the arms cut loose from the body, squirming like tails pulled from lizards we found in Dade's hibiscus bushes. I imagined the disk evaporating, becoming a cloud of debris. A cloud! The torpedo would create an anti-cloud to the TallaTec that filled this chamber, this fishbowl, this vessel.

But my Rad Sick paranoia wouldn't let go. What if the torpedo only did minor damage? New doubts gripped me: slightly cracking the crab's shell would only dissolve the cold capsules more quickly. The TallaTec would simply gush in one glob instead of extended release.

Alas, I prayed the missile would alleviate my fears.

If nothing else, I hoped the octopus needed to pull itself far upstream within the cavern system before releasing its mother-load, needed to swim far uphill to affect the widest swath of population.

Ryanna's hand slapped my shoulder. She stood beside me, her other hand on my elbow. She nodded. I grimaced. My palms were becoming numb. My fingers flared with an arthritic jolt.

She opened the launch tube's door wide.

"You told me you'd know how to set it," she said.

I did?

I tuned my ear to the future, finally using my Rad Sick hearing in a conscious way for gigantic good. This torpedo was truly old school. I heard myself unscrewing a lid at the nose. The detonator would be waiting, quivering. I would have to set the detonator by hand; it was hooked to a timer. The timer would go up in pitch when it was ten seconds from *boom!*

Again, I knew exactly what I had to do.

My arms shook; the biceps, triceps and rotator cusps strained to turn the projectile nose-up. I was breathing heavily, as if bench pressing weight beyond my strength. Hot sweat dripped from my forehead and warmed the back of one hand. My legs shook; I could feel my Rad Sick knees buckling.

With one hand I held the metal gator-baby tight against my gut. With the other, I searched for the lid at the snout. My fingers slid over the cold surface. I found the circular groove, dug into it with my nails, and turned counterclockwise. The lid screeched with every half-twist, then spun free and clunked on the floor.

A dial hid in the hole. I didn't need to jam my ear against the device, because I could hear into the very near future and know the sounds. I heard them loud and clear as if the timer ticked inside my ear canal. I turned the dial twice to the right, and the rusty ticking started.

We held our breaths. I counted the seconds into the future and recounted them as they became the present. My Rad Sick ear listened intensely to each croak from the beast. When the noise changed musical keys, I'd know when to jam it in the launch tube.

No, the tick was not a croak but like a spoon on a china plate. A clear clang, headache-producing. I could hear the vibrations of the exterior's molecules, slow dancing within the explosive's powder. It was like music by John Cage; I was waiting for the subtle key change from high C to C#. It would happen in ten seconds.

It did. The clink became a violin shriek. Fear made all pain vanish. Now was the time to move!

With a gigantic thrust, I jammed the torpedo into the tube. Ryanna slammed the door and raced to the control panel. It was evening inside the submarine. The black disk must have been only yards above us. I took a step back.

Water flooded the tube. Ryanna frantically flipped levers, turned dials and switches.

The Mother of all *Clicks* popped.

The missile flew like a bottle rocket in a fraction of a heartbeat. Inside my head I saw the misguided spy from 1980, having just pulled the trigger and mistakenly launching that Anti-H into the Miami sky. I could see the expression on his face falling from grim concentration to tragic desperation as he realized his mistake. How long had it taken? An instant? A minute? Had he watched the sky glow and bloom with hot light and orange, fiery plumes, and had he thought empty thoughts as the radiation spread like a dust storm? So many dead. So many steeped with radiation sickness.

Strangely, thirty seconds passed before anything happened.

Then.

The Mother of all *Booms* cracked.

Big Dismal sink emptied, the water shooting upward in a fat column.

The submarine began its descent through sky to dry bottom. But no: the cave mouth spewed water, refilling the sink, just as quickly as we fell.

Splashdown!

The sub tilted sideways, then rocked back the other way. Seesawed for minutes. Then we righted. The glass nose shrank, became the viewing window from before. The television on the ceiling glowed, but did little to fight the sudden darkness. I could see almost nothing. I couldn't see Ryanna.

Chunks of the gizmo rained around us, still burning, melting, disappearing in flames though we were underwater. I could hear the patter of the pieces striking the surface, tapping the sub's hull, then bubbling as they sank.

The door in the ceiling opened.

Ms. St. Nick looked down, smiling. She shook a scolding finger at her boot, then studied my face. Her eyes filled with apology.

She whispered something like *Verzeihung.*

"Sorry," she said out loud. "Too much kick in das boot."

Sunday, December 31st, 2000

I met Ryanna at Skull Springs. She wanted to say goodbye. Ryanna was leaving for New York. After placing her lovely piece in *the pacific,* agents were calling, saying she should move to Gotham.

She wanted to meet at the springs because she still had something to show me.

Oddly, the weather was warmer than when we'd cruised the spring in October. A mild breeze blew from the south. Though the north Florida winter was chillier than Miami's, we were still in Florida: warm weather could reign in T-town too.

I'd forgotten about kissing Ryanna those many months ago. Elly was everything to me now. I'd decided yesterday to leave the cinderblock walls of Alum Village for her tiny house on Sharkey Street. I'd asked Elly to come with us this afternoon, but she was feeling a little under the weather and wanted to rest before returning to work tomorrow.

Ryanna and I stood on the cement dock and watched the sun glimmer in the southern sky. A boat's motor putted at the far end of the dock; Ryanna was letting the engine warm up. The chugging echoed down the river, the noise eventually muffled by cypress.

We were the only ones there; Skull Springs was closed for the New Year's Eve holiday.

"New York, huh? Small town girl in the big city," I said. "Aren't you going to miss all this? The view of the Hudson won't be this pretty."

"Oh, I won't be gone forever. Don't worry." She'd plucked a piece of winter-brown bahia grass earlier and now stuck it in her mouth.

I'd told her about the Xmas Reception at the underground swimming pool, about what I'd experienced, about what Elly had said had happened.

Elly said I'd been trapped in the submarine for minutes, not hours. She said the vessel hadn't moved, everything had been normal, except for an initial strange 5 minute interval when the power went out and everything fell dark, and it sounded like the sub had taken a breath. A few dim candles were lit here and there in the room, and the crowd applauded. Then the lights flashed to life, everyone cheered, and all was ordinary. Elly said, after the light returned, Ms. St. Nick had struggled with the latch of the deck's door. When, after a minute, she'd had no luck, she'd hurried to the stern, oddly lowered herself into the water (hmmmm, lucky for her she'd been wearing a wetsuit), and grabbed a tool kit from a submerged compartment. She pulled herself back onboard and furiously fiddled with wrenches and screwdrivers to open the hatch.

According to Elly, when I'd emerged, I'd certainly looked dazed but not TallaTec stoned. I didn't remember any of this; I didn't start having recall until the moment Doc Primus started his Volvo to return us to Alum Village—except for a strange flashback of brushing shoulders with a crying Dr. Fish Hat as we exited. The man was talking angrily into a cell phone. And weeping.

I'd been gripping the 64 inch television as I'd stumbled from the submarine, and I'd still clutched it as I'd sat quietly in the backseat.

The breeze settled at Skull Springs. "Are you sure you weren't there in the sub with me? Can you steer a submersible?" I asked Ryanna.

"I think you must have bumped your head," she said. She smiled and looked out at the spring's lake. Something about her expression was pure feline, as if she held a secret that she'd never release, as if she'd become one of the stray cats that haunted the ruins of the Spanish fort near the Confluence.

We boarded the glass-bottom boat, and Ryanna stuffed the bahia grass into her pocket and steered us from the dock. She adjusted a few toggle switches on the dashboard and then inched the throttle. The motor bumped up in pitch. The diesel fumes entered my nose and stung my tongue. Ryanna guided the craft to the middle of the lake.

"You know," I began, "I never did *get* all that pseudo-science mumbo jumbo you've used to explain the whirlpools."

"What?" She pulled back the throttle. We idled.

"About molecules lining up. Nature wanting to disorder and re-order itself. You said something like, *Natural world wants to pull against something, create disorder, become reordered to a different form.*"

"You're close."

"Close to what? And anyway, what about the Second Law of Thermodynamics: all closed systems run down, charge headlong to chaos, yes?"

"But we have rebirth." She squinted into the glare on the river's surface. "Rebirth." She repeated the word as if it were more holy than God. "That's all we have to fight the chaos. And there's not a thing we can do to stop it. Doesn't that make you glad?"

"Huh?" She'd sidetracked me again.

"Look," she said, and pointed at Skull Spring's lake.

"You see the swirling bits of tape grass," she said, "the *Vallisneria floridana,* in the middle of the spring's surface?" She pointed. "I can guarantee you that's somehow lined up with the water shooting from the springhead below. Let's see if we can see the bottom."

We headed in the direction of the leaning cypress.

I squinted, staring at the view beneath the boat's glass bottom. I concentrated, aware of some glimpse of movement catching the light. Something danced in the deep's gloom, like streamers attached to a fan.

Glancing over my shoulder, I caught Ryanna leaning over the boat's starboard side, her eyes, as always, wide with wonder.

I stared down through the boat's windowed bottom, gazed deep into the cold currents, down where all became blurry. An angular shadow crept into view, maybe two feet long; it was attached to something bigger. The shadow halted. Maybe it was simply a corner of the boat's stern caught and distorted by sunlight.

"I don't see much," I said. "Even in bright sunshine, it's pretty murky."

Ryanna nodded. But she kept staring over the side.

Bubbles leaked from the cave mouth in a narrow cloud.

The circles of air twisted as they drifted up, eventually winking at the surface.

The bubbles then ceased.

The angular shadow grew, stretching for several yards. It slid from the cave's mouth at the bottom of the spring. From the shape of its head and the tapering of its long tail, it looked like a gigantic alligator. The creature circled the spring's nether zone, making tighter and then widening circles. I realized it was rising to the surface, as if following a labyrinthine tunnel of water only visible to creatures of the aquifer.

"What is it? An alligator? Is that the newer form? Is that what the spring has birthed?"

"Keep looking."

The shape made its winding, methodical way, closer and closer to the surface. The gator's shadow grew in size.

The mouth opened, cranking slowly, giving the impression that the beast was mechanical. The rows of sparkling teeth glimmered in the sunlight. One nostril released a ribbon of bubbles. As it circled into the better lit water, its skin appeared streaked with yellow lines. The lines weren't stripes, more like splashes of paint. The tail bobbed side to side.

As a thin layer of clouds cleared the sun's face, the water became brighter. Now every detail shone clear.

The eyes were oversized and their rims had a faint orange glow, as if the reptile were a mutant, some sort of warped beast that must have caught a swatch of stray radiation that had whipped the Everglades during the Accident. Though I knew this was impossible, I could feel a spark of heat emanating from the beast's thick hide, a hotness leaking from those glowing eyes. Yes, I could easily imagine the radiation leaking into nearby wilderness, creating Rad Sick beasts that would invade and eat all heaven and earth.

How would this mutant have gotten to St. Marks? I doubted a relocation experiment by the bloody marine biologists, but it was possible. Perhaps this "new" breed had slowly spread north for twenty years as a generation of rapidly growing gators clawed their way from Glades to Lake Okeechobee to Payne's Prairie to St. Marks. Were they following me? Or were they, like me, finally escaping their boundaries, finding "comfort" beyond home's borders.

Ryanna gave an explanation about a possible cross-breeding between caiman and gator had made this crocodilian with crazy eyes, and this was the disorder bursting into the newer form, but I *knew* this resulted from the Accident's radiation blast, and the radiation was the disorder that had given birth to this newer form, this goggle-eyed, glowing gator. And now I was really putting it all together . . . because it was now clear that I, we, all from *La Fiebre*, all us *hot babies*, had been the subjects of radiation's disorder, but we had been re-ordered to the newer form as a generation of Rad Sicks, each of us birthed with a new-to-the-human gift, our prescience through nonstandard sensory perception (NSP) that allowed us to hear, smell, taste, and feel the future. We were the new and better form. We humans, the dominators of nature, spinning toward disorder with a Cold War, bloody battles, radioactivity, and H-bombs . . . but look what this disorder has created: we are NOT the SICK. We are the new and reborn, the better species, the next better version of humanity.

I closed my eyes and tried to picture this better world. I wanted so much for it to be true. As I took a deep breath of the spring's humid air, I could feel my heart calming, my body, for maybe the first time in my life, growing completely comfortable with itself, all the Rad Sick bitterness evaporating into the cypress branches. Almost.

At this moment, Ryanna sat down, and I sat down beside her at the boat's console. We were silent for a while.

The sun cut through a new thin layer of clouds. My brain switched gears, and I contemplated the tentative Wings meeting that Rand had set for next week. I looked forward to it.

We will have the service for Van Gear's ashes tomorrow. A service somewhere.

I stayed silent as Ryanna began to talk. She told me of her antici-pation and dread of the writers life in Gotham. She steered us back to the dock, nervously chattering about New York.

Monday, January 1, 2001

We were at the Confluence to spread Van Gear's ashes. Willing-ton had the urn; the urn was shaped like a trophy. Rand had an old *Bible*. Jack had a dog on a leash; the beast barked at the stray cats until Jack shushed it. Ash brought a virgin joint of choice marijuana.

The joint was pure cannabis. Nothing else. TallaTec, the Thing, had disappeared from the scene. Vanished. The House that Tec Built had steel bars over the windows and doors. The shack was condemned. Empty. Dead.

The weather was warm. Elly had commented about it this morn-ing as we'd sipped coffee at dawn.

Her tiny house on Sharkey Street faced east, and we stood on the porch to watch the sunrise. I'd wanted to ask Elly to ride with us this afternoon, but she didn't want to miss a shift at Ravensview, and simply smiled and gave her blessing. Before I left, we threw the TV I'd "won" into a dumpster at an apartment complex a block down the street. We didn't trust the damn thing. Besides, we decided the best way to celebrate the new year was to spend a quiet night at home talking without background noise. When the television hit the dumpster's bottom, a flash struck as if fireworks; we heard it shatter, and something squeaked, but we'd ignored the din and walked quickly away.

The shock of Van Gear's death lingered for us. We were shattered, dry eyed but tears-minded. I held a hardcopy of a Van Gear story from his collection, the collection I'd celebrated with him the day we first met. I wanted to read from it before we spread the ashes. It was the piece we'd planned to talk about at the next Wings meeting, right before he died. Reading from his fiction felt fitting, but I wasn't sure we'd have time.

It was my idea to bring his ashes to the Confluence. After yesterday with Ryanna at Skull Springs, a Wings gathering to celebrate Van Gear at the Confluence's waters made sense. My idea sprang from when he and I and Willington had rolled out to the Confluence on a Sunday morning. The pair had arrived on motorcycles at Alum Village, after chowing eggs at a nearby Waffle Missile diner. Willington's wife had generously let him lark-off the day, so he'd had hours for roaming; Van Gear always had the hours. On that Sunday at the Spanish fort, the three of us had wandered the banks of the Wakulla, headed north, tromping on the dark sand. Van Gear had whipped out a harmonica and played so softly we could barely hear, as if the melodies drifted from a folk band at the oyster shack in St. Marks. His notes were bluesy. Willington and I hummed along. Van Gear led us along the river. I was behind him, and Willington trailed as the anchor. We hit a stretch of bank where the saw grass forced us into sluggish, gritty mud that later would take some time to wash from our shoes, but we didn't care. The three of us pushed upriver, as if searching for something, but we had no idea what. It seemed as if Van Gear were on a secret mission. I now realize he'd been searching for his spirt-self, or some version of such. A search for a marker in the river that was as much wind and grit as soul, as much water spiders and gulls as transcendence. When Van Gear had stopped and looked out at the river and put the harmonica in a pocket, I'd glanced back at Willington, and saw that he was slightly panting. I realized I was too. I wondered if most of the hike we'd been holding our breaths as Van Gear's harmonica sang. The three of us had watched an anhinga drying its wings on a stump on the opposite bank. We'd stood silently, entranced. Hiking back, we laughed and joked. Once in the parking lot, having found a hose to de-mud our shoes, we told childhood stories about first times seeing sharks or gators, dolphins or manta rays. We listened to each other with wonder, until the motorcycle engines kicked in which meant we were headed back to T-town.

Today we first wandered the San Marcos site as if we'd never seen it before, as if this ghost of a fortification could commune with the ghost of Van Gear and transmute him back to our reality.

I trudged along the inner circumference of the wall. I was searching for what I imagined to be the strands of the man's long, black hair; I pictured these strands interlaced with the moss that clung to a few of the site's small oaks. The smell of the Gulf of Mexico kept entering my head, making me want to strip and dive off the point that marked the confluence of the St. Marks and Wakulla Rivers. I imagined diving into the cold sea and treading the coastline until I dogpaddled to the old, white lighthouse a few miles east.

Jack's dog bumped my ankle. The small pup, some sort of Chihuahua-schnauzer mix, had pulled free of Jack's leash. I wondered if he'd found Van Gear's scent, the spirit's fragments toeing along the sandy earth and leaving footprints distinguishable only by dogs and psychics.

I scratched the dog's head, but then the pup caught sight of one of the site's felines, and he scampered towards an oak cluster, ignoring Jack's shouts.

"Look what I found," said Willington as he shuffled around one corner of the San Marcos.

We meandered toward Willington. He was leaving town soon too, but not until late summer. His desperate job search had come to a result. He'd landed a position after an interview at the humongous MLA conference in San Diego that always spanned between Christmas and New Year's. I suppose all English Lit types (maybe even us), more than the average person, needed to get away from family during the holidays, the pull of relatives leaving them mired and then unmoored in the pagan ruckuses of Philistines. O, what arrogant academic asses we all are.

The long-haired ex-journalist now held a palm-sized disc in his hand, held it above his head, up to the sun. In his other arm he cradled Van Gear's ashes, the urn pressed to his ribs like a football.

"Looks like a flywheel," said Ash.

"I think you are exactly right," said Willington. "In fact, I think it's the flywheel to a Harley road bike, very much like the one Van Gear used to ride."

"How the hell did it get here?" I asked.

"That's a good question," said Jack.

"It's some kind of sign," said Rand. "Turning and turning in the widening . . . *gear*?"

I laughed.

"Does seem somehow important. An odd coincidence," said Willington.

"You probably planted it," said Jack.

"No, I didn't, Jack," said Willington. He sounded defensive but then shrugged his shoulders when he saw that Jack was kidding. I think Jack, more than the rest of us, really wanted to break the super-somber mood. That's probably why he'd brought his dog. He eyed Rand's *Bible* nervously.

"A very weird coincidence then," Jack mumbled.

How coincidental had it been when Ryanna first showed me the Confluence and its mysterious whirlpool? That was certainly the first of a sequence of strange phenomenon that had interconnected and now had seemingly fallen apart, massively evaporated. Were we meant to toss the flywheel into the whirlpool and see what, if anything, would happen? We could watch it sink slowly like a doleful, fresh-released catfish still stunned by the hook. Or we could gape as the wheel floated (*a miracle!*) and turned in a Sisyphean circle it would never escape.

"Should we drop it in the urn?" asked Ash. "Let it mix with Van G.?"

No one disagreed.

Willington looked into the trees, considering the idea. I'm sure he, like the rest of us, suddenly felt super sad that, yes, Van Gear truly was dead. We'd loved the son-of-a-bitch half-to-death, and we'd probably not given him the credit he'd deserved, and we were all now feeling dismal and useless and would have liked to bury or cremate our current selves too so that we could each be reborn into some better self.

Willington unscrewed the lid. He clattered the flywheel across the urn's mouth, but then realized the opening was too small.

"Can't make it fit," said Willington.

"Wasn't meant to be," said Jack.

"Seems inappropriate to sprinkle him on the flywheel, as if he were a little paprika and pepper for a metal taco," said Rand.

"Sacrilege," mumbled Ash, soundly weirdly unphilosophical, strangely religious.

"We can toss it in with him," I said. "The wheel can be the last thing we throw."

"But who gets to toss it?" asked Jack.

"We should shoot hoops for it!" said Rand. Everyone laughed.

"Hey, I'm serious. I really want to be the one to whip that disk as far as it can go," said Rand.

"Ash would win that contest. It wouldn't be fair," said Willington. "And we got no hoop for miles."

Ash said nothing.

"Or maybe we could stand on the bank, each simultaneously put a finger underneath the flywheel, and flip it into the water together on the count of three," said Rand.

"That's a bullshit idea," said Ash. He sounded more wistful than scolding. Van Gear's death had changed him from a deconstructionist to a hard-core realist. And realism had made him even closer to my Ex. A good thing, I'd argue.

"That's not a bad idea, Rand," said Willington. "But I don't think it's too practical."

"Plus we would have to stand too close together," said Jack.

"Van Gear would have said . . . ," I began. Paused. "We should kiss it." But instead of Van Gear, I thought of Elly, wishing she stood beside me now, so I could grip her hand tightly.

I took the flywheel from Willington and fingered it with both hands. The metal was cold. The object was lighter than I'd imagined.

"Then Willington should probably drop it in the water after the ashes."

I wished Elly was there at that moment because I wanted to kiss her.

No one said anything for a full minute. We all stared at the ground.

A moment later Rand was cutting through the woods towards the point of the Confluence's Y crux. He held the *Bible* on top of his head with both hands. Willington followed, and the rest of us fell into line.

Within a minute we all stood at the water, looking out at the combined-river deltas that pushed to the Gulf.

"I truly loved the egotistical son-of-a-bitch," said Willington. His voice cracked as he spoke. "You know, I really did."

"We all did," said Jack.

I handed Willington back the flywheel. He put the urn down, and with a Herculean toss, winged the disk over the water. The thing sailed into the humidity of the warm January day, hovering just above the surface, and we lost sight of it. I wondered if the whirlpool would find it.

We were all wet-eyed now.

"Everybody," said Willington, suddenly looking ten years older, "hold out your hand."

We did. Each hand as cup, bowl, urn of flesh.

But first Rand placed the book upon the grass. Jack wrapped the dog's leash—the pup had finally returned—around a tree five yards behind us. Ash started to pull the joint out of this pocket, thought better of it and slid the spliff back.

The wind, as if on cue, ceased.

Willington dropped in each of our hands a handful of ashes. The ash was not like lightweight sand. Small pieces of what must have been bone and cartilage littered the cinders.

One or two of our crew mumbled something that sounded like prayer, but I couldn't tell who was saying it and what was being said. It didn't matter. Anyway, I had my eyes closed, head down.

I heard the sound of boots shuffling through grass, so I glanced up.

Ash dropped his handful into the water first. Next, Rand. Jack let his ashes sift through his fingers. Willington motioned for me, but I held back. He shrugged. He stood at the point of the bank and leaned over as far as he could, turned the urn topside down, dumping what remained into the sea.

A thin ash-cloud hung above the surface, circling, almost like a dust devil, a waterspout the size of a man. I watched, wondered if I was the only one who could see it. I suddenly wished my ear for invisible voices and sounds would tremble to life, go into full-intensity without the ultra-boost of TallaTec. On the wind, for just a heartbeat, I could have sworn I heard the deep mumble of Van Gear's humming, singing the same notes he'd played on the harmonica that day. And I thought I heard Taylor Velázquez's fingers drumming on the gunnels of an oar-filled boat somewhere in the North Atlantic—safe and sound. But then all faded.

One by one, the rest of Wings turned away, headed back through the woods to the fort and the parking lot. I stood there with my hand still full.

My face contorted. I sobbed. I must have looked like a monster facing and fearing the burned ashes, as if they might be isotopes made to sear themselves into my cells, the same molecules that'd irradiated me as I'd been born.

I fought to catch my breath, break the tears.

I stood where Willington had stood, and heaved the dust underhand as powerfully as I could. I watched and waited.

A film of ashes gathered on the surface, a river of soot atop the water. As the cinder-river reached a spot twenty yards off the point, it began to swirl as if caught in a whirlpool. The film turned slowly, like the swirl of colors in an under-stirred can of paint.

I watched for a minute.

"Hey!" someone shouted from somewhere behind me. Rand, I think. "Come on! Everyone wants to go!" I turned and stared into the trees, then swung to face the sea again.

The ashes had vanished.

At this moment, I sat down. I'd stopped crying.

The sun cut through a thin layer of cumulous clouds. I contemplated the tentative Wings meeting that Rand had set for next week, looked forward to it, even if Wings now all stood around the parking lot, impatiently waiting for me.

On a log on the far side of the St. Marks, an anhinga bird—Ryanna called them snakebirds—dried its wings in the warm light. The black feathers had a striking sheen. The bird appeared invulnerable but to me looked exposed. The breeze made the swamp grass sing in a throaty, harsh rattle. The wind brought in the smell of salt air mixed with gasoline fumes from two motor boats clicking to the sea. The sun now felt summer-hot.

A fathom from the log where the anhinga lingered, a dark spot rose to the surface, black ridges jutting from its top. The shadow had a crocodile-sharp front, as pointy as the tip of a V2 rocket. The front end of the shadow wavered as the sun stretched bright through the clouds. The dark spot hovered, drifted downriver, then disappeared.

Michael Trammell grew up in South Florida and currently lives in the Florida panhandle. His poetry collection is *Our Keen Blue House*; other work has appeared in *New Letters, The Chatta-hoochee Review, Pleiades,* and the *G.W. Review.* He is a Senior Lecturer at Florida State Univer-sity and an associate editor for the *Apalachee Re-view.*

HYSTERICAL BOOKS